MAY 19 2016

Avarice

by

Philip Soletsky

Avarice by Philip Soletsky

Copyright © 2015 Philip Soletsky

All rights reserved. This book or any portion thereof may not be reproduced or used in any manner whatsoever without the express written permission of the author except for the use of brief quotations in a book review.

ISBN-10: 1517783623

ISBN-13: 978-1517783624

To my readers.

All for you.

Also by this Author

Embers
A Hard Rain
Dirty Little Secrets
Little Girl Lost

After

Jason sat on the hillside near the tree line with his arms wrapped around his knees and watched the house burn. It was down the slope a little ways, surrounded by a lavishly landscaped expanse of immaculate lawn. A pool edged by a textured concrete patio abutted the house at the rear, the water turning milky with ash. Jason imagined the embers making small sizzling sounds as they rained down onto the surface of the water and died, but that sound, if it existed at all, was lost in the roar of the house which was by this time fully ablaze, punctuated occasionally by the tinkle of glass and at one point the crash of the big flat-panel television falling off the wall in the living room. And there he sat and watched it burn as the column of black smoke it generated wove its way upwards into the bleached blue sky.

A smoldering stub of a cigarette, held between the first and second fingers of his right hand, had dropped a waterfall of ash down his left shin, but his mind hadn't registered that yet. Last night's twenty minutes of rain, a rarity in this pricey residential neighborhood east of LA, had damped the gritty, sandy soil of these hills and was seeping into the ass of his Dockers. That too went unnoticed. His left palm full of cactus spines, no doubt gathered during his scramble up the hill to his current luxury box seating overlooking the contest of house versus oxidation, was a distant stinging. The vast majority of Jason's mind, as he sat there on the damp hillside with the last remnants of tobacco glowing against the filter and the cactus spines already festering in the flesh of his hand, was repeating 'Oh shit! Oh Shit! OH SHIT!' Echoing like a lunatic shouting in a small, tiled room. Underneath that some tiny fragment of his brain was still producing rational thoughts, primary among them: It wasn't supposed to end this way. It wasn't supposed to end this way at all.

The trail of events seemed so surreal now, and even having lived through them he had difficulty understanding the threads that connected them all. He remembered the beginning, the movie producer. That seemed clear enough to him, but where the hell had Ricky come from, and when had the DEA gotten involved? Maybe they hadn't been DEA agents at all. There was no way to know. And Chip, poor Chip. Sitting and watching the house go up in flames, he felt as though he were flying apart, scattering like burning scraps of paper.

He was startled by the explosion of the Porsche's gas tank in the attached two-car garage. One side of the garage's peaked roof lifted like the hinged lid of a child's toy box and belched out a ball of dense, black smoke with a roiling orange core. The ball spun upwards to join the cloud gathering over the house in the hot, still air. The roof slammed back down and hung askew from the shattered roof spine. The surge of heat caused the ornamental shrubs nearby to wilt and shrink back; two next to the garage burst into flames. The part of him that was still paying attention was surprised the explosion hadn't been more spectacular, but then recalled that after yesterday's drive from Palo Alto there had been very little more than fumes in the Porsche's tank. That was part of the reason he hadn't taken the car and headed out I-10 until he hit the Atlantic Ocean when the fire had started. That, along with the fact that he would have had to clean Deirdre and her brains out of the driver's seat – a task he probably would not have been up to on the best of days, which this clearly was not.

A lonely siren wailed in the distance. Because of the way sound funneled down the length of the valley, it was difficult to tell how far away the fire engine was, but it was definitely headed his way.

It was time to be going; past time in all likelihood. Jason was loath to hang around and face all the questions; questions he himself probably did not have the answers to. He stood and dropped the cigarette butt, at this point down to the filter, and ground it under the heel of his right shoe. He swept the ash from the leg of his pants with his right hand and the grit from the seat of his pants with his left. Only then did he notice the cactus spines buried in the meat of his palm, the sudden stab of pain bringing a gasp to his lips. He examined the spines, like tiny slivers of glass. Tongue clamped between teeth, he tried to grab the end of one with a thumb and forefinger, but succeeded only in driving it in deeper. “Fuck,” he whispered.

He worked his way down the hill, angling a little to the left into the backyard two houses over, and trotted around the side, hitting the street just as the fire truck was racing past, the scream of its siren pitching downwards as it receded. He watched as it lurched to stop, the doors all popping open simultaneously and firefighters spilling out. The first one out on the passenger side landed on the *‘For Sale By Owner’* sign stuck into the grass strip between the sidewalk and the road, both booted feet snapping off the wooden stake and mashing the printed cardboard rectangle into the dirt.

‘Good luck selling that sucker now,’ Jason thought ruefully.

Taking a left to the fire truck’s right, he jogged his way down the road and between the pillars that marked the entrance to the subdivision. At the main road he looked left, then right. Left? Or right? Flip a coin? He laughed wildly. It occurred to him that with seven million in cash burning in the trunk of the Porsche, he probably had less than five dollars on him. Water over the damn parade, as Deirdre would have said. He chose right (given the ache that was setting up residence in his left hand, left wasn’t his favorite direction just then) and started making his way eastward at an easy loping jog.

The slapping of the soles of his shoes on the pavement formed a rhythm in his head, and he started to sing a song to himself that was either an actual song or maybe was only a lot like a song he had heard somewhere. “Leaving it all behind. Baby, baby, I’m leaving it all behind.”

11 Days Earlier

Jason pushed back from the keyboard and pressed the heels of his hands into his eyes. 'I'm wasting my time,' he thought to himself. 'This place is as good as dead, and nothing I do is going to change that.' He pulled up an internet window and checked the stock price again. $1.15, down 6 cents so far for the day. A little applet in the corner automatically ground out its tiny formula – his shares were worth a shade over three hundred grand. The little clock in the corner of the applet read 2 years, 7 months, 2 days, 2 hours, 11 minutes, 16 seconds. That was how long it would be before his shares became vested, before he could cash them out. It hadn't seemed like that long when he had started the clock at five years, but now with a little more than two and a half years to go, it was forever for all practical purposes. Two and a half years throughout which he would work eighty to one hundred hour weeks without a paycheck, just as he had done for the past sixteen months.

He heard the whisper of someone treading on the industrial carpet in the hallway coming to a stop at the door to his office behind him. Without even turning around he knew it was Keith, who spent his days wandering the ever more deserted hallways like some agitated ghost. Jason didn't take his hands down from his eyes, didn't turn around, and hoped that Keith would take the hint and drift away to darken some other doorstep. Keith, ever clueless, instead came into the office and sat on the empty desk across the room with his feet on the seat of the desk chair.

"How many times a day do you check that, anyway?"

"Forty, fifty. The applet will automatically update every 15 minutes all on its own."

"Don't you think that's a waste of your time?"

Jason felt a wave of anger rise inside him, but couldn't find within himself a source of energy to maintain it. The wave ebbed, and he was once again a placid sea of depression. The silence stretched between them.

Keith took the lack of an answer on Jason's part as a cue to change subjects. "How goes the dog thing?"

By 'dog thing' Keith meant one of their current clients, an online dog toy supply company in its death throes. It was one of hundreds of companies online in that niche, and had been running in the red since the day it opened, the original seed money all but gone. In short, its whole business model was hopeless. That's what Jason's life had been for the last year. Working on pathetic e-commerce business models. Jazzing up websites, registering with search engines, making deals with other sites for banner space, arranging billing through credit card companies. But it was all just a thick coat of paint smeared over the ugly, cracked truth of online businesses – there weren't enough customers out there for twenty let alone hundreds of dog toy companies, and the internet giants like Amazon sucked all the oxygen out of the room.

Realistically, that was the same boat that Keith's dream, Not Your Father's Ecom, was in. The last time Jason had checked, there were over five hundred e-commerce companies, not counting small consulting firms and independents, and there just wasn't enough business to go around. And the business that was around, like the dog thing, didn't have any money. If they had money, or were making money, they probably wouldn't hire an e-commerce consulting firm, now would they? That was the flaw in Keith's business plan. The dog thing, like so many of their other clients these days, was paying their fees with stock of ever-dwindling value. Jason absent-mindedly tapped a few keys and brought up a stock price for that – 94 cents, down 4 cents so far today and seriously at risk of being delisted from the NASDAQ. So the agreement for a fee of a hundred thousand shares was now worth something slightly south of a hundred thousand dollars. Not exactly helping their own stock price any.

Back before the second tech bubble burst, this industrial park had been packed with businesses, this building packed with people, four packed into this very office. In truth, their clients had paid in stock back then too, but it was stock that was often doubling or tripling in value. Not Your Father's Ecom was flying high at its peak of $53.50 a share, Jason's shares worth in excess of $20 million his tiny applet had told him. But it was all a game; buying on credit, buying on stock, with no real money flowing into the system beyond the IPO. Everyone knew it was inevitable that the bubble would burst, that the first guy into the pyramid scheme would get out, and everything would collapse after that, but if only it could have lasted until his stock options matured. In retrospect, 5 years had been too long a time to expect the house of cards to stand.

He turned in his swivel chair to tell Keith just what he wanted to hear, that the dog thing was going fine, that everything would be fine, but he found the office empty. Keith, apparently tired of being ignored while Jason ruminated, had left, leaving Jason with his three ghosts of officemates past.

Jason thought Keith had it right, that leaving was a fine idea. The work would wait for him. He would come back later and do it, all night perhaps, for as long as it took. This job, as hopeless as it was, was all he had, and he would try everything he could to make it work. He tried to recall the energy that had kept him going when the company had first started. The hours had been just as long then, and in reality the pay just about as crappy, though back then there had been at least the promise of future riches as long as the stock price was high. In a way he had treated this job like an extension of college: a group of guys pulling endless all-nighters, surviving on pizza and Mountain Dew, solving hard problems. Though working essentially alone now, he tried to keep that spirit alive as best he could. It was the only way to get through his days.

He shut down his computer, after a quick glance at the

latest stock quote - $1.13, down under three hundred grand now, grabbed his Nike windbreaker, and headed down empty hallways to the parking lot.

There had been a time, Jason recalled, when parking had been tight, that they and the business in the other half of the building (a company that had tried to sell scented candles and potpourri over the internet, long out of business) had fought tooth and nail for spaces. Now Jason's silver Porsche was practically alone out there, keeping company with Keith's fire engine red MG and the secretary's forest green Corolla. Wisely she hadn't let the stock options go to her head.

He threw the windbreaker on the passenger seat and got into the car. He wended his way past dozens of 'Available for Lease' signs, out of the industrial park and onto the I-10 headed east away from LA. As he accelerated onto the freeway, he rolled down the window to let a hot breeze tornado through the car, shifted into 4th gear, dialed up *Everclear* on his iPod piped through the car stereo, pulled his cell phone from his pocket, and activated the speed dial – the LA freeway juggle, look ma, no hands.

"Hey, Chip?" He had to shout to be heard over the wind and music, had to press the phone hard against his ear to hear. "Yeah, I'm done for the day. It's, uh," he trapped the phone between his head and left shoulder and looked at the watch on his left wrist as he shifted into 5th and swerved around a truck hauling bottled water, "2:00 now. How about we meet at about 3:45?"

He braked slightly and downshifted as his radar detector chirped, "C'mon, you're your own man now. Get to the usual place, call Kelly and see if she can make it, and I'll meet you there." He pushed the end button without waiting for a reply and tossed the phone on top of the windbreaker. He noticed the police car along the side of the road and was well within the speed limit when he passed. Beyond, he popped back into 5th and accelerated.

Exiting the freeway, he wound his way around upscale strip malls and shady, manicured parks, finally passing between the pillars that marked the entrance to the development that contained his home. When he had first bought the house, the pool, the attached two-car garage, the three bedroom two-and-a-half bath mini-mansion, just driving between the pillars had engendered a sense of peace. Increasingly, however, the stress of wondering where the next mortgage payment was going to come from, how he was going to pay the taxes due next month, how he was even going to pay the electricity for the damn air conditioning, was making him almost dread coming home. His job produced literally zero income; the company couldn't afford to pay any salary. They paid him instead in stock options. He had gotten an agreement from Keith that allowed him to cash out some options six months ago; his choices had been that or declare bankruptcy. After taxes, what had remained was just about gone now. He'd have to cash out five times as many shares at present prices to buy himself even a month of breathing room, unless something changed soon. Clearly a case of diminishing returns.

With a slight squeal of tires he pulled to a stop at the end of the driveway. He jumped out of the car, grabbing a paper bag from the behind the passenger's seat as he did so. The '*For Sale by Owner*' sign jammed into the grass at the curbside was faded and curling at the corners. He yanked it from the soil like a weed and replaced it with a new one from the bag, rocking the shaft of the sign back and forth to set it solidly in the earth. A real estate seminar he had attended earlier in the year had stressed that an old sign indicted a house that had been on the market for some time, and that tended to scare away buyers who believed there must be something wrong with it. There were dozens of houses for sale within ten miles of here, three others in this very development; he would take any advantage he could get. He thought that perhaps he should try calling realtors again; it had been six months since the last one had dropped him. Tossing the bag with the old sign behind the seat, he climbed back into the car and pulled it the rest of the way into the driveway, braking to a halt in front of the single, wide door that covered both bays of the garage. He killed the engine and went into the house, jogging up the broad carpeted stairs to the master bedroom suite.

It was spacious if a little severe; off-white walls, different off-white carpet. The bedspread, also off-white, was subtly different from the walls and floor. Off-white lacquered dresser and bedside table, different from each other and the walls, floor, and bedspread. The walls were completely bare of artwork or photos of any kind. An artist that Jason had dated for a short time had dreamt up the decoration scheme. He suspected she had chosen it more for how she looked standing in the middle of all those different whites while wearing a black satin thong, than for how the room looked by itself.

He crossed to the louvered closet doors. It would have been bizarre if he had opened them revealing long racks of off-white suits like the *Talking Heads* used to wear, but instead it opened on an ordinary collection of jeans and Dockers, collared shirts and casual light-weight suits. Most of the closet was empty – Jason had never spent much money on clothes. This was the smaller of the two closets in the bedroom, the other being a large walk-in affair on the opposite wall. Jason currently kept empty cardboard moving boxes in that one, despite having moved in over two years ago.

After changing into blue jeans and a dark green button down shirt, he wandered out onto the balcony off the bedroom overlooking the pool. He rested his arms on the railing and stared down at the fractured shards of light rippling on the crystalline pool surface. He should have sold this house when the downturn started but he, like everyone else, wasn't willing to admit that the party was over, that the downturn was the beginning of a long slide that still wasn't showing a bottom. Now the development was so full of houses for sale, he couldn't get enough out of the house to even clear the mortgage.

Returning to the Porsche, he was back on I-10 streaking westward in minutes. A short time later he parked in front of a building that from the outside looked much like any upper middle class apartment structure in southern California, a pink adobe exterior with cobalt blue tiles pressed into the surface artistically. A concrete walkway lead up to oversized white oak doors with big glass panels and polished brass handles.

It wasn't until you opened the doors that you began to suspect anything.

Surprisingly, the first thing you noticed was not the smell, because a first-class air handling and filtration system and a thousand bouquets of flowers can more or less completely remove the commingled odors of antiseptic, piss, and shit. No, the first thing you noticed was far more subtle. The normal hum of human activity was muted; footsteps were hushed, conversation all murmurs, and no one laughed out loud. The people, sitting around in wheelchairs or propped up in the couches and chairs scattered around the lobby area, dozed or turned pages in books or often just stared off into space, occasionally drooling slightly. Jason always thought of all nursing homes, even one as nice as this, as waiting rooms to death's doorstep.

As soon as he was through the doors, a woman seated behind the long desk in front recognized him and gave him a big fake smile. "Mr. Taylor, so good to see you again. Your mom has been doing just great. I think I saw Mitzy just taking her into the garden."

"Thank you." He felt a stupid fake smile on his own face. Fake smiles were contagious that way.

He moved past the end of the desk and she reached out,

putting a hand on his arm, no smile now. "Mrs. Real wanted to see you when you came in."

Jason nodded tiredly. There was no point in trying to avoid it. He altered his route towards a plain wooden door with a brass nameplate that read "Gloria Real, Facilities Manager." He knocked softly twice, and then opened the door when the person inside called "Come."

The understated elegance of the lobby stopped at that door. To Jason, Gloria Real and her office were a perfect fit – a drab, no-nonsense woman in a drab no-nonsense office. The pale green walls were completely free of any ornamentation except for a simple calendar: no pictures of puppies or kittens, just perfect geometric rows of days and dates. The plain gray metal desktop was empty except for a yellow legal pad, one black pen, one pencil, and a black office phone. Mrs. Real wore her brown hair hanging straight to the collar of her white linen blouse buttoned to the neck. She wore no makeup with the exception of a vast abundance of lipstick, which today was a violent shade of red.

She pursed those lips as she saw Jason come in and close the door behind him. "Please, Mr. Taylor, sit down." She gestured to the green leather chair in front of her desk. She began her carefully prepared speech before he was even fully settled in the chair. "Mr. Taylor, this is very difficult for me to say, but not everyone can afford the level of care that we provide at this facility. There are many fine state institutions that we could place your mother in that-"

"No, please." He interrupted her. "I know I'm a little behind. I will get the money." He pulled a check from his wallet, took her pen, and began to fill it out.

"Mr. Taylor, I'm sure you appreciate the difficult position you put me in."

He signed the check, tore if from the booklet, and pushed it across the desk to her. It was made out for one thousand dollars. He was sure it would clear, but just barely. "Please, this is it. This is all I have right now. Just give me two weeks. I, that is she, I know she likes it here. She's happy here." He sat in the seat lightly, as if the whole office might fall away into a deep pit at any moment.

Mrs. Real picked up the check and fingered the serrated edge. Did he see a slight softening of the lines around her mouth, or was that wishful thinking on his part? "This isn't the whole amount."

"I know. I will get the rest. Just two weeks. That's all I need."

He held his breath while she silently debated. Never mind for the moment that he had no idea why two weeks should be any different from today as far as his finances were concerned.

He decided a play for her vanity couldn't hurt. "Please, Mrs. Real, I couldn't bear to have her in one of *those* places."

She made a big theatrical sigh. "Very well. Two weeks. But at that time the account must be paid in full. If it is not, you will have to place her in another care facility."

"Yes, thank you. I understand completely." He got up from the chair and had an almost overwhelming urge to bow and scrape as through before a queen who has just bestowed upon him some great honor. "I'll get the money. I will. Thank you."

He moved quickly out of the office and closed the door. In the lobby he found he was stooped over and had to straighten up. Had he actually bowed?

He gave a thin smile to the woman at the front desk in response to her big fake one, and walked to the open doorway at the back of the lobby that lead to the garden. Pebbled sidewalks wound around small trimmed islands of grass containing statuary of children at play. He passed a bronze boy with a kite and a little girl with arms stretched overhead holding a teddy bear aloft.

His mother was in a wheelchair, a tartan afghan in her lap covering her remaining leg. A small length of support stocking was visible at the hem, her only foot laced up snugly into a solitary white sneaker. Mitzy stood behind her in her crisp white nurse's uniform complete with white nurse's cap pinned in her bright red hair. Jason thought those caps had gone out of style right around World War II.

Jason heard Mitzy talking to his mother as he approached. "So there's Jessica, OK? She was Steve's daughter from his first marriage. She sees Trevor with Melissa. This is at the party at the estate. She can't hear what they're talking about, but Trevor is showing her something in this briefcase he's carrying."

It was "The Young and the Restless" or maybe "Ryan's Hope." Jason smiled to himself. Mitzy was an encyclopedia of soap opera plotlines. It gave her something to talk to the patients about though most of them, like Jason's mother, were in no condition to care one way or the other. Jason liked the constant human contact, even if it was just meaningless drivel, which was one of the reasons he had moved his mom to this place as soon as he could afford it, more or less.

"Hi, Mitzy."

She turned and smiled a genuine smile at him, the full thousand watts. He greatly admired her seemingly endless energy. She had very white teeth and a large spray of freckles across the bridge of her nose and her cheeks. "Hi,

Jason. We were just enjoying the sunshine after lunch. We had tuna casserole! Your mom really likes tuna. We got the flowers you sent on mother's day. The roses are beautiful! I put them in a vase in her room."

"Thank you so much, Mitzy. I'm just going to walk with her for a while if that's OK."

"That would be great! I'll be right over there if you need anything." She moved off towards an old man sitting on a stone bench in front of the crouched statue of a boy playing marbles. "Hi, Mr. Darby! How are you today? Did you have a nice lunch?"

Jason released the brakes on his mother's wheelchair and pushed it down the walkway looking at but not seeing the statues he had passed hundreds of times during other visits. As he walked he talked about work. He talked about his house and his friends. He talked about the weather. He talked about movies he had seen.

His mother took it all in, but what she did with it inside was anyone's guess. She had not said a word in many months. She used to speak occasionally, only a word or two, often words that had nothing to do with each other or what was being said around her. She would say something like "Table pink" or "Happy car," and then she would fall silent. The plethora of doctors he used to consult, because he hoped it might make a difference, had had a term for that behavior, but he had forgotten it. They had had a term for her entire condition as well, but what did that matter? In the final analysis, she was what she was, and all their diagnoses said she wasn't going to get any better. And though the doctors judged that she wasn't even aware of her surroundings, Jason refused to believe that and wanted her to be somewhere nice with people who cared for her. He just didn't know how he was going to continue paying for it.

He parked her wheelchair next to a patch of grass and

sat on the ground at her feet. He plucked a blade of grass and played with the tip, then tore it into tiny fibrous strips. He told her about a book he was reading as he looked up at her. Her face was slack, her brown eyes open but focused on nothing and everything at once. Her thin hair, still mostly brown though with some grey, was in a pony tail, probably because it was easy to care for that way.

This was his mom, and had been for almost as long as he could remember. Oh, she hadn't always been this far gone, but even when Jason was very young she had been forgetful and disoriented much of the time. His father, whom Jason hardly remembered, had seen the writing on the wall, decided he didn't want to be saddled with a teenager and an invalid wife, and ran off for parts unknown. A couple of hundred dollars in cash showed up in the mail every few weeks. As a way to pay off his guilt, Jason figured his father had gotten off cheap.

So it fell to Jason to be the man of the house, but seriously, what could a fourteen year old do? If maybe he had known about social services he might have gone for help, but he didn't. He kept the house himself. He cooked, he cleaned as best he could, he shopped, and he paid the bills. Of course the house deteriorated. The lawn was hardly ever mowed, the bushes grew wild, the paint peeled and the roof leaked. The fall of his sophomore year in high school, the ceiling of his bedroom had collapsed in a shower of sodden sheetrock and rotten wood. Unable to think of what to do, he had stuffed most of the debris into garbage bags, lay down plastic sheeting to catch the water when it rained, and closed the door to the room hoping for the best. He slept on the broken-down couch in the living room, the door to his bedroom remaining closed, from that day onward.

He managed to keep the lights on, his mother fed, and get through high school with a B average, but he could remember his face burning with shame for the month he hadn't managed to pay the water bill, with showers only once a week at school, without clean clothes, until it got so bad he could almost smell himself.

He never invited anyone to come over after school. They would see his house. They would meet his mom. He couldn't let that happen.

The herd instinct of high school students naturally singled him out as free game for jokes and insults. That had been bad. Worse still was when he had crossed some invisible threshold during his senior year, becoming so pathetic as to be beyond jokes and was instead completely socially ostracized. Unsurprisingly, he had intentionally missed his five-year reunion several summers ago.

He would never allow himself or his mother to fall back to that life. Never. He would find a way. He had to.

These were the thoughts that ran through his mind as he spoke to his mother, though he never let what he was feeling enter his voice. He told her about a trip he had taken to the San Diego Zoo. He talked about some really good take out Thai food he had eaten last week. He wondered if maybe he should start watching soap operas, because Mitzy never seems to run out of things to talk about.

When he checked his watch he noticed that almost an hour had passed and he had to be on his way to meet Chip and Kelly. He unlocked the wheelchair brakes and made his way back across the garden.

Mitzy was still with Mr. Darby, though she had transferred him to a wheelchair at some point. "So Morgan thinks Taylor is the father of the baby, but we know that it's really Jack. Of course with Samantha in a coma, she'll never tell, though the doctors think she might come out of it soon." She noticed Jason coming and switched conversations so smoothly that Jason felt for a moment as if his life had been transferred into the soap opera. "Did you have a nice visit? I know your mom loved seeing you. If you want to leave her right there I'll take her up to her room in a little bit."

"OK. And thank you, Mitzy, for taking such good care of her."

"Oh, Jason, I enjoy taking care of your mother. She's such a good listener."

A good listener. That certainly described his mother in a nutshell.

He left the nursing home and drove numbly, with the radio off, trying and mostly failing to get out of his sulk, until he pulled into a parking lot next to a small, rectangular concrete block building. A wide smoked-glass window on the front gave a shadowy impression of the room inside, people shifting about like wraiths. He locked the car and set the alarm. It give a double chirp in response to the signal from his keychain remote as he went inside.

The interior was dim and cool, almost like a cave, and it took a few moments for his eyes to adjust from the bright sunlight outside. A dark bar stretched along the left-hand wall, a row of booths along the right, and a scattering of tables in the space between. Even before his eyes had adjusted, he could make out Chip and Kelly at one of the tables. You could hardly miss Chip, a veritable mountain of a man, over six feet six and well over 350 pounds. Unshaven and generally unkempt, he looked like the prototypical hacker, and it was all he could do to check his Gmail account. He had been a supply chain manager at the same company where Jason worked, and had been one of the first let go when the downturn started. He had sold his stock options for more than twenty bucks a share, but due to his position had only a few thousand shares. No fortune, but he plowed the money back into his father's plastic injection molding company where he now worked. It wasn't as exotic as a high tech company, but it was solidly plugging along, which was more that you could say for just about any local high tech company you'd care to mention. Chip had never liked the plastic molding business, and liked it less so now, but a job was a job.

Kelly, Jason had to admit to himself, was still breathtakingly beautiful, with stylish chestnut hair, blue-green eyes, and a model's profile. She also had a computer expertise unmatched by anyone he had ever known. Jason and she had gone through a certain courting ritual when she had joined the company about a year after Jason had, but they had settled instead into an easy friendship. She had seen the writing on the wall long before anyone else, had sold her stock options out for the legendary price of forty dollars a share, and had started her own website design company with the money. While it would probably never allow her to get rich, she kept the company afloat with sheer force of will and raw talent. The long hours it required were clearly starting to take their toll, evidenced by dark circles around her eyes and a certain slump to her shoulders.

Jason pushed out the third of four chairs at the table with his backside as he sat down and signaled the waitress for a beer by pointing at Chip's glass and then at himself. "How goes?"

Kelly was picking grains of salt off a pretzel from the bowl in the center of the table, "Oh, you know, same old, same old. I spent the last two weeks doing a complete site overhaul for an online seller of women's shoes, and then they up and went bankrupt before they paid my fee."

"That totally sucks. You going to get anything?"

"They've said that they're very sorry, and they'll send me about two hundred pairs of shoes if I tell them my size." She sighed. "I could probably hire a lawyer and go after them, along with all the rest of their creditors, but in the end you can't get blood from a stone, right?"

Chip, who had been watching this exchange like a spectator at Wimbledon, said, "Hey, I've got some good news." He leaned back in his chair making its legs groan ominously while he dug in the front pocket of his jeans. He pulled something out and threw it onto the table in front of Jason, who picked it up to find it was a metal key ring with a little black plastic gun attached to it. The word "Deathblow" was printed across the barrel of the gun in red.

"Deathblow. That's the new Segal film?"

"Yeah, they include one of these inside the DVD case wrapper. We got the concession from the company doing the distribution. I'll make nine cents profit per key chain, twenty-five thousand key chains per film. They've signed us up for two dozen films this year."

Jason did a little quick math in his head – about $50,000. A pretty good chunk of change for keychains. He couldn't help but draw the comparison to the IPO for Not Your Father's Ecom. That had raked in $350 million in about 3 hours. Oh, how far they had come. "Can I keep this? I might need to rob a bank later."

"You can keep dozens of them. I've got a thousand in my trunk."

"Just the one, thanks." The waitress delivered Jason's beer, placed it on a coaster on the table, and left. Jason picked up the beer and took a long pull, then set the glass back down on the coaster. "I noticed the stock fell another fifteen cents today. I think it will be under a dollar before the end of the quarter."

"If you're looking to do tons of work for very little

money, you could always come work with me." Kelly tossed the first pretzel aside and started desalinating another one from the bowl.

Chip took his glass off the table, took a drink, and settled back in his chair with the beer resting on his stomach. "Aren't we a cheery group?" He brightened, "Oh, hey, I've got one for you, Jason. Loni Anderson and Mary Tyler Moore."

Jason thought about it for a moment, then rubbed the stubble on his chin. "That's a tough one."

"That's a tough one what?" Kelly asked.

"It's a game we started playing a few weeks ago when you were on that trip to Baltimore. Like six degrees of Kevin Bacon, you try and make a link from one actor to another through TV shows that common actors were on."

Kelly leaned forward with her elbows on the table and her chin perched on her hands, "I get it. Like Loni Anderson was on *WKRP in Cincinnati* with Howard Hessman."

Chip chimed in, "Right, but where does that get you?"

Kelly snapped her fingers a few times. "Oh, that show. What was it called? *Head of the Class.*"

"Yeah, and then?"

"Uh, I dunno." Kelly took a quick sip from her drink.

"*Head of the Class* was an evolutionary dead end. No one made it off that show with a career except Lisa Bonet." Jason eyed Chip through slitted eyes. "Our friend Chip is much more clever than that. Loni Anderson also starred with Lynda Carter on *Partners in Crime*. It's a devious link because that show was short-lived, and I'm sure Chip watched it because the boob factor was very high."

Chip laughed making the beer slosh in the glass balanced on his stomach. "You know me so well. Whence next, Holmes?"

"Lynda Carter was on, what else, *Wonder Woman* with Lyle Waggoner. Longer lived, and also a high boob factor. Lyle Waggoner was on *The Carol Burnett Show*." Jason stopped there.

"Stuck, oh sage?" Chip asked.

"Give me a minute."

"Carol Burnett played a part on *Magnum P.I.*" Kelly added.

"Only twice. The character has to show up at least three times for it to count." Chip waved her off and concentrated on Jason. Clearly a battle of TV trivia of epic proportions was gearing up.

"*Carol Burnett* was a variety show. Dozens of people were on it as guests. But who knows if any of them made three guest appearances? Did Harvey Korman have another series besides *Mama's Place*?" Jason was gazing upwards towards the ceiling, almost talking to himself.

The waitress came to the table and placed the check facedown. "I've got to cash out, could you pay this and open a new tab with the next waitress?"

Chip pointed to the check. "Bet you the check you won't get this one."

Jason smiled a little, "You're on. Mary Tyler Moore and Lou Grant were both on *The Mary Tyler Moore Show*.

Lou Grant was on the *The Closer* with Tom Selleck."

"But that gets you back to *Magnum P.I.*, and we already rejected that." Kelly pointed out.

"Right, right. Uhhh." Jason was back to staring at the ceiling again.

"Pay up, friend." Chip finished the beer and put the glass down on the table with a thunk.

Jason picked up his own beer and polished it off. "OK. I got it. I got it. Carol Burnett played Helen Hunt's mom on *Mad About You*." He looked over at Kelly and pointed to Chip. "What our friend here was hoping I wouldn't remember is that Carol Burnett didn't start that role. Marion Dussault did."

"OK, you got me." Chip pulled a roll of money out of his shirt pocket and peeled off a twenty and a couple of singles and dropped them on the check. "The change is yours."

"Thanks." The waitress took the check and cash and left the table.

"I don't get it," Kelly said.

"Elementary, dear Watson, "Jason said, "Marion Dussault was the mother on *Too Close for Comfort*."

Kelly finished for him, "And Ted Knight was the father, and he was also the newscaster on *The Mary Tyler Moore Show*."

Jason slapped his palm on the table, "Exactly!"

"You got me this time, Mr. Bond, but you won't be so lucky next time."

"Don't count on it, Blofeld. Anyone want to do dinner?"

"Not me." Kelly stood up, "I've got to get to a client meeting at five." She picked up her purse, which had been hanging over the back of her chair. "I'll have to take a rain check."

"I'm in." Chip stood, hitching up his jeans.

Jason, Kelly, and Chip walked out of the bar and into the parking lot, squinting in sharp afternoon sunlight.

"Thanks for calling, Chip. I needed the break." Kelly said.

"It was Jason's idea." Chip said.

"Well, thanks anyway. Jason, I might come by this weekend and do a few laps in your pool. You still own that giant house you can't afford, right?"

"Until I manage to sell it, or decide to burn it down for the insurance."

"No buyers?"

"Not even a nibble, and my current ask is more than a hundred grand under the mortgage."

"Keep at it. Things have to get better eventually," though she said the last part without enthusiasm. She waved, and walked away to her car.

Jason watched Chip watch Kelly walk away, her hips doing their magic under a pair of tight, faded Levis. He could see love in Chip's eyes, but also knew that Chip was a realist, and given how he looked and how Kelly looked, that it wasn't going to happen. He also knew that Chip would settle for friendship if that was all he could get. Jason wondered briefly if he was settling as well; if he and Kelly couldn't try again to be something more.

As Kelly's car drove by them she waved again, Chip raised his hand to wave back but then just kind of hung it up there, dropping it only slowly to his side as Kelly's car turned right onto the roadway and receded into the distance.

Jason spoke, breaking him out of whatever reverie he was contemplating. "So, Mexican?"

Chip turned to him, "Uh, Chinese?"

Jason tipped his head from side to side, bouncing the idea of imaginary mu shi pork in his mouth. "Sure, the place on Piedmont?"

"Yeah, I'll meet you there."

Chip lumbered to his ancient Toyota Tercel, wedged himself behind the wheel, and, after a little extended cranking and pumping, managed to coax it to life. Jason got into his own car, deactivated the alarm, and followed Chip out of the parking lot and down the street.

*****

Glue. Where the hell was the glue?

Rifling through his desk, Peter Ryder clawed his way past pens and pencils, folders and paperclips, half a ream of paper and a stapler.

Glue. Glue. Glue. The single word a forming thunderous drumbeat in his head.

He slammed that drawer closed and opened the next

one down. He pulled out fistfuls of pill bottles: amphetamines, downers, Viagra, blow, Oxy, legal, illegal, labelled, unlabeled. He scattered them out across the desktop like a gambler hurling bones. Snake eyes. No glue.

Only one drawer left. Only one hope left in the world.

He made a whimpering sound of joy when he found the white cardboard box inside, the blue metallic tubes of modeling cement lined up in orderly rows. Not the new American shit, but old school stuff imported from Thailand. Glue the EPA, or maybe it was the DEA, hasn't screwed with. Full octane. Harder to get than heroin. His palms sweating, he clutched at a tube, sent others skittering across the carpet, cracked the plastic seal.

He squeezed out a shimmering gelatinous worm two inches long into a sandwich bag and clamped it to his face like a man suffering a coronary clutching an oxygen mask. He inhaled and the bag collapsed, the glob of glue sticking to his nose. The top of his head blew off and he rocked back in the chair, his eyes rolled up to the whites, the bag fluttering to the floor.

He gulped his next breath in pieces, like a fish dying on a beach in the sun. The following thirty seconds were key. Hold the rush, ride the wave, or get rolled over, tumbled down, crushed to dust. Eyes closed, his fingers played across the collection of pill bottles on his desk with the nimble dexterity of virtuoso pianist. He jammed a pinch of cocaine up each nostril, rubbing the remainder into his gums. He took two Percocet, one Benadryl and a tab of ecstasy. Careful. Careful. He pressed two fingers against his carotid, opened his eyes and tried to focus on his Phillip Patel. As long as his heart rate stayed under two hundred, things were going fine as wine. Two fifty was bad news. If he hit three hundred, sell.

Hovering around one seventy five. Maybe trending

upwards. He needed something to level him off.

The intercom on his desk buzzed, a sound that cleaved into his head like a steel spike. He leapt for the button, sending pill bottles flying everywhere, fearing his skull would explode like shrapnel if it buzzed again. "Yes," he croaked.

"You're wanted on the set," Brenda, his secretary, informed him.

"Got it."

He released the button and staggered to his feet. He swayed, his pulse hammering in his temples, two oh five, two ten easy. "Got it," he slurred to himself. He grabbed the first bottle he saw, pried the lid off, tipped two pills into his palm, and tossed them back. He thought he caught a glimpse of Viagra blue in the moment they were airborne between his hand and mouth. Whatever, he could feel his pulse slowing.

Looking up he found he was presented with five doors leading out of his office. Maybe seven. Long experience had taught him to aim for the one in the middle. He staggered, rendezvoused with the door in more or less the expected location, and heaved it open with such excessive force that it almost came off its cheap hinges.

His secretary looked up at him, her typical welcoming smile dawning on her lips, but it died halfway through sunrise. "The cinematographer called. They're shooting in five," she said, her face crinkled with concern.

He said nothing, just stood there blinking, feeling like a helium balloon trapped inside, battering ineffectually against the ceiling when it yearned to be free.

"You, um, have something on your nose." She brushed

at her own nose to illustrate, which was actually pretty helpful, because he had been under the distinct impression he had left his nose somewhere on his desk, and was about to go back and get it.

He swiped at the blob with hands that had been transplanted onto arms half a mile long, mashing the glue against his face, smearing it across his upper lip. The next breath of air came with a fresh blast of fumes, and his head split open, beams of blinding light shining through the cracks. How his secretary managed to look at him without shielding her eyes was a mystery.

"You look awful. Can I get you an Ibuprofen or something?"

"Ibuprofen? Do you have any idea what that crap does to your liver?" he muttered.

He managed to find the door leading outside on the second try. It was still mostly dark, dawn the merest suggestion of pink in the distance. He lightly touched upon two of the three steps leading down from the trailer door and floated across the parking lot to his director's chair. Humming to himself, he settled onto it like a feather drifting to earth.

Everyone was staring at him. Did he have more glue on his nose? Had he accidentally knocked his nose off and left it inside? He had an urge to check it and was worried he would freak if all he found was a hole in his face. No freaking. Not allowed. Not this morning. This morning was too important, which was why he was so stressed out about it, which was why he had started in with the glue in the first place.

"I'm Peter Ryder, goddammit," he said to himself. "I directed *Undressed to Kill*. I've got a Hitchcock Award, and an MTV Popcorn Award, and was third or possibly fourth runner up for a best director Oscar. I can do this." It was all self-affirmation bullshit put in his head by his yoga dipshit girlfriend, and she was full of crap. She was flexible and a great fuck, but full of crap nonetheless. Still, it tamped down the craving to run back to his trailer for more glue, at least a little.

His assistant came up and handed him a cup of coffee, black. He didn't drink coffee, black or otherwise, and had told her dozens of times to bring him herbal tea. It never seemed to stick. Still, she was young and blonde and big chested, and useful for oh so many other things. Today she was dressed in a tiny T-shirt with strategic slashes all over the place that made it look like she had been attacked by perverted cats, shiny black leggings that hugged her like a thin coat of latex paint, and fuck me high-heeled ankle boots. She turned away from him in a move that looked casual, something off to the side of the set had suddenly attracted her attention, but was calculated to show him her ass and the distinct lack of any panty lines whatsoever. He sensed stirring in his Dockers, which told him the last pills probably had been Viagra after all.

He gathered himself together and sat up straighter, which felt like pushing together a heap of mashed potatoes into a statue shaped like himself. "Let's do this!" he said in an authoritative voice that startled him and set everyone else into motion.

This was it, the big finale shot of his movie. The money shot, literally and figuratively. It had cost almost a million dollars to set it all up.

He looked at the mirrored face of the famous Bonaventure Hotel in downtown Los Angeles. A window on the thirty-fifth floor was highlighted in green tape. Every camera, twelve of them, was pointed at this tape. The special effects guy assured him it would be removed without a trace in post-production.

The cinematographer kept one eye on the rising sun, another on a computer screen which showed him light meter readings from dozens of sensors placed all over the exterior of the building. The sun sliced through the thermal layers, a fiery sliver of red, a new smog-shrouded LA dawn. He slammed a hand down on a big panic button and an air horn sounded which made Ryder wince.

A moment later, the window exploded outwards as the stuntman's flailing, burning body broke through it backwards.

Then something really strange happened.

The shards of glass dancing like crystals in the dawn light around the stuntman as he fell all changed into dollar signs, little silver ones, like freshly minted coins. Next the heads of the people around him popped like cartoon bubbles, only to be replaced by more dollar signs.

The sizes of the symbols were proportional. The cinematographer, some celebrated Swedish prodigy who came in at a cool thousand an hour, had a dollar sign as enormous as an Easter Island head. His pack of assistants, probably no more than five hundred a day apiece, were like little dollar sign ducklings following their mother around. The twelve cameras, eleven grand a day each, were substantial dollar signs that looked like they were made of plates of steel riveted together like the hulls of tanks.

This trip was going bad, and Ryder gave a desperate glance back towards his trailer which had become a huge downy dollar sign, overstuffed like a poofy couch. Forty five hundred a week.

There was applause and his head snapped back. The blue vinyl and canvas airbag was deflating. He had missed the landing. Safety crews, a gaggle of dollar signs, rushed forward to cut the stuntman out of his Nomex suit. Two mid-sized dollar signs – runners, gaffers, sound guys, who the hell knew what – high fived each other. His assistant hopped into his lap, her arms around his neck and her derriere wiggling joyously against his groin.

It was then that he noticed the cinematographer still had his head underneath the replay hood. Ryder concentrated on him. With his head covered, he was the only normal-looking person in sight, but when he came up for air, his dollar sign looked distinctly unhappy.

It pivoted left and right, and gave out a mighty sigh. "We didn't get it."

"What do you mean you didn't get it?" Ryder cried, "It cost a million dollars!"

"The smog. There was too much of it. It muddied the light."

"Smog? This is fucking Los Angeles! There's always too much smog!"

"Not always, not at dawn."

Ryder slumped in his chair. "So what do we do?"

"What can we do? We can't use the footage. We'll have to try the shot again tomorrow." The man shook his dollar sign again and walked away.

How the fuck was he going to afford to repeat this shot?

Ryder was way out of his depth here; he could admit that to himself now. Back when he had started looking into financing his first movie, it had looked, well, not exactly easy, but he had done the ins and outs of bigger financial projects in the past. He had directed nearly a dozen successful films over the past fifteen years, so how much harder could financing one be? He had figured he could handle it. Way past handling now, eh Petey-boy? He was astonished how much the union guys wanted, and the local politicos wanted, the equipment rental guys – everybody had their hands out – and the $75 million, $75 million out of his own pocket, didn't go very far. Not as far as it had to. He was in this movie, in it up to his eyeballs.

A little math last night over several drinks showed his options dwindling. Of the original $75 million, only about three remained. He figured he had a couple million he could siphon out of stocks and other holdings, and he could pull another couple out of the house by refinancing. And that was about it. Seven million dollars give or take a little, but he needed more, much more – probably somewhere in the neighborhood of twenty million dollars to finish it right. More if the smog kept fucking him up. What he needed, was a plan.

And glue. A lot more glue.

*****

For a moment, neither one of them moved. Deirdre stood next to the bed wearing only black stiletto heels and a silver thong looking at the window, or rather the ragged hole in the broken glass where the window had been. Ricky stood in front of the closet door, the camera for the moment forgotten dangling from its strap on his left wrist.

She stepped forward cautiously and leaned over to look down into the courtyard in front of the hotel. The heels made her balance precarious and she had a moment of vertigo. Was this the tenth floor? No, it was the eleventh, she remembered now, and the body looked very tiny down there on the pavement, a small crowd gathering around it.

How had she misjudged so badly? It was, after all, supposed to be just a Badger Game. The setup was pretty simple. She would spot some guy sitting alone in the casino wearing a wedding band, sidle up next to him, and play it friendly. Ricky had taught her well. She could spool out the perfect mix of shy and aggressive, flirting and serious, reading the responses of the mark all the way. A flip of the hair, resting her hand on top of his as he gambled, the accidental brush of her breast against his arm, then the tantalizing whisper – she was a single woman looking for a good, uncomplicated, no-strings-attached fuck. Was there something the wife didn't like, wouldn't do because it was too dirty? She, he could rest assured, would do it all. A one-time and one-time-only offer. Was he interested?

It amazed Deirdre how quickly the vow "'Til death do you part" faded in the face of the slogan "What happens in Vegas stays in Vegas."

She'd take him up to her room – it wouldn't do to have the wife walk in if they were traveling together – and get busy. At the right moment, Ricky would pop out of the closet, camera clicking away. He brought a gun along just in case the guy got violent, but so far he hadn't needed to even show it. Deirdre intentionally picked guys who looked soft.

Some would curse. Some would call her a bitch. Some would cry. Some would beg. Some would swear they had never done anything like it before and never would again as long as they lived. All of them would hand over their money, take the memory card from the camera, and run like the building was on fire, though one had taken a moment on his way out the door to apologize to Deirdre, which for the life of her she couldn't understand.

In Reno it had gone smooth as silk, fourteen times at nine hotels over the course of a month.

Here in Vegas, it had all gone to hell on the very first play.

Tiny faces in the crowd turned upwards to look at the hotel and Deirdre stepped back from the window quickly, though certainly no one could really see let alone identify her from that distance.

"We have to go," Ricky said from behind her.

She looked over her shoulder at him. He had not moved from the closet doorway.

She looked at the floor strewn with clothing and started collecting hers. She scooped up her bra and shorts and tossed them in the general direction of her suitcase. Her shirt had gotten kicked under the bed and she had to kneel down on all fours to reach it.

"We have to go," Ricky repeated, flat and emotionless, like a commentator at a particularly boring golf tournament. His complete detachment frightened her a little bit. He stepped forward and lifted the wallet out of the pocket of the man's pants wadded up on the floor, leafed through it, took some of the cash, and put it back.

"I'm going as fast as I can." She could hear a tremor in her voice, panic nibbling at the edges of her self control. Releasing the hair clips, Deirdre stripped off the brunette wig she was wearing and shook out her own long blonde hair.

Did she have to worry about fingerprints in a hotel room? There were no doubt hundreds of them. The drinking glass from the nightstand went into her suitcase along with the wig and the wrapper from the condom. The condom itself was on the body in the courtyard. There was nothing she could do about retrieving that. She stepped out of her stilettos and pulled on a pair of ripped jeans. She was in such a rush to put on her shirt that she accidentally misaligned the buttons and tucked it into the jeans without catching her mistake. She crammed her feet into white sneakers without socks.

Ricky came out of the bathroom where he had flushed the camera memory card down the toilet. He zipped up her suitcase after piling in her clothing and throwing the camera and her heels inside.

They took one more look around the room for anything they may have missed. A glance out the room door showed that the hallway was still empty, though that wouldn't be true for long. They ran to the stairway, up three flights, and down the hallway to the elevator. Deirdre pressed the button and they waited an interminable time for it to arrive. She resisted mashing the button rapidly, repeatedly, but just barely.

They scurried into the empty elevator the moment the doors slid open and Deirdre pressed the button for the lobby.

She leaned against the handrail and tried to slow her breathing. "Shit, I didn't think he'd kill himself. Did you think he'd kill himself? Because I sure didn't."

"Of course I didn't think he'd kill himself." Ricky shook his head. "Where's the angle in that? We've haven't even made our expenses yet, and now we have to get out of town."

"You think someone saw us together?"

"It doesn't matter. The casino is full of cameras, and even with the wig I'm not taking chances. No, we're out of here. Your shirt is buttoned wrong."

Though her hands were shaking, Deirdre had the shirt fixed as they reached the ground floor. They walked through the lobby at a leisurely pace, arm in arm, Ricky carrying the suitcase, a couple at the end of a relaxing vacation. Two empty police cars were stopped in the entryway, their light bars popping blue and red, their radios filling the air with chatter.

Across the parking lot Ricky threw the suitcase into the trunk of a black 1963 Buick Rivera as Deirdre got in and buckled her seatbelt. "Where are we going to go?"

He got in and twisted the key, the big V-8 roaring to life. "I've got a thing I want to try in Los Angeles."

*****

Scott's earpiece emitted a burst of static, and then his partner's voice came through as though he was standing right beside him, "You in position yet?"

He depressed the button on the radio in the left breast pocket of his jacket with his left hand, and spoke softly down into his coat as if holding conference with his own armpit, "Give me another minute. It's darker than shit back here and there's garbage everywhere."

"Roger," was Miller's reply.

Scott picked his way around the piles of trash strewn in his path. The light of the streetlamp at the mouth of the alley behind him penetrated only weakly down this far, the way ahead darker still. As his eyes adjusted, he passed what he was pretty sure was a cat, dead and bloated lying on its side near the wall, and for a moment was thankful that it was as dark as it was. He continued moving, careful not to kick broken bottles or cans on the ground, until he came to a spot about 20 feet from the end of the alley. Three concrete steps lead up to a door painted some dark color, indistinguishable in the minimal light. Iron pipe sunk into the concrete formed a banister along the left side of the stairway. Above the door there was a wire cage enclosing a light socket, its bulb long gone. The back of the building was without a fire escape. That was probably a violation of fire code, but it meant that Scott had only one exit to worry about.

Scott hunkered down between a small dumpster and a row of overflowing garbage cans. He had a good view of the door. Across the alley from his position was a poster on the wall for some toothpaste brand, the model's teeth glowing white in the darkness. "In position." He whispered into the radio. The broken concrete of the alley was slick beneath his feet with some unidentified slime. Scott breathed through his mouth to minimize the stench.

"Moving in, leaving radio engaged," was the reply.

Scott heard the sound of his partner's breathing in his ear, the rate increasing as he approached the door on the other side of the building. Scott drew his own weapon from his shoulder holster and rested the butt on the dumpster lid. The pounding on the front door sounded tinny in his ear. "DEA! Open up! We have a warrant to search the premises!"

A light went on in a room on the second floor throwing a yellow, rectangular streak into the alleyway. Scott's eyes were drawn behind him to the lump in the alley, which in the light could definitely be identified as a dead black and gray cat, insects energetically crawling over its face, its eyes mostly gone. He felt his gorge rise, swallowed it back down, and returned his attention to the door.

"DEA!" His partner shouted over the radio, "On the count of three I will enter through force if necessary. One... Two..."

The alley door burst open revealing two men back lit by a bulb somewhere on the ceiling of the hallway behind them. Both were white. One was very thin, shirtless, his ribs showing in stark relief from the light behind him.

Barefoot in white boxer shorts, he hopped up and down on his left foot on the landing at the top of the concrete stairs while trying to stick his right through the leg of a pair of jeans. Stringy hair hung into his face. The other was also shirtless, but larger and well-muscled, wearing jeans and sneakers.

"I think they're coming your way," he heard his partner panting as he entered at the front of the building.

Now there's a newsflash, Scott thought to himself.

Scott crouched over with most of his body behind the dumpster, his right arm extended over the top and gun pointed at the larger of the two. "DEA! Put your hands up!"

The skinny one straightened, dropping the jeans and putting his hands up, the jeans comically tangled around his right ankle. The big one hesitated less than a second, leaping off the landing and hitting the ground heavily at the bottom of the stairs. He pounded down the alley towards Scott.

"Stop!" Scott yelled. He tried to bring the gun over to aim at the man but found the sleeve of his jacket caught on some kind of cleat on the top of the dumpster. He wrenched at it and heard the fabric start to tear.

As the man ran down the alley, he drew a small gun from the waistband of his jeans, which looked even smaller in his large hand. Something low caliber, Scott figured, maybe a .22. He pictured the bullet entering through his eye and ricocheting around in his skull like a marble in a clothes dryer. Scott had turned now, crouched with his back flat against the brick wall next to the dumpster. He wrenched his right arm again, the fabric of the jacket separating near the shoulder. His arm suddenly coming loose ruined his balance and sent his feet out from under him. He landed hard on his ass, his legs out straight in front of him, and felt the slime seeping through the seat of his pants.

The man skidded to a halt in front of the poster and pivoted towards Scott. As he brought the weapon up, his feet slid a little on the slick concrete, and his first shot hit slightly to the left of Scott's head. The bullet slammed into the wall, throwing hot chips of brick into his face.

Scott fired from his sitting position, the gun almost resting on his right thigh, bringing up the barrel as he fired. The first bullet passed through the man's right knee causing him to buckle to that side. The second shot caught him in the stomach. It passed through the meat of his abdomen and exited to lodge in the cheek of the model on the poster behind him. Scott fired a third and final time as the man fell, this time hitting him in the neck, tearing out the side and sending a spray of bright, arterial blood into the air. The man spun and fell face first into the poster, sliding down, smearing blood across it, to end in a fetal heap against the wall.

Scott rolled away from the wall and lay in the alley on his left shoulder, the gun in his right hand pointed around the dumpster at the man still on the landing at the top of the stairs with his pants twisted around one ankle. "Don't you fucking move!" his voice rasping in his throat.

The man laced his fingers on the top of his head – he had done this before, "Easy, man! Easy! I'm not moving!"

Miller came out of the door behind the man, grabbing hold of a big fistful of greasy hair and hauling the man in front of him as a shield. He quickly took in the scene in the alley. "You OK?" He called out.

"Fucking fine." Scott pushed himself into a sitting position, his left hand sinking into something wet and nasty, already feeling a little jittery and nauseous as the adrenaline passed. He shook his hand to fling off whatever was on it.

"Move, fuckhead." Miller shoved the man, who stumbled down the staircase with his pants dragging behind him.

When they reached Scott, he was standing with his hands on his knees taking long, shaky breaths. Miller holstered his own gun and bent to check the man on the ground. "He's done." He picked up the gun next to the body by the barrel using a handkerchief to preserve any fingerprint evidence, but didn't think his partner would have any difficulty with the shooting review board on this one. The thin man took the opportunity to hastily pull on his pants.

Scott holstered his own weapon, noticing the tear in the sleeve as he did so. "I really liked this jacket." He kicked the body on the ground once in the chest. The three returned to the stairway, Scott turned to the thin man. "We're not going to have any problem with you, are we?"

The man's Adam's apple bobbed up and down as he glanced down the alley at the body of his partner. "No, man."

"Good." Scott took hold of the banister on the stairs with both hands and wrenched at it, swaying his body back and forth. Satisfied that it was solid, he took out handcuffs and locked one on the man's right wrist and the other to the pipe. "Don't go anywhere."

"Get me my shoes while you're in there," the handcuffed man called to them as they climbed the three steps and went in through the door.

Miller had passed through the building on the way to

the back door and hadn't run into any other occupants, but better safe than sorry – both men drew their guns again.

The short hallway beyond the door opened into the kitchen lit by a single bulb screwed into a fixture that was meant to hold three. Empty soda and beer cans were scattered across the scratched, cream-colored, Formica top. The sink was full of dirty dishes, a few roaches working on the leftovers. A garbage can stood in the corner filled with pizza boxes folded in half. They both passed through into the living room – sprung couch with a blue threadbare blanket thrown over it, yellow plastic coffee table scarred with cigarette burns, and new 60" flat panel TV and satellite receiver on the floor. They moved up the stairs, keeping to the outsides of the treads to minimize creaking. The bedroom nearest the stairs had a stained mattress on the floor with a pair of dirty Converse sneakers next to it. The closet was empty, lacking even a door.

Scott pointed at the shoes with his gun, "Found his shoes."

"We'll bring them to him on the way out." Miller replied, and they continued down the hallway.

Beyond the bedroom was a bathroom. The toilet seat was missing and it looked like it hadn't been flushed in roughly ten years. The smell was beyond belief.

"How do people live like this?" Miller asked.

Scott didn't know and only shook his head in response.

The hallway ended at another bedroom. This one also had a stained mattress on the floor, a sawed-off, pump-action shotgun resting nearby. Scott holstered his gun and picked up the shotgun, operated the pump several times ejecting four shells, and put the empty gun back down. He picked up a copy of Grisham's *The Pelican Brief* off the mattress. "He's never going to know how it ended."

"I read it. It sucked." Miller looked around the room, "Where do you suppose the stuff is?"

They checked the closet in that bedroom as well, finding clothing, some free weights on the floor, and a generous collection of porn magazines, mostly bondage, on the upper shelf, but not what they were looking for. Overturning the mattress they found a narrow incision in the underside.

"Paydirt." Scott carefully pulled back the edge of the mattress cover the reveal banded stacks of money, two bags of white powder, probably cocaine, and one larger bag of marijuana. "How much do you figure?"

"Those are, what, hundreds?" Miller peered over Scott's shoulder.

Scott shifted his head left and right to get a better look at the tops and bottoms of the banded stacks, "Some hundreds, some fifties."

"I think Dorado's onto us. I'm sure he can't prove anything, but still. We'd better just take a stack or two."

Scott nodded, "OK." He reached into the mattress and pulled out two of the stacks and flipped both to his partner who put them into his breast pocket. Initially Miller had been uneasy about taking the money; Scott always saw it as well-deserved hazard pay. Besides, if they didn't take it, it would just end up in the state coffers where politicians would deal it out to their cronies.

The two of them turned the mattress back over, and replaced the Grisham on top. Scott grabbed the sneakers off the floor of the other bedroom. In the front hallway they separated. Miller went out the front to their unmarked car to call in the crime scene, and pack the money up under the driver's seat to retrieve later.

Scott went out the back to keep the suspect company and clarify for him how much money had been in his stash. In general it didn't matter if there was a discrepancy between how much cash a suspect said he had and how much was actually found at the scene – who would trust the accounting of a cokehead? Still, enough discrepancies could cause some problems, bring down an internal audit, even for two agents as decorated as Scott and Miller. It was better if the suspect could be convinced to alter his numbers before he was officially questioned. Scott was sure that this one could be convinced. The alternative was that the suspect would be fatally wounded. Scott, unbeknownst to Miller, had exercised that option a couple of times in the past.

Scott went out onto the landing and lit a cigarette. The suspect was sitting on the bottom step, his right hand up at shoulder level because he was handcuffed to the railing. Scott tossed the sneakers down at the man, bouncing them off the back of his head.

The man hunched his shoulders like a turtle, "What the fuck, man." He then realized that the sneakers lying on the steps next to him were his. "Oh, thanks, man." He reached for the sneakers with his right hand, coming to the end of the chain before realizing that he was still handcuffed to the railing. He lined the sneakers in front of him and then pushed each foot in without untying them by rocking his ankles and using his thumb as a shoehorn.

Scott looked out over the alley – the dead body, the dead cat, the stinking garbage, the stinking suspect. He hated this fucking job, but you couldn't beat the take-home pay.

10 Days Earlier

James Dorado leaned back in his chair, steepled his fingers on his ample stomach, and pondered. Being the director of the LA field office of the DEA had its perks: company car, nice parking space, good secretary. It also had more than its share of ulcers, two of them staring up at him from the open folder on his desk at this moment – Agents Miller and Scott. On the surface, they were two of the most decorated officers in LA, and personally responsible for more drug seizures than any other agents in California. Underneath, Dorado knew though couldn't yet prove, they were skimming.

He thought it had begun about two years ago when Miller had shot a street dealer to death during a bust. It was a good shooting; no one doubted that. The problem was that the dealer had had a small pharmacy on his person, but pretty much bupkus for cash. The DEA had thousands of drug bust cases logged and analyzed – if you found X drugs, you typically found roughly Y dollars.. Oh, sometimes you found a dealer who had just used all his money to buy drugs, or one who had just sold all his drugs, in which case the X to Y ratio was all screwed up, but such cases were the exception rather than the rule. It was really a matter of simple economics. And maybe that particular dealer two years ago had been one of the exceptions, but since that date, nearly all of Miller and Scott's busts were coming up light.

Dorado knew they were taking it home with them, and he started digging. The company rumor mill was unstoppable, so even his discrete inquiries got around, and Miller and Scott probably knew that he knew. And so began the dance. Dorado had to be cautious. Even as director, it was a risk making waves against two such decorated officers who regularly had their faces in the papers without sufficient proof. Dorado's position wasn't helped by the fact that he was one of only two minority DEA field office directors in the entire US of A, the other being an Irish woman in the Atlanta Division. The perception was that he had gotten his job because of misguided diversity quotas and his mixed black and Mexican heritage. While he couldn't speak for the woman in Atlanta, in his instance that was probably true. Coming up past an unremarkable start as desk agent, Dorado knew he had advanced through the ranks far more quickly that his skills and record merited. Despite this, Dorado saw himself as a good director, on the whole well thought of by those under his command, and he planned on keeping his office clean. Which is why Scott and Miller gave him such a bellyache.

His job had cost him his marriage to a fine woman. After years of dinners interrupted, weekends at work, and vacations cut short all for the sake of some crisis at the office, she had finally had enough. The straw that broke the camel's back was a "highly credible tip" concerning a big shipment of drugs, the proceeds of which were expected to fund terrorism both domestic and abroad. It came while they were on their fifth wedding anniversary getaway at Niagara Falls. The intel turns out to be bad, and she was gone less than three weeks later. He didn't blame her, though he missed her often. She had remarried to an accountant about a year later, a really nice guy Dorado grudgingly liked, who never had an emergency spreadsheet catastrophe hit during dinner.

Her ex-wife and her new husband had had two girls. Though not by nature a man who dwelled in the past or fretted over old regrets, the Christmas photo postcards he received of the shiny happy family that could have been his rested like an enormous boulder on his chest while he lay in bed at night.

Having sacrificed his marriage on the altar of his job, he certainly wasn't going to risk losing his job as well, but he wasn't going to let Scott and Miller slide either. He kept his notes and he compiled his folders and built his case carefully. Which brought him to today's entry: a bust late last night that resulted in one dead guy, one live guy, a kilo of pot and two of cocaine, and about seventy-five hundred bucks, about five thousand less than should have been there, by the numbers. The running tally he kept showed, conservatively, the two agents had pulled in approximately nearly two hundred thousand dollars apiece in the last two years. A lot of money.

Dorado admitted to himself that the temptation was great. He knew that if banded stacks of untraceable cash regularly passed through his hands, that some would probably have found its way into his pockets. But it didn't, and it wasn't, and he would be damned, clichéd though it sounded, if it was going to happen on his watch.

The buzzing of the intercom on his desk interrupted his thoughts. He reached forward and punched a button, "Yes, Helen?"

"Agents Scott and Miller here at your request."

"Send them in."

He opened the center drawer of his desk, slid the file inside, and was just pushing it closed again as the two agents walked in. He put a smile on his face, stood, and reached across the desk to shake hands with both of the agents. "Gentlemen. A morning's congratulations for good work last night."

"Thank you, sir," Scott replied.

"Please, sit down," he said, indicating the two wing back chairs positioned side by side across from him. He settled his considerable bulk back into his own seat with a sigh. "Coffee?"

"No, we're good," Miller said.

Dorado pulled a file from his 'In' box and flipped it open, "From your reports I don't think you'll have any problem with the shooting."

Scott leaned back and crossed his legs at the ankle, "We just finished our statements."

"Good. I've tentatively scheduled the shooting review board for," he leafed through pages on his desk calendar, "Monday morning at eleven. That good for you?"

Scott and Miller looked at each other, that silent communication that partners have passing between them.

Dorado noticed it, "Problem, gentlemen?"

Scott turned to him, "I'm going to have to turn in my gun, stay off the streets until then."

"That is standard procedure. You've been through it before. We'll have you back on active the middle of next week."

Scott leaned forward, his elbows resting on his knees, gesturing with his hands, "That bust last night was just a fluke. I heard from a reliable source that there were drugs at that address, and the source was good, so we moved on it."

"And you got a good arrest. I don't see a problem."

"We've got a real high-visibility bust set for tonight. One of those parties up in the hills. We've been setting up for it for months."

Dorado leaned back in his chair. Now he saw the problem. The media was screaming that all the drug busts were poor minority folk, while the wealthy drug users went unpunished. What the media didn't realize was that the poor drug users and dealers did their business in parks and schoolyards and on street corners, places where they were almost bound to get caught. The wealthy did it in their luxury high rise apartments and fancy homes in the hills, behind enormous, expensive walls and out of sight. Their dealers were discrete, catering to a very specific clientele. Upper crust arrests like this were too few and far between to pass up. He ran through the lists of other agents available to him in his head. Several were on loan to the San Diego field office to cover a shipment supposedly coming in by boat this weekend. One was on vacation, another on sick leave after breaking an ankle tackling a suspect on a staircase. These guys watched way too many reruns of *Walker, Texas Ranger*. There were many big investigations all going on at the same time.

Scott and Miller waited while their boss ruminated. They knew the manpower problems he faced as well as he did, and were pretty sure he would have little choice but to leave them on the case. Better, they thought, to let him reach that conclusion on his own.

Dorado leaned forward again and rested his arms on the desktop, "Hollywood Hills case, right? No knowns, no priors?" People who didn't have criminal records rarely got into shootouts. The risk was an officer supposed to be inactive awaiting a shooting review board getting involved in another shooting.

Miller shifted in his seat a little, "We plan to go up there and watch the place and see who shows up. We won't really know what we're dealing with until then.

Dorado didn't like it. He weighed the risks of sending Scott into a position that might require shooting versus the publicity that would come out of a non-minority drug bust versus the price of passing on the chance entirely. Politics, politics.

"I could turn in my gun, and go in with my partner armed," Scott suggested.

Dorado turned that suggestion over in his head. Scott would then technically be in compliance with the directive requiring him to turn in his weapon until the shooting review board had obtained its findings. It also left his partner without backup. The fallout from one or both of them being killed because Scott didn't have his weapon would be considerable. Still, what were the chances? Besides, Scott was certain to bring a personal weapon along just in case regardless of the rules. Of that Dorado was certain.

Dorado drummed his fingers on the desktop, "What's your read on it."

Scott leaned back in his chair and looked at Miller. "High cash, low risk sales to upper crust buyers. I don't see it as the sort of thing someone would bring a gun to."

Miller interjected, "Unless the dealer has a bodyguard."

Scott nodded, "Unless the dealer has a bodyguard. He could be armed. Probably would be armed. But would he start a shootout with DEA agents?"

Miller tipped his head from side to side, "Unlikely."

Scott agreed, "Unlikely."

They both turned back to Dorado who echoed, "Unlikely. Still, we have to clear one case before we start the next one, so I'm going to have to ask you to turn in your weapon pending the outcome of the review board. The risk of you involved in another shooting before that review, in fact less than 24 hours after the last shooting, is more than I'm willing to bear. Officially." He lowered his voice and continued, "Unofficially, you're both big boys, and your partner has a gun. If you want to go in to what you see as a low risk situation unarmed, I'm not going to order you not to. Clear?"

Both men nodded. “Crystal,” Scott said. Dorado had managed to maintain his deniability should the whole thing go sour on them, and yet left himself well positioned to pick up some of the glory if they made an arrest. They expected nothing less of Dorado who they saw as a marginally competent boss but a superior politician. They both stood, shook hands again with Dorado, and left.

After the door to his office closed, Dorado signed the requisite papers in the folder on the shooting, closed it, and threw it into his ‘Out’ box. He opened his center desk drawer and pulled out the other folder. Those two were very cool for officers on the take. Still, Dorado thought, had he seen a gleam in Scott’s eyes as he spoke of the high amount of cash that a dealer at a glitzy party could have?

Maybe a high-end dealer could be persuaded to testify against Scott and Miller as to how much money had actually been in his possession at the time of the arrest. Better to let the dealer slide and get Miller and Scott, allow Dorado to clean his own house, right? Although maybe Scott and Miller knew this, and were going to restrain their greed on this particular arrest, though Dorado didn’t think that would be the case.

This could be the one that would allow him to nail those two once and for all.

*****

Ricky guided the car down the road, his left wrist resting over the top of the wheel, his right on the seat beside him holding a cup with the words ‘Mountain Grown’ printed on it in green. His sunglasses cut the morning sun, coming directly at them as they headed east, to a manageable glare. Deirdre leaned back in the passenger seat dozing lightly and watching the scenery flash by, her own cup of coffee warm between her thighs. They passed the main entrance to MGM studios on their right. A man standing next to a yellow Ferrari parked in the gateway was yelling at the guard, the cords on his neck bulging out above the collar of his shirt. A second man stood behind him, balding with the last strands of his hair grown long and pasted flat across the top of his skull. He had the man by his shoulder and was trying to coax him back into the car, but the man continued to yell, now poking the guard in the chest with his finger. Deirdre watched the exchange recede to a spot in the side mirror without resolution.

Ricky swung a hard left, passing through a traffic light just as it went from yellow to red, the rear tires squealing in protest. Deirdre slid over towards the door, the lap belt digging into her hip. He then took a right a couple of blocks down and retrieved a sheet of paper from the inside pocket of his coat. With the cup in one hand and the page in the other, for a time neither hand was on the wheel, Ricky steering with his knees. He glanced from paper to roadway and back to paper again as he drove.

"Hey, Dee, catch an address for me."

Deirdre straightened up in the seat and looked out the window. They were off the main boulevard now, passing among warehouses and machine shops. They drove by a gas station ("Tires Rotated While U Wait") and a welding place, a shower of sparks coming off something a man was working on over a barrel alongside the building. In a small wrecking yard, Deirdre noticed a starfighter from some old TV show, Deirdre thought it was *Battlestar Galactica*, its paint peeling and one wing cracked and bent downwards. A 7-Eleven was next to the wrecking yard, its address in black block lettering on the glass door. "That 7-Eleven was number two-sixteen."

"Two-sixteen. Two-sixteen." Ricky looked from paper to road. "There, there. That was it." Ricky dropped the page, letting it flutter to the floorboards. He let go of the coffee cup and pulled a U-turn in the middle of the street. Deirdre barely managed to keep his coffee from overturning by pinning it to the seatback with her hand.

The car thumped over the track of a wide chain link gate that was open, and into a beaten dirt parking area where Ricky pulled in next to a battered blue pickup. When he shut off the engine, the whine of power tools could be heard outside even with the windows closed, a soundtrack like a migraine waiting to start.

Ricky turned to her, “Dwight’s a little sleazy, but I’m going to need his in if I’m going to make this deal happen. Just ignore him and let me do all the talking, OK?”

Deirdre put both coffee cups on top of the dashboard and slung the strap of her purse over one shoulder. “Sure, Ricky, whatever you say.”

They got out of the car and walked towards a cinderblock building with a dented metal door. Outside of the car, the power tools were every bit as deafening as Deirdre had expected, a piercing shriek that cut to the bone. Inside the building was a little quieter, but not much. The interior was smaller than one would have thought from the outside, with barely enough room for a single battered metal desk and a row of filing cabinets along one wall. The air was hot and dry, pushed around unenthusiastically by an oscillating fan on top of one of the cabinets. A man in jeans and a blue work shirt sat on one corner of the desk flipping through papers attached to a clipboard. He looked up when they entered and spoke in the loud tones of a man used to working around all the noise, “Can I help you folks?”

“I’m looking for Dwight Day,” Ricky shouted.

“He’s, uh,” the man rifled the papers on the clipboard, “back section, building area seven. If you want to go back there to see him, I’ll have to take you.”

Ricky surreptitiously squeezed Deirdre’s elbow, a signal she knew well. She smiled and subtly thrust her chest at him, "I would appreciate that if it wouldn't be too much trouble."

The man blinked at her, "How's that?"

"I said, I would appreciate that," Deirdre found herself shouting, standing up on the toes of her boots and leaning forward as if to physically propel her voice across the short distance between them.

He shied back from her a bit, probably her morning coffee breath, "I'd be glad to."

He led them out of the office and locked the door behind him with a key ring attached to a chain on his belt. They went down a wide alleyway towards the sound of the tools. The ground was loose, soft dirt. Ricky grimaced as dust built up on his highly polished shoes. Deirdre walked leaning way forwards, walking on her toes, to keep her heels from sinking in and pitching her on her ass.

As they passed an opening in the cinderblock wall on their right, the whine climbed to a fever pitch, a noise that washed over them like a physical wave. Inside Deirdre saw three men wearing heavy headphones like the guys on the runways at airports wear. They were feeding boards into the maw of some kind of machine, pulling ornately beveled molding out the far side and stacking it against one wall. The air was hazy with sawdust, the smell of pine and machine oil. Beyond the opening, the whine reduced, gradually replaced as they walked with an orchestral percussion section of hammering and drilling, equally as loud, and not an improvement.

The alley continued, passing a series of bay-like areas separated by sheets of corrugated metal where sets for movies, like whole rooms, were being assembled. Their guide turned to them, "We're pretty busy here working on the sets for the new J. J. Abrams film. Very sci-fi. Wild stuff."

Deirdre smiled, fascinated.

They stepped out of the alleyway into one of the bays. Its floor was poured concrete. Ricky stomped several times to try and knock some of the dust off his shoes. Deirdre was glad to be back on solid ground. The man made a 'wait here' gesture to Ricky and Deirdre and walked across the bay to tap the shoulder of a man on his knees using an air hammer to drive finishing nails into the frame of a door. The man put the air hammer aside and stood, wiping dust from his jeans and taking off his safety glasses. Dwight was short, but very broad, with the sleeves of his work shirt rolled up over considerable biceps. His black hair was oiled and combed straight back on his head like a helmet. He recognized Ricky and smiled with his mouth open, swaggering across the bay to shake his hand, "Hey, Ricky," he said loudly, "I was wondering when you were going to show up." He turned to the other man, "I've got them Carl. Just give me five minutes."

Carl looked at his watch, "I need this set on a truck to Paramount at four today."

"Not a problem. You have my word on it."

Carl seemed satisfied with Dwight's word, and turned and walked back the way they had come. Dwight pivoted to Ricky. "You look like life's been good to you," he said, noticing the Rolex on Ricky's wrist. He hiked a thumb at Deirdre, "This the girl you're seeing?"

Ricky shouted introductions between Dwight and Deirdre. Dwight's eyes met Deirdre's for exactly one millisecond before dropping to her chest. He shook Deirdre's hand with the enthusiasm of a sheltie going to town on her leg, no doubt pleased with the show he was giving himself by shaking Deirdre's boobs around, and causing one bra strap to slip off her shoulder. Yeah, Dwight was quite a piece of work. When she retrieved her hand, she transferred her purse from one shoulder to the other, sliding the bra strap back into place at the same time.

Dwight leaned towards Deirdre, "No reason to shout at each other out here, let's go somewhere quieter and a little more private." For a moment Deirdre thought he meant just the two of them, and wondered how far Ricky would let Dwight go to get what he needed. Dwight did a two-handed 'after you' gesture towards the alley they had come from, and they turned and walked in that direction. Dwight hung back, Deirdre was certain, to check out her ass. Flustered and getting angry, she stepped off the concrete pad of the bay into the alleyway, only to have her heel sink into the soft ground a good two inches. Falling backwards, arms starting to pinwheel, Dwight was suddenly there, his hand around her left biceps to steady her, the back of his hand rubbing against the side of her breast. "Nice shoes," he glanced down at her boots, "but not good on ground this soft. I'll help you."

They continued down the alleyway, Dwight holding Deirdre's arm and copping a feel. Had to hand it to old Dwight; he knew all the tricks. Deirdre remained stone faced. Ricky tagged along behind.

Shortly Dwight opened a door in the left-hand wall and ushered them inside. It was a small break room with several round Formica tables on metal legs scattered about, blue molded plastic and chrome chairs in loose clusters around them. A refrigerator, yellowed with age, stood in one corner. A counter next to it had a coffeepot, microwave, and a collection of snacks. When Dwight closed the door behind them, the room was surprisingly quiet; there must be soundproofing in the walls. As they sat down, Deirdre thought she had gone deaf after the barrage of noise outside, but then heard the wheezing of the ancient fridge in the corner.

"Can I get you anything?" Dwight asked.

Ricky answered for both of them. "No, we're good," he began loudly, before clearing his throat and answering in a more normal tone of voice.

Dwight went over to the counter, picked up a package of Oreos, and returned. He spun a chair around and sat on it backwards, his heavy forearms resting on the chair back. He noisily opened the cellophane package and popped a cookie in his mouth, spoke with his mouth full, "Before I give it to you, and I'm not saying I won't because we've got a deal, what do you want it for?"

Ricky smiled broadly, clearly a question he was prepared for, "Heck, look at this girl," he indicated Deirdre with an open palm, "she's going to be a star."

Dwight tossed another cookie in his mouth, chewed, and leaned back in his chair to inspect Deirdre around the table. His eyes roamed slowly up and down making her skin crawl.

"She's got a nice rack on her, and her face is good," Dwight said, making Deirdre feel like the two men were appraising a race horse and wondered when they would make her open her mouth so they could inspect her teeth.

"She might need to drop a few pounds," Dwight continued, "Getting a little thick in the waist. Whatever. It's your thing." He leaned forward in the chair, fished a fancy envelope out of his back pocket, and tossed it on the table. Even folded over and grimy, Deirdre could tell the cream-colored paper was of very high quality. She couldn't contain her curiosity and picked up the envelope. Inside was an invitation to a party for that night at some address she didn't recognize. 'A special thanks to the crew for their outstanding job.' Ricky took the invitation from her and read it to himself with his lips moving.

Deirdre didn't get it. Dwight must have seen the look of confusion on her face, "Your boyfriend didn't tell you? He's taking you to a big Hollywood party tonight. Your big chance to be discovered!"

"They invite the set builders to those parties?"

Dwight scratched his head, sliding his fingers around in the oil, "Not usually, but rumor has it that the producer's account is slipping into the red so he's doing it to grease some union reps. Networking, favors, seeing and being seen; that's the stuff this whole town runs on. That, and money, right, Ricky?"

"Right, Dwight." Ricky said. He put the invitation into his jacket pocket and brought out a thick envelope. He slid it across the table to Dwight. Dwight picked it up and flipped through the bills inside. Those that Deirdre could see were hundreds, and it looked like there were quite a few of them.

"Good enough," He snapped the edge of the envelope against the table top and flipped another Oreo in his mouth as he stood up stuffed the envelope into his back pocket, "enjoy your party." He crushed the cellophane package with two cookies still inside, the muscles in his forearm bunching and writhing like snakes, and threw it into the garbage can near the door as he walked them out.

Back in the alley they were assaulted by the noise of the saws and hammers, even more shattering after the quiet of the break room. Dwight again held Deirdre's arm as they walked, fingers stroking the side of her breast. In the parking lot, he released her arm and smacked her on the ass hard enough to sting through her jeans, "You won't forget old Dwight when you're famous, will you?"

"Not even if I wanted to," she gave him a fuck you glare as she climbed into the car and slammed the door hard.

She folded her hands across her chest and slouched down in the seat, certain her cheeks, both sets, were burning.

Dwight shrugged and talked to Ricky over the top of the car as Ricky opened the driver-side door, “If anyone asks, you’re with carpenter’s local 415, not that anyone is going to ask. I don’t think many of the working guys are going to the party. Who wants to hang out with a bunch of Hollywood snobs? But there will be plenty of people there no one knows so the invitation should be all you’ll need.”

“OK, Dwight. This should work out fine.” He got in and closed the door.

Dwight slapped the roof twice as they pulled out of the parking area and turned into traffic.

Ricky drove hunched over the wheel, shoulders tight. “Dwight,” he growled. “If I didn’t need him for this deal, I would have punched his face in.”

“Deal to what? What are we doing in LA, Ricky?”

“Have you ever seen one of these Hollywood parties, Dee?”

He glanced over at her and she shook her head.

“I worked for a caterer years ago, right after high school. We did this party at the house of some record executive. Huge fucking house, living room half the size of a football field. Right in the front hall on a table, just as you came in the door, there were these two bowls. One was full of pills, all kinds; the other was full of money.”

“What? I don’t get it.”

“The party was on the honor system. People would take what they wanted and leave money in the bowl. There were thousands of dollars in that bowl, Dee."

"And we're going to steal the bowl?"

Ricky shook his head, "No, will you listen to me? I think if I work some connections, figure out how it all goes together, I can supply those parties. I'm talking about going legit, giving up the con."

Deirdre almost laughed at the thought that Ricky considered selling drugs in the same realm as going legit. "Look, Ricky, I know we've had a bad run of luck. Vegas was my fault; I picked the wrong mark. We can get on track. Let's go back to Reno. We were doing great there."

Ricky frowned. "We weren't doing great in Reno, we were treading water. I'm tired of treading water all the time. I can make this work."

"So you think you're just going to walk into this party and start selling drugs?" She was incredulous. Ricky actually thought this was a good idea.

"Let me take care of it," Ricky raised his voice. "I know what I'm doing."

Deirdre raised her voice as well. "Christ, Ricky! Didn't you learn anything from San Francisco? Drug dealers have guns, Ricky. Drug dealers shoot people, Ricky. Are you trying to get us both killed?"

When Deirdre considered it later, she was surprised to realize that there had been almost no warning at all, at least none that she could read. Maybe there had been a slight change in the set of his face or the angle of his body, but that was it.

The back of his hand caught her just below the cheekbone, a casual whip-crack of his wrist that snapped her head over, banging it against the passenger window.

Ricky suddenly swerved sharply to the curb. A car he cut off blasted its horn at them. With the car still rocking on its springs, Ricky turned angrily towards her, his hand fisted at his side. Deirdre spun in her seat to face him, shrinking away from his fury, her back against the door. "You really must think I'm an idiot! Do you think I'm an idiot?"

She shook her head quickly, the quaver in her voice, "No, Ricky, I don't think that at all."

"Goddamn are you stupid sometimes!"

"It's just that," she froze, uncertain exactly what she had intended to say next, but fearful he would hit her again.

With a visible effort Ricky unclenched his hand. He took a deep breath and let it out. Deirdre watched him and kept herself pressed flat against the door. "Look, Dee, I've got everything thought out. This is what you might call reconnaissance. You heard Dwight, see and be seen, networking, maybe grease a few palms. I'm going to look around, get the lay of the land."

"Uh-huh."

He leaned towards her, his mouth set in a grim line, and she tried to shy back but had nowhere to go. He took her hand in his, grinding the small bones in her fingers together for emphasis as he spoke, "This is THE big opportunity, MY big opportunity, and you're going to stand around and look pretty, and stay out of my way, and not fuck it up like Vegas, right?"

She shrank back, trying to pull her hand free, trying to melt into the car door, "Right." She felt tears threatening.

Ricky let go, pulled his wallet out of his hip pocket, took a wad of money from it and stuffed it into her aching hand.

Deirdre looked down at the money dumbly, "What?"

His right hand whipped out close to her face and she flinched away from it. His finger pointed past her nose and down the road. "Get out."

"What?" she repeated.

"Down this street about a block on the right is a beauty parlor, Chinese place, I looked it up last night. Go get hair, nails, make up, the whole nine yards. Put this on," he reached into the back seat and picked up a large white box off the floor that he shoved at her, "and I'll pick you up out front at five."

"OK, Ricky." She fumbled open the door with her hand behind her and backed out onto the curbside. The box almost fell from her lap as she stood up, but she trapped it against her knees with her hand.

He reached out and pulled the door closed. She had to jump back to keep from being whacked by it. The box fell to the ground and opened. She got a glimpse of some silver material before she quickly bent over and swept it closed, clutching it to her chest. As she straightened up, Ricky pulled away from the curb in a squeal of rubber. She stood on the sidewalk and watched him drive away.

*****

Ryder sat hunched over the table, his left hand moving papers around the tabletop while his right massaged his forehead. The remnants of a hangover thumped a hard bass beat deep within his brain, and he had a nearly overwhelming urge to reach for some help of the adhesive variety, but this was too important. He had to get this right. It was consuming all his willpower to keep his shit together.

The papers told him his earlier figuring had been pretty much dead on; he had a little over seven million dollars that he could scrape together. That included everything, every dime of cash he could lay his hands on.

The clack of heavy, sensible shoes on the patio made him raise his head. Maria, his maid, was walking towards him carrying a large glass pitcher of orange juice.

"Would you like more juice, Mr. Ryder?" She spoke in English heavily accented with Spanish.

"Sure, sure," he waved at his half-empty glass, which she had begun refilling before he had even replied.

"Anything else? You should have breakfast. I have very good mango fresh from the market today."

The thought of the sweet, slimy flesh of a mango in his mouth made his sour stomach turn over. "No, nothing else."

"Yes, sir." She started clomping off across the patio towards the house.

He took a large swallow of orange juice, wishing he was washing some pills down with it. Oxy, Vicodin, something to just take the edge off his headache. Sobriety and clear-headedness was a rarity for him, and he didn't much like it. The world was too real and too close, too in his face all the time. He stood from the table and skirted the pool to lean against the railing and overlook Los Angeles. Past the railing was a sheer drop of over a hundred feet to the next house below his down the hillside. He looked for the woman who lived there and liked to sunbath nude by her pool, but she wasn't there today. Beyond her house, the hill continued downwards, the houses clustering more tightly together near the bottom as if they had all slid down there in a heap during the last earthquake. Perhaps they had.

Even this early in the day a considerable layer of smog had collected over the city, making the scene look like an aged photo in sepia tones. Later in the day the layer would thicken until the air up here near the top of the hill would become unpleasant unless a strong breeze from the ocean managed to push it more inland, in which case it was Pasadena's problem to the east. He took a breath of fresh air that only the wealthy in Los Angeles could afford and reluctantly returned to his papers.

He needed about twenty million dollars to finish his film. In truth, he needed more like thirty million, but he was reasonably certain that he could delay many of the bills until after the opening. Then he would start to get box office receipts and he could pay off the debts, provided the opening was big. Despite the fickle, movie-going public, he liked his odds. He had good special effects, a pounding soundtrack, and a passable plot. He also had a topless scene with a hot, new female singer. She was 21 but looked 16 and, despite some early arguments about the artistic merit of the nudity, she had peeled off her top and shook her cans like a pro. She fancied herself an actress. In Ryder's opinion, she couldn't act her way out of a paper sack, and he was none too fond of her singing, either, but he knew hot when he saw it. Geeks on the internet had been Photoshopping her head on nudes for years, and the buzz created by the rumor that she was appearing topless in his film was priceless. Yeah, this film was a winner.

Finishing it required him to find a way to take seven million dollars and turn them into twenty. He had already been over, and rejected, all the legal ways there was to raise that kind of money. He could have, for example, asked to borrow the money from friends with the promise to pay them back, and maybe an associate producer credit on the film. He would have taken this route if all he needed were five million or so, but he knew that he couldn't collect the kind of money he needed that way. He thought about trying to get funding out of the usual groups that funded movies, venture capitalist types. But since *Battlefield Earth* and other big-money debacles, it was hard to get money that way without surrendering the lion's share of the profits, which was something he wasn't willing to do given how big he was sure the movie would be. On top of it all, he was afraid of starting rumors that the film was over budget. Such rumors had more or less killed *Waterworld*, and *The Abyss*, and frankly had been none too good for *Titanic*. Ultimately, of course, *Titanic* had risen above the rumors, but Ryder had to admit to himself that his film was nowhere near another Titanic. He just had a zinger of an action flick with probably at least one sequel on deck.

The phone on the table rang shrilly, and he picked it up. "Ryder."

"Peter, honey," Phyllis, the caterer for tonight's party, cooed.

"What can I do for you, Phyllis?" he said tiredly.

"It's what I can do for you, darling. I was down at Jean Claude's, and he has a new shipment in of the red caviar. The rarest of the rare! And a steal at only seven hundred fifty and ounce! He has eight pounds, and I reserved it because I knew you would have to have it for the party tonight, but I had to call because the check you gave me won't cover it. How soon can you send another one?"

That was the thing about money in Hollywood. Everyone was always eager to spend someone else's. Peter could hear the lilt of greed in her voice along with the subtle sneer that he might dare as to be so gauche as to turn down such an offer. Still, this party was important to smoothing lots of union feathers, and in for a penny, in for a pound. He rolled the numbers through his head, almost one hundred grand in caviar. Jesus! He had to show some responsibility somewhere. "Too much caviar, dearest. I don't want to overwhelm the canapés, now do I? How about two and a half of the black, and two and a half of the red? I'll send another thirty thousand to you this afternoon."

"Yes, of course, darling. You're right as usual." Peter could hear the fall in her voice. With her percentage, he had just clipped thousands off her profit. He hung up the phone and sat back down in the chair, rolling the cool juice glass against his forehead.

So, given that he had no legal options open to him short of buying seven million lottery tickets and hoping for the best, illegal was the way to go. That wasn't a problem for him. He'd bought prostitutes and drugs for actors, bribed city councilmen, and once paid a judge to screw his first ex in the divorce. Still, the magnitude of what he would have to do to get the kind of money he was talking about was daunting. He considered going to a loan shark for the money, but suspected that the vig on thirteen million dollars would be more than he could ever pay off. That left... Frankly, he didn't know what that left, but he was going to have to figure something out, and soon.

*****

Deirdre stood on the sidewalk with the money crushed in her right hand and the box pinned against her chest like she was holding a load of books in junior high school. She continued staring down the street long after Ricky's car had receded from view. The throbbing counterpoints of her cheek and the side of her head were setting up a resonance in her skull, pushing towards what she was sure would become a beauty of a headache. How the hell had her life come to this?

When Ricky had picked her up two years ago, it seemed to Deirdre like she was finally getting to go somewhere.

Anywhere had to be better than her dirt poor parentless existence in Red Mountain, California, and Ricky exuded smooth confidence and charm with the same casual effort with which the sun gives off heat and light, and in roughly the same quantities.

They had traveled together, and he had taught her simple scams at first like the Pigeon Drop and the Spanish Prisoner. They did a variant of the Bejing Tea Ceremony in Arizona to snobby tourists from Connecticut with the help of an Indian who said his name was Freddy Ironbird, or something like that. She and Ricky did The Lady and the Briefcase in Sacramento, and two plays of The Long Pity Tale in San Bernardino. They had hooked up with a crew in Portland, three guys and another woman, for A Gathering Of Pearls.

They never got caught, never even close. But as the saying goes 'a fool and his money are soon parted,' so it is also true that perpetually conning fools inevitably hits on a lot of people who don't have much money to lose. Cash was always tight, and when the occasional con went bad it got even tighter.

Ricky decided that he needed to hit bigger marks. That was when things had started to go seriously wrong.

They went to Santa Barbara where he tried going with a straightforward Replicas scam. He bought one real Rolex watch – a move that just about left them penniless after weeks of successful plays – and a stack of knockoffs. The plan was to show the genuine article, sell the fake, and vanish into the wind before anyone realized the switch. They managed to pull it off exactly once on some Eurotrash heir, or maybe he was actually a genuine Prince of somewhere. On the whole, however, though rich, such people were generally not stupid, and the sales rarely completed. Besides if you were worth a bazillion dollars you could afford to walk into a store and pay some stupendous amount of money for a watch. That was maybe even part of the fun of being atrociously rich.

From there Ricky had insisted they try working drug dealers, his reasoning being that such people had a lot of money and were unlikely to call the police after being conned. To Deirdre it sounded like a stupid idea as the true currency of a successful con is trust on the part of the mark, drug dealers almost completely lacking in that particular trait. But Ricky had been doing it a lot longer than she had, he was driving the car, and she had few options open to her other than to go along for the ride.

He went with the classic Pig in a Poke, a play that took a dealer in San Francisco roughly ten seconds to discover using some chemicals in a test tube. Shots had been fired – a lot of shots if Deirdre's nightmares were at all accurate – and she thought they were both lucky to have gotten away with their lives. Ricky lost the seed money, the small amount of cocaine he had bought as the front, his gun, and even the nice briefcase he had carried to the sale. He was angry and sullen for days afterward.

Then he had announced that they were going to Reno and then Vegas, and the shit that had all turned into. Now he wanted to crash some Hollywood party and start selling drugs. And he had hit her! Was he losing his mind?

She began walking along the baking sidewalk with her head down. The exhaust and noise of the cars speeding past was making it hard to think. The heat of the sun pressed on her, mica flecks in the concrete throwing painful glints into her eyes.

Maybe the time had come for her to cut and run. The more she thought about it, the more attractive the idea became. She opened her fist and looked at the wad of money in her hand. She counted it: two hundred dollars. How far could she get on two hundred dollars? She pushed the money down into the front pocket of her jeans with her thumb.

Where could she go? Where would she live? What would she eat? What would she do? She needed to earn enough to make rent, give her some breathing room, time to put together a con of her own or find a job. She had never even graduated from high school; all her employable skills involved lying on her back. She laughed cruelly at herself.

She stopped and looked back she way she had come. There was an appliance store, its gate shut and the windows soaped over. There was a tattoo parlor, and right in front of her, a beauty salon. Red Chinese characters (at least Ricky had told Deirdre they were Chinese; they could have been Korean or Japanese for all she knew) on the glass were above the English name 'Beautiful You.' Bamboo slats and tall plants in the window kept her from seeing much of the inside.

She put her hand on the doorknob and thought again about where two hundred dollars could take her. She knew where it could take her. It could take her home. Deirdre also knew she could never go back to Red Mountain, could never face her friends who had told her she was nuts to leave with Ricky, some guy she knew nothing about who had just blown into town in a big black car. She shook her head.

If she was careful, she was sure everything would be OK. She just had to watch out for herself. Deirdre knew how to do that; she had been doing it for most of her life.

The wind chimes mounted above the door tinkled delicately as she entered.

The door closed behind her with the soft whisper of its hydraulic cylinder, shutting out the noise of the traffic outside. There was the plinking of some Chinese stringed instrument coming from speakers mounted near the ceiling. Somewhere in the profusion of plants near the front window a fountain made low gurgling noises. The air was filled with a delicate scent, the result Deirdre thought of the incense stick smoldering in a long, narrow porcelain dish on the front counter. The room had a few simple wooden chairs lined up along the wall. She didn't see anyone.

"Hello?" She advanced a few steps away from the door, the sound of her boot heels on the wooden floor sounding sharp and alien in this quiet place.

A small oriental woman came through a curtained passage at the back. She was dressed in a black satin shirt and slacks. Her hair was dark as coal and wound up on her head in a bun with two red lacquer chopsticks woven into it. She struck Deirdre as grandmotherly, though she didn't look old. She was less than five feet tall, and she had to tip her head way back to look Deirdre in the face, who was near five-eleven in her heels.

"Can I help you?" She spoke in clipped tones, so that 'help' sounded more like 'hep.'

"I," Deirdre didn't know exactly what to ask for. For a moment, she wasn't sure what she was doing here at all, and felt like running away and leaving this woman to her peaceful surroundings.

The woman waited patiently for Deirdre to say something with a confused smile on her face.

Deirdre tried again, "I'm sorry, I, that is, could you," she looked at her fingernails, then ran her fingers through her hair.

"Are you Deirdre?" the woman offered.

"Yes, I am."

"Ricky called. He said to make you beautiful."

"Yes, thank you."

She took Deirdre by the hand, hers as small a child's, and walked her towards the curtain in the back. She turned to smile at her, "Make you beautiful. You make my job easy."

Deirdre laughed and felt herself blushing.

She was led to a room with a long wooden bench draped with clean, white towels. The music in here was different, softer, reminding her of sea breezes and rushing water. The air was warm and humid and smelled of sandalwood.

The woman took the box, which Deirdre had forgotten she was holding, and placed it on a table near the door. "Please undress."

"What?"

"Please undress. Massage first. Relax inside, beautiful outside."

Deirdre sat down on the bench and ran the zippers on her boots. She tugged them off and set them aside. One teetered on its heel for a moment, and then fell over knocking the other boot over as well. She wanted to stand them up again, felt such disorder an obscenity in this place. Instead she pulled her shirt off over her head and slipped off her bra. The woman was taking a variety of bottles of oils and lotions out of a cabinet on the wall and placing them on a shelf near the bench. Deirdre wrapped her bra in the shirt, putting them on top of the box. She wriggled out of her jeans and placed them on top of the shirt and lay face down on the bench. The towels were wonderfully soft, and smelled slightly of flowers.

The woman turned rubbing oil between her hands,

"You relax now."

She covered Deirdre with a sheet to the waist, then put her hands on Deirdre's back and began to work at the knots in her shoulders that were such a constant in her life that Deirdre didn't even notice them anymore. Resting on her chin with her arms down at her sides, she saw a red lantern made of impossibly thin paper hanging at her eye level.

The woman's hands were much stronger than they looked, expertly finding tension and working it away. Deirdre breathed in the scented air, the humidity warming the insides of her lungs. Tassels hung from the bottom of the lantern in an intricately woven pattern. She wanted to reach out and tease the tassels with her fingers like a toddler grasping at a mobile above its crib, but her arms were heavy, her breath slowing. She started to realize that she was dozing off. Afraid of breaking the spell the massage and the music were weaving, she forced her thoughts away, and fell into a deep sleep.

She was home, in Red Mountain, in the simple dilapidated trailer that she and her mother had called home. Her mother had a hand on her shoulder and was shaking her gently. It was Saturday morning and that meant pancakes shaped like Mickey Mouse's head with butter and syrup. Afterwards they would go for a walk in the hills where her mother would point out birds and plants she knew the names of. In this dream – and Deirdre knew it was a dream – her father was still gone. Deirdre's father had split when she was only four, and she seldom thought about him. But her mother was still wonderfully alive, and it was years before the pancreatic cancer left her a sallow shell with her eyes sunken deep in her face, had made her retch and moan and shit herself before taking her life ten days before Deirdre's fifteenth birthday.

Deirdre squeezed her eyes shut and tried to hold onto the final wisps of the dream, an image of her mother standing on the hillside, her blonde hair shining gold in the bright desert sun and with a big smile on her face. Her last thought as she awoke was *I have my mother's eyes.*

The woman was gently shaking her. Deirdre felt so completely relaxed she felt like laughing, and she felt like crying. "I'm sorry, I fell asleep."

"I let you sleep, long time. We must hurry now."

Deirdre looked at her watch. Hours had passed. She rolled into a sitting position, dragging both hands through her hair. She took a deep breath, feeling the looseness of her massaged muscles, and let it out a pleasurable moan. As she stood, she remembered she was wearing only her panties. The woman approached with a dark blue silk robe, holding it as high as she could reach to get it over Deirdre's shoulders. Deirdre put it on and tied the sash, noticing white cranes delicately embroidered on the front as she did so.

They went down the corridor to another room, this one with a barber-style chair that could be tipped back towards a sink mounted on one wall. The room was lit only by dozens of candles burning in small holders on shelves all over the room. As soon as Deirdre sat in the chair, the woman tipped her back, laying her head into the sink, and began working warm water and then soap that smelled like lilacs into her hair. She felt herself falling asleep again, and resisted the urge this time.

A young girl, perhaps all of ten, came into the room. The woman's daughter? Granddaughter? Deirdre didn't know. She began giving Deirdre a pedicure. She couldn't see what color the girl was painting on her nails with her head in the sink.

Later, the woman dried and styled Deirdre's hair, piling it up in golden ringlets on her head and draping down around her shoulders. The girl had moved to Deirdre's fingernails at the same time, painting them a pale lavender color, the same color as her toes, Deirdre could now see. The young girl applied Deirdre's makeup while the older woman gave instructions. If Ricky had left any marks on her face neither one of them commented on it. When they were finished, they spun the chair around to face her towards a full-length mirror hanging on one wall that she had not previously noticed. As she focused on herself, she took an involuntary breath and mouthed 'Oh my God.'

The young girl said something to the older woman in Chinese. The woman translated. "She says you are very beautiful, like a woman in a music video."

Deirdre laughed, "Tell her, thank you."

The woman spoke to the girl, then said a quick phrase that was clearly an order. The girl ran from the room, and came back a moment later with the box, Deirdre's clothing still piled on top. "You must change. Hurry."

Deirdre looked at her watch and was again surprised to see how much time had passed. She set her clothing aside and opened the box. On top was a pair of silver high heel sandals with straps long enough to wind around her ankle and partway up her leg. She tucked them to one side and lifted out a dress. It was also silver, made of a material like heavy satin and was long enough to reach all the way to the floor. A tiny flesh-colored thong fluttered to the ground like a discarded tissue.

Deirdre shucked her underwear and pulled on the thong under the robe, then removed the robe and draped it over the chair. She was careful not to mess up her hair as she shimmied the dress on over her head. It was vaguely oriental, with a high neck that left her back bare. The dress cinching in at her waist and had slits up the sides to her hip. A diagonal slash across the chest revealed a whole heap of cleavage. It was exactly Ricky's taste. She stepped into the heels and looked at herself in the mirror. The candlelight raced sensually along the material. Deirdre thought it was slutty, but tolerable. She'd certainly worn worse, or at least less.

She noticed the two women staring at her with what she thought was disapproval and became suddenly self-conscious. She sat back in the barber's chair and quickly wound the sandal straps around her ankles and calves. The young girl bowed slightly and left. The older woman waited patiently.

Deirdre stood and collected her clothes, which she placed inside the dress box. She walked with the woman to the front room where she had first entered. The woman went behind the counter and Deirdre remembered that the money was in the pocket of her jeans inside the box. She fumbled to get it open, spilling her clothing onto the floor. The woman started to come around the counter to help her.

"It's OK. It's OK. I've got it." She collected the money from the jeans as she swept her clothing back inside. She noticed that the side slits rode up high when she crouched, and she was going to have to remember that or give someone quite a show. She stood and handed the two hundred dollars to the woman. The woman put the money in a cash box behind the counter, offering several twenties to Deirdre in return.

"Please, you keep it," Deirdre said, pushing the change back at her.

"Too much! Too much!" The woman insisted.

"No, really. Please? I've had the most wonderful time."

The woman looked uncertain for a moment, and then smiled and put the money back under the counter, "Thank you."

"Thank you."

Deirdre turned and walked outside. Hundreds of cars streamed by as the evening rush hour got rolling. The sun was low in the west, but the heat of the day, seared into the concrete, radiated up at her in a stifling cloud.

She stood on the sidewalk waiting for Ricky. The sickly, yellow light filtering through the smog fell on her, making her feel like a hooker working the street. She pulled on the slash in the dress trying to close the gap over her cleavage, but the material was too snug at her waist and neck to give much. A passing car honked at her, the driver yelling something she didn't catch out the window at her, though she could well imagine what it was the driver had yelled, and she felt her face burning with humiliation.

Two more car horns and another shouted comment (this one she did catch), and Deirdre wanted to run back into the salon and hide there, but she was suddenly afraid to turn around, afraid she would find it wasn't there, that it had never existed. Like some tiny slice of heaven on earth she would only get to experience once, her own private, pleasant *Twilight Zone.*

Ricky pulled up while she struggled with her thoughts, and he rolled down the window and barked at her to get her attention. "Hey, baby! Can I get a blow job for twenty dollars?"

She was about to respond with something choice when she realized it was Ricky. She opened the car door and got in, recognizing as she did so how it must look to the other drivers passing by. The thought made her sick and angry.

She folded the dress underneath her as she sat down. Ricky tried reaching up the side slit to grope her crotch and she slapped at his hand. He laughed and pulled away from the curb before she had the door completely closed.

"You look good, babe."

"Thank you," she said quietly.

"You have some change for me?"

"My roots were coming in dark and she had to bleach them," Deirdre lied.

Ricky considered her suspiciously out of the corner of his eye, and then shrugged, "What the hell. You look like a million bucks. I figure that's worth at least two hundred. What about me?"

She examined him and noticed that he was wearing a new dark suit, white pressed shirt, and small gold and diamond cuff links at his wrists. He was freshly shaven and his hair was cut and combed. She also noted that the car had been completely cleaned and detailed, the midnight black exterior looking as hard and dangerous as it had when Ricky came rolling into Red Mountain.

"You look good," Deirdre said, and he did too.

"Nice of you to say," he reached over and slid a hand inside the slit again. She used the excuse of putting the box in the back seat to twist away. He frowned and put his hand back on the steering wheel. "At the party, you eat, drink, whatever the fuck you want to do. Keep other guys' hands out of your dress though," he winked at her. "I'm going to be poking around. Just stay out of my way and don't cause any trouble."

"OK, Ricky."

He turned the car off the main drag and onto a secluded roadway that wound up into the hills. "And smile, this is our big chance."

Deirdre smiled and thought *I am in incredible fucking trouble.*

*****

Jason sat at the redwood patio table next to the pool, his laptop open in front of him and a can of ginger ale beside it, the table's umbrella angled to keep glare off the screen. A wire trailing from the back of the computer ran off the table, across the patio, and through the open sliding glass door into the house. Jason knew how easy it was to hack wifi and didn't trust it at all. He had a second chair pulled over in front of him, his feet resting upon the seat. A file was open on his lap. Kelly lay on her stomach on the diving board over the pool, a towel spread underneath her with a glass of iced tea perched by her head.

She reached down and drew circles in the water with her fingers. "You've been working on that all morning. Take a break."

"In a minute."

"In a minute. In a minute. You've been saying that for the last hour. As least take your shirt off."

"OK, but it won't be pretty." Jason pulled his shirt over his head and tossed it on the patio next to his chair. He sat still for a moment, letting the sun warm his pale skin.

Kelly had turned her head and was looking at him through her sunglasses. "You need to get out in the sun more."

"What I need to do," Jason said typing on the computer, "is make a four thousand dollar mortgage payment and a five thousand dollar property tax payment by next Friday."

"It is a lovely house, though."

"Thank you."

"That's what they can put on your tombstone. 'Here lies Jason, he had a lovely house.'"

"I get it, I get it." He closed the laptop screen after saving his work. "But it sounds funny coming from a workaholic like yourself."

"It's Friday, Jason, and I'm here by your pool. Do you see a computer anywhere on me?"

Jason let his eyes slide up the golden line of her legs, shining slightly with tanning oil in the sun, over the rise of her back along the liquid surface of her dark blue tank suit, coming to rest on her face. He could see everything in sharp detail: the soft curve of her shoulder, the halo of small hairs at the back of her neck, even the reflection of himself in the lenses of her sunglasses. He smiled at her.

She smiled back at him, "Well, do you?"

"Do I what?"

"See a computer?"

His mind was empty of witty retorts, "No, no computer."

She laughed at him, a melodious sound that reminded Jason of wind chimes. "Go put on a swimsuit. We'll take a swim, make some lunch. The work will be there later."

She picked up the iced tea and lifted her head from the diving board to drink. Jason watched the muscles in her back stand out through the thin material of the swimsuit as she arched. She put the glass back beside her and turned towards him, lying on one hip. She smiled again, but Jason thought this time the smile was a little different, the question of friendship or maybe more hanging between them unspoken. Jason wanted to see what her eyes looked like at that moment, wanted to walk to her and tear the sunglasses from her face and hurl them into the bushes that edged to pool. He wanted to stare down into her blue-green eyes of unfathomable depths, cup her face in his hands and kiss...

A loud clattering from inside the house interrupted his thoughts. Both he and Kelly turned to the open door, the moment between them broken, to see Chip come outside carrying a red and white cooler. "Sorry. I knocked over the lamp beside the couch," he looked behind him into the house, "but I think it's OK." He stepped over the wire running through the door unnoticed with his right foot, but then hooked his left ankle on it and pulled it taught, dragging the computer across the table by the wire.

Jason jumped up, scattering the papers from the folder on his lap, and pinned the computer to the table top with his palms. Kelly sat up and turned quickly on the diving board, knocking the glass of iced tea into the pool.

Chip stopped in the doorway hopping on one foot, the other hanging in air with the wire around his ankle. "Sorry again." He shook the foot to free it, and then walked over to one of the chaise lounges and put the cooler on the ground next to it. He turned back to Jason, "Did I break it?"

Jason opened the laptop and punched a few keys, "Still connected." He knelt next to the chair and gathered the papers from the ground back into the folder. Chip went inside to check on the lamp.

"Oh, Shit!" Kelly said from the diving board.

Jason had the file open on the table, holding papers in each hand and trying to get them back into the correct order. He turned to look at her. She was back on her stomach looking down into the water. "What's wrong?"

"I knocked the iced tea in the pool."

Jason put the papers down, walked to the edge of the pool, and looked down. The glass was resting on the bottom, a brown cloud of iced tea snaking above it like smoke. "Don't sweat it. I'm pretty sure the chlorine will take care of it. Besides, what's a few ounces of tea in a whole swimming pool?"

"OK." She stood up on the diving board, took off her sunglasses and tossed them to him. Jason caught them easily one handed. She jumped high off the board and dove lithely into the pool, scattering the cloud of tea with the passage of her body. After retrieving the glass, she pushed off the bottom to shoot to the surface near the edge where Jason was standing, splashing water on his shoes.

She hung one arm over the concrete lip of the pool, reaching up with the glass towards Jason. He took the glass from her, and she climbed out. Jason stepped back awkwardly at the last moment to give her room to stand on the patio. She swept her hair back off her forehead and gathered it over one shoulder to ring the water out of it with a twist between her hands.

She took the glass from him, the moment their fingers contacting around the glass sending an electric shock through Jason, and walked past him towards the house leaving dark, wet footprints on the white concrete. "You want anything? I'm going to get more iced tea."

"I could use another soda."

She looked towards Chip who had come back out of the

house and was sitting on the chaise lounge. He thumped the cooler in front of him, "I've got drinks in here."

She placed the glass on the tabletop and took the towel that had been on the back of Jason's chair. She wrapped it around her waist like a skirt, picked up the glass and Jason's empty soda can, and strolled into the house. Jason and Chip both watched her walk away.

Chip turned the cooler around so the opening side was to him. He tipped up the lid. "The lamp's fine. I brought you guys sandwiches in case you hadn't eaten yet."

Jason put Kelly's sunglasses on the table next to the computer, "What have you got?"

Chip pawed around inside the cooler, "Chicken salad, ham and swiss, smoked turkey and provolone."

Jason thought about it for a second, "Chicken salad."

Chip pulled a sandwich from the cooler, inspected it through the Saran wrap, and tossed it to him. Jason unwrapped it and took a bite as he sat down in the chair, leaning forward with his elbows resting on his knees.

Kelly came out of the house with a fresh glass of iced tea and a can of soda, "What are you two thinking of for lunch?"

Jason spoke to her around a mouthful of sandwich, "Chip brought sandwiches."

"Ham and swiss or turkey and provolone?" Chip offered.

"Turkey and provolone, please."

"Your wish is my command," he presented the

sandwich to her with a flourish.

"Thank you, good sir," she took the sandwich with a curtsey and sat down on a chair at the table near Jason.

Chip picked up the remaining sandwich and a soda from the cooler. "Hey, Jason, I've got another one for you."

"Another sandwich? Really, one is enough."

"No, TV trivia."

"OK, let's hear it."

Kelly spoke quickly around the bite of sandwich she had just taken, "Ooh! Ooh! I want to play!"

"Donna Douglas and Bill Bixby."

Kelly frowned, pushing a piece of lettuce into her mouth with her finger, "Who?"

"Bill Bixby, he played the guy on *The Incredible Hulk*"

"Not him, I know him. The other one. Donna something."

"Donna Douglas. You know her, Jason?"

Jason took a drink of soda, "She played the daughter on *The Beverly Hillbillies*."

Kelly put down her sandwich on its wrapper and started sketching lines in the air, "OK, OK, I've got it. Buddy Ebsen was the dad on *The Beverley Hillbillies*, and he was also *Barnaby Jones*. *Barnaby Jones* had Lee Meriwether, who was also Catwoman on *Batman*. There were lots of other stars on *Batman*; Penguin, the Riddler – they were all big stars, right?"

"There are two problems with that," Jason held up a finger, "One, Lee Meriwether was only Catwoman in the *Batman* movie. On the TV series it was Eartha Kitt and Julie Newmar. Two," he held up a second finger, "all the villains were big stars, but they were big movie stars. Lots of guest shots on lots of shows, but few repeat performances of the same character to count in our game, except on *Batman* of course." He looked at Chip, "I think *Barnaby Jones* is the wrong way to go."

Chip smiled, "I'm not saying anything."

Kelly leaned back in her chair and talked to herself, "What else was Buddy Ebsen on?" She snapped her fingers a few times, "Oh, what was it called? That crappy PI show set in Texas? The millionaire oilman. Austin? No, Houston! *Matt Houston*!" She looked over at them, "*Hart to Hart* was about millionaires too. Do you think being a millionaire is so boring that you can't think of anything better to do with your time than solve crimes?"

Jason swallowed, "Believe me, I have a few million bucks, I'm not spending my time solving crimes."

"Amen, brother," Chip said.

"OK, so *Matt Houston*. The secretary on that was also the bimbo on *Buck Rogers*. Hemsley something."

"Pamela Hensley," Chip corrected. "She played Princess Ardala. I'm sure it doesn't say bimbo on *Buck Rogers* on her resume."

"Whatever."

"*Buck Rogers* is a good call, Kelly. The high bimbo quotient I'm sure fixed it in Chip's mind."

"Did I ever tell you guys that I went out one Halloween

as Wilma Dearing back in college. I've got to say, I looked pretty hot. The only problem was I couldn't wear any underwear or you could see the lines. I carried my ID in my cleavage."

Chip looked at her with wide eyes and swallowed dryly, "A photo or it never happened."

Kelly laughed, wind chimes again, "Oh, there were plenty of photos. I'll look around when I get home."

Jason was finishing the last bites of his sandwich, "So, where were you, *Matt Houston*?"

"No, Pamela Hensley gets me to *Buck Rogers*, which gets me to Erin Gray, which gets me to *Silver Spoons*, which gets me I don't know where."

Jason looked at Chip, "I just got it. You're right there, Kelly."

"Right where? *Silver Spoons*? I dunno, Ricky Schroeder? He was on *NYPD Blue*, wasn't he?"

"Have you ever heard of Ray Walston?"

"*My Favorite Martian*?"

"Yeah, Bill Bixby was on that too."

"Ray Walston was on *Silver Spoons*?"

"He played Ricky's uncle for a year or so."

"I didn't know that."

"Well, there you go, you made it."

"Yeah, I did, didn't I? With a little help."

"Hey, what are friends for?"

Chip leaned back in the chaise lounge and unwrapped the last sandwich. He took a bite and settled in, "Aaah. This is the life. You're white as paste, Jason, you have to get out in the sun more often."

Kelly pointed at Jason, "That's what I've been telling him."

"Yeah, well, work, work." Jason turned to the table after crumpling up the sandwich wrapper and opened up the computer.

"You know what you need?" Chip asked.

"Nine thousand dollars by the end of next week."

"Huh?"

"Never mind. What do I need?" Jason asked without turning from the computer.

"You need a fishing trip. I'm going out on my dad's boat tomorrow. Take a day sailing and fishing around, spend the night at anchor, come back here on Sunday. What do you say?"

"I'd say it sounds great, but I've got to get this website finished by Tuesday at the latest."

"How about you, Kelly?"

"Oh, I'd love a day of sailing, but I have to pack this weekend."

Jason looked at her, "Pack? Where are you going?"

"Didn't I tell you? Not going. Moving. The high rent at

my current place is killing me. I'm moving to a new apartment next week. "

"Need help moving?" Chip asked.

"Nah. It's just a couple of miles from my current apartment, and I don't own that much. I'm paying a couple of guys to come in and move all the big stuff. I just have to throw it all in boxes."

Jason opened the contact list on his phone, "What's your new number?"

"I don't have one yet. I'll get it to you when I do."

"You know," Jason said, "you could just get a cell phone and keep your number with you when you move. You're probably the last person I know on earth living with a land line."

"Uh-uh," Kelly shook her head. "I'm not getting a cell phone. Do you have any idea how unsecure they are? And I read an article about people walking into traffic while their brains are sucked into those damn things."

"You sound like my grandmother." Jason closed the phone book and reopened his work files, and was soon too involved to pay much attention to Chip and Kelly, who had started a discussion of whether Julie Newmar or Eartha Kitt was a better Catwoman, which led into an argument of whether or not Eartha Kitt was still alive. Kelly lay in the sun while Chip did a cannonball off the diving board that sloshed an inch of water out of the pool and onto the pool deck.

The three of them ate mushroom and sausage pizza for dinner on the patio. As the evening air became cooler, Jason and Chip put their shirts back on. Kelly wore a University of Santa Barbara sweatshirt she borrowed from

Jason that came down to mid-thigh. Jason ate the pizza one-handed, pecking away at the keyboard with his other one. He worked into the evening, waving goodbye to Kelly when she said she had to go home and start packing. Chip left a little later to see a Warner Brothers cartoon retrospective playing at a theater on the UCLA campus.

Jason worked on the computer until well after dark, making notes in the file by the light of the screen, finally shutting it down near midnight. He went into the house and put the file and laptop on the countertop in the kitchen, unplugged the LAN cable, and wound the cord up into a ball. He put the ball on top of the laptop, and closed his strained eyes, rubbing them with his fingers.

He walked back out to the patio with his eyes still closed, breathing in the scent of the night air laced with honeysuckle which grew wild at the edge of his property. He realized he had never taken a swim.

When he opened his eyes, he took two running steps across the patio, launched high in the air, and landed in the pool fully clothed. He closed his eyes and sank to the bottom, holding his breath, feeling the tiny currents of the pool filter system eddy around his body, under his shirt, waving his hair. When his lungs became tight from a lack of oxygen, he swam to the surface and stroked to the shallow end of the pool, walking up the concrete steps and into the house. He left damp footprints on the stairway, in the upstairs hallway, and into the master bathroom where he stripped off his sodden clothes and threw them into the empty Jacuzzi tub with a splat. He toweled off and went to sleep nude, his hair wet against the pillow.

*****

The road Ricky drove on followed the contour of the hills, weaving in and out of clefts, and circling back upon itself as it switchbacked upwards. Occasionally there was a break in the thick vegetation beside the road, giving a panoramic view of the city lights below, more impressive the higher they went. The uphill side of the road was an almost continuous barrier of bushes, fencing, or wall, broken only sporadically by imposing-looking wrought iron or wooden gates. They drove in silence, the last of the day bleeding out in purple-hued dusk.

Deirdre sat with her thoughts. Thoughts of what stupidity Ricky might be up to and how much trouble it could get her in, mingled with some wonderment of what a Hollywood party might be like.

Ricky turned in at a heavy, iron gate that had been pushed back on its track. A huge man with a crew cut wearing a tuxedo leaned into the car as Ricky slowed and rolled down his window.

"Invitation," the man said.

Ricky reached into his inside coat pocket and drew out the invitation, which he handed to the man, who looked at it using a small flashlight.

He handed it back to Ricky, "Thank you, sir. If you would just follow the road to the portcullis in front of the house," he pointed, "the valets will park the car for you."

Ricky closed the window and drove up the wide driveway, a sweeping lawn on their left and a mile of white stockade fence on the right. Two horses stood against the fence watching the car go by. The house rose in front of them, a gargantuan, sprawling ranch of glass and light. The driveway twisted into a large circle near the front door around a fountain tossing streams of water tinged by colored lights into the air.

Ricky slowed just as a gleaming yellow Ferrari was driving away. Two men in red jackets and black slacks approached the car from either side and opened the doors, the one on Ricky's side handing him a ticket stub as he slid into the driver's seat. The other one helped Deirdre from the car with a hand delicately holding her wrist. He closed the car door behind her, and stepped aside as the car drove off.

Ricky came to her, took her by the elbow, and together they walked up the wide stone steps to the front door. The door was open, strains of jazz music floating out and over the lawn.

They entered a high atrium, an enormous crystal chandelier above and a polished white marble floor below. A waiter with a silver tray offered glasses of champagne or wine, white or red. Deirdre took a glass of white wine. Ricky took a glass of champagne. A man in a casually cut charcoal suit came up to them.

"Hi. I'm Pete Ryder. Welcome to my home. There's a hot buffet in the living room, and a cold buffet out on the pool deck along with a bar. Help yourself to anything you like, and if you need anything I'm sure one of the servers can help you." He quickly shook Ricky and Deirdre's hands, and then was gone to greet the next people coming in the door.

"Chummy guy." Ricky said. He led Deirdre into the living room. A long buffet table was set up along the wall, a jazz quartet playing in one corner. The liquid blue of the pool was visible through the sliding glass doors at the far end of the room, throwing rippling light and shadows on the ceiling.

They walked towards the pool. Ricky glanced at the buffet as they went by. Deirdre was looking out for stars she might recognize, but didn't see any.

The outside was lit primarily by the luminous blue of the pool. A bar was set up near the house, multicolored lanterns hung from a frame around it. Couples and small groups sat at glass-topped tables, each with a centerpiece of votives glowing softly.

Deirdre walked to the railing, admiring the view of the city below. She wasn't sure what she had been expecting for a big Hollywood party, but she didn't think this was it. She maybe expected bigger-than-life stars, a red carpet and reporters and flashbulbs. And maybe, she admitted to herself, she had been expecting some producer to come up to her and tell her she was beautiful, offer her a role in her next picture. It would have solved a lot of her problems. *Keep dreaming* she told herself.

Ricky stood next to her with his back against the railing, resting his elbows on it, and surveyed the pool deck. "This is where the money is, Dee. All we have to do is make some connections." He noticed a group of three young men in suits standing around one of the tables, and leaning over it occasionally. "Just what I was looking for. Stay here." He handed his empty champagne glass to her and walked over to them.

Deirdre watched him approach and noticed a small pile of cocaine on the tabletop. The men were pushing it into lines using credit cards and snorting through rolled-up bills.

"Where can I get some of that?" Ricky asked when he got close.

One of the men turned to him. He was very good looking in that soap-opera sort of way. He had a ring of powder around one nostril and his eyes were shiny bright. "Want some? Good shit." He held out the rolled bill to Ricky.

"Not for me. For my woman over there." Ricky gestured with his head back her way.

The man leaned to the side to peek around Ricky and gave Deirdre a long leering look she felt from ten feet away. She tried to turn her shoulders inward, put a little less of her tits on display. "Nice," He said, "Bring her over. Plenty to go around."

Ricky tipped his head. "Maybe it's a little too early for coke. Got any pot?"

The man took a moment to process this question, "No, I don't. Go see Tommy inside. He can set you up with anything."

"Tommy?"

"Yeah, second floor. Follow the crowds."

"Tommy. Thanks a lot." He slapped the man on the shoulder and walked back to Deirdre. "All set. You wander around. Have a good time. I've got business." He walked off into the house, stopping at the bar to get a beer.

Deirdre didn't ask what kind of business he had meant. She had seen the coke, and knew that Ricky was about to do something stupid. Like waiting in the car back when Ricky had been trying to con the drug dealer in 'Frisco, this was maybe time for her to make a decision. The Clash song was drifting through her head: 'If you want me let me know-awo-awo-awo, should I stay or should I go.' She took a deep breath and turned to stare out at the city lights below.

*****

Scott and Miller were in a van parked one switchback up the hillside from the gated entrance. They had driven up and down the road much of the afternoon looking for a spot that gave them a good vantage point of the road and as much of the house grounds as possible. The spot they had found was pretty good but not great. By using the camera with telephoto lens mounted on a tripod between the front seats, they had managed to read and photograph about half the license plates of the cars as they drove in. They now had requests into the state department of motor vehicles to identify the owners. Despite priority status, they knew those requests would take hours to come back on a Friday evening. Then they would have to request a search to see if any of those owners had previous drug offenses, which would take even longer. They both figured this whole thing was probably an exercise in futility.

They knew the house belonged to a movie producer named Peter Ryder, and that he had one prior for possession of marijuana. They also had from a good source that there would be considerable drug dealing and use at the party. Big surprise. You hardly needed an informant to know that. What they didn't know was who the dealer was. They hoped that he had a long list of priors. If they could find him through that, maybe when they leaned on him he would sell out some of his clients. But even if he did turn, and that was unlikely because these guys pretty much made their living being discrete, anyone they managed to bust tonight would be out tomorrow on some plea with a fine paid, and probably a fat headline on TMZ. The media and ACLU howled for the arrests of some rich folk who used drugs and to stop picking on the poor drug users in the projects, but everyone knew it was nothing but free publicity and street cred as far as this crowd was concerned.

As the flow of cars into the house had slowed to a trickle, Miller passed the time looking through the camera at the party. Scott was tipped back in the driver's seat with his eyes closed.

"Shit," exclaimed Miller.

"What?" Scott asked without opening his eyes.

"Check out the three guys doing coke at one of the tables on the patio."

Scott grudgingly roused himself from the seat. Miller stepped away from the camera so Scott could look through the eyepiece, "Yep, that's what they're doing."

"We should call it in."

"For what? Even if we could get a judge to sign off on a warrant, which I doubt we could, by the time we got down there the drugs would be long gone. And if we get the pictures admitted as evidence in a trial, their lawyers would just say they were snorting flour. A total waste of time."

"Doesn't that piss you off?"

"Lots of things piss me off. Three guys doing coke at some party in the hills is way down on the list." He swiveled the camera around scanning the rest of the patio, "Hello, who's this?"

"Who's who?"

"Oh, man! Look at the tits on that one!"

"Where?"

"Broad at the railing. Poured herself into a silver dress, big cutout on the front. Oh, baby, you just made the whole night worthwhile." He snapped off a half dozen shots.

"Let me see," Miller tugged on his shoulder.

"In a second, junior. Her man's walked over to the druggies. Are you lonely, honey? I wouldn't leave you alone for a second." He ran off a few more shots.

He finally let Miller take a look.

“Hey, she’s turned around,” he complained.

“Your loss, but I’ve got pictures.

“Nice package in back too. Twenty dollars says she has no underwear under that dress.”

Scott laughed, “I’m not taking that bet. Besides, how would you prove it?”

“Bust her coming out of the party. Give her a quick strip search,” Miller smiled lewdly.

Scott actually considered this for a moment. It brought to mind a stint he did in sex crimes when he got freebees from hookers. “Nah, there’s a guy with her. That’s a hassle we don’t need.”

The radio crackled and gave out their call sign. Scott picked it up. The dispatcher notified them that motor vehicles had come up with a list of owners, and that the names were being run through the computer now for priors. Scott acknowledged the message.

*****

Ryder had been greeting people on autopilot for more than an hour now, the bulk of his mind, or at least that part of it not pining for the tubes of glue in his study, still working on the money problem without solution. The tension of the whole thing was killing him. He walked away from the front door almost in mid-greet, and made his way across the atrium to the stairs. He was planning to huff some glue, and then get something from Tommy to smooth him out, maybe some Quaaludes. Enough of this sober shit. He needed to get high and think! Time was running out. He pictured the face of a giant clock, like Big

Ben swathed in fog, closing in on him.

He looked at all the people he didn't know hanging out in his house; writers, directors, grade-B actors. Few of the union rank and file had shown up at the party; he hadn't really expected them to. He saw at least three union heads here, though, and he had a dozen prostitutes plying their trade. Some good was going to come out of all of this.

Upstairs he made his way down a line that had formed in the hallway outside a bedroom that Ryder had converted to an office, which for the purposes of this party had been converted to a pharmacy. Tommy worked from the desk dispensing pills and powders, joints and tabs with one hand, sweeping cash into a desk drawer that Ryder had emptied for him this morning with the other. Tommy noticed him and held up a finger in a "one sec" gesture. Ryder nodded and let him keep working.

He watched Tommy sort and sift, give and take, with the speed of a Vegas dealer. The open desk drawer held tens and twenties, fifties and hundreds. Jesus! There had to be ten grand in that drawer, and the night was just getting started. Ryder did a little math in his head. He licked his upper lip and stared at the stacks of money. How crazy was the idea that was forming? He had always been a man to trust his first instincts in business, and his instincts told him he could make this work.

He stopped Tommy just as he was about to sell to a tall blonde, breasts lifted by a tight gold bustier almost to her chin. "Need to talk to Tommy for just a minute." He took the blonde by the shoulder and turned her towards the door, his arms spread wide to move the line of people ahead of him. He closed and locked the door on a crowd of frowning faces. He turned back to Tommy who was taking the lull in the action as an opportunity to neaten up the stacks of bills in the drawer.

Tommy looked up from the money, "What's up, Pete?

Is there a problem?"

Tommy watched Ryder check the balcony and then close and lock the balcony doors. "You didn't want me to sell to the blonde? I had already sold her some speed earlier, and I was thinking maybe she was having too much myself."

Ryder looked at him, "What? No. No. We've never had any problems while you've been here. You can decide who you want to sell to and who's had too much."

"Then what's up? Your guests are waiting."

Ryder was pacing back and forth in front of the desk. He couldn't think of a good way to start. How much did he trust Tommy? What he was planning could cost him everything.

"Pete?"

Ryder turned suddenly to him, "How much money could you make here tonight?"

Tommy held his hands up, palms forward, "Hey, if this is about the split, I've always given you 15% of my profit in the past."

"No. It's not about that. How much money can you make?"

Tommy dropped his elbows onto the desktop and rested his chin on his hands. He toyed with a pale green capsule on the desk in front of him with one finger. "Hard to tell this early in the evening. I once made about twenty-five at this rave in the valley. Must have been 1000 teenagers there."

"And your highest profit comes from?"

"That's easy, coke. I buy it from a guy. If it's pure, I can cut it down a little. You have to cut it down a little. Too pure, and your guests will all fry their brains. What's this about?"

"In a second. And the guy you buy coke from, how much does he make?"

Tommy smiled, "This is like research for a movie, right?"

Ryder didn't say anything and Tommy, seeing something in his eyes perhaps, answered him, "Don't know exactly. He's taking a lot of risk getting it into the country, and then there's more risk dealing it out to little guys like me. But he can cut the product a lot because it's sure to be ultra-pure when he gets it."

The amount of money to be made in the drug trade was staggering. He could be looking at prison. He could be looking at his only chance. He could get himself killed. He couldn't see any other way.

"I'd like to buy."

"You don't have to buy. I'll comp you. You know that."

"I don't want drugs for myself. I want to buy from your guy, and sell it to you to sell at these parties."

"What? The movie business isn't profitable enough for you?" Tommy started laughing, and then stopped when he saw the look on Ryder's face. "Shit. You're serious."

"Listen. I buy from your guy and sell it to you completely uncut. I set you up as the dealer at parties all over town. You keep what you make, no percentage. I make money, you make money."

Tommy's mind whirled at the amount of money he could make in a week. Still, he saw a problem. "Why would my guy want to sell to you if he can sell it to me for more profit?"

"You said it yourself, there's risk making all the little sales. I would buy it all. One big sale."

"He might for one big sale, but that's a lot of money."

"Seven million dollars?"

"Yeah, that kind of money. You're serious about this, right? This kind of guy, you don't fuck with."

"Completely serious."

"OK, let me make a call." Tommy pulled out a cell phone and dialed a number from memory. "Nick? Tommy. No, I'm still working through the last stuff you sold me. But I have a guy here, straight, wants to make a big buy."

Ryder stepped away from the desk to look out the window at the night. He felt suddenly ill. He wondered if he wasn't making a big mistake. His palms were starting to sweat and he could hear his pulse in his ears. Tommy continued behind him. "Seven million. Yeah, no shit. Cash."

Tommy looked over at Peter, "Yo, Pete." Peter continued staring out the window as if he hadn't heard him. Tommy whistled, "Yo, Pete!"

Peter turned to him. "Yeah."

"My guy wants to know how soon you want to do this. He has product in now he was going to deal out, but if you want it, he'll sell it all to you for seven."

My God! I'm really going to do this. He'd have to pull in the mortgage, sell the stock portfolio. He could do that tomorrow morning. Clean the home accounts out. Pull in every dime. "I could maybe do it late tomorrow."

Tommy relayed that information into the phone and came back to Peter, "Sunday morning?"

Ryder took a deep breath, "Sunday morning."

Tommy spoke into the phone again, then listened, and then hung up. "Sunday morning, 4 AM. The Santa Del Ria marina. Just you, and just him. This goes bad, I don't know you, you know?"

Ryder acted like he hadn't heard him. He was looking out the window again, talking to himself under his breath, "I can do this. I buy it for seven. Call in Fred over at Grandview Productions, get Tommy in at his parties, call Sid over at Beacon, run his parties." He turned back to Tommy, "How long you figure it will take you to sell it all?"

Tommy had been running the numbers through his head himself. With that kind of money he could make from this, he'd be out of here and on some beach in a heartbeat, maybe with the blonde in the gold bustier. But whatever, wherever, he would be done with the reaping machine that was Los Angeles. Peter's question interrupted his train of thought. "Pretty long time. I'm not sure how many parties you're talking about, but I'm just one guy. Even if the parties are good, it might take a couple of years."

A couple of years? Peter felt his heart skip a beat. What the fuck had he just done? He needed the money in months. Now he was like some fucking drug kingpin storing cocaine in his wine cellar for the next two years while he went bankrupt. Shit, he definitely had not figured this through. He thought he saw some motion on the balcony out the window, but when he looked outside he didn't see anyone. His nerves were shot. He noticed that Tommy was still talking.

"What did you say?"

"I said, that way I could sell it faster."

"What way?"

"Weren't you listening? If you offer the same deal to some friends of mine, low price, no split of the profits, and if you can supply the parties, I think we could sell it all in six months."

Six months. Like music to his ears. He could move seven million dollars of cocaine into the sinus cavities of Hollywood, make his movie, clear his debts, and never think about making a movie or a drug deal again in his life. He offered up a silent prayer to God, though he hadn't set foot in a church since his third wedding.

"Set up all the guys you can. This is Hollywood. There are ten parties every weekday. Twenty on weekends. You're going to work them all. You and I are going to make a lot of money." He dragged a hand down his face and noticed that it came back wet, though he wasn't sure if it was his hand or his face that was sweaty. He walked back to the door drunkenly, adrenaline washing through his system, his heart pounding, his throat dry. He opened the door to find the blonde standing right in front of it, a glazed and hungry look in her eyes. "Help yourself," he said to her, and she practically knocked him over running into the room on her heels.

His shirt felt damp up the sides and along the ribs, and he realized that he was covered in flop sweat. He went towards his bedroom to change it.

*****

Ricky made his way upstairs and arrived at the room just as Ryder was pushing people out of it, an anxious blonde with porno breasts barely contained in her gold bustier at the front of the line. Past her Ricky could see the guy who had welcomed him to the house closing the door, and behind him another man counting money at a desk. Then the door was shut.

He was certain this was a meeting he didn't want to miss.

He made his way down the hallway, checking rooms on the same side of the hallway. The next door down was a linen closet. The one beyond that was a huge bathroom. The next was a bedroom. Checking quickly that it was empty, Ricky entered and closed the door behind him. He crossed the room to a pair of French doors and peeked outside. A deserted balcony spanned the back of the house overlooking the pool. A pair of doors at the other had access to the room Ryder was in.

Opening the door wider, he crawled outside. Keeping low, he was mostly hidden by a heavy stone railing if anyone chanced to look up from the pool, though he was uncomfortable because there were a lot of people down there. He worked his way towards the other end, moving silently, and crouched against the wall beneath an open window. He could hear the conversation inside as clear as day.

Ricky had nearly shouted out loud when he had heard Ryder mention seven million dollars. His mind had instantly spun into a frenzy. Fucking seven fucking million fucking dollars! He couldn't even wrap his head around that many zeroes. He had written the place and time of the drug deal on the back of the invitation with a ball point pen and then practically run off the balcony and back to the bedroom.

He stood in the bedroom hyperventilating, his thoughts

wild. He started pacing and muttering to himself. "All I have to do is figure out some way to get the money away from the producer before he makes the deal. Ryder hasn't met the dealer yet, so maybe I could go with an Impersonator scam." Ricky shook his head. "No, the time and place are already set, making my chance to get in, make a fake deal, and get out before the real drug dealer shows up too slim for comfort. If Ryder wasn't already locked in on doing a drug deal, he would be ripe for a play of Too Good To Be True, but that took time to set up, and a lot of props, and at least two other players. Maybe the government would offer a big reward, like half or something, for turning the deal over to them. No, probably more like some crime fund reward, ten grand or less."

Ricky stopped and tried to take a calming breath. He would have to think this through carefully; there was no way he was going to fuck this up. He had more than a day to work out the details. He would just take his time and think it all over. He suddenly realized that he was standing in a bedroom in Ryder's house without any good explanation. He went to the door and opened it a crack. The guy was headed his way!

He considered hiding back on the balcony or into the closet, but then dismissed both as too obvious. As the doorknob turned, he quickly dropped and scrambled under the bed, crawling into the shadows near the wall as best he could. Ricky saw the light go on, and watched the closet door swing open. He breathed softly through his mouth.

The man was humming. A shirt hit the floor, and Ricky heard the chimes of hangers banging against each other. After a rustle of fabric, the light switched off, and the door swung closed.

Ricky stayed under the bed, counting slowly to sixty before he crawled out. That had been way too stupid of him. He was going to have to be a lot smarter than that if he was going to pull this off. He quickly went to the door and checked the hallway. There was the crowd at the other door, but no one was really looking his way. He left the bedroom, closing the door behind him, and went downstairs.

Ricky came back out onto the deck with a peculiar look on his face. Deirdre watched him as he went to the bar and got a drink, and then came over to her. He looked very happy. Too happy.

"Something up?" Deirdre asked.

"Nothing you need to worry your pretty little head about. Everything's great!" He swirled the tumbler of scotch he was holding, the ice rattling in the glass.

Deirdre tried to read his expression for some hint of what had him so happy, but came up dry. She noticed something clinging to the sleeve of his jacket and pulled it off. It was a ball of carpet fuzz. "Where have you been? What's this?"

Ricky took the fuzz from her. "Do you see any more?" He turned back and forth in front of her for inspection and looked down at himself, brushing his hands along his jacket front.

Deirdre shook her head.

"It's nothing." He threw the ball of fuzz over the railing and into the abyss of the valley. "Why don't you go get us something to eat? I saw some shrimp at the cold buffet on my way by." He pushed her away from the railing and smacked her on the ass causing her to stumble a few steps in the high heels.

"OK, Ricky." She said to him over her shoulder.

As she stepped up to the buffet and took a plate from

the stack, she tried to imagine what could have happened to make Ricky so happy, but she couldn't think of anything. Could he have made some deal to sell at these parties so easily? There was certainly some other dealer at the party; the guys with the coke proved that. Had he made some deal with Ricky?

Looking at the food she realized that she was very hungry. She took a pile of cold cocktail shrimp for Ricky and some pasta salad and several tiny quiches for herself. She went by the bar on her way back and exchanged her glass of wine, which had become warm, for a cold one.

When she returned to him, Ricky took the shrimp. He became almost unbearably smug as he ate and drank, and it set warning bells off in Deirdre's head, but he could not be drawn into telling her what had happened. Deirdre just couldn't figure it.

Ricky was smiling on the outside, but on the inside he was a pool shark calculating angles and forces. If he could somehow intercept Ryder after he got the cash but before he made the deal, any number of cons could be used to get the money away from him, but how to do it? He couldn't wait on such a narrow road in an upscale neighborhood like this; the cops would roust him in minutes. Put some kind of tracking device on his car? Where could he get such a thing? Could he afford it? This whole setup had cost him nearly all the cash in his possession. How could he intercept the guy if he didn't even know what kind of car the guy drove? He had a sudden thought as he saw the producer come out onto the pool deck.

He walked over and interrupted his conversation with one of the servers, something about red caviar. "Someone here told me you were quite the car buff?"

Ryder turned to him, "Who, me?"

“Yeah, this guy said you had a garage under this place full of sports cars.”

“No, sports cars are toys for middle-aged men. I thankfully have a few years to go before that.”

“Then the yellow Ferrari I saw coming in wasn’t yours?”

“No! No. I spend a lot of time in my car and I like to spread out. I have a Lincoln Navigator.”

“The SUV?”

“Yeah. I know, you never need four-wheel drive in LA, but the engine has such power and the leather seats are amazing. It’s like driving around in my living room.”

“Let me guess. Green?”

“Well,” he leaned towards Ricky conspiratorially, “I do have one vice where cars are concerned. I don’t want to drive one that looks like everyone else’s. I paid a little extra and got it in metallic purple. Custom color. Looks great! Hey, if you’re a sports car guy, the yellow Ferrari belongs to, “he stood up on his tip toes to look over the crowd of the party, “the guy by the fireplace,” he pointed into the house. “Balding, looks like Friar Tuck.”

Ricky had no idea who Friar Tuck was, but thanked him for a great party and headed into the house, veering off once he was sure the producer wasn’t watching him. He pulled the invitation from his pocket and wrote ‘Lincoln Navigator, metallic purple.’ One problem solved.

*****

Scott got back into the van through the side door, having stepped outside to take a piss off the edge of the hill. As he slid the door closed on its track, the radio squawked.

Miller picked it up, "Miller here. Go ahead."

"We've finished running that list of names through the computer for you."

"Anybody stand out as our dealer?"

"One of the cars, a blue 1997 Ford Mustang, California license Tango-Charlie-Alpha-3-5-1 is owned by an Andrew Thomas Malta."

Scott heard the name and started snapping his fingers, "Andrew Thomas Malta. Thomas Malta? Tommy Malta?"

Miller looked at his partner, "You know him?"

"Oh yeah," Scott said, "that guy's got a rap sheet ten feet long. I busted him the first time when he was fourteen. Been years since I've seen him, though. I figured he was dead."

"Not quite, just gone upscale." Miller spoke into the radio, "Do you have a current address for him?"

The dispatcher gave it to him. Miller signed off.

Scott whistled to himself, "That's a pretty trendy high rise. Tommy's done OK for himself." He climbed through the gap between the front seats and into the driver's seat and started the engine. "What do you say we wait for Tommy at his place? It has to be more comfortable than this van."

"You read my mind."

9 Days Earlier

Scott drove the van into the parking lot of Tommy Malta's apartment building. It was a high-rise covered in peach stucco that in the glow of the parking lot sodium vapor lamps looked jaundiced. Scott pulled into the darkest corner of the lot farthest from the building, where he stopped and turned off the headlights, but not the engine.

"So, what do you think?" Miller asked.

Scott ducked his head to look up at the apartment building through the windshield. "Seventeenth floor, right?"

Miller checked the information given to them by the dispatcher, "Yep."

Scott considered the face of the building, most of the windows dark, a balcony for each apartment. "We should be inside."

"That's what I think."

"We'll try around back." Scott put the van back in gear and glided across the parking lot towards an alley that ran down one side of the building. They parked next to a dumpster.

Scott reached behind his seat and retrieved a green nylon backpack. "Let's try it."

As they got out of the van and made their way around the dumpster towards the door, Scott pulled an electric lockpick from the backpack. It looked like a small electric drill, but with a segmented bit that tensioned the cylinder and worked against the tumblers until the lock opened. There was almost no lock it couldn't pick, though some might take several minutes, and it made a high-pitched grinding noise that tended to attract attention. When they got to the service entrance, they found the door propped open with a wedge of wood. Miller smiled and gave Scott a slight butler's bow and an 'after you' gesture.

Scott shoved the pick into the backpack. "I never get to use my toys," he mock grumbled.

The concrete hallway beyond had a line of bare light bulbs in the ceiling, a service elevator near the end.

Miller pushed the elevator call button, "How much money do you figure he'll have?"

"After a party like that? Could be twenty grand."

They were silent waiting for the elevator to arrive, counting money in their heads. The elevator creaked and rattled its way up to the seventeenth floor. When the door opened they stepped out into the hallway and stood in the silence of the sleeping building. Satisfied no one was awake to be a witness, they turned right and walked down to apartment fourteen. They made a note of the nearest emergency stairway entrance on the way.

Scott knocked on the apartment door and waited, knocked and waited again. No one answered. He pulled the pick from the backpack. The lock was a good one, and it took nearly thirty seconds of scraping and grinding before the door opened. He put the pick back into the backpack. "They've got to make a quieter version of this thing." He looked at his watch. "That party should be breaking up soon. Tommy will be one of the last ones to leave. Forty, maybe forty-five minutes to drive here. I figure we've got an hour."

They spent half that time searching for the stash of money they knew had to be there, but thirty minutes isn't much time to search even a modest apartment and Tommy's apartment was large with two bedrooms, a living room, kitchen, and a study. They weren't particularly surprised when they came up empty.

Near the time they thought Tommy would arrive, Scott told Miller to go wait in the stairwell one flight down. When Miller closed the door, Scott locked it and went into the kitchen and got a beer, sat on the couch with his feet up on the glass coffee table, and turned on ESPN to wait.

Another hour later, Scott had finished four beers and had a steady buzz on. He threw his suit jacket over the back of the couch and opened the sliding glass door leading out onto the small balcony to cool off. He paced, and then settled back on the couch, finally finding *Striptease* on HBO. The movie sucked, but he could watch Demi Moore all night long. Twenty minutes later he heard a key turning in the lock.

Tommy came through the doorway carrying a briefcase. Less than a step into the room he froze, realizing the lights and TV were on. He saw Scott on the couch and ran back out. From where he sat Scott could hear the stairway door bang against its stop and slam closed again. He drank from his fifth beer and waited.

Miller shoved Tommy into the apartment a minute or two later.

Scott raised his beer, "Tommy. Sit down. Relax. Have a beer. Mi casa, su casa." Scott thought he might have slurred some of that. He wasn't sure. He noticed his partner looking at the line of beers on the tabletop. Fuck him. He stood up a little unsteadily and came across the room.

A light dawned in Tommy's eyes, "Scott? Jesus! What the fuck are you doing in my apartment?"

"Hey, he remembers me!" He looked over at his

partner, "That's nice, isn't it?" He walked close to Tommy "It's nice to be remembered." He punctuated this with light slaps to Tommy's cheeks. Scott stopped and thought that might be a little over the top, like some stupid Mafia Don. He shrugged to himself and took the briefcase from Tommy. Tommy said "Hey!" but then realized he was in dangerous waters and was silent.

Scott laid the briefcase on the back of the couch and opened it. Inside there were several sandwich bags of different colored pills, another containing pot, a very small amount of cocaine twisted into another. No money. "You still a small time drug dealer, Tommy? I figured you'd be past that by now to killing old ladies for their social security checks."

Tommy looked indignant, "You can't use that. You didn't have a warrant, and you're in here illegally."

Scott dropped two sandwich bags he had been holding back into the briefcase. "We have photos of you, Tommy, dealing at a party in The Hills. We roll some of your clients, you're looking at a long time of trouble."

Tommy said nothing.

"Of course, you roll on them, maybe we could cut you a deal."

Tommy chuckled and shook his head. He knew that if he turned on his clients that the nice apartment, the car, the women; it was all over. He would rather take his chances with a couple of grainy photos taken at night with a zoom lens from half a mile away in a court of law any day.

Scott waited for Tommy to say something, but it was clear he wasn't going to. He spoke to Miller, "What does he have on him?"

Miller stood motionless for a moment, and then reached out and started patting Tommy down.

Tommy waved his arms around to brush Miller away, "Hey, get the fuck off!"

Miller came up with Tommy's wallet, which he flipped through. "Sixty-five dollars, three credit cards, a driver's license."

Scott frowned. "No money on him?"

Miller shook his head, "Sixty-five dollars."

Tommy looked over his shoulder at Miller and back at Scott. "Money? You're hustling for money? You knew this bust wouldn't hold water. You were looking to steal a quick buck! Shit! And you're calling me small time? Skimming nickels and dimes like a corrupt meter maid? Nice life you got for yourself there."

Scott's face turned crimson, "Where is it, Tommy? Where's the money?"

Tommy started laughing, "The money? The money? I put it into the bank, what the fuck do you think I did with it? I'm not driving around town with twenty grand in a briefcase. You clowns used to busting morons who keep their money stuffed in their mattress? You want money? There's sixty-five dollars. Take it. Go buy yourself a new suit."

Scott, despite his somewhat drunken state, moved with the speed of a man long-trained in hand-to-hand combat. He grasped Tommy by the lapels and spun him, pushing him backwards off balance across the living room. Tommy wrestled with Scott's grip on his jacket and had almost broken the hold when they passed through the sliding glass doors onto the balcony, the curtain billowing around them like a cape. Scott drove his knee up into Tommy's groin and hoisted him in the air. The balcony railing caught Tommy in the back of the knees and he went over, Scott still holding onto his lapels. Instead of trying to break Scott's hold, Tommy now clamped onto his wrists. He bent his knees and tried to wedge his feet into the railing, but the spacing in the lattice was too narrow.

Tommy looked up into Scott's face, red, cords standing out on his neck, his hot, beery breath washing over him through gritted teeth, muscles bunched in his upper arms against the roll of the dress shirt sleeve from the strain of holding the other man over the railing.

Miller fumbled his way through the curtain onto the balcony. He put his hand on his partner's shoulder, afraid of jarring him and causing him to drop Tommy. "Come on, Scott, let him go." He looked at Scott's rictus smile and frowned inwardly at his poor choice of words.

Scott's smile widened, "Let him go." He looked down at Tommy, "Should I let you go?"

Tommy shook his head spastically. One loafer slipped off his foot unnoticed, bounced on the balcony floor, and slid under the bar at the bottom of the balcony railing to fall seventeen stories to the pavement below.

"You know you were sixteen the first time I busted you? Frankly, I'm getting tired of it. What say we save me and the taxpayers of this fine state the hassle and expense of putting you through the system again?"

Tommy's grip on Scott's wrists tightened, his knuckles white, the sweat on his and Scott's hands making him start to slip, "You want money? I'll get you money!"

"I'll get you money! I'll get you money!" Scott sneered. "You got a million dollars? Because I think that's what it might cost you to keep me from dropping your ass."

The seam at the back of Tommy's jacket split halfway. "Seven million!" Tommy squeaked.

Scott hauled Tommy back up onto the balcony so quickly his jacket separated almost completely across the back. Tommy's knees sagged as they tried to support his weight. Scott held him up, their faces close together.

"What did you say?" Scott hissed.

Tommy shifting his eyes, trying to look at other things besides Scott's wild face, but they were so close together is was difficult, "Let me look around here. I think I've got ten grand stashed."

Scott shook Tommy by his lapels until his teeth rattled. "You said seven million dollars."

"I, uh, I, um."

Scott whirled Tommy back through the sliding door into the living room, almost running down his partner on the way. He threw him onto the couch and stood over him, hand rested on the butt of his gun at his hip. Miller wandered back in off the balcony, unable to grasp or control the events whirling around him. He felt disconnected, like a man watching a movie.

Tommy panted, but said nothing.

Scott crossed the room to the mantle over the living room fireplace and took a bronze statue of a replica of The Thinker in his hands. He hefted the statue as if testing the weight. He turned the statue towards Miller "This guy is called The Thinker, right?" He turned it so it was facing him "He looks constipated to me." He walked back to stand across the coffee table from Tommy. "Still, he's a good role model for you right now. Thinking about the future. Thinking about the consequences of his actions. Are you thinking right now, Tommy?"

He let the statue fall from his hands. It smashed through the glass top of the coffee table to thump heavily on the carpeted floor beneath.

Tommy jumped. "OK. OK. But you didn't hear this from me, right? Right?" He looked from Scott to Miller and back again. Neither said anything.

"There's a drug deal. A big one. On the docks, Sunday morning. OK? OK?"

"Seven million dollars? Cash?"

Tommy nodded quickly.

"Who's buying?"

"Movie producer. I think he needs it to pay for a movie."

"Peter Ryder? The guy whose house you were at tonight?"

Tommy squirmed but didn't answer, which was answer enough for Scott. He turned to his partner and grabbed him by the shoulder, which seemed to snap him out of the spell he had been under.

"Holy shit! Seven million dollars!" Miller whispered. "What a bust!"

Scott looked at him like he was crazy. "Bust? Think about it. Seven million dollars. Only you and I know about it. Some movie producer, a dealer, maybe a couple of heavies." He let the thought trail off to see if Miller was on the same wavelength.

Miller leaned in close, "How much are you thinking of taking?"

"All of it."

Miller started to stutter, "Al-ala-aaa-alll?"

Scott pointed at Tommy on the couch, "Don't move a fucking muscle." He walked his partner over towards the sliding glass doors. For a moment Miller had the crazy thought that Scott was going to throw him off the balcony.

"Get a grip, Miller!"

"Easy does it, Scott. I'm with you on this, believe me. But we can't pull shit on some movie producer. Too public."

Scott thought about this for a moment, and then walked back to Tommy. "Who's the dealer?"

"I don't know his full name. Just Nick, that's all I call him."

"How do you find him?"

"I don't. I call a cell phone number, and he tells me where to meet him."

This presented a problem. It was possible to track the position of a cell phone using the tower network, but it required a court order.

"Where's the deal going to be?"

"Santa Del Ria marina, at four tomorrow morning."

Scott stepped into the frame of the coffee table, the glass crunching underneath his shoes, to tower over Tommy "This is all straight, right, Tommy? You wouldn't lie to us."

Tommy sat sagging on the couch. "Straight up. I swear."

"We check this out and find that you've been lying to us, you know that we'll finish our conversation on the balcony."

Tommy nodded weakly.

He reached towards Tommy who shrank back into the cushions. Scott took his jacket off the couch next to Tommy and put it on. He picked up the backpack off the floor near the coffee table. He gestured towards the door, "Let's go."

"We're just going to leave him here?" Miller asked.

"He just turned on his dealer and his market. We're not going to be seeing much more of Tommy around here, are we Tommy?"

Scott and Miller left and closed the door behind them, returning to the van. Miller drove around the building and out into the street.

"So, where now?" Miller asked.

"First we get some coffee. It's going to be a long day. Then we'll go and check out the site for the deal. We can go by headquarters and pick up a telescopic mike and some video equipment. I think the best plan is to take down the dealer just after the deal goes off, but we're going to have to make it up as we go along."

Miller had been warming to the idea of over three million dollars in his pocket, but worried about what form his partner's adlibbing might take. The money they had been taking so far had been harmless, squeezed from drug dealers who would have used the money to buy more drugs to sell. It was almost like a public service they were doing. He still thought of himself as a good cop, but knew that somewhere out in the landscape of taking money there was a line between being a good cop, and not being a good cop. He didn't know exactly where that line lay, but he was certain seven million dollars was way over it.

*****

After the agents had left, Tommy sat glassy-eyed.

He thought briefly about calling Nick and Ryder to warn them, but realized that Ryder would never let him deal one of his parties again, and Nick would probably just kill him. He was utterly burned in LA. He got off the couch and went into the bedroom. He emptied the dresser into a suitcase pulled from his closet. In the bathroom he collected his toiletries.

Back in the living room with the full suitcase, he went to the stereo. There was an *REO Speedwagon* CD box set on the shelf. Folded inside was fifteen thousand in running away money. He had always wondered what he would have said if a guest had picked it up and found the money inside, but it had never come up.

He planned to drive to Baha and get a hotel room, and watch the papers for the outcome of what he had set in motion. If Nick and Ryder were both killed, maybe he could put things back together again; the drug trade would go on. But if Nick somehow survived and found out he had talked and came after him, he could hop across the Mexican border and disappear into South America. He'd just have to wait and see.

*****

After leaving the party Ricky had unfolded a map under the meager illumination of the dome light in the car, tracing the winding mountain road in both directions with his index finger. While the road continued up over the hill and down the other side, that direction led away from the heart of LA into less populated areas. Towards LA, there was really only one way to go.

Ricky drove out of the hills and found a Circle K parking lot that gave them a good view of the first intersection that roadway hit.

They spent the night sleeping in the car, the interior bathed in yellow by the Sodium vapor security lights. Ricky woke early the next morning, stretched, rolled his neck to work the kinks out, and settled in for the long haul. When Ryder came out to get his cash, Ricky was betting this road would be the way he would do it, and Ricky would be waiting.

He slouched down in the driver's seat, a cup of coffee purchased two hours ago held in his hand and resting on his knee. He looked out the windshield and through the crossing traffic at the half dozen or so cars waiting at the light. Nothing.

The light cycled to green and the cars dispersed themselves into the circulatory system of the LA freeways. Ricky poured the last of the coffee from the cup into his mouth and swirled the cold bitterness around before swallowing. The light turned red again and cars began piling up. He shifted in his seat to keep his butt from falling asleep. He had never done any kind of a job that involved waiting like this. He had spent countless hours setting up marks, watching people, observing their every move, but all this waiting went against Ricky's grain, and he had a hard time keeping still.

It would have been better if Ricky knew which bank Ryder used. Then he could have simply watched the bank. But he didn't know, and while he had thought about a quick rummage through Ryder's home office during the party to try and find out, he figured he had pushed his luck about as far as it would go in the snooping around Ryder's house department.

He drummed his fingers on the steering wheel and looked over at Deirdre asleep in the passenger seat. Her feet were drawn up underneath her and her forehead rested against the window. Her mouth was open a little and she was breathing softly. At some point Ricky was going to have to tell Deirdre what was going on, but he was going to wait until his plan for getting the money had solidified. On the other hand, maybe Ricky should just ditch her. It was the first thought that had crossed his mind when he began planning of what he would do with seven million dollars, trading up for a younger and more pliable model. But for the time being, he might need her for something, so it was best to keep her around. Like now, for instance.

He reached over and swatted her on the hip. She turned her head quickly and her blue eyes flew open in that expression of surprise and confusion that was Ricky's favorite. It meant that he was fully in charge. She had a red splotch on her forehead from where it had rested against the window.

"I've got to piss like a racehorse. Keep an eye out for me," he told her.

"OK, Ricky. What am I looking for?"

"I told you when we parked, a purple Lincoln Navigator."

"I know that. I mean why?"

"That's on a need to know basis, Dee. You don't need to know."

He got out of the car and closed the door. Deirdre called to him and he leaned over to look at her through the window.

"Can I have the keys to listen to the radio?"

He dug into his pants pocket, tossed the keys to her, and headed off in the direction of the Circle K.

Deirdre sat up and put the keys in the ignition. She pushed buttons until she found a classic rock station, dragged a hand through her hair, and wiped at the corners of her mouth with her fingers. The light changed green and she watched cars stream into the traffic. No Lincoln Navigator, purple or otherwise.

Deirdre was pretty certain that Ricky wanted to follow the Lincoln when it turned up, or what sense did watching this intersection since dawn make? But Ricky hadn't told her to follow it if she saw it. What if he came out of the bathroom and she told him he had missed it? What if he came out of the bathroom and she and the car were gone because she had followed? She was in a delicate situation, and hoped she wouldn't have to choose. Why did Ricky want to follow the SUV in the first place?

Deirdre drank the cold dregs of coffee from her cup and tried to figure it all out. They went to the party, good food, but otherwise a bust as far as she was concerned, and her feet were still killing her from the sandals. Ricky had gone inside to check out the drug dealing operation, and then come back out smiling with carpet lint on his jacket. And now they are watching a road that came out of the hills for a purple Lincoln Navigator. The only person that lived up this road that she knew of was the guy who had owned the house, the movie producer.

As the light turned green and cars surged into the intersection a flash of metallic purple caught her eye, but it was a Plymouth Roadster. She returned to her thoughts, trying the puzzle from a different direction.

Carpet lint. Where did Ricky get the carpet lint? He must have lay his jacket on the floor, or lay on the floor himself while wearing the jacket. She watched the light cycle green to red and back to green again while she formed a picture in her mind of Ricky lying on the floor. Someone could have pushed him down. No, then he wouldn't have come back outside smiling. He lay down himself somewhere to do something. To pick something up? Then he would have gotten fuzz on his knees, but not his jacket, probably. Unless that something was under something else, like under a bed. He looked under a bed and saw something and crawled under to get it? Then what are they waiting here for? And why was he upstairs looking around under the beds anyway?

Under a bed. Ricky could have hidden under a bed. And heard something? That was a story she was starting to believe in.

And yet, it still left some holes. Ricky walks into a room, crawls under a bed, and then people walk in and start talking? What would make Ricky walk into a room and crawl under the bed in the first place? Maybe Ricky snuck into a room and under a bed where a conversation was already taking place. But then he should have been able to hear it from the hallway or whatever and not risked sneaking into the room. And at the top of it all, what did Ricky hear that had them waiting for this car at this spot at this hour of the morning? Deirdre was convinced she didn't know enough to even guess, but she was pretty certain it involved money because that was all Ricky really cared about.

She was startled as he opened the car door.

"Anything?" he asked as he settled into the seat.

"Nothing."

"I got you some more coffee."

"Thanks." Deirdre took the offered cup. She tore the plastic tab out of the lid and watched as a column of steam rose out of the opening. She debated asking how long they were going to sit and wait, but Ricky had a determined look on his face and a set to his shoulders that said they would be there for as long as it took. Whatever Ricky was waiting for must be very valuable. If she only had some way of figuring out what that was.

Ricky leaned back in the seat and blew on his coffee to cool it as he watched the cars go by and time passed.

Three hours later nothing had changed, and Ricky was started to wonder if the producer might have gone to some small bank out in the backcountry, meaning he wouldn't be coming down this road at all. His plan was to wait until noon right where he was. If nothing happened by that time, he would find a cheap motel and crash for a few hours. And then? As passing cars sent hot chrome reflections across the lenses of his sunglasses, Ricky started to consider going instead to the location of the deal and trying to work both the producer and the dealer there. Though he had never worked an Undercover Cop play before, maybe that was worth a shot, but where would he get a convincing badge, and did he need an actual police car to pull it off? He wasn't sure, and it wasn't like there was a phone support hotline he could call to get help figuring it out. Ricky knew he had exactly one chance to get this right. He also recalled the drug dealer in San Francisco and the disturbing speed with which he had started shooting, and Ricky didn't even have a gun anymore, though that problem could be rectified easily enough. And if the dealer brought bodyguards as well? That was starting to add up to a lot of people, which made running a play exponentially more complicated, some of them probably professional shooters. If at all possible, getting to Ryder before the deal was definitely the better approach, but where the hell was he?

Ricky, a man who had never had a bank account, was entirely unaware that almost all modern banking could be done without ever setting foot in a bank.

*****

Ryder sat at the desk in his study. The surface was completely covered in printouts, financial statements, the LA Times business section, and three yellow legal pads with notes scrawled on them. The layer of paper continued on the floor around his chair; piles of bank statements, cancelled checks, and stock trade records, so that it looked like he was sitting in the impact crater of a large paper meteorite.

He had gotten up early this morning, though actually he had had very little sleep last night, and run all the numbers out to the last penny. With Friday's closing stock prices he could pull together seven point six plus million dollars, less trading fees and penalties for early withdrawal from certain accounts. Much of the money was in simple cash accounts or mutual funds which would be easy to move. Money in individual stocks would be somewhat more difficult to move on a weekend, but it could be done with some loss of value in foreign markets or through after-hours trading boards.

The ringing phone startled him. He had to shift some piles of papers to find it on the desktop. A large fanfold near the edge of the desk teetered and then fell over the far side trailing paper like a slinky. He fumbled the handset out from under the papers on the third ring.

"Pete. It's Michael. I'm at the office. What's the

emergency?"

"Hey, Michael. Sorry to drag you into the office on a Saturday morning. I need to sell stock – raise some money."

"And it couldn't wait until Monday? You know selling on weekends is a bad idea. It's a buyer's market. What stocks are you looking to sell?"

"All of them."

There was silence on the other end of the line while Michael digested this. "Pete, I know the market is down right now, but you know this correction has been in the pipeline for some time. Now is not the time to sell. Hold, and wait this one out. It might even be the time to buy as there are many indications that the worst is over."

"I know all that, Michael. But I need the cash now."

"OK, I'll start looking on the Singapore market. How soon do you need this?"

"Today."

Silence again. "Pete, I've been your broker for what, about fifteen years now? If you need a loan, we can arrange something based on the balance in your portfolio. I couldn't do that today, but I could get you the money first thing Monday morning."

"Michael, I don't have the time for this right now. Just sell the stocks. I've got other things to do, but I'll call you later today to see how you did. OK?"

Michael sighed in resignation. "OK, Pete. I'll get on it."

Ryder hung up the phone and put a check mark on the

list of items on one of the legal pads. He was doing very well. It had helped that his banker had been at the party last night and had been able to arrange the mortgage on the house on the spot with one phone call. Now all he needed to do was figure out how to handle the actual money. At a little before ten it was still too early to do anything about that yet.

He showered and shaved, and had poached eggs overlooking the smog collecting in the valley. He finally headed out at a quarter of noon, passing Ricky a scant ten minutes before he was going to give up the vigil. Ricky dropped in smoothly behind him and Ryder was much too busy to notice a tail, not that in his wildest imaginations would he have been expecting one.

*****

Ricky and Deirdre followed Ryder easily. They kept several car lengths behind, often with one or two cars between them. To say the large SUV, half a car higher and wider than anything on the road that wasn't a box truck and bright purple to boot, stood out in the sparse afternoon traffic was an incredible understatement. All was going well until Ryder turned through the gate of a movie studio. At the last moment Ricky veered off and pulled into Marv's Reliable Used Cars lot across the street. There was a guard at the studio gate, and Ricky fumed that he was unable to follow Ryder inside.

He stopped the car with a jerk that made Deirdre brace her hands against the dashboard. Ricky slammed the gearshift into park and clamped his hands on the steering wheel. Ryder needed the money in just over twelve hours. What the fuck was he doing wasting time at a movie studio? He couldn't pick up the money there. Unless... What if he were going to pick up prop money and try to use that in the deal? Would Ryder take that kind of a risk? Ricky thought he himself might have tried it if the money looked real enough, but based upon the few moments

Ricky had spent talking to Ryder, Ricky didn't think he had the balls.

A man in a suit jacket made of some shiny blue material and gray slacks walked up to the car and leaned in Ricky's open window.

"Nice car. Hello, little lady." He nodded to Deirdre. "I can get you a good trade-in price towards any car on the lot."

Ricky turned to him with a look of such venom that the man actually stumbled back a couple of steps. He opened his mouth to say something, took another look at Ricky, and walked quickly to the farthest point on the other side of the lot.

Ricky went back to staring at the gate of the movie studio. What was Ryder doing at the studio? Maybe he keeps some money there. Ricky pictured him taking banded stacks of money out of a safe built into the wall of his office. The picture looked right to Ricky, though he couldn't imagine Ryder keeping the whole amount in some wall safe.

None of this changed Ricky's plan. He was going to stick with Ryder until Ricky was sure he had collected all the money together.

Deirdre had given herself a mental point for her detective work when they set out this morning. She had been right that Ricky had wanted to follow the producer. But what now? She didn't know where Ricky had been expecting him to go, but from the sudden downturn in Ricky's mood she knew this wasn't it, which confused her. A movie studio seemed like a perfectly good a destination for a movie producer.

*****

The alleys of the studio back lot were choked with all manner of movie-making equipment; partial sets, camera dolly tracks, scaffolding, a pile of fire hydrants, a stack of telephone booths, statues, and a collection of park benches in various styles. Ryder maneuvered his car at a crawl, afraid that he was going to scratch the paint at some of the narrower spaces. He finally reached his destination and parked next to a rusty trailer home that looked a lot like the one that Jim Rockford had lived in during *The Rockford Files*. It could have been the exact one for all he knew. He climbed up the three rickety aluminum steps to the door, the middle step tipping under his weight and almost dumping him on his ass, and entered the trailer without knocking.

The interior had been hollowed out to make one large room with the exception of a bathroom near the far end. It was decorated in a style best described as college dorm room. Three sprung overstuffed couches in clashing colors and designs took up much of the space. A single desk in the room was dominated by a large model of the starship *Enterprise* about three-quarters completed, a confusion of multicolored LEDs blinking in the saucer section. Nearby stood a life-sized cardboard cutout of *Seven of Nine*, a flowered plastic lei draped around her neck. *Smashmouth* was playing on a stereo system heaped on the floor.

Two guys in their twenties sat at a folding table on folding chairs banging away on laptops. A third stood at a whiteboard on which was written a flow diagram of boxes and arrows, the boxes containing text like 'Tom and Sara meet for the first time,' and 'Sara wrecks car in the rain.' No one had noticed Ryder enter. He stepped over to the stereo and tapped the power button off with his toe. Three heads turned to him nearly simultaneously.

The one at the whiteboard spoke, "Hey, Mr. Ryder. What brings you here? We're not rewriting anything for you," he looked at one of the seated men, "are we Jerry?"

The seated man shook his head, “Not that I know of.”

“No, guys. No rewrites. I’m working on the outline of a movie script and I’d like to run some plot points by you.”

The one standing at the blackboard, Ryder was pretty sure his name was Sam, shrugged. “Sure, we’ve got some time. Take a seat.”

Ryder came forward and perched on the edge of the desk after sliding the Enterprise to one side to make room. “OK, here’s the story. Ordinary guy ends up needing a lot of money fast. He sets up a big drug deal and plans to sell them later for a profit.”

“How big a drug deal?” Jerry interrupted.

“Seven million dollars.”

“Wow, that’s a pretty big deal. How is he going to sell all those drugs?”

“That’s not important.”

“Not important?” The other guy at the table asked. “That’s your whole character motivation. He needs the money quickly. How can he turn seven million dollars in drugs into money quickly?”

“Ordinary guys don’t get involved in big drug deals,” Sam added, “You’ve got to have a whole network to distribute it.”

“That’s right,” Jerry said. “I don’t think you’ve thought out your plot very well.”

“OK. OK. Let’s say for the sake of argument that the drug deal is already set up; that there’s no way to back out of it.”

Jerry tilted his chair up on the two rear legs, "OK. It's your movie."

"That's right," Ryder sighed, "it's my movie."

Sam had taken a red marker pen and moved to a clean space on the whiteboard. He drew a box and wrote 'man needs money fast' inside. He then drew an arrow from that box to another box in which he wrote 'sets up drug deal.'

"So," Ryder continued, "my question is, how does the drug deal happen? The guy and the dealer meet at some pre-arranged place and time. Does the guy bring a suitcase full of cash and exchange it for one filled with drugs?"

"Sure, that works," Jerry nodded.

"It does not work." The other guy at the table said, rolling his eyes. "Ordinary guys do not carry seven million dollars in cash to a drug deal. That's crazy. Do you even know how big a stack of money seven million dollars is? How much it weighs?"

Sam drew another box on the whiteboard. Inside this one he wrote 'afraid of getting killed for money.' Ryder swallowed hard. Those boxes pretty well summed up his life. He gestured at the board, "That's it exactly."

Jerry asked "Guy has seven million dollars for a drug deal, but what's to stop the dealer, or anyone else for that matter, from killing him and taking the cash?"

"He could bring a gun," the guy across the table said.

Sam wrote 'bring a gun' on the whiteboard.

Jerry nodded, "Sure, he brings a gun. He feels more secure with it. But he doesn't want to end up in a shootout with the dealer. This is just some ordinary guy; the dealer is probably a professional killer."

"He brings a friend to cover his back," Sam said, as he wrote 'bring a friend' on the whiteboard.

"Absolutely not. The dealer specified just the two of them."

Sam drew a line through 'bring a friend.'

"Dealer's going to have friends almost certainly even so. Guys with high powered rifles watching the whole deal." Jerry pointed out.

"Does the guy die in your movie?" The third guy asked. "Someone doing something this stupid really needs to die. The audience is expecting it."

Ryder shook his head. He didn't like where this was going at all. "Look. We agree that the guy's not going to walk around with seven million dollars in cash. But the dealer has to see this as a business, right? He imports and sells, that's what he does. He can't go around shooting everyone who buys from him."

Some nods from around the room, not as strongly as Ryder would have liked.

"So, how does this deal happen so our man comes out alive?"

The three writers were silent for awhile.

"OK, so it's a business," Sam said. "Write him a check."

Jerry laughed, "A third party check from an out of state bank. No, wait! I can see it now. 'Excuse me, will you take travelers checks?'"

Ryder cupped his face in his hands.

"How about a wire transfer to like the dealer's Swiss bank account?" The third guy said.

Everyone turned to look at him.

"Drug dealing involves millions of dollars. The dealer would have to have a Swiss bank account. Wire transfers in and out all the time. You bring a laptop with a cellular modem to the deal, and wire the money anywhere the dealer wants."

Ryder took his face out of his hands, "That works. You just pile all the money in a single account and wire transfer it away."

"What's to stop the dealer from killing the guy after the wire transfer?" Jerry asked. "Or even before the transfer? With the laptop and the account numbers he could do the transfer himself."

"Nothing," Sam said, "But he won't as long as he gets his money. He doesn't want to kill needlessly. And this way no one else can steal the money, probably. At least our man's not walking around with millions of dollars in cash."

"It can work." Ryder said. "I can do this."

Jerry nodded, "Yeah, I think it's believable. I still have problems with the whole average guy turned drug dealer thing, but otherwise it works."

"Yeah, that's what I've got to work with. Listen, you guys are lifesavers. I've got to go." Ryder headed for the door.

As he opened the door and stepped through, he heard Sam saying, "So imagine the whole drug deal goes sour.

The guy gets his head blown into a pink mist by a high power rifle." Ryder closed the door and walked shakily back to his car, again stepping on the weak middle step and having to catch himself when it tipped.

He got into the car and leaned his head back against the leather headrest. "It's not bad. It's a business deal. Wire the money, pick up the drugs. Easy." He tried taking a couple of yoga-shit deep cleansing breaths, but they didn't calm him any. He knew what he needed; it came in little tubes from Taiwan. Sobriety was for the fucking birds.

He started the car and drove back out of the studio where Ricky again picked him up. He drove to a computer store and bought a laptop with cellular modem and arranged for the cellular service. He then returned home where he called his banker who instructed him on how to download and install software on the computer that would allow him to make wire transfers using the laptop. It was easy, and the banker assured him was a completely secure way to transfer money from account to account.

These mundane activities did nothing to relax him.

*****

As Ryder returned home, Ricky followed him all the way up the winding road to the house, keeping a switchback or two between them at all times so he wouldn't be noticed, and then continued past the house when Ryder turned in. He made a U-turn a little further on using an ungated driveway, and headed back down to return to the Circle K parking lot.

Ryder had never gone near a bank, and Ricky didn't know what to make of that. Maybe he had arranged to have the money brought to him at home, and some car that had passed unnoticed had done so. Maybe someone was going to deliver it to him early tomorrow morning, and he didn't have it yet. Maybe he had picked up fake money at the movie studio and really was going to go with that. Hell, for all the Ricky knew, maybe he had kept all the money he needed in a safe at the movie studio, or maybe even in his house. Maybe. Maybe. Maybe. Maybe. Ricky ground his teeth.

He came to a decision, started the car, and headed for the nearest motel. It all came down to the money, and Ricky wasn't going to do anything until he saw it; it was as simple as that. He couldn't risk moving on Ryder until he knew the money was there, and the only time he could be absolutely sure of that would be at the deal. So be it.

Ricky would be at the deal too, and he would do whatever was necessary.

*****

Jason woke early on Saturday morning. He dressed in dark blue UCONN shorts with white piping and padded downstairs barefoot, his feet sinking into the deep pile carpeting on the stairway. The smell of coffee greeted him as he came into the kitchen from the coffee machine he had loaded and programmed the night before. He poured coffee into a 'World's Greatest Grandmother' mug, added a teaspoon of sugar, and took the mug and a box of *Cap'n Crunch* peanut butter cereal from the pantry to the dining room table.

Returning to the kitchen he collected the bills from the place where they hung from a magnetic clip on the side of the refrigerator, and the checkbook and pen from a drawer. He sat down at the table and took a handful of cereal from the box, munched on it, and washed it down with coffee.

He opened the checkbook and got down to business. One thousand bucks to the nursing home, the phone bill, internet bill, electric bill, gas bill, car payment, Discover card, Visa, lawn service, student loan, and the whoppers: mortgage and property tax payments. The balance in the checkbook steadily dwindled. Jason at one point had tried to calculate exactly how much money it took to maintain his lifestyle for a single day. He was up near three hundred dollars a day when his growing horror had overwhelmed his curiosity and he stopped.

By the time he was done with the bills, he was also done with the box of cereal and the cup of coffee. He went and got himself a second cup of coffee and returned to the checkbook. The balance stood at $193.16 – really not even enough to get him through a single day if his aborted calculation had been correct, but the miracle of credit would let him carry on a little longer, though in two weeks he had to make some kind of payment to his mother's care facility. He would have to talk to Keith on Monday about selling some more stock, but it was just a stopgap measure. He hadn't had a call from anyone interested in even taking a look at his house in weeks. He knew that eventually, and probably not that long from now, something would have to give.

*****

The white fiberglass V of the hull sliced through the light chop. The deep blue of the water became a paler blue against the hull, and where the water sprayed up against the chrome deck railing it became a mist, fracturing the bright sunlight into a faded rainbow that hung just off the bow.

Chip stood at the wheel of the 'Morning Mist,' a twenty-eight foot sailboat owned by his father. Chip's father, near seventy-five now, did not sail much anymore, but Chip still took the boat out as often as he could. It would sleep four, but Chip usually took the double bed in the fore cabin for himself given his size, leaving two single fold-down bunks for sleeping in the main cabin. He had been planning to sail with Jason and Kelly up the coast to fish near Catalina, spend the night at anchor, and then sail back on Sunday. With neither Jason nor Kelly along, the prospect of a night on the boat felt less like a sleepover party and more than a little lonely. And, truth be told, while he loved the sailboat, he disliked the tiny bulkhead bathroom greatly.

He turned the wheel and tacked, ducking slightly as the boom passed overhead. Across the wind the sail filled again with a sharp snap of canvas, the boat heeling over to that side as Chip gripped the wheel firmly. He had been sailing most of his life, and felt completely at ease on the boat alone.

The weather service was reporting that the wind would pick up speed later in the day due to a storm out at sea. That might make a night aboard a boat as small as the 'Morning Mist' at anchor a little rough. His modified plan was to fish a location closer to home and be back at dockside by nightfall. At the dock he could hook to public utilities, which would allow him to watch the 42" TV in the main cabin that was really too large for the small onboard generator to handle. He could go ashore and rent movies if he wanted, and maybe get a pizza delivered. Finally, at the dock he could use the much larger and nicer bathrooms that were set aside for the use of slipholders.

He switched on the sonar unit, watching the profile of the sea floor slide underneath. When the bottom became irregular he spun the wheel hard over, driving the ship into irons. He walked along the narrow deck beside the cabin to the bow where he threw the anchor overboard, pulling back on the line to set it firmly. He wound the main sail down; bundling it against the boom as it lowered. The boat was anchored over the site of a brick barge that had overturned in a storm back in the 1950's. The bottom was littered with bricks and made an ideal breeding ground for fish.

A variety of casting and trolling rods and reels were

stored in a ceiling rack in the main cabin. Chip pulled down a simple spin caster with moderate weight line. He skewered a sandworm, taken from a Chinese take-out box of worms he had bought from a vendor on the dock, onto the hook and let it drop into the water. Easing himself into a deck chair, he put his feet up on the railing with the tip of the fishing rod hanging over the side.

He sighed.

He knew that Jason had money troubles – big money troubles. He had seen the 'for sale' sign weathering for months at the curb outside his house. The tech bubble had long ago burst. All that remained of the halcyon days was a war of attrition, like post-apocalyptic survivors in *Mad Max* engaging in bloody battles over the dwindling supplies of gasoline. That Jason's company had survived this long was a testament to his skill, and though Chip had not come right out and asked, he was pretty sure Jason was working without a paycheck. And Kelly's company couldn't be going all that well either. Chip wished there was something he could do for his friends. He hummed 'If I Had a Million Dollars' by the *Barenaked Ladies* as he played the fishing line in the water.

Who was Chip kidding? His father's company was still afloat, but just barely. And good as it was to have the job, Chip hated working at the plastic factory with all the noise and heat and everything pervaded with the reek of hot plastic which to Chip smelled like burning hair. As a fish nibbled at the edges of the worm, not yet ready to take the bait, Chip frowned at just how much things sucked all over.

*****

Miller drove into the parking lot of the Federal Building on Yorba Linda Boulevard. Scott got out and leaned in the window.

"Drive down to the Marina area. Check it out. See if you can find a good place to set up."

"OK. You going to get equipment?"

"Yeah. A telescoping mic, a better camera and tripod than we've got with some night vision capability. Can you think of anything else we might need?"

Miller drummed his hands on the steering wheel, "No. No. I think that's about got it."

"Come back here and get me in," he looked at his watch, "about an hour. We'll try to get a few hours sleep before tomorrow morning. I want to be there early." He slapped the window frame and stepped back from the van.

Miller started to drive away and Scott trotted to catch up. "Whoa. Whoa."

"What?

"Fill up the tank. We might have to follow people around a little and I don't want to risk running out of gas."

"Right."

Scott stepped back again, and Miller pulled out of the parking lot an back into the traffic. He ran his tongue around against his front teeth. This was going to be a crazy night.

*****

Ryder came into his home office carrying two inches of bourbon in a cut crystal tumbler in one hand and a stack of financial statements in the other. He dropped the stack of papers on his desk where they added to the growing mound, and shifted the other stacks around until he found the power switch for the computer and toggled it on.

The chair springs and Ryder made simultaneous wheezes as he sat down heavily. It was late, very late. He'd been combing over the whole deal in his mind all day. Ryder thought he had everything covered. He hoped.

He leaned forward and rested his elbows on the desktop, rolling the glass of bourbon between his hands as he watched the computer go through its boot up sequence.

He thought for the thousandth time of not going through with it. The money that was in his account now could set him and his wife up in any number of countries; countries from which extradition was very difficult. In fact, fuck the wife – take the mistress. Or try one of the islands down by Trinidad and find some native girl who wore coconut shells on her tits. He could almost feel the warm sand between his toes. The Windows startup chime brought him back. Where else could he live but LA? He liked being a big shot. He liked mingling with stars and politicians. He liked fucking starlets with the promise of a movie role and then dumping them cold. All he had to do to keep all of it was a simple business transaction about five hours from now. No big deal.

He called up his account software and connected to the bank computer. After a lengthy negotiation the balance came up – six point two million and change. Where the fuck was the money?

He grabbed the phone off the desk sending a pile of papers sliding to the floor. He jabbed out the phone number of his broker with his index finger and fumed as he listened to it ring. It was finally answered.

"Michael, where the fuck is my money?"

"Peter. I'm glad you called. The pre-opening of the

foreign exchanges was so low that I couldn't sell all your holdings. You don't understand the loss you'd be taking. Give it just a couple of days; you'll get another hundred thousand easily."

"I don't have a couple of days. I don't need the money Monday. I need the money now, and I don't care what loss I take to get it."

"Peter, you don't understand."

"No, you don't understand. I need everything converted to cash now. Everything. Sell. Now. *Capish*?"

"OK. OK. Everything. I'll get on it. It might take a few hours, though. Only a skeleton crew left at the office at this hour."

"A few hours I have. I'll check the account around 3:30AM. It had better all be there."

A sigh from the other end of the phone. "It will be, Peter."

Ryder hung up without saying goodbye. He had been considering not bothering to check the balance in the account. It was a good thing he had! With all the other things he had to worry about, you would think his broker could have handled something as simple as liquidating his holdings. Clearly, Ryder thought, he had to watch every little thing himself. It was the little things that were going to get him killed if he weren't careful.

He took a swallow of bourbon wishing that it was something stronger, forcing the liquid fire down his throat, and ran through the entire deal again in his head.

8 Days Earlier

The effects of the storm blowing out to the west were diminished in the harbor, so it caused only a slight rocking of the boats tied to the dockside. Still it was enough to unsettle the pizza Chip had had for dinner, leaving him with a faint queasy feeling that made sleeping difficult. He lay quietly in the forward cabin hoping the sensation would pass, but finally gave up and, with a sigh, hauled himself into a sitting position. He dragged his hands down his face and rested his forearms on his thighs. He had debated briefly with himself earlier about simply driving back to his apartment and sleeping there, suspecting that he might have trouble sleeping even through the storm was far away. Ultimately, he had stayed, and now as dawn neared he regretted it, but tomorrow, today he corrected, was Sunday and he could always take a nap on the couch while watching football.

He felt around on the floor with his feet for his shorts, his car keys rattling in the pocket as he pulled them on. He made his way along the short hallway and up the stairs to the deck.

The storm had pushed cold air in from the Pacific, a thick fog hanging over the harbor. Chip sat on the bench seat along one side and sucked in the cool, damp air, settling his stomach somewhat.

A pair of high beams cut into the fog and swept along the side of Chip's boat. A large SUV pulled alongside and stopped. The motor died, and a moment later the headlights shut off. Chip sat on the deck and listened to the tinkling of the cooling engine.

*****

Ryder sat rigidly in his SUV, his guts alternately loose and watery and then seizing in a twisted cramp. He slid his hands along the steering wheel slick with sweat and tried to calm his breathing. In less than an hour, this would all be over – that was the thought that sustained him. That plus the complex blend of drugs and alcohol he had fueled up with before coming to this meeting. Ryder, who considered himself something of an expert on the intricacies of illicit drug interactions, admitted to himself that he was way off the reservation. There was numbness in his hands, almost a feeling they weren't his anymore, that had him nervous. When the film was done, he planned to take his fifth stint in rehab.

He looked over at the passenger seat at the laptop and cell phone attachment piled there. A small chrome-plated semi-automatic with a pearl handle rested on top. It was his wife's gun and he couldn't imagine using it, but still, better to have it and not need it, etcetera, etcetera, right?

Opening the car door, his frazzled nerves jumped at the chime reminding him the keys were in the ignition. He wrested the keys out and jammed them into his pants pocket. The gun went into the right pocket of his windbreaker. He gathered up the computer equipment and got out of the car, closing the door with his knee. The night was peaceful, the creak of boats tied up at the dockside, lanyards and pulleys and other sailboat crap clinking almost musically. The boat nearby had all its edges softened by the fog, a great white looming shape.

He put the laptop on the flat top of a garbage can on the dock and pulled out his cell phone. He dialed the number of his bank from memory and spoke to the voice-activated menu system. "Ryder, Peter, Account Number 08239866." He waited while the computer verified that information. The balance in his account was in excess of seven million dollars. Everything was in place.

He wired the cell phone to the computer and placed it on top of a nearby piling. His computer dialed the bank computer and connected, bringing up a screen that showed the current date and time and the account balance. He typed in some commands and set a program he had been given by his banker running. A timer appeared in the corner at twenty minutes and started counting down.

*****

Ricky left Deirdre in the motel without explanation and went to get a gun. It had taken a dozen phone calls through a long and tenuous line of acquaintances, but he had finally found a leathery old guy, ancient would be a better description, who sold him a beat up .38 automatic. The man had rattled on about the good old days on the grift while he cleaned the gun for Ricky. He used to be a fair Glim Dropper in his day, he confided in Ricky with a wink of his one good eye. Jesus, Ricky thought, when was the last time anyone did a Glimmer Drop? It had probably been during Prohibition, and Ricky added another dozen years to his estimate of the guy's age.

Did Ricky know Carol from Modesto? How about Phyllis from Simi Valley? Ricky made a noncommittal grunt. She had been arrested a couple of months back for insurance fraud, slip and fall, something like that. The old man started in on a long and winding story about two guys running a Land Scheme in Tijuana who ended up on the run from the *policia*. Ricky thought he might talk until dawn, but managed to cut him off by telling him that he was running a con on a very tight schedule and had to go. The guy nodded and winked again as if he had one in play himself.

Ricky picked up Deirdre on the way to the marina. She fell asleep almost immediately, like taking an infant for a ride in a car. As he drove into the quay he killed the headlights and the engine, coasting the car to a silent stop between two large boats up on wooden storage frames. He sat in the car letting his eyes adjust to the dark, then leaned over and pulled the gun quietly from under the seat and put it in the pocket of his leather jacket. He shook Deirdre roughly to wake her.

"Stay in the car. Don't go anywhere. Don't do

anything. Don't make a sound. OK?" He pointed a finger at her an inch from her face.

Disoriented she shied back in her seat and looked at his finger, becoming slightly cross-eyed as she did so, "Right, Ricky."

He got out closing the door silently and made his way towards the dock. The fog was so thick that he had almost walked into the SUV bumper before realizing that the dark shape in front of him was Ryder's car. He backed away quietly and hid behind the deserted dock master's shack. He could barely make out Ryder pacing back and forth.

Ricky couldn't understand how Ryder, as far as he could tell, had never picked up the money. His only option as he saw it was to watch until the cash showed up and then make his move, though he had no clear idea what that would be. Ricky was not adverse to a little improvisation, so he hunched down to wait.

*****

Miller and Scott were parked in the van on the hillside above the harbor. They sat with the side door slid back on its rail. Miller crouched behind a camera, now useless because of the fog, while Scott held a parabolic dish connected to a box pointed in the direction of the marina. A wire ran from the box to a pair of headphones that hung around his neck.

"Shit! This place was perfect this morning. You could see the whole marina and the access road. Now we can't see shit!" Miller slapped the side of the tripod in disgust.

"Shhh. Quiet!" Scott had grabbed one side of the headphones and was holding the cup to his ear. "He's calling his bank." He listened.

"Should we move? I think we should move closer so we can see what's going on."

"With this fog we'd have to be standing right next to them to see anything. I think the best we can do is wait for the deal to go off, and then catch the dealer coming out the access road." Scott consulted his interior map of the area in his mind, "This road T-bones the access road just down the hill."

"OK. Let me know if you hear anything." Miller leaned back in his seat behind the camera.

"Will do."

*****

Ryder was pacing back and forth very quickly, making himself nearly dizzy and he spun around and around. He kept looking at his watch, checking the timer on the computer screen, checking his pulse, and fondling a tube of glue that he carried in his pocket for luck.

The fog brightened in the direction of the access road, the glow resolving itself into a pair of headlights on a chopped-down, light-colored BMW, white, maybe yellow. It stopped and the motor shut off. The lights remained on, blinding Ryder.

A man got out of the driver's side and walked into the beam of the headlights. Ryder held a hand up to shield his eyes from the glare. The man had his hand on the butt of a gun in the front of his waistband. Ryder kept his own hands far from the gun in his pocket, certain that even touching it would lead to his death.

"He-hello?" Ryder said.

"You have something for me?" The man's voice was

very deep, slightly accented, maybe Greek?

"You have something for me? Are you Nick?" Ryder replied.

The man stood silently for a moment looking around and then nodded to himself as if reaching some decision. He walked around to the trunk of the car, opened it with a remote attached to his key ring, and pulled two hard-sided suitcases from inside. Walking over to Ryder he placed them on the ground next to the trashcan, noticing the computer open on top for the first time. His eyes narrowed.

Ryder tipped one of the suitcases onto its side. He undid the clasps and flipped it open. Inside were packages of white powder shrink wrapped into plastic blocks about the size of a brick. He worked one out of the suitcase and hefted it; the weight felt right. He tried to push his thumb through the plastic. It was very tough, and he reached into his pocket to get his keys, going into the pocket with the gun instead. His hand touched the cool, smooth pearl inlay of the handle and he froze for a moment. Fresh beads of sweat broke out on his forehead and a tremor started in his hands that he couldn't seem to stop. He dug his keys out of his pants pocket, using the end of one key to punch a ragged hole in the plastic. He fumbled his keys back into his pocket and pushed his index finger through the hole, his sweat causing the tiny white crystals to cling to the fingertip. Putting his finger in his mouth he rubbed the crystals into his gum line, lacerating the inside of his lip with his fingernail. Cranked nearly to the moon on what was already in his bloodstream, Ryder, somewhat a connoisseur of cocaine, knew it was the purest he had ever tasted.

The man was still looking at the computer screen. "What is this?"

Ryder turned from the suitcase to look at him, "A

computer," he answered dumbly.

"Where is my money?"

Ryder looked at the screen. The counter was flashing at zero and the account balance was zero. "Oh, the money has just moved to another bank account." He turned the laptop towards him and connected to a different account at another bank. The display again showed the balance, the counter running down from a little over seventeen minutes. Ryder turned the screen proudly to the other man. "There it is. The computer program automatically moves it every twenty minutes."

"What the fuck is this?"

"Your money."

"My money is cash!" The man bellowed. He shoved Ryder back roughly and kicked the top of the suitcase closed.

"No," Ryder's voice came out as a croak. He cleared his throat and tried again. "No. Just tell me where you want the money. I can wire it anywhere in the world from this computer."

"Fuck wire. Cash! Seven million dollars, cash! Don't you understand what cash is, asshole?" He bent over and spun the suitcase angrily, slapping the clasps shut.

Ryder felt it all spinning away from him. He needed this deal. He needed to complete the movie or he was ruined. "No. Please. Look at the computer." He prodded the screen leaving a greasy, sweaty smear. "The money is all there."

The man had finished locking the suitcase and stood with one in each hand. "The money needs to be all fucking

HERE!" He turned away from Ryder and snarled, "Tommy is fucking dead!"

Ryder felt his hand go into the pocket of his windbreaker and draw the gun out as if it had a mind of its own. "Stop, please." he heard himself say as if from very far away.

The man sensed something in Ryder's voice and turned. He saw the gun and dropped the suitcases. They hit the dock with a loud thump that made Ryder jump.

"You going to shoot me with your fucking toy gun?" The man took a step towards Ryder who stepped back, putting the trashcan between them.

Ryder thought that maybe it was a trick of his eyes, but the man looked enormous, the fabric of his shirt barely containing his huge biceps and massive chest. His hair was long and dark and shaggy and unkempt; he looked like a madman. The gun in his hand seemed ridiculously small. "I have the money. I can get you the money," his voice took on a pleading tone.

A low, animal growl started deep in the big man's chest. It came out as a roar, "I'll take that gun and shove it up your fucking ass!" He lunged at Ryder across garbage can.

Ryder jumped back and the gun went off.

The small-caliber round passed between two ribs low on the man's left side, clipping a lung and passing out his back. Blood started seeping into the lung. The man stared down at the small, spreading stain on his shirt in disbelief. Ryder looked down at the gun in his hand, looked up at the man, his mouth worked soundlessly.

The man pulled out his own handgun, a cannon in comparison. Ryder dropped his gun and clutched the laptop to his chest like a talisman.

"You!" The man shouted, his shout punctuated by a gunshot that smashed through the computer screen in a shower of sparks and hit Ryder in the stomach. Ryder fell on his back, the computer lying open on his chest, half the screen dark. "Stupid!" and another gunshot, this one slamming into the body of the computer, the bullet ferrying shards of plastic and metal into Ryder's chest. Ryder waved his arms and legs feebly, as if pinned to the ground by the weight of the laptop. The man changed his aim upwards, "Fuck!" The final shot caught Ryder full in the face, smashing the bridge of his nose into a spray of bone shards that blasted into his brain, killing him instantly.

The man stood over Ryder breathing heavily, wetly. He spat on Ryder, noticing that his saliva was bright red. He hitched his chest and spat again, this time tasting copper in his mouth. A coughing fit overtook him. The nick in his lung tore, becoming a sizable rent. Blood flowed into the lung freely. The gun fell from his hand unnoticed to the ground. The huge man hunched over as he gasped for air. He dropped to his knees and doubled over, hands slapping the deck planks, the pressure in his lungs becoming excruciating, a thin stream of blood and drool running from his mouth. One lung foundered near collapse and began spilling blood over into the other lung.

He fell onto his side, blood splashing up his throat and out his nose and mouth. He coughed weakly, rolled onto his back, and began to drown. His breathing hitched repeatedly, his massive arms and legs drummed on the thick planks of the dock shaking it to its pilings, and then he was still.

The creaking of the boats at anchor seemed very loud in the sudden silence.

*****

Scott and Miller sat with their heads together, each with one half of the headphones held to their heads.

"What the fuck just happened?" Miller asked.

"Shhhh!" Scott listened intently for a moment, then "I think we had better get down there."

Miller slammed the door shut on its track while Scott jumped into the driver's seat. The engine roared to life, and they were off down the road like a shot.

*****

Chip peeked over the edge of the boat, his eyes very large, the forms of the two dead men ghostly in the fog. He noticed the cell phone on the piling almost right in front of his face. He thought quickly.

He put a hand over the gunwale and grasped the cell phone. Leaping onto the dock he landed solidly on the balls of his feet and ran towards his car faster than he had ever run in his life. The cord from the cell phone to the computer popped out as he ran.

In his car he missed the ignition twice with the key before driving it home. The old Toyota turned over tiredly at first, finally gaining momentum and catching, a plume of blue smoke belched from the tailpipe. Chip clomped the gas pedal all the way to the floor, the engine revving insanely in neutral. He jammed the car into gear, the gears grinding, throwing the car forward with a lurch and a squeal of tires.

*****

After what Ricky had seen he had slouched back on his heels. No cash? What could he do now?

He was trying to work through that question when he saw a man jump over the side of a boat tied to the dock. The man was large and fat, his shirtless torso glowing pale in the foggy light. He ran close by with astonishing speed, and Ricky, without knowing exactly why, ran after him. Before Ricky could catch him, if actually Ricky had wanted to catch him which he himself was not certain, the man got into a car and sped off.

Ricky ran across the marina, climbed into his own car and slammed the door, getting a surprised squeak from Deirdre in the passenger seat. He started the car and U-turned in a wide fishtail of gravel, and sped off after the other car, the taillights of which were just visible in the distance through the fog.

Inland the fogged thinned, and Ricky was able to drop back a fair distance without fear of losing the other car.

"Ricky," Deirdre began.

"Quiet! Let me think." Ricky didn't know what was going on, but he was pretty sure the guy he was following was his last chance at the money, if in fact there was any chance left at all.

*****

Scott and Miller sped into the marina parking lot having just missed the other two cars speeding out. They drove the van out onto the dock, stopping behind the other two cars already parked there. Scott left the lights on and the engine running as they got out of the van. They stood in silence looking down at the two bodies for a moment, listening to the sounds of the water slapping against the pilings. Tendrils of fog swept across the dock, eddying around the bodies like a curious animal.

"So, there wasn't any cash?" Miller asked in disgust.

"Doesn't look like it. The money was in some bank account somewhere"

"So, where's the money now?"

Scott stepped carefully over the body of the drug dealer. He looked down at Ryder, the computer open on his chest with the screen half dark, acrid smoke rising from a hole in the keyboard. The counter in the corner of the screen was flashing zero, the balance in the account showed zero. He took a deep breath and said, "I don't know."

They searched the bodies and the dock area in the glow from the headlights of the van and the drug dealer's car. They were careful to touch things as little as possible, not quite certain how they wanted to handle this yet.

Miller had pulled a wallet from one of the bodies and the registration from the SUV. "This gentleman here," he said, pointing with his foot, "is Peter Anthony Ryder."

Scott nodded, "The movie producer whose house we were watching last night."

"Yep. Looks like Tommy told us the truth."

"Altitude will do that. The deal was set, only Ryder tries to play some game with wiring the money around, this guy doesn't like it, and here we are."

"Yeah," sighed Miller, "here we are." He paused, "So the money's gone?"

"But not forgotten. You heard Ryder on the headphones. If he wasn't lying, and I can't think of any reason why he would, that money is going to bounce around in cyberspace every twenty minutes for all eternity. In fact," he checked his watch, "it's already bounced twice."

"So we call it in. It's a pretty good bust. This guy," he gestured to the dealer, "must have been a major guy to move millions in product." He walked around to the driver side of the van and reached in for the radio handset. "Too bad we let Tommy go." He keyed the mic, "This is agent Miller, come in Central."

Scott put a hand on Miller's shoulder, "Wait a second."

The radio squawked, "This is central. Go ahead."

Miller put a hand over the mic, though without the button depressed it wasn't active, "What?" he whispered.

"We might still have a shot at this thing."

"How?"

"This is central. Go ahead," the radio repeated.

Scott took the mic from Miller, "Central, do you have the correct time?"

"Oh-four-forty-two hours."

"Thanks, Central. Out." He tossed the radio back onto the seat and turned to Miller, "I don't know exactly, but I think we need to think about this."

"OK, so think."

Scott walked over to Ryder's body and looked down at it. He looked around at the boats in the marina. "No one's come out of their boats."

Miller looked around, "So? It's late in the season. Maybe no one is staying on the boats. All this gunfire, someone would have come out by now if they were here."

"So, no one knows about this crime scene but us."

Miller bobbed his head from side to side, "OK, I see what you're saying, but I don't see where you're going with it."

"I don't know yet either, give me a minute to think it through." Scott walked over and looked at the body of the dealer. He then went and checked out the BMW and SUV, then examined the guns lying on the dock. "Ryder's gun is small caliber, a 22. What are you carrying?"

"A 38. I've got a 22 in the glove compartment, my backup."

Scott crouched down and lifted the edge of the dealer's shirt to peer at the wound, turning the body slightly "Looks like the bullet went clean through. Get me the 22 out of the glove compartment."

Without understanding what Scott was doing, Miller went and got the gun from the van. When he came back, Scott was holding Ryder's 22 in his bare hands.

"Hey, you're leaving fingerprints."

"Not a problem," Scott said. He threw it.

Miller watched as the gun turned end over end as if it were happening in slow motion. It disappeared in the fog, and then a moment later hit the water with a splash.

"Now shoot your gun."

"What? Where?"

"Just out over the water."

Miller shrugged and fired the gun once pointed out to

sea.

"There. You just shot him. Gunshot residue on your hands will prove it."

"Now you've completely lost me. We have another body here. How do we explain that?"

"By not having the body."

"I don't follow."

"We came down here using a lead from the party, ended up in a shootout. It's a good shooting – he was armed. End of story."

"And the second body?"

"Nobody is looking for a second body. Nobody is looking for the money, either. I want to keep it that way. We take Ryder, and dump his body in a canyon somewhere. We park his car at LAX long-term parking. If someone finds the car they think Ryder took a flight somewhere, and if someone finds the body it would probably take a week just to get him identified with that face wound. That should give us enough time to find the money."

"OK. It makes sense. But how do we find the money? If we start using official channels to track this guy's accounts, it's going to raise some flags."

"The information has to be on that computer somewhere."

"I don't think you could even play a game of solitaire on that computer right now."

"No," Scott considered, looking down at the smashed

keyboard, "but I think the lab boys might be able to help us there. We can tell them we took the computer off the dealer and we're trying to find information about his sources from it."

Miller smiled and shook his head, "Shit! Did you ever think maybe you should have gone into a life of crime rather than a career in law enforcement?"

Scott laughed, "Hey, I'm young yet."

Now that they had made their decision, they both realized that time was against them. If they waited too long, the discrepancy between the estimated time of the dealer's death and the time they reported the shooting would be too large to account for. Hurriedly they wrapped Ryder's body in a plastic painter's drop cloth they found in the van and loaded him into the back of the Navigator. Scott washed down the dock where Ryder's body had been with sea water using a bucket he found on a nearby boat. Someone on the lab team might notice the water, and while he couldn't think of a way to explain it, it would be easier to explain than Ryder's blood all over the dock. They would cover that problem if it came up. If he had learned one thing in his years of dealing with criminals, it was never give an answer to a question no one has asked.

They looked at the scene that remained with a critical eye. Dead drug dealer, gun lying on the dock, bullet that had shot dealer in the ocean somewhere, probably. The computer, bullet riddled and covered with Ryder's brain and bits of his face, was a problem to their story. They decided to put it into the trunk of the BMW. It was difficult to explain what a computer with bullet holes and blood was doing in the trunk of the dealer's car too, but that was really the dealer's problem, and he wasn't up to explaining anything, was he? As an afterthought they shut off the power switch on the computer. The screen had gone completely blank when they moved it, and they were concerned of further electrical damage occurring, if that were possible.

Scott, wearing gloves, drove the Navigator to a Shipley's donut shop nearby while Miller called in the shooting. He parked in the far corner of the lot, bought a dozen donuts, and walked back to the marina. He got back just as the crime scene techs were arriving. The donuts made him very popular.

*****

Sundays were the only day that Jason took things slowly. He purposely didn't set his alarm, allowing himself to wake up whenever he did. He would then wander downstairs in favorite UCONN shorts and a T-shirt, collect the Sunday newspaper from the front steps, and lie around on the couch with sections of the paper spread around him in a heap, a lazy cup of coffee growing cold on the end table.

It was all the more jarring then when Chip came screeching up into the driveway near dawn, jumped out of the car, leaving the engine running, and pounded on the door a dozen times before remembering the doorbell. He leaned into the doorbell steadily, shifting from foot to foot like a child that has to pee.

Jason made his way downstairs adjusting the UCONN shorts as he came, and sleepily looked out the living room window to see who it was, opening the door when he realized it was Chip. "Easy on that doorbell, I'm still making payments on it." But he was talking to the empty doorway, Chip already having darted by him and inside.

"Jason! You won't believe it! These two guys shot each other right next to the boat! One of them had seven million dollars! Look! Look!" Chip said, waving the cell phone at Jason so quickly he couldn't see what Chip was holding.

"Hold it! Slow down!" He grabbed Chip's flailing hand and looked at the cell phone. He looked Chip in the eyes speaking very slowly and evenly, "Chip, this is a cell phone."

"I know it's a cell phone. But, Jason, I," Chip began, flustered.

Jason held up a hand, "Hold on a second. Come with me." He led Chip into the kitchen and started the coffeemaker. When it was finished, he poured coffee into the 'World's Greatest Grandmother' mug and added three tablespoons of sugar, because Jason knew Chip took it that way. He led Chip into the living room and sat him on the couch, took the cell phone from him and gave him the mug, and settled into the chair opposite him. "Now, take a sip, and start again. You were on the boat yesterday morning fishing."

Chip took a big swallow of the coffee, which was probably too hot to drink that fast, but Chip didn't notice. He told Jason the entire story, starting from the fishing trip, the storm out at sea, sleeping on the boat, the shootings, the laptop and the money jumping from account to account, and ending with him taking the cell phone and driving to Jason's house. He spoke utterly without pause, and when he finished he was out of breath.

"And that brings us to now."

"Yes." Chip panted.

Jason shook his head as if trying to clear it. "Could you go through that one more time? I'm not sure I heard you correctly; I think the sun was shining in my ears."

Chip started through the story again, but Jason stopped him, "I got it. I got it. That was a joke."

"Oh," Chip smiled slightly, really nothing more than a small spasm of facial muscles, clearly too strung out for a joke.

"Do you want me to go the police station with you?"

"What? No. Jason, think about this for a second. These two guys killed each other, and now the money is just out there." He gestured with his hands in a waving motion as if the money was flying around in the air outside. "No one is looking for it. No one else even knows it exists." He said that last in a harsh whisper, like telling a ghost story around the campfire.

"So?"

"So? Jason, look at this house you can't afford. Look at me stamping out keychains at my father's company. Think of the money!" Chips eyes were fever-bright.

"You think we should go after this money?"

Chip nodded slowly.

"That's nuts."

"Why is it nuts? You use your computer to find the money and transfer it into your own account. No one is ever going to come looking for it."

"What makes you think that?"

"Because after the shooting it was like a graveyard. These two guys were alone."

"What about their families or partners or whatever?"

"I told you, the money is bouncing around from account to account. I think the one guy set the deal up that way. If it went sour, the money would never be found."

"And it won't be." Jason looked at the clock on the cable box. "That money has jumped four times already, and we don't even know where to start looking."

Chip smiled, though it looked a little maniacal, "But we do." He picked up the cell phone from the coffee table where Jason had put it and punched redial. He held the phone against Jason's head until Jason held it there with his own hand.

The phone rang twice and was answered by a computer, "Welcome to the Bank of America automated account information system, please speak slowly and clearly: say your name, followed by your account number."

Jason hung up the phone and dropped it back on the coffee table, "OK. Bank of America. Without a name and account number, we're stuck."

"Ryder, Peter, Account Number 08239866"

"How do you know that?"

"He called that number standing next to the boat. He must have been checking his account. His name stuck because I had a crush on a girl named Amy Ryder when I was high school."

"And the account number?"

"08239866."

"OK, 0823. August 23. That's your birthday. But the rest of it?"

"9866."

"Yeah?"

"Come on, Jason. September 8, 1966."

"Should that mean something to me?"

"The premiere date of *Star Trek*!" Chip looked hurt.

Jason laughed, "You would know that!" Jason again picked up the phone and hit redial. He waited for the computer to play its message. He said "Ryder, Peter, Account Number 08239866," and waited while the computer reported the balance. He hung up the phone. "There's nothing in the account."

"You knew there wouldn't be."

"I didn't know there wouldn't be. I suspected there wouldn't be. Now I know. Big difference. "

"So what do we do?"

Jason thought for a moment, and then went over and turned on the laptop which had been sitting on the dining room table. He opened an internet window and brought up the home page for the bank. He examined the source code for directory routing information.

Chip leaned over his shoulder, "What are you doing?"

"I'm trying to find a way into their account records so I can see where the money was transferred."

"You can do that?"

"Not legally. In fact, it's probably a federal crime, but I'm not changing anything, just looking." He kept typing while he was talking.

After fifteen minutes Chip wandered into the kitchen and grabbed a box of Wheat Thins and started munching on them. Ten minutes later the Sunday paper hit the front steps with a whump and Chip went to retrieve it. He sat on the couch reading the comics, then the TV guide, then the 'Lifestyle' section. He was flipping through a Best Buy circular when Jason said, "I've got it!"

"You've got it?"

"Here." He pointed to the screen that showed the past 30 days of account information. "At 4:20AM the money was transferred out to an account at the Union Pacific Bank in San Diego. It would have been there until 4:40."

"And then were did it go?"

"I don't know. This account doesn't say." Jason was jotting down the account information on the corner of the folder containing the online pet company project.

Chip took Jason's wrist to look at his watch, but he wasn't wearing one. He dropped the hand and went into the kitchen to look at the clock on the microwave. "It took you 45 minutes to find that out."

"That's not bad for cracking a bank computer."

"But the money jumped twice in the time it took you to find that out! We'll never catch up to it!"

"Not this way we won't. But I don't happen to have a better idea. Do you?"

"Me?" Chip asked.

"You."

Chip looked around as if the answer might be written

on the walls. "No."

"Well, then, I think we might as well keep going. Maybe if we're lucky the transfers will develop a pattern and we'll be able to get ahead of it."

"You think that's possible?"

"It's definitely possible. As for probable, eh." Jason held his hand out flat, seesawing from side to side. He got up from the keyboard and went into the kitchen. He dug a frying pan out from under the stove and took eggs and butter out of the refrigerator.

"What are you doing?" Chip asked.

"Making breakfast. I always think better when I'm fed."

"But the money!" Chip pointed to the computer.

"Will just have to keep jumping around without me while I eat. We're quickly going to end up so far behind it half an hour won't make any difference."

"OK" Chip said glumly. "I'll make scrambled eggs."

"I think there are some English muffins in the fridge."

Despite Jason's belief that the money was already as good as gone, that they would never catch up to it, he only ate a little of the scrambled eggs that Chip had made for him. He returned to work on the computer, the breakfast growing cold beside him. The list of account transfers and other notes trailed down the cover of the work folder, and then on the backs of the pages inside. He had to admit it, he was hooked.

*****

Ricky drove slowly by the house, his eyes narrowed like those of a predator, missing nothing. The battered Toyota was parked diagonally in the driveway, the driver side door open and the engine running. There was no one in sight. He let the car glide down the street to the end of the block before U-turning and going by the house again.

"Dee, write down the address of that house." He said, passing her paper and a pen from his jacket pocket.

Deirdre jotted down the address, noting that she was writing on the back of the invitation to the party in the hills. Also written on the back was 'Santa Del Ria Marina, 4AM' and 'Lincoln Navigator, metallic purple' in Ricky's cramped, blocky writing.

They came to the pillars that marked the entrance to the subdivision and turned left. The first strip mall that they came to Ricky pulled in and parked. He arched his back, his vertebrae popping audibly, and leaned over the steering wheel looking out the windshield.

Deirdre looked out and noticed that the majority of the strip mall, the section they were parked in front of, was a women's gym, the plate glass window before them filled with stair climbing and treadmill machines facing away from them. Even near dawn on a Sunday, toned women worked the machines, bodies wrapped in spandex. She turned slyly to Ricky, expecting to find him leering, but found instead is eyes unfocused and looking at nothing at all. Deirdre knew that usually Ricky would have brought a sandwich and made an afternoon of watching the asses pumping in front of him. She was beginning to think that whatever he was on the trail of was bigger than she imagined. It all began, she thought, with the invitation that she was holding in her hands.

"Did anything about that car and house strike you as strange?" Ricky asked suddenly.

"You mean like we started out following a nearly new Lincoln Navigator and ended up following a beat-to-shit Toyota Tercel?"

"No, not that."

"You mean like a beat-to-shit Toyota in the driveway of a nearly new house probably worth about a million bucks?"

"Yeah, that's it. It's not his house. He's gone to see someone, but who?"

"You're asking me? I don't even know who we're following, or why, let alone who he would visit. Ricky, honey, you want my help, you're going to have to tell me what's going on."

Ricky sat thinking about that. Deirdre waited silently, holding her breath.

He broke his silence and shook his head, "No. Not yet. But soon."

He started the car and they continued down the road, the area crowded with fast food places and large shopping areas and office buildings, mostly closed this early on a Sunday. They finally came to a Walmart that was open, and Ricky went inside, Deirdre following with a growing sense of apprehension. Manipulative Ricky she was used to dealing with; Secretive Ricky was new to her.

As they headed towards the sporting goods area, Deirdre thought Ricky might be going to buy a gun. Didn't Walmart sell guns? Ricky didn't currently have a gun that she knew of; he had lost the last one during the abortive drug deal in 'Frisco. He instead ended up talking with the salesman about binoculars, eventually buying a fairly expensive set with a credit card. Deirdre knew that Ricky didn't like using credit cards, that they 'left a paper trail'

Ricky often said. Clearly his current plan was tapping Ricky dry. She watched as he signed the name 'James Holland' on the credit slip without comment. How many stolen credit cards did Ricky have on him, Deirdre wondered?

They returned to the strip mall, parked the car, and walked back to the subdivision. Walking hand in hand along the sidewalk past pristine houses with manicured lawns, Deirdre noticed children were playing on some of the lawns or the man of the house was out mowing the grass. Ricky had left his jacket in the car and unbuttoned the first two buttons of his shirt, the binoculars on their strap around his neck, and Deirdre almost laughed at his attempt to try and blend in, to try and look just like another couple out for a morning walk. Ricky, tall and broad, dressed in black slacks and a white dress shirt, looked more like a Spanish soap opera star than anything else. Deirdre, herself almost as tall as Ricky in her high-heeled black boots, in black jeans and a white undersized half shirt, looked like a bimbo from an auto parts calendar. Yeah, they were blending.

Still, a couple jogging the other way, colorful running tights and matching Disney sweatshirts, said good morning to them. So, although they didn't look like they belonged here, at least they didn't look too scary. Not too scary was good.

Ricky slowed as they passed the house with the Toyota in the driveway. The driver side door was still open but the engine was no longer running. With the keys dangling in the ignition, Deirdre presumed that it had either stalled or run out of gas. As Ricky slowed to a near stop, Deirdre grabbed his upper arm and moved him along. She was sure that standing in front of the house and gawking at it was going to look odd to anyone who saw them.

They walked to the end of the block and turned and walked back. Ricky stopped when they got reached the pillars. Deirdre leaned against one of them and massaged her aching foot and ankle through the boot. These boots were not made for walking.

"See anything?" He asked her.

She looked up at him from her bent over position and had to toss her head to get her hair out of her face. "Nice house."

"Yeah." He said, and then went silent.

Deirdre finished rubbing her other foot and stood leaning against the pillar.

She could only think of two reasons why he wasn't telling her anything. Either he didn't trust her, or he was planning to ditch her. As little as two days ago if she had learned that he was planning to ditch her, she would have done everything she could to help him. Now she was beginning to wonder if whatever he was attempting was worth her hanging around for. Just how valuable could it be? The other thought, that he didn't trust her, frankly terrified her. Deirdre realized, at no small blow to what was left of her ego, that she was firmly under Ricky's control for as long as he wished, that her need for money and an unmistakable raw animal attraction left her effectively without alternatives. How obsessed by this plan he must be in order for him not to realize that.

Ricky took a pack of filterless Camels from his shirt pocket and shook a cigarette out of the pack. Deirdre lit it for him using a hot pink plastic lighter from her purse. He took a long drag, letting the smoke bleed out of his nostrils, and handed the cigarette to Deirdre who took a puff of her own. The habit disgusted her, especially in light of the fact that her mother had died of cancer, albeit not lung cancer. But Ricky had smoked when she met him, and now she smoked too. She handed the cigarette back to him and he slouched against the pillar, the cigarette dangling from his lips.

They stood that way for a long time.

A family drove by in a large minivan. Deirdre watched the rows of windows go by her, the face of a child sealed behind each one, a teenage boy in the back craning his neck to look out the rear window at her as they drove away. Probably going to church, she guessed.

With a grunt, Ricky heaved himself away from the pillar. "Too many people around here on a Sunday." He dropped the smoldering butt and ground it beneath the toe of his shoe. "We'll have to come back after dark to take a look at the house. We'll find a motel somewhere around here for the day." That pronouncement made, he set off walking back to the where the car was parked.

That sounded just fine to Deirdre, whose feet were killing her and who hadn't slept well in the car last night. Maybe when they came back tonight she would be able to learn something.

*****

It wasn't until much later, after the techs has swabbed Miller's hands and bagged the swabs, after they had both given and repeated their statements numerous times, that they finally got back to the body in the Navigator. As Scott had hoped, the high traffic at the donut shop had left the SUV unnoticed throughout the day.

Getting into the truck he gagged. Ryder had ripened considerably during the moderately warm day. He would have left the windows cracked, but of course a car smelling like a decaying corpse was much more likely to attract unwanted attention. Rolling down the windows, he headed north, into the hilly scrubland of the San Gabriel

Mountains, Miller following behind.

The sun was low in the west when the Navigator crunched to a halt overlooking a ravine on one of any of a number of nameless dirt roads that wound through the Angeles National Park. The two of them got out of their cars, walked to the edge, and looked down. The deep shadows below allowed them to make out few details. It appeared free of furniture and appliances, meaning it was farther off the beaten path than most ravines, which often became a dumping ground for LA garbage.

They went to the back of the SUV and retrieved the body still wrapped in plastic sheeting. The sheeting was anonymous, sold in thousands of home improvement stores across the state. They threw the body into the ravine. It rolled and slid down the incline, tangling up in some bushes about halfway down. Not exactly out of sight, but good enough.

Miller stood and prayed, silently mouthing the liturgy that had been drummed into him since childhood.

Scott watched him with a frown on his face. He slapped Miller on the shoulder, "Come on. We still have to go by the airport. I've got to get to sleep, and I want to be at work early to see what the lab thinks of that computer."

Miller was unhappy, thinking of the body down in the ravine that would never get a proper burial. "Yeah, it would be a real shame if we couldn't get the money after all this."

Scott didn't like the tone in Miller's voice. "Hey, you're with me on this, right? You have to understand how far we've stuck our necks out. That crime scene stinks, and with a little poking our whole story is going to come apart. You don't think come Monday morning Dorado's going to be going over those reports with a fine-toothed comb?

Damn straight he is! He's not stupid; he'll figure it out. We've bought ourselves some time, maybe a week or two depending on how long our friend down there stays lost. We have to find that money now, or we're in all likelihood fucked. And whatever we have to do to get it, we're going to have to do."

Miller took a deep breath, "Yeah, right. I'm sorry. Won't happen again."

Scott looked at his partner closely like he was examining some previously unknown species of insect. It made Miller feel particularly uncomfortable. "OK, then, let's get to the airport."

So to the airport they went. Miller drove to arrivals, flashing his badge to the traffic cop who wanted him to move along, telling him that he was waiting for his partner.

Scott pulled into long-term parking, keeping the sun visor down and his face out of sight of the video camera at the entrance. He took the parking ticket and put it into his pocket. He slotted the SUV somewhere in the middle of the lot; cars left out near the ends for long periods of time always catch the eye of roving security personnel as abandoned. On the parking shuttle bus, he crumpled the parking ticket and dropped it beside his seat where it would be cleaned up and thrown away at the end of the shift.

Passing through the airport, he came out the arrivals doors and climbed into Miller's car. "Piece of cake. Drive me home, and I'll see you tomorrow morning. Right, partner?"

"Right, partner." Miller repeated softly, but he was already having second thoughts.

*****

Dusk had come and gone, and night had fallen. Chip, realizing that asking Jason lots of questions was just slowing him down, had wandered around the house listlessly, flipping through sections of the Sunday paper and watching pieces of various football games on television. He had gone outside about an hour ago, and, as near as Jason could tell, had fallen asleep on a chaise lounge by the pool.

Jason's eyes were severely strained, his back hurt, he hadn't eaten anything since breakfast this morning, and he hadn't brushed his teeth yet that day. Yet he couldn't seem to break himself away from the computer, despite his assurances to Chip that another hour wouldn't make any difference, and despite his prediction, now coming all too clearly true, that they would fall farther and farther behind the money as time went by. In point of fact, Jason had successfully tracked the money through eleven transfers; in the same amount of time the money had moved more than thirty times. So far all Jason knew, if eleven transfers could be considered a good statistical sample, was that the money was moving around banks all contained within the state of California. If there was a pattern other than that, Jason didn't see it.

A quick check online showed over a thousand banks and branch locations in California. Among that many banks the money could hop around the state for almost three weeks without repeating a single bank twice, and then move on to other states afterwards.

He had originally approached this as a mental exercise. Could it be done at all? And yet as he had worked, he thought of the stock options he had worked years for, now virtually worthless. He thought of the less than $200 left in his bank account, the nursing home planning to transfer his mother to some godforsaken state hole unless he came up with the fees, and the mortgage and car note payments that were due in 30 days. Why couldn't this money be his and Chip's?

Well, for one thing, he argued with himself, it's not as simple as transferring the money into his account electronically. Perhaps it could be done that way, but that sudden appearance of money in his account could not be explained, to the Federal Government least of all. No, if he actually managed to find the money, he would have to be more circuitous in taking possession of it, maybe by creating a series of fake accounts online and letting the money bounce around those for a time. But while such an approach would distance the money from its origins, it wouldn't help explain its presence in his account when it landed there. That was a problem that he had not yet solved.

For another thing, his argument continued, the money isn't yours. He pictured himself as a small child in church on Sunday morning, the priest railing about 'Thou shalt not steal.' But as near as Jason could tell, if Chip was right, the money wasn't really anyone's anymore, at least not anyone living. Why shouldn't they have it?

As he worked onward, ignoring the grumblings of his stomach and the ache of his neck and back, Jason knew that he couldn't let this go. He was already building a whole life around this money in his mind, with his mother securely cared for, maybe even giving a few more doctors a try, with the mortgage paid off and the Porsche too, and the sixty- or seventy-hour weeks of staring at a computer screen behind him.

Chip woke up a few hours later and made both of them macaroni and cheese, of which again Jason ate very little while sitting at the computer, following the money off into the night.

*****

Ricky and Deirdre returned to the subdivision after dark. They had both changed their white shirts. Ricky wore a dark gray sweatshirt with a WWE logo on the front, and Deirdre a black sweater. They walked between the pillars and down the street past houses, the occasional bedroom or living room window framing the cool blue glow of a television. At a house that appeared completely asleep they paused, looking for signs of movement, perhaps an elderly grandmother with insomnia, or signs in the yard that a dog might live there. Satisfied, they made their way quickly around the side to the backyard, and scrambled up the loose dirt of the hillside to the ridgeline above.

The storm to the west had blown itself out, and left in its wake a clear night sky, but the moon was not yet up, and the stars offered meager light by which to navigate the weeds and low bushes on the hillside. Though Deirdre had changed her boots for a pair of black sneakers, making their way along the hillside that ran behind the houses was proving treacherous, her ankles frequently tangling in the long grass.

"Shit!" Ricky hissed in a whisper.

"What?"

"Some of these bushes have thorns!"

"They're cactus, Ricky."

"Fuck!"

They counted the shapes of the houses below, finally coming to the one Ricky wanted. The houses in this area of the subdivision, indeed the entire subdivision, all looked alike, cookie-cutter copies with only a gable here or a porch there to distinguish them. This one had a single light on in what Ricky figured was the dining room. A man Ricky didn't recognize sat working at a laptop computer at the table. He scanned around with the binoculars, but didn't see anything else of interest. He dropped the binoculars on their strap and tried to think of what to do next. Maybe they should go around and check to see if the Toyota was still there?

"Can I have a look?"

"Sure." He handed her the binoculars.

She looked at the house, the liquid reflection of the lit window on the pool outside, the guy working at the computer, kind of cute in a thin, Tom-Cruisey sort of way. Someone walked up behind him to look over his shoulder at the computer, but before she could get a good look at that person Ricky grabbed the binoculars away.

"Hello, Moonpie," he said as he focused on the house, "so you're still there."

That he hadn't lost the trail of the money was a relief to Ricky, but that still didn't tell him what his next move should be.

7 Days Earlier

Ricky stood on the hillside, binoculars held to his face, staring at the man working on the computer through the window. He stared with a single mindedness that frankly Deirdre found unnerving, his body taught as a wire, humming in resonance like an antenna to signals that she couldn't sense. So far the only things that she had seen attract Ricky's attention for any length of time were topless dancers and sports on which he had bet money, and that made her even more curious as to what could possibly be going on. Yet despite her watching him watch the house for hours standing on that sandy hillside, and then sitting carefully among the low mesquite brush and cactus that dotted the ground when she became tired of standing, she was no closer to understanding. Attempts she had made to talk to Ricky, questions she had asked, were met with either noncommittal grunts or complete silence.

And so she waited. And waited.

She pulled a long spine off a cactus nearby, its shaft as narrow as a pin glowing ghostly in the moonlight, the end bending over upon itself to form a tiny barb. Her mother had pointed out cactus like these during the long walks they would take in the scrub desert near their home. She told Deirdre that once stuck the spine would break off leaving the barb behind under the skin where it would itch and burn.

Her eyes were drawn by a sudden brightness to one side. A window on the second floor of the house next door was filled with light, the line of shower curtain and tile visible clearly marking the room as a bathroom. Deirdre checked her watch: 4:45. They had been out on this hillside all night. That sudden realization brought with it a number of pains that until then had gone unnoticed. Her neck was sore, her ass was asleep, and her throat ached, she realized, from a number of cigarettes she had smoked during the night, almost without noticing, and snuffed out in the sandy soil by her feet throughout the night. She counted eleven cigarette butts all in a row.

She looked up at Ricky still standing motionless, and thought for a minute that maybe he had died from some massive coronary that had left all his muscles locked until rigor had set in, and would remain standing until someone came and pushed him over. She then thought of the scene from the *Terminator* movie in which Schwarzenegger stood guard, camera tricks making the sun set and rise behind him. And here Ricky had just about done it, no camera tricks required.

Another light went on in the house three over on the other side, Deirdre's angle through the window too steep to pick up any detail from inside. She also noticed an almost imperceptible lightening of the sky in the east, from black to dark blue to a hue something like deep lavender.

She looked around herself at the hillside – some rocks, cacti, small bushes.

She tried to talk to Ricky but her voice came out as a rasp. She cleared her throat and tried again. "Ricky, honey, the sun's coming up. All those houses down there, and not a lot of cover up here." She left the thought unfinished.

He lifted the binoculars from his eyes and looked down at her as if aware of her for the first time. She noticed his eyes were shining red with irritation and wondered how long it had been since he had blinked. He then looked east.

"We'll come back tonight. No point in staying here anyway. He gave up on the computer hours ago."

Deirdre looked at the house they had been watching and could see the light on in the window, the computer sitting on the table, but the man was gone. She hadn't remembered seeing him leave the computer but her mind had wandered a bit, and maybe she had even dozed a little while sitting.

Ricky helped her stand up, her knees and ankles complaining with a damp stiffness the first few steps she took. They made their way back the way they had come, Ricky again cursing the cacti quietly as they went. It was becoming brighter rapidly now near dawn, and there were lights on in many of the houses, so they moved quickly, stumbling over occasional rocks or partially buried roots that were still hidden in shadows, plowing through a few patches of grass that had grown long and coarse. They cut through at the first house that was dark that had houses on both sides of it that were also dark. Deirdre nearly jumped out of her skin as a dog barked loudly from the house on their left as they wove between them, but no lights came on in either house. They squeezed past a large air conditioner sitting on a concrete pad that nearly filled the alleyway, Ricky snagging the sleeve of his sweatshirt on an edge of sheet metal, and then emerged on the sidewalk.

It was lighter still on the open street and Deirdre looked down at herself and over at Ricky. Both dressed entirely in black, weeds, dirt, and brambles clinging to their pants all the way up to their knees, and by turning around Deirdre could see pale dust on the seat of her jeans that firmly resisted brushing off. Even to the casual eye, she thought, they must look very suspicious on this orderly suburban sidewalk shortly before dawn.

She took Ricky's arm and they walked. She wanted to run, but was certain that two people dressed all in black and running this early in the morning would catch someone's unwanted attention. Knowing their luck it would probably be a cop who lived in the area looking out the bathroom window as he shaved.

They saw only a single jogger puffing his way along the street on the opposite side. Ricky tensed, and then made as if to dive into some ornamental bushes at the edge of the yard they were near. Deirdre, certain they had already been seen, pulled Ricky close and leaned her head on his shoulder. She hoped maybe they looked like a couple out for a romantic walk, at the crack of dawn, dressed all in black and having already walked through dense weeds, fragments of which clung to them. OK, she admitted it was a dumb idea, but it had to be less suspicious than two people in black diving into bushes that were probably too small to hide them anyway. As they passed the jogger, Deirdre saw him out of the corner of her eye turn to look at them. For the first time in her life she hoped that he was checking out her ass.

They made it out of the development and back to their car without a police cruiser pulling up to them, lights on top twirling, radio crackling, demanding to see some ID.

Ricky drove in silence. Deirdre leaned her head against the window and tried to think of what they could have done to look less suspicious. They needed dark clothing at night on the hillside so they wouldn't be spotted, but come morning it was a problem. Bring a change of clothing and swap in an alleyway between houses with some dog barking at them? Unlikely. She shivered in the blast from the car A/C, her clothing damp with sweat and dew, and thumbed the vent in front of her closed. Her thoughts turned back to why Ricky was watching this guy work on the computer in the first place, but she nodded off without any answers.

The property values held for the first several miles, upscale strip malls and tasteful boutiques, but then fell precipitously into older strip malls and fast food restaurants, security shutters drawn down across the storefronts. Traffic was still light just as dawn broke, the sky a deep blue before the serious smog set in and turned it yellow-brown.

Ricky pulled across the cracked concrete apron and into the parking lot of a motel with a red neon sign out front – the Sea View Motel. As she dozed with her eyes partway open, Deirdre saw the sign and tried to figure out how far they were from the ocean, but drifted on to other thoughts, and then fell into a deeper sleep. Jouncing across the potholed parking lot bounced Deirdre's head against the window, smacking the exact same spot on her head that she had hit when Ricky had slapped her several days earlier. The stab of pain was surprisingly fresh from her still-bruised scalp, and it brought her fully awake as Ricky brought the car to a rocking stop.

Ricky left the engine running as he went into the office. Deirdre could see him talking to the guy, long hair held back in a greasy ponytail, behind the desk through the large plate glass window that faced the parking lot. When he came back, Ricky drove the car down the lot and parked in front of room 5.

Deirdre's legs were still stiff as she got out of the car, rubbing the sore spot on her head. She paused trying to think of how long it had been since she had slept, not counting any sleep she might have done while sitting on the hillside. Ricky went around and opened the trunk. He took out a battered canvas duffel bag in which he kept his clothing and walked to the room door. He unlocked the door using a key attached to plastic tag twice the size of a credit card, and went inside leaving the door open.

"I'm getting in the shower," he called out to her.

Deirdre went around to the trunk to get her things. When she had left home with Ricky, she had simply stuffed what she could carry into green plastic garbage bags. Travel light, and never look back. That was Ricky's motto and she had embraced it whole-heartedly. Looking into the trunk now, seeing the same ratty green plastic bags made her feel lonely instead of independent, unanchored and insecure rather than a free spirit.

Next to the bags was the white box the silver dress had come in, the lid ajar, a corner of the dress hanging out like molten metal. She went to tuck the dress back into the box, noticing as she did so that there was a grease stain on the fabric, probably from the car jack jammed in next to it. She ran the cool, slick surface of the material between her fingers, the ugly black smear of the grease made her feel as if she were breathing with a heavy weight on her chest, the serenity of the beauty parlor very far away. She pushed the fabric back into the box, fitting the lid on firmly, and putting the lug wrench on top to hold it in place.

She grabbed two of the garbage bags, slammed the trunk lid down with her elbow, and went into the room.

Stepping from the gray light of dawn to the complete darkness of the room was disorienting at first. As her eyes adjusted, she could see the outlines of the furniture. A brighter band of light was coming from the crack under the bathroom door, the sound of water running within. She kicked the room door shut with her heel and tossed the bags and her purse onto a chair that stood nearby a small, round table against the windows, and opened the blackout curtains. The light flowed into the room weakly through the filthy glass, hesitantly illuminating the chair, table, double bed, battered chest of drawers, and TV mounted on a stand bolted to the floor.

She sat on the edge of the bed, sinking almost to the box spring against the sagging mattress, and took a deep breath, looking at her feet. The carpet was mottled green shag, beaten almost completely flat. The bedspread had maybe once been orange or red, but had faded to threadbare pale pink.

She pulled her purse from the chair and rummaged inside, finding a crumpled pack of cigarettes and the hot pink lighter. It caught on the third try and she held the flame to the cigarette clamped between her lips. She tossed the lighter onto the tabletop, where it rattled and slid to a rest next to a square glass ashtray. She drew on the cigarette and tried to find answers in the patterns of smoke in the still air.

After only a few puffs, she ground out the cigarette in frustration. Two days ago she was sure she was going to leave Ricky if she could only find a way, certain he was on a collision course with disaster with her along for the ride. Now she felt that he might be onto something. His silence, his severe focus, his quiet intensity, all pointed to something big, bigger perhaps than he had ever dreamed. She ran it around and around in her head and realized she didn't have a fucking idea what it might be. Two years spent pulling endless scams and moving city to city with nothing to show for it, and now she was afraid that he would finally score big. Some stupid plan of his wouldn't be a complete failure, and he was leaving her out.

"Fuck." She mouthed silently.

She got up and closed the blackout curtains once again, plunging the room into near darkness. She dug the toe of her left sneaker into the heel of her right and worked off the right shoe, and then did the same with her left. Peeling off her jeans, she worked off her bra without removing her sweater, and climbed between the sheets. They smelled stale but clean. She found herself settling into a large depression in the middle of the mattress, the pillow lumpy beneath her head, and stared at the ceiling. A large brown waterspot on the ceiling was shaped like Australia.

Her frustration was strong at first, causing her to grind her teeth, but it waned as exhaustion overtook her, draining away with her consciousness.

When she rolled over restlessly in the bed an hour later, hot now because of the sweater she was still wearing underneath the covers, she sat up and blinked sleepily in the dim light leaking around the blackout curtains. She pulled the sweater over her head and threw it onto the table nearby, her hair showering in a frizzy cascade around her shoulders.

The bathroom was dark and silent, the space in the bed

beside her empty. Ricky had left.

*****

Miller sat with his forearms on the desk, a styrofoam cup of coffee between his hands on the desktop. Scott was in his chair, tilted back on the rear two legs against the wall, apparently asleep. The cubicle they shared was about eight feet on a side; their two desks pushed front to front forming one large surface; the ruined computer on the surface between them. It was nine o'clock on Monday morning.

They had both gotten into work a little after six, arriving at the evidence lab to find it almost entirely dark. A lone technician was seated in the pool of light cast by a work lamp putting dabs of blood from a rack of test tubes onto microscope slides with a long, glass pipette.

He had glanced at the computer only for a moment, fingering the hole in the keyboard distractedly with a latex-gloved hand, "That puppy's a gonner."

"But if the hard drive isn't damaged, can it be moved to another computer and accessed?" Scott had asked.

"Oh, I suppose." And with that he turned back to his test tubes.

Scott and Miller had waited while he prepared more slides. Time crept by.

Finally Scott spoke, as if the possibility that the technician had forgotten they were standing there existed, "So, should we leave this here for you? When can you get on it?"

The technician didn't even turn away from the slide he was working on. "Oh, you don't want me working on it."

He paused while he lowered a cover slip onto a slide, his tongue clamped between his front teeth and lower lip. That done, he turned back to them, "I totally fried my girlfriend's computer last month trying to install a new video card. Plug and Play, my ass. You want Jerry."

"And when does Jerry come in?"

The technician looked at the clock on the wall, "Maybe nine." Then he sat with his lips bunched up, running thumb and forefinger around in the razor stubble on his chin, considering his answer, "It's Monday. Probably closer to nine-thirty."

So Scott dozed, while Miller stared at the computer on the desktop waiting for nine-thirty to roll around.

Miller pictured the computer as a treasure map written in some arcane language, the unfathomable code of ones and zeros left like a trail of breadcrumbs on the magnetic surface of the hard drive. If they could follow that trail to the money it was possible that they would find it before anyone even knew it was out there to be found. But he felt that they had to work fast. He had had a brief moment of clarity as he lay in bed last night in the hazy moments before falling asleep, a certainty that someone hiking around at night had stumbled across the body of the movie producer at the bottom of the ravine. Miller had rushed into the office this morning and searched the local police activity for a report of a John Doe found in the hills, but nothing had turned up. Still, he was certain that it was only a matter of time before the body was discovered, before it all started to come unraveled.

Then there was the problem of the shooting review board later in the week. As the evidence technicians had dusted and swabbed, measured and photographed the scene on the dock, Miller had tried to put himself into their heads. What did the scene look like? What matched his story and what contradicted it? Despite Scott's assurances that the shooting would pass muster, Miller knew there were inconsistencies that could hang him.

Scott told him that he was experiencing a criminal's vision – because he was involved in the crime he could see how all the clues fit together, convinced that they formed a clear picture of the crime as it had been committed. Like a carpenter that builds an entire house is certain every flaw in the construction is glaringly obvious to all who look at it, Miller is sure each discrepancy in the crime scene is highlighted with hunter orange paint. It is this guilt reflex that they hope to see when questioning a suspect. The way they can stare into the eyes of a suspect who knows how the crime was committed, the suspect convinced that they know it too. Miller is going to have to suppress feeling this at the shooting review later in the week.

They both know that the thousands of tiny fragments collected at a crime scene, actual clues inescapably mixed with the general detritus found in any location, often form a clear picture once the crime has been solved, but at first blush frequently raise more questions than they answer. It is this confusion that Scott hopes to exploit, add to if necessary, to gain the time needed to recover the money.

That is, if they can get off the starting line, if any useful information can be recovered from the roasted electronic junk in front of them.

Scott leaned forward suddenly, his internal clock having told him it was nine-thirty. The sharp rap of the front legs coming down on the gray industrial tile flooring startled Miller from his thoughts.

Scott picked up the laptop before Miller had finished collecting himself, "Let's go."

The lab at this hour was considerably more active. White-coated technicians worked at numerous stations analyzing and cataloging evidence. At a bench to their right as they entered, a man was bent over the contents of vacuum bags emptied onto fiber-free sheets, sifting through piles of hair and dust with long metal tweezers. He had a surgical mask over his face, and a pair of magnifying spectacles and a light held on his bald head with a black plastic strap. Next to him another man moved bits of china around on a tray, probably trying to determine what it had been before it was shattered.

Miller touched the shoulder of a stern looking woman passing by carrying a clipboard, her short, dark hair and the shapeless lab coat combining to make her almost asexual. "Can you direct us to Jerry?"

She looked at him distastefully, perhaps considering filing sexual harassment charges for touching her shoulder, "I think he's in the ballistics lab," and she moved on before Miller could thank her, or ask her where the ballistics lab was, as neither he nor Scott was certain.

Scott shifted the computer from one arm to the other, "I think she liked you."

"You think so? I thought there was some real chemistry there between us too."

They ended up hovering over the man sorting carpet lint until he noticed them. He directed them back out into the hallway and down to a doorway adjacent to the indoor shooting range.

The walls and ceiling of the ballistics lab were covered with acoustic tile. One man was pulling thick sheets of high-density plastic off of the target at the far end of the lab. Another was standing next to a gun mounted to a holding frame bolted to the floor and writing on a clipboard.

The man from the far end of the lab called out, “Twenty-five feet, penetration to the, uh, seventh sheet.”

"Seventh sheet,” the other man echoed as he wrote on the clipboard.

The man worked the bullet out of the plastic using a pair of tongs with rubber sleeves on the tips. He walked over to the other man to show him the bullet still held in the tongs, rotating it in the light of a small penlight he pulled from his breast pocket. “I don’t see the double stripe pattern of the other round. This isn’t the right gun.”

The man with the clipboard held the tong hand of the other man and canted his head, looking at the bullet as he tilted it, “Probably not, but put it under the stereo microscope anyway.”

“Right.” He walked towards Scott and Miller to leave the room.

“Are you Jerry?” Miller asked.

The man gestured back over his shoulder with his head, “He is,” and left.

They approached the man who was finishing writing on the clipboard. He looked up at them, “What can I do for you?”

“Are you Jerry? We’ve been told you’re the resident computer guru.” Scott said offering up the computer in his arms.

“That I am. I just help out with ballistics from time to time.” He took the computer from Scott and carried it to a lab bench along one wall of the room. “What do we have here?”

"Computer confiscated from a drug dealer. We think there might be some information on it about his contacts. Can you get any data off it?"

Jerry shone the light of his penlight into and around the hole in the keyboard and display panel. Then he opened a drawer in the bench and pulled out a set of small screwdrivers in a plastic case. He flipped back the lid of the case and selected a Phillips head. He put the computer on its back and started removing screws from the rear panel, whistling tunelessly through a gap between his front teeth.

Eight tiny screws stood in a line beside the computer when he lifted the panel off, his whistle pitching downwards and trailing off as he got a look at the interior. "You gentlemen have a problem."

"What?" Scott leaned over the other man's shoulder to get a look.

"Right here." The man pointed with the screwdriver at the bullet hole.

"So, it's got a bullet hole in it. We knew that coming in here." Miller said.

The man's voice took on the tones of the scientifically adept lecturing to the scientifically inept, "The bullet hit the hard drive."

"And that's not good?" Miller asked. Technologically, anything more complicated than his TV remote control was beyond him.

"No, that's not good," Jerry said.

"So, that's it." Scott turned away.

“Maybe.” Jerry said, “But maybe not.”

“Is there any way to get something off a hard drive with a bullet hole in it?” Scott asked.

“Let me show you something.” Jerry put the panel back onto the computer and replaced the screws. He picked up the computer and led them out of the ballistics lab and down the hallway. They stopped at a locked steel door that looked like any other along the hallway. He handed the computer to Scott and pulled a ring of keys from his pocket. Selecting one he unlocked the door and ushered them inside. The room was dark until Jerry flipped a switch on the wall and banks of fluorescent bars on the ceiling hummed to life.

The room was a stark gray concrete box with racks of electronics along the walls. In the center of the room stood a massive steel cylinder with smaller cylinders radiating off at all angles. The machine was covered in patches with tin foil. Thick bundles of wires ran from the electronics racks, up along a steel frame near the ceiling, and back down to the machine. To Miller it looked something like the lunar lander.

“Wow.” Scott said.

“Yeah, uh, wow. What is it?” Miller added.

“This is a pet project of mine,” Jerry walked over to the machine and ran his hand along the curve of one of the cylinders lovingly. “There is an increasing problem in law enforcement with data recovery from damaged media. Disks intentionally destroyed, cracked in half, thrown into the harbor, buried underground for weeks or months.”

“With a bullet hole through it?” Scott asked.

“That has never been tried. Still, the theory should

hold. See, the format that data is stored on a hard drive, or almost any magnetic media really, is relatively delicate. Knock a few zeros off here, a few ones off there, and suddenly the entire disk is unreadable by the operating system file manager despite the fact that most of the data is still OK. Still, there are programs that can then be used to simply stream the data off of the device if the device is still functional but only unreadable." Jerry stopped. "Am I going too fast?"

Scott smiled tightly, "Could you boil all this down for me?"

"Well," Jerry started again, "If part of the disk is damaged because it has been burned say or had acid spilled on it-"

"Or is missing because of a bullet hole," Scott said hopefully.

"Or perhaps missing because of a bullet hole, then the rest of the data may be recovered from the undamaged portions. That's what this machine does."

"How long will that take?" Miller asked.

"That's hard to say. I'll have to insert a slug made of nickel into the hole in the hard drive to allow it to spin in balance. That should only take a day or so. Then, if the data can be recovered at all, it will have to be read off onto another computer. How long that will take depends on how big this hard drive is, how much data it holds, and how widespread the damage." Jerry did a little mental mathematics, "Probably a week. Maybe a little less."

Scott and Miller did a little mental math of their own. The body almost certainly would not stay lost a week. The face wound would have made identification difficult for anyone without a criminal record and hence had never had their fingerprints taken. But, as Scott remembered while they drove home last night, Ryder had been arrested for some petty drug possession, and therefore probably had his fingerprints in the system. Scott was cursing himself now for not having chopped off Ryder's fingers. The body would be identified almost as soon as it was found, and that would send some investigative bean counter digging after his bank accounts shortly after. But the money would have jumped a couple of hundred times by then, leaving the bean counter with a long trail to follow. With the data from the computer, hopefully, they would be able to figure out where the money was and head straight to it. They might still get there first.

"When can you start?" Scott asked.

"Right now, if you'd like. I'll keep you posted on my progress."

"That would be a great help," Scott smiled. "We'd really appreciate that."

*****

Monday morning found Jason sleeping face down on the living room couch, his head propped on his arm, his left leg in fetal position up against his chest, the right flung out straight so the foot hung over the end of the couch. Chip came down the stairs having fallen asleep on Jason's bed watching *Jurassic Park 3* on TV. He looked from Jason on the couch to the computer open on the kitchen table.

He walked over to the computer and picked at the scraps of paper scattered around the tabletop. Bank names, account numbers, mathematical equations that Chip frankly didn't understand – there didn't seem to be any order to it at all. He noticed a road map of California open on the seat of another chair at the table and picked that up. There were small x's marked on the map in black felt tip pen that were numbered one through thirty. Seven other x's were not numbered.

Jason stirred on the couch and rolled himself into a sitting position. His hair was pointing every which way and his forearm had left a long red splotch on his forehead. He snorted and ran his tongue around on the gunk built up overnight on his teeth. He got up took several steps towards Chip, then changed his gait so he was dragging the left leg a little.

Chip turned from the map and noticed him limping, "Are you OK?"

"My leg fell asleep. We might have to amputate." He blinked his eyes sleepily and pointed to the map in Chip's hands, "That's all the banks I tracked the money through last night."

"Where is it now?"

"Don't know." Jason shuffled past him into the kitchen and took a glass from the cupboard. He ran water into it from the sink faucet. The first mouthful he swished around and spit out. He drank the rest of the glass, rinsed it, and put it upside down in the dish rack. "But I've cracked thirty-seven banks. Not a bad day's work."

"But the money has moved hundreds times."

"Uh," Jason looked at the clock on the microwave that read 7:38 in green LED bar numerals, "eighty-three, eighty-four in another minute or two. I told you yesterday that we wouldn't catch up to it. We have to find the pattern that the money is being moved around in and get ahead of it."

Chip looked at the map, "I don't see any pattern."

"Neither do I, but it could be almost anything. Bank addresses, phone numbers, zip codes, order they appear in the phone book. Who knows? Maybe he's going through banks alphabetically by the last name of the bank manager."

"Do you think so?"

"No, I don't. When we do see the pattern it's probably going to be very simple, but until then there are so many variables that it is going to take a little while to pin down."

"So what do we do now?"

"Now? It's Monday morning. I'm going to work. You might as well also. We're not going to find this money today, and we're probably not going to find it tomorrow, but if no one else is looking for it, we will find it."

Chip stood silently thinking about that as Jason went past him and up the stairs. Jason took a quick shower and brushed his teeth twice because they felt so gross. When he got back downstairs Chip was sitting at the table with a ruler and pencil drawing lines between the various x's. The connect the dots picture that was forming didn't look like anything at all, even with a lot of imagination mixed in.

"I don't think that's it." Jason said.

"No, but it was worth a try, wasn't it?" Chip looked up at him hopefully.

"It was as good a guess as any." Jason replied.

He went over to the coffee machine and realized that it was empty. He had forgotten to fill it the night before.

"Lock up when you leave." Jason shouted at Chip over his shoulder as he went through the interior door into the garage, grabbing a windbreaker from where it was slung over the banister as he went by. The garage door rattling upwards, he jumped into the Porsche driver's seat and fired the engine to life. He blasted out of the garage in reverse, the door not quite all the way up yet, and stopped just in time to avoid hitting Chip's car, which was still parked diagonally across the driveway.

Jason blew out a long breath. That had been pretty close. He put the car in neutral and set the parking brake.

He went back into the house. Chip was still sitting at the table looking at the map.

"Hey, I need you to move your car."

"Shit! I forgot all about it." Chip went past Jason at a fast walk, patting his pockets looking for his keys. Out in the driveway, Chip found he had left the driver's side door open, the keys dangling from the ignition. "I had a feeling I had left those there," Chip muttered to himself. He wedged himself behind the wheel and tried to start the car, but the battery was stone cold dead.

"Need a jump?" Jason leaned in the open door.

"Wouldn't help. It ran out of gas."

"You left the motor running when you came in yesterday?"

"And the lights on." Chip smiled sheepishly.

Jason went into the garage and grabbed the gas can for the lawn mower. He shook it, but from the weight he could tell that it was empty. "No gas."

"Never mind. I'll call triple A. Just give me a hand pushing it out of your way."

The two of them with some pushing back and forth got the car straightened out in the driveway enough so that Jason could squeeze by.

Jason got back in his car and buzzed the window down, "You sure you're OK?"

"I've got it. I've got it. Go. Go."

Chip stood with his hands on his hips as he watched Jason pull out of the driveway and down the street.

*****

Ricky came out of the bathroom, the bare light bulb inside over the sink throwing a weak rectangular shaft through the doorway and onto the faded carpeting. A towel around his waist, he used another to dry his chest and shoulders. His black hair was matted against his skull, his dark eyes fully dilated, gathering the meager room light. He saw Deirdre in the bed, her pale skin glowing against the darker coverlet. Taking a deep breath he expanded his chest, flaring nostrils sifting out her scent from among the ghosts of stale cigarettes, the mildewed shower, and industrial cleansers. He watched her sleep, savored her scent, an erection tenting the towel in front of him.

He controlled his urges. He had more important things to do.

Padding back into the bathroom he used a towel to clear a large oval in the foggy mirror. He shaved using an old-style razor, the type with a double-edged razor blade stored in a head that ratcheted open by rotating the handle. He had stolen it from an antique store as a teenager thinking it was real gold; the razor was gold plated. He hissed through his teeth at the alcohol sting of the aftershave.

He dressed in worn blue jeans, sneakers, and a plain white T-shirt. He combed his hair straight back. He didn't know what he would be doing today, but he wanted any witnesses to think of him merely as some nondescript guy in jeans and a T-shirt. "Guy without distinguishing features" was the fashion template for the day. He took his wallet, keys, watch, the room key, and his gun with him when he left.

Stepping outside he was momentarily blinded by the bright sunshine. The air was warm, clearly headed towards uncomfortably warm, and filled with the sounds and smells of the cars and trucks driving past the motel. An aged and dented LA Times newspaper dispenser was standing against the wall near the motel office. Ricky went to the machine, fumbled three quarters from his pocket, and purchased a newspaper. He then folded the newspaper around the gun because he had seen it done in a movie once and, passing his car, crossed the small parking area and went into a diner next door.

A wind chime made of strips of hammered tin hung on the back of the door announced his entry. The interior was all brushed stainless steel and metal-flecked white Formica, arranged as a wide hallway, booths to the left, counter to the right. A wall separated the counter area from the cooking area. Ricky could see the slender, leathery cook working at a griddle through a wide window in the wall. The sole customer was a man with long, stringy blonde hair in a stained green army jacket. He sat at the counter arguing a call in last night's baseball game with the cook through the window, who shouted his replies above the clatter of dishes and the sizzle of the griddle. The ease and style of their banter placed green army jacket as a regular fixture in the diner.

Ricky perched on a chrome stool with a red leatherette seat at the counter, leaving an empty stool between him and other man. He placed the newspaper on the counter beside him, rested his elbow on it, and picked up the menu from where it was wedged between a ketchup bottle and a napkin holder.

"Get you something?" The cook was leaning his forearms on the shelf that ran along the bottom of the window cutout.

Ricky glanced over the menu, "Three eggs, over light, toast, dry, and coffee. Regular, not decaf."

"Bacon? Sausage?"

Ricky weighed this decision carefully, his lower lip thrust out. "Bacon, crisp."

"Just a couple of minutes." The cook expertly split the eggs against the edge of the griddle without breaking a single yolk. He then came out of the kitchen through a pair of swinging doors at the end of the counter, picked up a glass urn of coffee and a cup and saucer, and poured a cup that he placed on the counter in front of Ricky.

"Milk? Cream?"

"Black's good."

"OK, then, man knows what he wants. Refills are free. One cup or twenty makes no difference to me. I'll have your breakfast in just a minute."

The cook went back around through the doors to the kitchen and Ricky clasped his hands around the coffee cup and stared into its depths.

The guy in the green army jacket continued, "Rodriquez was safe by a mile. They have a picture of it on the front of the sports section today. His foot on the bag and the ball in the air. You mind?" He reached over the empty space towards the newspaper by Ricky's elbow.

With only a flick of his eyes to the side, Ricky brought his arm up and quickly drove his elbow downwards, catching the other man's hand between his elbow and the countertop. The man howled and pulled his hand back, cradling it with his other hand while flexing the fingers. The cook looked up from the griddle and through the window at Ricky. Ricky went back to looking into his coffee cup.

"What the fuck, man? What's your problem?" The man's voice was shaky, running up and down in pitch.

"My newpaper." Ricky replied quietly.

"I know, man, but what the fuck? I just wanted to see the sports section."

The place was very quiet except for the sizzle of the eggs and bacon on the griddle. The cook looked at Ricky and then flicked his eyes down to the paper. He could just make out the edge of the butt of the gun between the folds. The cook felt a low-grade tremor starting deep in his gut. While the man didn't look like he was ready to use the gun, he didn't look like he was not ready to use it either. Staring at Ricky he said, "That's the man's paper."

Green army jacket turned to the cook, his voice becoming plaintive now, "But I just wanted to see the sports section. He's not even reading it." His words came out softly and slowly near the end, a music box near the end of its wind.

"Man likes his paper crisp, like his bacon. That's his right. You better get to work. You don't want to be late."

Green army jacket's Adam's apple bobbed up and down. He glanced from Ricky to the cook and back again. Even if he didn't understand what was happening, the pressure that had gathered suddenly in the air was intense, explosive, like a dark thunderhead on the horizon. He began speaking slowly, then picked up speed, his words tumbling over each other near the end. "Right, right. I gotta go. Sorry about your paper, man. No harm done, right? I gotta go."

He left swiftly, without receiving or paying his check.

The cook deftly slid the eggs and bacon off the griddle and onto a plate with a wide metal spatula. He grabbed four slices of toast as they came out of the toaster, and came around through the swinging doors. The plate chattered against the countertop as he put it down, his hands shaking slightly. He and Ricky locked eyes, an unspoken understanding passing between them, as he reached slowly under the counter and pulled a knife, fork, and spoon wrapped up in a paper napkin. He went to refill Ricky's coffee cup before realizing that the Ricky hadn't touched his coffee yet, so he dropped his hands to his sides.

"Well," he said uncertainly, "you need anything, you just call. I'll be in the back." He pulled a check pad from a pocket of his apron, scrawled a couple of quick lines on it, tore off the sheet and slid it onto the counter face down, and disappeared through the swinging doors. The cook didn't care if the man paid or not. He thought long and hard slipping out the back door, but in the end decided that if he kept his head down and his mouth shut the man would eat his breakfast and leave. It certainly wasn't the first time someone had brought a gun into the diner and left without shooting anyone; this was, after all, Los Angeles.

Ricky chewed through the food methodically. He ate all the eggs first, picking up the yolks and popping them into his mouth whole where he punctured them with his tongue, feeling the warm, viscous yolk run throughout his teeth. Next came the bacon, his teeth nipping off precise one inch pieces from the strips, like some kind of machine, which he would chew and swallow before biting off another one. He then ground up and swallowed the toast dry, the muscles in his jaw working steadily, and finally he drank the cup of coffee, stopping every so often to swish some around like mouthwash. The entire meal was complete in than ten minutes.

When he was done he wiped his mouth with the napkin, glanced at the check, and paid leaving less than a ten-percent tip.

Ricky had to admit as he took the newspaper and left the diner that bringing the gun with him had been a stupid thing to do. He was going to have to be smart if he was going to figure out a way to get the money. He decided then and there that he was going to leave the gun in the car if he didn't think he would need it, or to wear a jacket and keep the gun covered if he was going to carry it.

Once back in the car he put the newspaper on the passenger seat and wedged the gun down beside the seat. He drove back the way he and Deirdre had come earlier in the day, and again parked in the strip mall in front of the gym. He took the binoculars from the car, and he left the gun.

*****

Jason cruised down the expressway at seventy, *Nickelback* blaring from the speakers, a large cup of coffee that he had gotten at a local grocery store in the cup holder. The coffee had gone a long way to clearing out the cobwebs that had grown in his mind overnight.

What had he been thinking? He had a job, albeit one that probably wouldn't be around all that much longer, and yet he had spent yesterday cracking banks, committing god knows how many felonies, in this crazy chase after drug money. Admittedly the chances of getting caught when he routed the bank hack through multiple VPNs, and only logged on long enough to get the next bank and account number, were remote, but still, there was a risk. He planned to go to Keith today to get his signature on the forms that had to be filed with the SEC in order to sell shares in the company, get himself some breathing room, and get back to work, maybe chop another fifty grand off the asking price on his house and see if that did any good. When he got home tonight he would tell Chip to forget it and toss the notes he had made so far. The risk was just too great.

As he pulled into the parking lot he noticed that Keith's car was there, but the secretary's was not. Jason wondered briefly whether she had been let go, found another job elsewhere, or was just out sick today. He walked past three empty offices to get to his own. He turned on the computer and, while it booted up, opened and spread out the folder on the pet supply company on his desk.

The project was just about finished, and he had to admit to himself that it looked pretty good. A neat interface made purchasing and checkout much less cumbersome than it had been, but his changes to the site went beyond cosmetic. He had found out early on that the site had never set up keywords for the major search engines, and doing that alone should increase their traffic considerably. He was also recommending that they raise the minimum on their free shipping offer from ten to twenty dollars. The statistics showed that the difference, while not scaring away too many consumers, should raise their cash flow.

Still, he had to admit to himself, none of this was likely to save the company, only slow its demise. Perhaps if it survived long enough, if enough other pet companies on the web went bust first, the narrowing of consumer market choice might save it. That was what competition was all about, right? Only time would tell. He cleaned up and ran test cases through the site the final few times, checked the code for errors, and checked the priority rating with the search engines. Twice he felt Keith standing in his doorway, but he chose not to acknowledge him and Keith left without saying anything.

At about noon his stock applet showed him that the stock price of Not Your Father's E-commerce company had fallen from $1.03 that morning to ninety-one cents. He pulled up a copy of the form to sell stock that he had used the last time. He had had a lawyer prepare it for him about a year ago. To Jason it was full of legalese bullshit, whereas and therefores abounded throughout, but it let him sell shares of stock before he was completely vested to keep from going bankrupt. He changed the date in the appropriate slot in the form, and debated over the slot that indicated the number of shares he was selling. He wanted trying to give himself a cushion about six months long. The problem was that filling out the form today would probably allow him to sell the shares in a week, and what would the share price be then? He decided to go with 50,000 shares, which should leave enough room for some price fall. Worse comes to worst he would end up with more money than he planned. Too much money was never a problem.

He sent the form to the laser printer at the end of the hallway and swept the pet supply company folder together. He planned to give the form and the folder to Keith at the same time.

Snatching the form from the printer, he scrawled his signature on the appropriate line as he went past a dozen empty offices to Keith's. He found Keith sitting at his desk, the desktop completely empty except for a phone, a Dilbert desk calendar, and a 'World's Greatest Golfer' mug.

"Hey, Keith. I finished the pet supply company. They'll be happy with the work." Jason dropped the folder on the desktop. Keith made no move to pick it up; he sat silently slouched in his chair, hands steepled on his stomach.

Jason waited uncomfortably in the silence.

"Well. Anyway, my last mortgage payment totally wiped out my bank account. I'm going to need to sell some shares." Jason put the form on top of the folder, put a pen he had been carrying on top of that. Keith still made no move.

"Keith? Hello?"

Keith finally heaved himself to sit up straight. He took the pen and signed his name on the form. "Sure, I can sign it."

Jason couldn't quite figure out the tone in Keith's voice, "But? And?"

"What?" Keith asked, looking directly at Jason for the first time.

"Your tone. It seemed to indicate that there was something more. I can sign it but- I can sign it and- Something like that."

"But," Keith began, but then stopped.

"Yeah, like that. But?"

"With that little stock applet of yours I'm surprised you haven't found out already."

Jason had a sinking feeling that he knew exactly what Keith was referring to, but he had to ask to be certain, "Found out about what?"

"The pet supply company announced about half an hour ago that it is filing for bankruptcy, and, as they're currently our largest and almost our only customer, our stock has lost a third of its value."

As Keith talked Jason did a little mental calculation and figured that he ran the applet near zero priority on his computer. The lag could be ten or twenty minutes, explaining why he hadn't seen the precipitous fall in the stock price yet.

Keith continued, "We could see as much as a fifty percent hit today, and when that happens the stock will probably halt trading."

Jason looked up from his internal arithmetic as what Keith was saying sank in. "Halt trading?"

"Just for a couple of days," Keith said quickly, "as soon as I can convince the SEC that the company has stabilized they'll allow trading to resume."

"How can you convince them? You probably can't convince me!" Jason's voice was rising.

"Jason," Keith tried to get a word in edgewise.

"I worked all fucking weekend on that pet supply company! And at fifty cents a share what difference does it make? I'll have to sell 80,000 shares to buy myself six months! If I try and dump 80,000 shares the price will fall still farther. I could sell every share I own and still be bankrupt by the end of the year! And how long before the stock is delisted at that value? How long, Keith?" Jason had run all that out in one angry stream without pause, and it left him winded.

Keith was silent, the sound of Jason breathing heavily was very loud in the empty building. "I don't know," he said quietly.

"Well," Jason said and then paused. "That's it then."

"No, Jason, there are other companies out there. I'm

already in talks with a company that sells camping gear." Keith let the thought trail off, just kind of float out there, hoping Jason would pick it up and run with it as he had always done in the past.

"Keith, please, let it go. We've been working, what, nine months without a paycheck? Even if we had enough work, which we don't, you and I alone can't hold this place together."

"But what else are you going to do? It's not like there are any other jobs out there."

Jason thought about that for a moment, "I have something I'm working on at home. It's high risk, but the payoff could be huge."

Keith looked down at the desktop and spun the pen on the surface a couple of times. "Yeah, well, I'm going to stay here and keep trying."

"OK. I'll be seeing you." Feeling awkward, Jason stuck out his hand.

Keith looked up at him, ignored Jason's hand extended between them, his eyes those of a lost child. "If I get more work than I can handle, can I call you?"

Jason remembered how powerful and commanding Keith had been when the stock has been seventy bucks a share, Keith's shares worth over a hundred million dollars. That vision was difficult to reconcile with what was left of Keith sitting before him, all sunken eyes and pale skin. "Sure."

"Thanks." Keith took Jason's hand and shook it, the four-year dream of Not Your Father's E-commerce dissolving between them.

The handshake ended, Jason turned and left. Keith came to the doorway and watched him walk down the deserted hallway, "Take care of yourself."

"You too." Jason waved at him over his shoulder without turning around.

Jason went back to his office and shut down the computer. He picked up his windbreaker and looked around the room. As he had never put any personal effects around as decoration, he didn't have anything he needed to take with him when he left. He finally grabbed a Not Your Father's E-commerce mug off the desk. They had had the mugs made to give them away at some convention a couple of years earlier. The mug was probably a collectable now; maybe Jason could sell it on Ebay.

He walked out into the parking lot, squinting in the bright sunshine until he could get his sunglasses onto his face. Unlocking his car he tossed the windbreaker on the passenger seat. He again wondered where the secretary was. He had forgotten to ask Keith and now it was bugging him, but only a little, and not enough to make him walk back into the building to do so.

He pulled his cell phone from his pocket and dialed Chip's work number. The machine at his office picked up; Jason hung up without leaving a message. He dialed his own home number. Chip answered on the second ring.

"What are you still doing there?" Jason asked.

"Well, triple A didn't get here for about an hour, and then I got to staring at the map, and I got wrapped up in thinking about it."

"I figured. I'm headed home."

"What about your job?"

"There isn't any job. Not anymore."

"I'm sorry, Jason." Chip's voice was full of sympathy.

"Don't be. That company was dead half a year ago, but no one had the decency to stick a toe tag on it and make it official. I'll be home soon and we can get to work seriously on tracking that money."

Jason heard Chip's excited "Cool!" as he hung up the phone and chucked it onto the passenger seat on top of the windbreaker.

He stood with his arms folded on the roof of the car and looked at the building where he had spent more hours than he could count; dinners, evenings, weekends, a few times even sleeping at his desk. Jesus, it had been so much frigging work. Jason estimated it had once held three hundred people, and now it held only Keith.

"Thank you ladies and gentlemen. Good night." Jason said to himself.

*****

Jason moved the investigation, which is what he now thought of it as, into the upstairs guest bedroom. The desk upstairs was smaller than the dining room table, but it presented a smaller risk for major soda spills, such as Chip dumping over a glass of Orange Crush onto the papers, which he had during lunch. And while Jason didn't get many visitors to his home, could not in fact think of one besides Chip and Kelly in the last several months, the pile of papers was becoming increasingly more incriminating. Forty-four felonies so far and counting, and Jason just felt better with it all upstairs and out of sight.

When he first thought about the money, he figured that he and Chip would have essentially forever to track it down, but the more he considered it, the more he believed that their time was limited, perhaps very limited. That much money was hopping around as often as it was doing was sure to catch the attention of banking regulators in short order. A week, Jason figured; if he hadn't managed to find the money in a week, the risks became astronomically higher.

A couple of hours ago, when he had come to the conclusion that a week was his deadline and he had circled the date with a red felt marker on the desk calendar, a week had seemed like all the time he could possibly need. The pattern of the bank transfers had to be a simple one. Find the pattern and find the money. It had sounded so easy.

Yet as he looked at the list of forty-four banks he had collected so far, he had to admit that he had nothing. The money hopped all over California – Los Angeles, San Diego, San Francisco, Redondo Beach, Oakland, Santa Ana. Big banks and small, international, national, and local. The money traveled through giant bank branches in major urban centers, and tiny credit union offices in the middle of nowhere with probably one bored employee sitting behind a desk. Banks that commanded billions, and credit unions with net assets of less than a million dollars. How had Ryder expected to withdraw seven million dollars from a bank with only a million in assets? The answer was obviously that he hadn't, at least not as cash. He had planned to wire the money to the drug dealer directly. Ryder had the money hopping all over the place as a way to protect himself from the drug dealer simply killing him. It hadn't worked, but that had probably been the plan, Jason guessed. But there was something beyond that, something else that Ryder had been planning that Jason felt he could almost grasp.

Jason closed his eyes and tried to picture the wharf as Chip had described it. He could see Ryder opening the laptop, the glow of the screen causing a dim halo in the air laden with sea mist. Ryder shifting his eyes around furtively, tapping the keys to set the program in motion. The click of the keys sounding alien among the nighttime sounds of the dock area, the musical clanking of lanyards, the creaking of the hulls. Ryder nervous, sheathed in a cold sweat beyond the mist-damp air, trying to plan a way to come out of the drug deal alive.

The floor beneath Jason's feet vibrated slightly with the closing of the front door. He heard the louder pounding of Chip coming up the stairs and down the hallway to appear at the bedroom door. He was carrying a long cardboard tube, like the type that posters come in, and a small paper bag.

"How goes?"

Jason crumpled up the image of the marina in his head into a ball and threw it into the corner of his mind. The thing he was missing would come to him; he had to just let it flow, not pressure it. He turned from the computer, "The last bank I hacked took almost an hour. I think I'm getting tired."

"This might help."

Chip pulled a plastic cap off of one end of the cardboard tube and shook out a large laminated sheet that had been rolled up. He stood on the bed and held one edge of the sheet against the wall where it joined the ceiling and let go of the roll. A map of California unrolled, reaching the floor at about the Oxnard level, the remainder of the roll bouncing and unrolling along the floor.

"Wow," Jason said, "big map."

"Um, yeah," Chip replied, looking at the length of map lying on the floor, "ten feet."

"Eight-foot-six ceilings."

"So I noticed."

"We'll hang it sideways."

Chip tore open the paper bag. Inside was a small plastic box of multicolored pushpins. With Jason on one end and Chip on the other they managed to get the map hung sideways on the wall, Nevada up and the Pacific down. It covered almost the entire wall.

"I'm glad you didn't get one in actual size."

"Yeah."

The two of them stood and looked at the map of California. Chip finally picked up the box of pushpins and looked at the road atlas on the desk. He jammed a pushpin into a suburb of Los Angeles, then went back and looked at the road atlas again.

"Oh, Chip?"

Chip looked away from the road atlas, "Yeah?"

"While you were gone I tracked the money through a bank in New York."

Chip looked from Jason to the map of California on the wall and back to Jason again.

"You did?"

"No, I'm just fucking with you. They're all banks in California."

"Oh, good." Chip went back to looking at the road atlas.

"So far." Jason said, smiling to himself as he sat in the chair in front of the computer.

Chip hung his head and sighed.

"I'm just fucking with you again. There are almost 1300 banks in California. The first forty-four were all California banks. I can't see any reason why the next 500 won't be, and by then we should have the money. Of course, I could be wrong. There's a pattern in there somewhere, and it might as well be changing states every fifty banks or something. Still, I don't think so."

"1300 banks? How did you find that out?"

"Federal bank registry on the internet. There are lots of fun facts on the internet like that. You want to know some other fun facts that I found out?"

"Shoot."

"I did a little digging into Peter Ryder. For one, it's been more than twenty-four hours since the shootout on the pier, and no one has listed him as missing, let alone dead."

"What about the shootout?"

"That went onto the police wire less than an hour after it happened. It's a national news story by now, big drug shootout in the LA basin. No mention of Ryder's body being there."

"Maybe the cops are holding that back until they can notify his family."

"Maybe. Maybe he wasn't dead. Could he have dragged himself away from there?"

"I told you, the guy blew his head off. Maybe they don't know that the body is his."

"I don't know, but even if you blow a guy's head off, he would still have fingerprints, a wallet, and his car was parked right there. There's no mention of a John Doe corpse either. I'm not sure what that means."

"Could it be bad?" Chip asked.

Jason thought about that. "I don't see how. It actually works for us, because I suspect as soon as Ryder is listed as missing or dead all his accounts will be frozen, or at least monitored. No, the less anyone is looking for Mr. Ryder, the less anyone will be looking for his money."

Chip stirred the pushpins around in the little plastic box with his index finger while he considered that.

"And another thing," Jason said, "seven million dollars may seem like a lot of money to you and me, but it was also apparently a lot of money to Ryder. Records show him taking out a big mortgage on his house and cashing out lots of stocks, bonds, other securities. He cleaned out a couple of bank accounts also."

"So it was just about every penny he had on earth?"

"Relatively speaking. He still shows three cars listed with motor vehicles, and I can't tell if he hocked his furniture or not, but I wouldn't think so."

"And he was some big drug dealer?"

"That's the other thing I can't figure out. The only arrest listed in the state of California is for marijuana possession a long time ago, a misdemeanor. He wasn't a drug dealer; he was a movie director."

Chip snapped his fingers. "That's why the name was familiar. He did that thing last summer with the vigilante stripper. *Undressed to Kill.* Pretty good film."

Jason shrugged, "I must have missed that one. Anyway, I don't know much about making movies, but I don't think it involves seven million dollars in cocaine. It doesn't make sense." He sat quietly and thought about it.

"But it doesn't have to, does it?" Chip offered.

"No, I guess it doesn't. As long as it doesn't come back to bite us on the ass. But what if, for example, he was working for the government or something. It might explain why a film director would get stuck in a giant drug deal. It might also explain why the police didn't report the body – because the feds are covering it up."

"Oh, shit!" Chip's eyes became large in his head.

"No, no," Jason waved his hand in the air, "I know that's not it. The government doesn't use civilians for undercover work, and it doesn't send in undercover guys without backup. The marina would have been full of cops before the echoes of the gunshots died away. All I'm saying is that there's something going on here we don't understand, and we have to be careful."

"Oh."

"But fast."

"Why fast?"

"Because all that money jumping around has to be raising regulatory flags all over the place. I figure in about a week that money is going to be attracting so much attention that there's no way we'll be able to get it without someone somewhere noticing. And that's provided that

Ryder stays buried."

"Buried? Buried where?"

"A figure of speech."

"Oh. Can you find it in a week?"

"I was just thinking about that when you came in. I'm not sure I can. I've been doing pretty well so far, but I don't think I can keep up this pace. We're going to need some help."

"I can help."

"No, I mean computer help. I think we should call Kelly."

Chip unhappily looked away from Jason, staring silently at the map on the wall.

"Hey, Chip, Kelly's the best. She can probably figure out a way to find this money that I've missed. Without her, frankly, we might not even get it."

Chip turned back and smiled, "You're right. And it's not like there isn't enough money for all of us."

"So I call her?" Jason picked up his cell phone from where it has been resting on the desktop next to the computer.

"Yeah, of course."

Jason hit the speed dial and waited for Kelly to answer. "Hey, Kel, I- What's that?"

Chip watched Jason listen to Kelly talking.

"He what? When? Yeah, I left. He said he was going to keep going. Yeah, I guess so."

Jason took the phone away from his head and spoke to Chip, "Kelly saw a report on the newswire. Keith closed the company down. He announced it just after I left."

He put the phone against his head and talked with Kelly. "What am I going to do with myself? Well, that's actually what I wanted to talk to you about. What Chip and I wanted to talk to you about. No, I'd rather not over the phone. Can you meet us at the bar? Twenty minutes? See you there."

Jason hung up the phone. "Let's get going."

They left the bedroom, went down the hallway, down the stairs, and into the garage. While Chip wedged himself into the passenger seat of the Porsche and the garage door trundled upwards, Jason spun through the list of music on his iPod, finally settling on *Alien Ant Farm.* Chip was still fastening his seatbelt when Jason blasted out of the garage and onto the road.

On the freeway with the top down the wind was swirling through the car. Chip had to shout to be heard over the wind and stereo. "What do you think she'll say?"

Jason gave no indication that he had heard, and Chip was about to lean over and ask again when Jason leaned over towards him and said "She'll probably say we're crazy."

*****

The sun was high in the sky, the air hot and dry as Ricky walked past the pillars and into the development. He wasn't sure he could continue to just walk around this quiet, upscale suburban neighborhood without attracting attention, but he couldn't think of a better way to keep track of the guy who was tracking the money. Also, he figured that eventually, probably tonight, he was going to have to get some sleep, but he didn't like the idea of not keeping an eye on the guy. He didn't know what he was going to do to get the money. And finally, he wasn't sure what to tell Dee, if anything. All the things he didn't know were starting to make him nuts.

On the first pass, Ricky noticed that the same crap car was in the driveway, but didn't see any movement in the house at all. Ditto on the second pass, and the third. Ricky realized that not only was this walking up and down the block damned suspicious, but it wasn't allowing him to study the house for any length of time. On the forth pass he saw a house diagonally across the street that seemed to offer a solution.

It was a smaller house but with the same overall architectural featuring and clearly built by the same builder. The two-story salt box with detached two-car garage behind it was neat and well-kept but the lawn looked downright shaggy compared to the golf-course quality greens that surrounded it on all sides. Ricky left the sidewalk on a hunch and went up the walkway that was made of bricks angled and set into the soil forming a repeating chevron pattern. He stopped at the front door and noticed on the stoop a newspaper in a clear plastic bag, the paper already somewhat yellowed with age. Turning the newspaper over with his toe of his sneaker, he saw the date was over a week ago. He cupped his hands to the leaded glass window beside the front door and looked in. The floor in front of the door had a healthy accumulation of mail. The house was definitely unoccupied, which suited Ricky just fine.

He went around the back, looked for obvious alarm wires on the back door and, when he didn't see any he jimmied open the door using a flat strip of metal he kept in his wallet for just such occasions. He opened the door and examined the jam looking for hidden alarm contacts, and then stood listening for either the sirens of an alarm system or approaching police. After several minutes had passed he went into the house, closing the door behind himself but not locking it. He went to one of the front windows that gave a view on the street. He resumed his waiting and listening there, figuring that if a police car went by he could be out the back in less than a second.

He waited and watched the house. Nothing changed. As time went by, he became more certain that his little breaking and entering hadn't been discovered, and he pulled a chair away from the dining room table to the window to give him somewhere to sit while he watched the house across the street do nothing. He used the binoculars to scan across the front every so often. If anyone was home he didn't see them, but most of the blinds were drawn in the upstairs windows. The thought briefly passed through his mind that perhaps they were not home at all, and while it angered him that maybe he had missed them and they had already gone to get the money, he couldn't think of anything better to do than wait, and so wait he did.

Near one o'clock, he went into the kitchen to see if there was something to eat. The refrigerator had been completely cleaned out and turned off; whatever reason the occupants had for being away was planned to be a lengthy one. In a cabinet he found a box of Ritz crackers, a can of Cheez Whiz, and a warm six pack of Dr. Pepper, which seemed like as good a lunch to Ricky as any. While rummaging through the pantry he found forty dollars consisting of a twenty and a bundle of smaller bills stuffed inside a cookie tin. He took it.

He resumed his vigil, the food arrayed on the floor at his feet.

He was firmly settled in, his butt and legs falling asleep, and just starting to wonder if he should call it a day and come back later to see if they were home that night, when the garage door across the street started up. A silver Porsche came out of the garage with the thin guy driving and the fat guy in the passenger seat.

Ricky was up like a shot and ran towards the front door. His tingly legs responded imperfectly and he stumbled in the front hall on the piles of mail and slid into a decorative end table which slammed against the wall. Two of its delicate legs cracked, and the table fell, a white vase upon it shattering on the floor into hundreds of pieces. Ricky regained his balance, ignored the mess on the floor, and wrestled with the unfamiliar combination of locks and deadbolts on the front door for several seconds before finally tearing the door open. He sped down the front walk and stood on the sidewalk, the Porsche already disappearing around a bend down the road.

He was certain now that somehow he had missed his chance. They were off to get the money, and they probably weren't coming back. They would catch a plane, get out of the country. That's what Ricky would have done. His car was more than a mile away so he couldn't follow them. Maybe he could catch them at the airport? He stormed across the street and up to the front door and, finding it solidly locked, went around to the back of the house to the sliding glass door. The sliding glass door had no locking bar that Ricky could see, only a thumb lock. The little strip of metal came in handy again.

Ricky stepped quietly into the interior of the house, only then considering that perhaps there was some other occupant of the house that he had not seen, some other person who remained home while the others went out. He stood scarcely breathing, and the house returned his silence tenfold; no one was at home.

With a burglar's instincts he searched through the house quickly. A short stack of mail on the counter in the kitchen indicated that the sole occupant of the house, and apparently the owner as well as indicated on a mortgage statement, was Jason Taylor. A car payment book in a kitchen drawer also showed him to be the owner, well, part owner anyway as a loan company owned the majority of it, of the Porsche. Ergo, the fat man drove the shitbox. A bank statement in the same drawer listed a net balance in the neighborhood of two hundred dollars. As he moved from room to room Ricky noticed that most of the furniture and electronics were less than three years old, many near top-of-the-line models, and most having seen very little use.

One of the upstairs bedrooms interested him the most. The map on the wall of California populated with pushpins, the scrapes of paper and notes on the desk and bed, and the open computer. They were tracking the money through the computer, though exactly how they were doing it Ricky had no idea. He had not expected that it would take them long to find the money, but given how this room was set up they were clearly planning to be in this hunt for the long haul. Nothing in the room seemed to indicate that they had found the money yet at any rate – no red 'X' on the map, no address circled on a piece of paper – and it relaxed Ricky to find that wherever they had gone, they were almost certainly coming back to continue the search. He raised the blinds in the room a few inches. It wouldn't let him see what was going on in the room exactly, but he could at least see if there were people in the room.

He wandered back downstairs and made one more circuit of the first floor, front hall to living room to dining room to kitchen. It disturbed him that the best he could do was watch the hunt for the money through binoculars. As long as he did, he figured, he was at risk of losing them the minute they found it, and yet he couldn't think of another option.

He exited through the sliding door, closing it behind him but unable to relock it using the metal strip trick. Since the door was undamaged, he hoped that would go unnoticed.

Back in the house across the street he relocked the front door, returned the chair to the dining room, and put the food back in the kitchen except for the empty soda cans, which he carried with him, stuffing them into a plastic garbage bag he took from under the kitchen sink. He looked at the broken table and vase in the front hall, but figured that there was nothing he could do about it. It would all be attributed to petty vandalism whenever the owners came back and discovered it. He stood near the back entryway and tried to think if he had left anything significant behind. He couldn't think of anywhere that he had left fingerprints that concerned him, he had the binoculars and his wallet and keys, and he hadn't brought anything else in with him. Good enough, he shrugged. And so, wiping off the doorknobs as he relocked the back door, he left.

*****

Kelly put down the beer bottle she had been holding onto the table with a clunk so loud that Jason was surprised the bottle hadn't cracked. "That's the craziest thing I've ever heard."

Jason turned to Chip, "Told you."

"Technically she simply said that's crazy. She didn't specify that she meant us."

Jason bobbed his head from side to side, "Good point."

Kelly looked from one to the other, "You two are serious."

"As colon cancer," Chip took a drink from his own bottle.

Hammering from the other end of the room caused Jason to look that way. Two men were assembling a stage;

the tables had been pushed back to make room. This early on a Monday afternoon all the other tables were empty except for one couple seated at another table. Clearly tourists, she dug into a woven bag on the floor at her feet while he fiddled with an expensive looking camera with a long lens on the table in front of him.

A waitress came over with a fresh bottle of beer for Jason. He touched her arm as she put the bottle down. “What’s all that about?” He gestured to the workmen.

“We’re starting live shows here this Friday. Jazz, blues, that kind of thing. No cover, at least to start. You should come down. That’s three-fifty for the beer.”

Jason handed her a five, “Maybe we will. Keep the change.”

“Thanks. Call if you need anything else.”

As the waitress left he looked back at Kelly, who was running her index finger around in the condensation on her beer bottle. She looked up from the bottle and their eyes met in the silence.

“OK, tell it to me again. More slowly this time.”

So Chip began with feeling seasick, ordering pizza, and watching *Star Trek*, all the way up through the shooting and driving to Jason’s house. Jason picked up at that point and in low tones, leaning across the table towards her to be heard, told her about using the cell phone Chip had brought him to find the first bank, and tracking the money through the banks thereafter. At the end Jason leaned back in his chair, giving her room to think.

“I was right the first time. You’re crazy.”

Jason turned to Chip, “That time she said specifically

that we were crazy."

"Too true."

Kelly turned away from them with a sigh of exasperation and looked out the smoked front window of the bar. She unconsciously swept her hand through her hair, folding it behind her ear. Jason noticed her earring was silver, some odd geometric shape that deceived the eye like a mobius strip.

She looked back at them, her lips tight, a little pouty, "I don't know what you expect me to say."

Chip frowned at his bottle.

"I thought the same thing you did when Chip first came to me. At first glance, it seems nuts."

"At second glance too." Kelly cut in.

Jason leaned forwards started again more firmly, "At first glance, it does seem nuts, but I think if we're careful, the risk is minimal."

"Minimal?" Kelly snorted.

"Yes, minimal." Jason heard his voice rising. "And we may never find the money," he realized that he had said that very loudly in the empty bar. He looked over at the tourist couple. He was still engrossed in the camera, now with the manual open on the table next to the camera body, but she had stopped digging in the bag to look at Jason. Their eyes met. Jason smiled slightly, "I lost my wallet." The woman smiled back at him understandingly and went back into the bag. Jason continued more quietly, "but I think we might, especially with your help. And I know what you're thinking: How do we get the money once we've found it? I don't know that one yet, but I swear to you I won't do it if it isn't one hundred percent safe and sure."

Kelly sat chewing on that. Jason watched as the two workmen laid down a sheet of plywood as the stage decking.

"I need this, Kel. I don't want to pressure you, but the company is gone, my job is gone, the stock is gone, and I'm probably going to lose the house in a month."

Again their eyes met, this time Kelly's face expressing anxiety and sympathy.

"Let me think about it, OK?"

Jason leaned back again, his hands resting open on the tabletop "That's all we can ask. But don't take too long. I'm giving us a week to find the money. I think if we don't find it in that time, we never will.

"OK. I'll call you tomorrow." Kelly got up and took her purse from over the back of the chair and slung it over one shoulder. With her free hand she reached out and squeezed Jason's hand. "Be careful."

"Always."

She shucked a couple of singles from the pocket of her jeans onto the table and walked out.

Jason picked the bottle up from the table and took a long pull.

Chip swirled the base of his beer bottle against the table, making Spirograph patterns in the condensation. "That went well."

Jason took another swallow of beer. "I guess so. I hadn't expected her to jump on board, but the more I think about it, the more I don't think we can do it without her."

"You don't think you can find the money?"

"No, I don't."

"Oh."

They were silent, each with his own thoughts. The workmen banged away at the far end of the room. The man finished assembling his camera monstrosity and the couple left the bar.

"Hey, Jason, I've got one." Chip said suddenly.

"One what?"

"Patrick Duffy and Dawn Wells."

Jason thought about it for a moment and then shook his head. "Not now, Chip. I'm not in the mood for games."

"OK."

Jason leaned back in his chair, his legs splayed out straight in front of him, the beer bottle resting cold against his thigh, and ran the banks through in his head trying to find the pattern.

6 Days Earlier

Dorado stood at his office window looking out through the venetian blinds at the traffic on the roadway below. His tie was off, hanging on the coat rack by the door, the top two buttons of his shirt unbuttoned. He flexed his fingers around the coffee cup he was holding in his hands.

The shooting Sunday morning on the dock had had his phone ringing off the hook all day yesterday from reporters and politicians. He had gotten a call from the White House thanking him for doing his part on the war on drugs, and he had watched himself give a press conference on the six and eleven o'clock news last night. This morning things were a good deal quieter. It gave him an opportunity to look over the reports on the shooting and, as was par for the course where Miller and Scott were concerned, what he read he didn't like.

Scott and Miller had reported to dispatch that they were on stake out as planned Friday night. They had called in a request for license plate checks with the DMV, and then for an address for one Thomas Malta at 1:25AM. Records cross reference showed Malta to be a repeat juvenile offender, mostly for drug possession and some dealing, followed by some years of apparent criminal inactivity, with nothing more on his record than a couple of speeding tickets, which probably meant he had simply become smarter about the crimes he committed.

After calling in for Malta's address, Scott and Miller had come by work to renew their requisition of surveillance kit – the van, an IR camera, a tripod, a telescoping microphone, the whole deal. Scott and Miller then made themselves scarce until 4:42 on Sunday morning when they had called and asked for the time. Then they reported the shooting at 5:03. Miller had not yet filed his report on the shooting, which would presumably shed some light on that. Scott had stated in his morning log that he had been unarmed during the conflict by request of the upcoming shooting review board, and so had not been involved in the actual shooting. His report about the stake out had also not yet been filed, but a stake out is a low priority event, and his report was not necessarily due or expected for at least a week.

On a whim Dorado had tried calling the phone number listed for Malta, and only a machine had picked up. Dorado chose not to leave a message. He then called an LAPD cruiser to do a stop-by. Knocking on his door had likewise gone unanswered. The cruiser at the scene radioed no sign of forced entry or other information to give them probable cause to enter the apartment, and so they hadn't. The police officer called shortly thereafter on his own cell phone to report that inside the apartment a glass coffee table had been shattered by dropping what appeared to be a bronze replica of 'The Thinker' through it. Dresser drawers had been emptied and most of the toiletries were missing from the bathroom. It was the officer's opinion that Malta had flown, the broken glass table indicating perhaps a threat of violence. Dorado had thanked the officer for his unofficial assistance. Where had Malta gone and why?

The shooting itself also presented many unanswered questions. Nick Sandesci had been bad news, of that Dorado had no doubt. His arrest record was extensive, almost exclusively for drug dealing but with some assault and assault with a deadly weapon thrown in for variety, and it was only through legal gyrations that would have made a Romanian gymnast proud that he had managed to stay out of prison. So there he was, out on the pier alone at the crack of dawn, a monster pile of drugs but only a few hundred dollars in his pocket, and Scott and Miller come along, and he decides to shoot it out with them? Only it hadn't really been a shootout. Ballistics reported that his gun had been fired three times, Miller's gun only once. None of the dealer's rounds had been recovered. Where had they gone? There was a grand mystery.

The medical examiner's report showed that the single bullet fired by Miller had nicked Sandesci's lung, one rib, and passed out the back never to be seen again. The lung had filled with blood, and the man had drowned. According to the medical examiner, this would not have been a quick death, the man being up and around for perhaps several minutes after having been shot. It seemed unlikely to Dorado that Miller would have shot the man just once, but instead of shooting him again or even shooting at him again, had instead waited for the first wound to become fatal, and Miller had no way of knowing his first and only shot would be fatal until the man had dropped from it. Another mystery.

Finally, the crime scene team had reported a large amount of salt water on the dock. The seas had been calm that night, and the dock was in a clearly marked no wake zone so it was unlikely a speeding boat had thrown the water onto the dock on the way by. How had the water gotten there? That much water on the dock looked to Dorado like someone trying to wash something away, but what? He didn't expect Miller's report to help answer that question. The very fact of whether his report even mentioned the water or not would perhaps be a clue, but Dorado couldn't think of what he could do with such knowledge one way or the other.

And so Dorado had many questions, few answers, and very little to go on, but he did have the luxury of time to think about it, and he did know a great deal about the way Scott and Miller operated. Also, he had read literally hundreds of mystery novels over the years and, laugh if you will, fact and fiction weren't always all that far apart.

As he thought about it, gazing out the window of his office at the last stragglers of morning rush hour, it looked to Dorado like there had been a drug deal planned between Malta and Sandesci. Maybe it had gone wrong, maybe they had shot it out and killed each other, and then Scott and Miller had come along and cleaned up. It wasn't a bad theory. It explained the seawater as being used to wash away Malta's blood, and it explained why Malta was absent from his apartment. But the theory wasn't without its holes either. Where, for example, was Malta's body, or his clothing and toiletries for that matter? Why had Miller fired his gun at all? Why would Scott and Miller feel the need to confuse the crime scene by getting rid of Malta's body? And, perhaps most significant of all, where was the money from the drug deal? Narcotics estimated the drugs were worth somewhere in the neighborhood of seven million dollars. If Scott and Miller had walked off with seven million dollars Sunday morning, Dorado was sure they wouldn't be around today waiting for someone to discover that fact.

There was still plenty that didn't make sense.

There was one more thing that seemed noteworthy, Dorado recalled, as he turned back to his desk, put down the coffee mug, and used one thick index finger to push the various papers around on his desk. Scott had reported a laptop recovered from Sandesci's car, damaged, but possibly salvageable. The computer was in the tech lab now for analysis. He thought to himself, as he buttoned his shirt buttons and grabbed his tie off the rack, that maybe there was something on the laptop that could answer some of his questions.

*****

The copper-colored disk of the hard drive spun slowly, no more than a few hertz. The slug filling the hole in the disk surface was dull silver and slightly less than the diameter of a penny. Three long scratches that cut through the copper-colored surface to the lighter core underneath ran circumferentially for perhaps an inch near the outer diameter of the disk. Small square sensors arranged around the disk hovered an infinitesimal distance from the surface, wires leading off in all directions. The inside of the vacuum chamber was bathed in a strange orange light.

Miller leaned away from the port window he had been

looking through and stood up. “Looks crazy to me. Is it working?”

Jerry spoke without looking away from the computer screen before him, “It seems to be so far.” He clicked the mouse and highlighted a group of numbers that was flashing by, the computer performed a quick calculation and he nodded to himself at the result. He turned to Miller, “The bullet was a solid round, not a hollow point or frangible one. The hole it made in the surface was very well defined, seemed to produce minimal mechanical shock in the surrounding surface, and left behind very little metallic ion debris.”

“And that’s good?” Miller prodded.

“Yes, from a data recovery standpoint, all that is very good. On the downside, the drive appeared to have been in motion when it was hit. There is significant damage from surface contact with the read head.”

“Those are the scratches on the surface?” Scott interrupted.

“Yes, the head cut through the recording surface to the substrate. That data, like the data where the hole is, is completely lost. There is furthermore some smearing near the hole caused by the debris from the bullet and the spin of the disk.”

Miller sighed and sat with one buttock on the corner of a nearby desk, “Bottom line, can you get data off it?”

“Oh, yes, we’ll get some data off of it. The question is how much, and from what portions of the disk. We might, for example, manage to recover the entire operating system, but I don’t think you care about a copy of Windows. Pictures from his last vacation, games, downloaded porn. There’s probably lots of data on this hard drive that you don't want. The drive is half a terabyte, by the way."

"But a lot of it could be blank." Scott added hopefully.

"Yes, a lot of it could be blank, but unless we can recover the file allocation table, we're going to have to read all of it to figure out the parts of it that are."

"So, how long?"

"Right now I'm trying to align to the track and sector grid. Once that's done, I'll see if I can find the FAT – that's short for File Allocation Table, a listing of what was on the hard drive – and then we start pulling data. If I can get the FAT, I'll be downloading tomorrow. If I can't, I'll be downloading tomorrow anyway, I just won't know what it is I'm downloading."

Scott pulled one of his business cards from his wallet. He scrawled a phone number on the back using a ballpoint pen, and handed it to the Jerry. "We're trying to track some drug money through bank accounts and we're afraid it might be moved. If you come across anything that looks like a list of bank accounts call me. That's my personal cell phone number on the back."

The scientist took the card and slipped it into his shirt pocket after looking at the number on the back. "Will do."

At that moment Dorado came into the lab. He surveyed the three men standing together and then approached Jerry with his hand extended, "I'm James Dorado, and you are?"

Jerry extended his own hand which all but disappeared into Dorado's large one "I'm Jerry Sikes, resident tech guru, call me Jerry."

When Dorado released Jerry's hand he walked over to the machine to look in the port that Miller had been looking in earlier. "What do we have here, Jerry?" he asked without looking up from the window.

Scott didn't give him an opportunity to answer. "The drug dealer that we nailed yesterday had the computer in his possession. We hope there might be some information on the hard drive about his associates."

"And who shot a hole in it?"

"We don't know, it was like that when we recovered the computer," Miller said.

"Uh-huh." They were quiet while Dorado thought this over. "I haven't seen your report on the shooting yet."

"I'm still working on it. I can have it for you in a couple of days, by Friday for certain."

"How about first thing tomorrow morning for certain?"

Scott and Miller exchanged a glance, "No problem, I'll get right on it."

Miller tapped Scott on the shoulder and the two of them left, the heavy metal door closing with a solid thunk that echoed in the small room.

Dorado turned to Jerry when the door was fully closed. "What were you going to say?"

Jerry blinked in confusion as if jarred from other thoughts, "Excuse me, what?"

"Before Scott cut you off, what were you going to say?"

"Um, I don't know. Nothing important, something

about the bullet hole, I think."

Dorado nodded slowly and digested this. Jerry pulled a calculator from his pocket and began punching keys. Eventually Dorado turned from him and went to the door, placing his hand upon the knob, but not twisting it. He stood like that for a moment, trying to fit the pieces of what he knew to what he suspected.

He took his hand from the doorknob and walked back to Jerry. Dorado pitched his voice down several octaves, his already deep voice coming out like the low rumble of heavy machinery.

He stood close to Jerry, towering over him, and whispered, "What did they tell you they hoped you would find on the hard drive?"

Jerry started to look at Dorado, but at the last instant looked away, staring at the calculator in his hands as if he could find the answer in the LCD screen, "Um, I think. They told me they were looking for, um, bank accounts."

"Bank accounts," Dorado repeated, raising his eyebrows, his voice that of the giant from *Jack and the Beanstalk* chewing up boulders, "not possible associates?"

"Nn-nno." Jerry stuttered.

"Fascinating." Dorado drew the word out as if it had far more than its four syllables, the first s like the hiss of a ruptured steam pipe. "And they wanted you to give this account information to them?"

"Yes, sir. Scott gave me his cell phone number."

"Just between us, I want you to give to me everything you give to them. Call me when you have something." He drew a card from his pocket and slipped it into Jerry's hand underneath the calculator.

Dorado turned away again and went back to the door, placing his hand upon the knob.

Jerry shook his head as if waking from a trance, "Look, is there some problem?"

"No problem," Dorado twisted the knob and opened the door, "What we have here is a failure to communicate." He smiled, his white teeth shining from his dark-skinned face.

The door again closed heavily, the sound echoing in the room around Jerry before dying out.

The hard drive spun slowly.

*****

Last night, after leaving Jason and Chip at the bar, Kelly had intended to put in a full night of work, but with the computer in front of her, she had found her mind a complete blank. OK, that wasn't quite right. It was a complete blank as far as her work was concerned. In almost all other respects her mind was a flurry of activity.

The jumble of her thoughts had continued through the sleepless night, the flutter of moths circling around a streetlight outside her window, the occasional shadowy form of a bat streaking through for a snack. She tossed and turned, the pillow alternately too warm and then too cold beneath her head, the sheets twisted around her legs, the coverlet abandoned in a heap on the floor beside the bed. She dragged herself downstairs in the morning wearing shorts, a blue T-shirt, and a pair of suede moccasins with faux rabbit-fur lining.

Kelly sat on a stool at the counter in her kitchenette surrounded by moving boxes in various degrees of packing.

She stirred a cobalt blue mug filled with tea on the counter in front of her absentmindedly, the ringing of the spoon against the sides of the mug having a soothing almost hypnotic effect. A half-filled clear plastic squeeze bottle of honey shaped like a bear stood on the counter.

She picked up the hot mug with both hands and scooted her stool back with her feet, the stool chattering along the sandstone tile floor. She crossed the room, rested the cup on a windowsill in the living room, and leaned her forehead against the cool glass, her eyes closed. She opened her eyes and looked through her own reflection at the street below.

At the Mexican restaurant across the street a waiter unfolded and then spread a white tablecloth over one of the wrought iron bistro tables. Diners sat at other tables, breakfasting over huevos rancheros and cups of coffee and sopapillas drizzled with honey. She twisted the lock and the window swung open on a vertical hinge. Hanging her head out the window, she could smell the cooking across the street, hear the clacking of heels of early morning shoppers walking on the sidewalk below, brightly colored shopping bags swinging at their sides.

She loved this area outside of L.A., an upscale suburban mix of apartments, restaurants and stores. In many ways it reminded her of her college apartment back in Boston near Newbury Street, only without the Spanish flavor obviously. She loved the pulse of the place, the music that drifted up from the restaurant in the evening as she sat working on the computer at the desk near the window. The monitor sat there now, the screen dark, its cord bunched up near its base, ready for moving. The CPU was on the floor by the desk.

She picked up her tea and turned, resting her butt upon the windowsill. The breeze through the open window at her back ruffled the fine hairs at the nape of her neck as she surveyed her life packed into boxes. Most of the furniture in the apartment wasn't even hers; it had come with the place.

She went and knelt by one of the boxes, placing the mug on the floor beside it, and lifted the flap. Inside were cups and glasses wrapped in sheets of newspaper; this wasn't the box she was looking for. She folded the flaps over again and moved to a box next to that one.

Right on top were her high school and college yearbooks. She put those aside. Underneath was a scrap book with a blue leatherette cover and 'Memories' embossed on it in gold. She lifted it from the box and rocked back to sit on the floor with her legs crossed. Opening the cover she was greeted with a wad of photographs all jammed into the front page. She smiled to herself. She had never finished organizing the book, or really even started it.

The photos near the top of the pile were from the last Christmas party at the Ecom company. She picked up a picture that showed her and Jason smiling at the camera, her holding a glass of something blue and frothy, the camera flash having turned his eyes red, and a Santa hat upon his head. He had one arm thrown over her shoulder, she was saying something into his ear; she can't remember what. Chip was not in the picture. That's right, she nodded to herself. He had been laid off in October.

Chip was in the picture of the company picnic and softball game from the previous summer, though she could barely make him out among the over one hundred other people in the picture. It was hard to imagine a company that big was completely gone. Where had all those people gone? Had they found other jobs?

Another picture: Kelly holding the bat awkwardly, Jason leaning over her shoulder, his arms around her, his hands over hers on the bat, trying to teach her how to swing.

The next picture showed Kelly holding the bat like a sword, feigning an overhead blow. There was a jagged line running down the image, the two pieces of the picture not quite lining up. The first softball she had hit in her entire life had struck Chip directly in the chest where the camera hung by its strap. Chip was uninjured; the camera had taken the brunt of the blow, cracking the lens and breaking the flash. The camera was ruined and had been worth over five hundred dollars, but nobody had cared. It was a company camera and they could just buy another one. There was plenty of money.

It all came down to money, she thought as she picked up the mug and finished the tea. She sighed. She didn't have enough money to stay in her apartment. Jason was stuck in his house because no one would buy it, and she was sure he would lose it to the bank soon. And Chip, he was working at his father's plastics company, a job that she knew he hated, but he had to earn a living somewhere.

And then Chip and Jason came up with this crazy plan. And yet, as she thought about it, maybe it wasn't so crazy. The money *was* out there, just bouncing around in electronic banking space, and maybe no one was looking for it. Or what if someone was looking for it? Kelly thought about that as she got up and carried the mug into the kitchen, rinsed it, and put it upside down in the drain rack.

She went back into the living room and knelt to gather pictures from the various piles she had sorted them into.

Kelly and Jason would look for the money from a distance, across the internet, and she planned to route their activities through so many anonymous servers that even if someone else was looking for the money, it would never lead back to them. That was important to her. Seven million dollars she realized was easily enough money to kill over, in fact someone already had, and she for one wasn't willing to lose her life over it.

The other thing that she wasn't willing to do was crack into banks, committing hundreds of electronic banking felonies along the way. That was the approach Jason was taking and, while it worked, she wouldn't go that route. She didn't think she had to. During the night she had figured out a better way to track the money. While it wasn't strictly legal, she didn't think it was all that illegal either. Certainly people were doing the exact same thing every day. She would have done a quick test this morning using her own bank account and computer, but the computer was already packed up, and it wasn't worth going through the trouble of setting it up again. She didn't need to test her theory; she knew it would work.

But the thing that had finally made her decide to help Jason and Chip was simple. They needed her. The fact that Jason had asked her in the first place meant that he couldn't do it alone. Her friends needed her, and she would help them.

She was a realist, though. She knew that it might get dangerous. In that case, she would be the one to tell Jason that it was time to let it go. Chip and Jason would get so caught up in it; they wouldn't be able to restrain themselves. By getting involved she could make sure things didn't go too far. The minute, no, the second it looked bad, she was going to call the whole thing off.

She finished gathering the pictures and jammed them back into the photo album. She put the photo album back into the box, followed by the high school and college yearbooks. Then she thought of something and pulled the college yearbook out again.

She rifled through the pages, stopping at the occasional photograph that had been stuck inside. She stopped when she found a picture of herself in a blue spandex bodysuit her hair teased into a huge 80's style, blue high-heel boots and blue nail polish to match. The zipper on the bodysuit was open clear down to her bellybutton. She laughed;

Jason would love it.

She closed the yearbook and put it back into the box. She put the photo on the counter with her car keys so she wouldn't forget it, and then she went upstairs to shower and get dressed. She wanted to get to Jason's before noon.

*****

The hammered metal pieces of the wind chime rattled against each other as Deirdre opened the door to the diner. The low morning sun sent slanting bars of light through the windows across the front, illuminating dust motes that floated in the air. She walked halfway down the length of the counter past the diner's sole patron, a lanky guy with a large Adam's apple in a dirty green army jacket, and sat on a stool opposite the window that opened into the kitchen. Without looking over she could feel the eyes of the guy in the army jacket roaming all over her. Hell, she could practically hear the patter of his drool hitting the countertop.

The man working the grill called through the window when he noticed her. "What can I get you, ma'am?"

"Two orders of eggs, one scrambled, one sunny-side up, bacon crisp, toast, and two large coffees to go."

"Be just a couple of minutes." The man moved away from the window for a moment, and then moved back and spoke to the man in the army jacket, "Give the lady a break, Sam. She's not on display."

Sam swallowed audibly, and mumbled "Sorry." to no one in particular. He stared down into the white mug in front of him instead.

When cooking smells drifted to her from the kitchen Deirdre felt her stomach rumble in anticipation. It reminded her that she hadn't eaten much of anything the day before.

She had slept through most of the morning yesterday and had awoken to find Ricky and the car gone. His stuff was still in the room, so he hadn't skipped, but she didn't know where he was. Not that she had expected a note or anything, and it was far from the first time he had left without explanation.

Without the room key she would have had to leave the room unlocked, or lock herself out. As neither alternative appealed to her, she hung around. First she watched game shows on the room television, an ancient console model with far too much green in the picture that made everyone look sick. Then, as the morning rolled into early afternoon, she ate some ice cubes from the motel ice machine, and a Snickers bar from a vending machine that she had bought with a dollar she found in the pocket of a pair of Ricky's jeans. Four days ago she had been at a party in a house worth millions with a battalion of waiters throwing hors d'oeuvres at her, and now she was lunching on a Snickers bar and ice cubes. Yeah, her life was pretty fucked up.

Afternoon had turned into evening, and Deirdre had switched to the news. On some level she always thought about the day that she would turn on the news and see Ricky being loaded into a police car or an ambulance or a hearse, and what that might feel like. She often thought that it might feel like nothing at all. As the weather forecast trailed to a close (hazy, sunny in the high 80's, some rain possible early next week), Ricky had come through the door.

Deirdre extended her senses trying to pick his mood; the hunch of his shoulders, the cast of his mouth, the angle of his eyebrows, and the set of his eyes. He was so preoccupied with whatever he was planning that he gave out no signals at all that Deirdre could read. It unnerved her after she had become so used to being able to read his every subconscious tick. He was so turned inwards that it was almost like he wasn't there at all, that the room felt somehow emptier with him in it.

There were only two things that Deirdre could tell about Ricky for certain. One, whatever he was after it was completely consuming his attention, more and more so as time passed. The other thing was that he smelled of cheese, tomato sauce, and some kind of spicy meat. He had had pizza, most likely pepperoni. She thought about asking him for some money so that she could get something to eat, but the way he was behaving it would be a struggle just to get his attention, let alone get any money out of him. It just wasn't worth it. Besides, the majority of her clothing, selected by Ricky to be skin tight to begin with, had seemed a little more so recently. Skipping a meal or three wouldn't kill her.

And so she had gone to sleep last night without dinner, Ricky an empty, brooding stillness in the bed beside her.

"Black?"

"What's that?" She came out of her thoughts and was almost surprised to find herself sitting at the counter in the diner.

"The two large coffees? You want those black?" The cook had come out of the kitchen and was filling two Styrofoam cups on the counter in front of her from a glass coffee pitcher. The throaty gurgle of the coffee pouring into the cup sounded almost like laughter.

"Uh. One black, one with cream."

He put the pitcher back on the burner and put a waxed cardboard container of cream on the counter. "Help yourself. The food will be done in just another minute."

As he went back into the kitchen she poured cream into her coffee, sipped it down a little ways, and added more cream on top. She put a fitted, plastic lid on each cup.

When the cook came back with two Styrofoam takeout boxes in a white plastic bag she thanked him and paid him with a twenty Ricky had given her that morning. She wondered briefly where he was getting money and how much more he had, then decided she was probably better off not knowing. On the way out, she again felt green army jacket's eyes all over her.

The air outside was already warm and unpleasantly thick with smog.

Back at the motel room the drapes were open, the light streaming into the room showing how truly shabby it was. Ricky was sitting in one of the chairs next to the small table smoking a cigarette. He was wearing a jacket though it was already quite warm in the room, which Deirdre thought was odd. She put the food on the table and he snuffed the cigarette out in an ashtray and dug right in.

She sat in the chair opposite him and opened the other takeout container. A billow of warm, salty steam drifted up towards the ceiling. A plastic spoon, knife, and fork, along with a napkin, salt, and pepper were all contained in a small cellophane packet. "We should have eaten breakfast at the diner," Deirdre said taking a bite of toast. "It looks like a nice place."

"Whatever." Ricky shrugged his shoulders.

Ricky ate in silence. Deirdre was content in the quiet, happy just to be getting some food in her stomach. She noticed that Ricky ate the unbroken egg yolks whole, like a snake on a nature show swallowing a chicken egg. Creepy. Had she never noticed that before?

She again ran through what she knew and what she suspected about Ricky's plans in her mind as she had done at least a hundred times the day before. Her conclusion this time was the same as all the other times: she just didn't have enough information.

When Ricky had finished he threw the plasticware into the takeout container, closed it, and stood up. "Let's go."

Deirdre was starting her last slice of toast. "Where are we going?"

"Out." Ricky said over his shoulder. He was already opening the door and stepping through it.

She stuffed the toast into her mouth and got up, grabbing her purse as she did so, and headed after him.

They got into the car, Ricky pulling out of the lot before Deirdre was done closing the passenger door. She had no idea where he could be in such a hurry to get to, but she didn't have to wait long to find out.

Ricky parked the car in the strip mall in front of the health club. He picked up the binoculars as he got out of the car. Wonderful, another day of walking up and down the street of that subdivision, Deirdre thought. She had at least had the foresight to wear sneakers.

Between the pillars and up the street, the shitbox Toyota was still in the driveway just as it had been the previous day. It might not have even moved as far as Deirdre could tell. Just shy of the Toyota, Ricky cut across the street and went up the driveway of another house and around the back.

Ricky took a piece of flat metal from his wallet and slid it between the door and jam. He wiggled it for a moment, and then pushed the door open and went inside. That was a pretty neat trick. She wished he would show her how to do it. Deirdre looked around at the neighboring houses to see if anyone was watching them, but the house itself blocked the view from the neighbor on one side, and high hedge effectively blocked the other. She followed him into the dark interior.

There was a small tiled mudroom just inside the door. Ricky went through the mudroom, and the kitchen beyond, to the dining room with Deirdre trailing behind. He pulled a chair from the dining room table and put it in front of the window, sat down, and made himself at home.

Deirdre looked over his shoulder and saw that this house gave a pretty good view of the front of the house they had been watching, although most of the shades there were drawn so it was impossible to see what was going on indoors. "Whose house is this?"

Ricky held the binoculars to his face and was sweeping the front of the house across the street, "I don't know."

"Are they coming home?"

"I don't know. The fridge is empty and unplugged. Now, would you sit down and be quiet?"

Deirdre shook her head and left to look around to see if she could figure out what had happened to the occupants. The mail in the front hall didn't give any immediate clues. She frowned at the broken table and vase, but didn't know what to make of it.

The upstairs held three bedrooms. One was decorated like the bedroom of a teenage girl: all pinks and flowers, music posters on the walls, a school banner, cheerleader trophies – the noble undertakings of any teenage girl in southern California. But the room seemed unlived in. For one, it was far too neat for any teenage girl Deirdre had ever known, and for another the posters on the wall, one of Madonna and one of the New Kids on the Block, were more than twenty years out of date. The closet held very little clothing. Maybe the daughter had moved away after college and her parents had left the room untouched. Whatever, she wasn't living here.

The second room along the hallway was the master bedroom. Filled with dark, heavy furniture of a sort of antique-y quality, it spoke of a going-towards-retirement couple, which meshed well with the furniture downstairs and a daughter who would have left for college in the late 80's. There were photos wedged into the frame of the mirror in the master bedroom. The daughter at graduation, big hair and the excess of eye liner; a family gathering in the dining room downstairs with some relatives present; a head shot of the couple, a beach in indistinct focus behind them. There weren't any papers on the dresser or nightstand that told Deirdre where they might have gone.

In the third room Deirdre struck paydirt. It had been redone as a home office, with a large desk, computer, and metal three-drawer filing cabinet. She sat at the desk chair and started looking through the drawers. Very quickly she found a current travel itinerary for an Alaskan cruise.

She took the itinerary with her and went back downstairs. Ricky was sitting in the chair spreading Cheez Whiz on a cracker.

"We're OK here, I guess. They don't come back for ten days."

"How do you know that?"

She waved the itinerary in the air, "Travel schedule. They're on a cruise."

"Good girl." He patted her on the ass. "Get yourself a chair. We're going to be here for a while."

Deirdre pulled a chair from the table and put it next to Ricky's. They sat and shared crackers and Cheez Whiz. It was as close to a Hallmark moment as they had ever enjoyed together, Deirdre thought. How fucked up was that?

Still, it was likely the best mood she was going to catch him in, and he was acting so strangely about whatever plan he was working on, that it was worrying her. "Ricky, honey, can you give me a hint why we're watching this house? Maybe I can help." And maybe she could help, or, if the plan was utterly insane, run for her life before all hell broke loose.

Ricky had woken up that morning certain he was going to tell Deirdre everything, and he had just been waiting for her to ask. He couldn't keep up the schedule he had been on for several days now. He needed Deirdre to take a shift on watch.

"We're watching this house because the guys there are going to lead us to some money, a whole lot of money. About seven million dollars." he said as he drew a curlicue on a cracker with Cheez Whiz.

He had said it so casually, the can of Cheez Whiz in one hand, that the magnitude of what he had said didn't register. It was more money than she would have possibly imagined. She tried to come up with a question that would help her to understand. She opened her mouth, and then closed it again, rejecting "Whose money is it?" as pointless. She shook her head and tried again, still nothing came to mind.

What thoughts she had managed to collect were scattered as Ricky jumped out of the chair and grabbed the binoculars off the windowsill. "Who the fuck is that?" he muttered to himself.

Deirdre looked past him at the other house. A blue Volkwagon had pulled into the driveway and a brunette woman got out, walked up to the front door, and rang the bell. Deirdre guessed she was a somewhere in her mid-twenties. Otherwise, she couldn't tell much more about her from this distance without the binoculars. The cute guy she had seen at the computer opened the door, and he scooped her up in a bear hug. He swung her back and forth a few times before putting her down. They went inside together and the door closed.

They hadn't kissed. That might be significant, Deirdre thought.

Ricky banged the binoculars down on the windowsill and slumped back into the chair. He pulled at his lower lip with his thumb and forefinger, shook his head. "Who the fuck is that?" he muttered again.

*****

Jason sat on the couch wearing blue jeans and a green T-shirt. His bare feet were propped up on the coffee table in front of him crossed at the ankles, a map of California and a yellow legal notepad full of calculations on his lap. Papers were piled up on the rest of the couch around him. He had his head resting against the couch back, his face tilted up towards the ceiling, his eyes closed.

Chip came in from the kitchen carrying a bowl of cereal. "You asleep?"

Jason groaned, "No. Just thinking."

Chip sat down in the recliner on the other side of the coffee table and set the cereal bowl down on the top.

Jason took a deep breath and lifted his head, opened his eyes and flipped through the stacks of papers around him listlessly. "I don't know, Chip. The money's been out there for, what," he checked his watch, "fifty-five hours now give or take, and we're not getting any closer to it. If there's a pattern in all this, I don't see it."

"How many accounts do you have so far?"

Jason dropped his hands on the piles of paper next to him, "I've lost count. Sixty-something I think. It doesn't matter. There should be plenty of information here to find the pattern. Phone number, address, location, size by number of customers, size by held assets, none of it matches. I'm starting to think that maybe there is no pattern."

"Is that possible?"

He shook his head, "I don't know. I guess anything is possible. He could have just pulled a list of banks together from the phone book and entered them into the wire transfer program, but then you would think they would be in alphabetical order, or something like it. The guy was a movie producer – maybe he made up the list when he was stoned, and it orders the banks by their altitude above sea level. No, now that I think about it, the list I have so far has hopped in and out of the LA basin a dozen times. That has to be the lowest area other than Death Valley, right?" He started tracing around on the map in his lap with an index finger, "Does this map even have topographic data?"

"Where does that leave us?"

Jason drummed the fingers of one hand on the map, "Well, we can't catch up to the money. We've been falling steadily behind since hour one. If we can't find the pattern, then I guess at some point we give up and go back to our lives." He then remembered that he had no job to go back to and added, "Whatever that is. I'll tell you one thing: I'm burned out on the computer. I've got to take a break."

"You're a smart guy. You'll think of something. You want some breakfast? I bought bagels."

"Yeah, sure, why not?" Jason put the map and pad on one of the piles beside him and stood up. He stretched, his knees popping audibly. As he headed for the kitchen, the doorbell rang, and he veered off course to answer it.

When he opened the door and saw Kelly standing there he shouted, "Kelly, you came!" and swept her up in a bear hug, swinging her side to side.

Chip came to the front door, "Kelly! Are you going to help us?"

"I will as soon as Jason puts me down," she said, over Jason's shoulder.

Jason put her down and ushered her inside, closing the door behind her. "Wow, Kelly. I really need your help. I'm completely burned out."

"What are friends for? But there's one ground rule I want to get straight right out."

"Before you say anything," Chip said, "Jason and I already discussed it, and we're going to split the money evenly three ways. That's about two point three million dollars each."

"That wasn't what I was going to say. I don't care about the money."

"But we want you to have it."

She shrugged, "Whatever. What I was going to say was

that I wasn't willing to do anything illegal."

Jason ran a hand through his hair, "I don't know, Kel. The information we need to find this money isn't exactly publicly available."

"That's what I thought when you first told me yesterday. But last night I had an idea."

*****

Across the street Ricky was pacing back and forth in front of the dining room window. Every couple of laps he would stop in front of the window, look out at the car parked in the driveway of Jason's house, mutter "Who the fuck is that?" to himself, and then return to pacing.

Deirdre had moved the two chairs back against the dining room table to keep Ricky from heedlessly walking into one as he paced. She didn't know enough to make any constructive comment, and so decided that silence was, as usual, her best option.

"That's probably his girlfriend, right? He hugged her like a girlfriend." Ricky had turned to her.

"I don't know," she said slowly, uncertain if it as a question he wanted her to answer. "That wasn't a romance hug. It was more like hugging a friend he hadn't expected to see."

Ricky turned away from her and looked out the window. He rested his hands against the windowsill and hunched his shoulders. "Think he's telling her about the money?"

"How would I know?' Deirdre asked from behind him.

"He's telling her about the money." Ricky said, his

voice firm.

Deirdre said nothing.

"We can't stay here. We have to get involved or we'll miss the money when they find it. It's as much ours as theirs, right?"

Deirdre had only the vaguest idea what he was talking about. "Uh, right." She added, almost as an afterthought.

He tore himself away from the window and headed for the front door. Deirdre, caught unaware, was several steps behind him and had to move fast to catch up. Ricky crunched through the mail on the floor in the front hall as if they were autumn leaves and, opening the door, headed down the walk and across the street. Deirdre closed the door after herself and followed behind.

As he reached the driveway Ricky came to a stop so suddenly that Deirdre practically ran into him. He straightened his jacket and finger combed his hair and took a moment to compose himself. He then casually walked up to the front door and rang the bell.

*****

Kelly had grabbed a piece of paper and pen from the couch and was sketching as she spoke, "The information we want isn't exactly public, but it isn't exactly private either. Lots of companies have access to people's bank records: credit reports, mortgage applications, college loans." She had drawn a box in the center of the page labeled 'Bank' with arrows radiating outwards to smaller boxes labeled 'Credit,' 'Mortgage,' and 'Loans.'

Jason was starting to see where she was going with this, "Home equity loans, car loans, credit card companies."

Kelly was nodding, "Right. All those companies have the perfectly legal right to look at your bank records, recent deposits, balances, and-"

"And withdrawals." Chip said.

Kelly looked at him and smiled, "Right."

"All those requests happen over the internet." Jason said, trying to think it through. "There must be some common request format that the bank computers recognize and respond to automatically. There's almost certainly not a person involved in the loop; it would take too long and there must be millions of requests a year. But how do we find that format?"

"OK. I've got one idea. I think we can," she began.

At that moment the doorbell rang.

"You expecting anyone?" Kelly frowned.

Jason shook his head. Visions of federal agents dancing in his head, he got up slowly, walked to the door, and opened it. A tall well-dressed man with broad shoulders, black hair, and handsome Spanish features stood next to an attractive blonde woman. He looked at Jason expectantly.

"Can I help you?" Jason asked.

The man's face lit up with a warm smile. "I'd like to think of it more like us helping each other."

"Are you selling something? I'm really very busy."

The man laughed, "Selling?" He turned to the woman, "He thinks I'm selling something." The woman returned his smile uncertainly. He leaned towards Jason conspiratorially and spoke softly, “Could we come inside and talk with you? It’s about the money.”

Jason paused as his heart stuttered for a few beats. When his brain finally restarted he realized that his shot at the easy denial ‘What money?’ was long in the past. He tried instead, “I don’t understand.”

The man spoke even more softly, Jason almost having to strain to hear it, “Relax. I’m not a cop, I’m not with the dealer down on the docks, but I do have an interest in the money, Jason, and I do want to talk with you.”

Jason was staggered by the use of his name. So much so that he actually stepped back from the door, which Ricky used as an invitation to enter, Deirdre following behind.

Deirdre closed the door gently and pressed her back against it. She felt out of control, as if the events of the past few days were picking up speed and she was being pulled along in their slipstream.

Ricky walked right into the living room, completely at ease and all smiles, like a seasoned politician working a room. He saw the brunette sitting on the couch next to the fat man. Papers were scattered around them on the couch, the coffee table, and spilled on the floor. “Hi. I’m Ricky. That’s Deirdre back by the door. And you are?” He held a hand out to Chip.

“I’m Chip.” Chip automatically responded and took the offered hand, Ricky pumping it vigorously once contact was made.

“Excellent. And you are?” He extended his hand towards Kelly.

“Um, Kelly.” She took his hand uncertainly.

"Um, Kelly, a pleasure to meet you. Though we should probably cut these pleasantries short, all this talk isn't getting us any closer to finding that money."

Jason had followed him from the front door and now stood in the living room archway with his arms crossed, "Look, would it upset you if we said that we have no idea what money you're talking about?"

"No, it wouldn't upset me," Ricky said, his smile not dimming in the slightest, "mostly because I know it's not true. The fact that you let us in here proves that."

Jason frowned but said nothing.

"OK, here's the deal. You're working on your computer to find seven million dollars jumping from bank account to bank account. The money was for a drug deal by a movie producer named Ryder, but instead of drugs he got himself killed. Chip was at the dock when the deal went to hell, and now with Ryder dead that money is ours."

Jason, Chip, and Kelly were shocked. This guy knew almost everything!

Things were falling into place quickly for Deirdre. Maybe too quickly. She almost couldn't fit the pieces of the puzzle together in her head fast enough, and the picture she was managing was full of holes that she was sure she could fill if she only had a little time to think about it.

Jason moved across the living room to stand near his friends, a little psychological backup. "That's a wild story; thanks for sharing. If all that money is out there, you'd better get looking for it."

Ricky shook his head, "I don't know anything about banks and computers."

"Then, if that story is true, and that's a pretty big if, why should we share the money with you?"

"I was there that night, on the docks. I know all about that money, and that gives me as much right to it as you. Right?"

The three of them looked at him without comment.

"Look, I may not know anything about banks or computers, but I'm a guy with a lot of connections. Just about anything we might need, I can get it. We can go after it separately, but doesn't it make more sense for us to work together?"

Jason pursed his lips, but then said nothing.

"No?" Ricky shook his head sadly. "I'm sorry you feel that way. Here I thought we could help each other. We'd all get the money and everybody goes away happy. But if you want to go it alone, there's nothing I can do about that. Maybe I'll take what I know to the cops. Big drug shootout at the docks, reward for any information, blah, blah, blah – I saw it all on the news. Maybe that's the safer bet anyway. You guys keep looking, and I'll go for the reward." He crossed the living room back to the front door, "Come on, Dee. It was a mistake coming here."

Deirdre opened the door and took several steps down the front walk and then stopped when she realized he wasn't following her.

"Still, you know the thing that really sucks?" Ricky took several steps back into the room; Deirdre came back to the open doorway. "I'll go to the cops, get the reward, probably only be ten thousand or so, and me and Dee will get by. But you, you're down to your last two hundred bucks. You'll lose the house, the car, all of it. Or, all you have to do is say OK, and we can split this money five ways.

That's a million plus each. But, never mind." He waved a hand in the air loosely. "You want to be greedy, see what that gets you." He started walking towards the door again; Deirdre again moved out of the doorway and a few steps down the walk.

He walked slower and slower as he got near the door, certain they were going to tell him to wait. Jason stood in stunned silence, his mind furiously trying to find an angle.

Ricky finally admitted to himself that the cool movie scene in his head wasn't going to happen so he turned back on his own, "Did I hear someone say 'Wait'?"

Jason swallowed dryly. If he had another option, he didn't see it. He licked his lips, "Wait."

Chip and Kelly both tried to talk to Jason at once. He paused them by holding up his hand, index finger up in a 'one second' gesture. "I need to discuss this with my friends."

Ricky shrugged, "Go ahead."

"Could you, uh, wait outside?"

"Sure. No problemo. We'll be out by the pool." He and Deirdre crossed the living room and through the sliding glass door to the patio. As he stepped outside and slid the door closed behind him, he said to Deirdre, "I like the sound of that. I'm going to have to get a house with a pool." The closing door cut off what he was saying mid-sentence.

Kelly was already shaking her head as Jason turned back to talk to them, "I don't know who this guy is, but you can't be serious about trusting him."

"Kel, he was there. He knows everything. How can we

cut him out? Right, Chip?" He looked at Chip who had a pained expression.

Kelly put a hand on his shoulder, "Jason, I don't like it. We don't know who this guy is. Maybe he's a cop. Maybe he was part of the drug deal. Maybe we get the money and he kills us all. Maybe we don't manage to get the money and he kills us all anyway. We-don't-know." She said these last three words slowly, pausing between each word for emphasis.

Jason didn't have an answer to that. "I need this money," was all he could think to say.

She put her other hand on his other shoulder and turned him to face her, looking up into his eyes, "You don't need this money. Not this way. You can come work with me. We'll scrounge up enough business to make it by. And Chip has his father's plastics business."

Jason backed up so Kelly's hands fell of his shoulders. She let them drop bonelessly to her sides. "But I'll lose the car. And this house! I can't sell it, I can't keep it. I'll be in debt for thirty years to pay it all off. I've got to do this."

Kelly folded her arms across her chest, her face set stubbornly, her eyes fierce. "Fuck this house!" She shouted so loudly that Ricky and Deirdre could hear her outside and looked her way.

Jason hung his head. "Chip, can you hold the fort? I have something I have to show Kelly."

"You're going to leave me here alone? What am I supposed to do with them?"

"Leave them outside."

"What if they want to come in, maybe get a drink of

water or use the bathroom?"

"Tell them there's a gas station down the street. Just don't let them in. Can you do that?"

Chip sighed, spared a glance at Ricky and Deirdre out by the pool, looked back at Jason and gave half-hearted shrug. "Sure, I guess."

"Kelly, would you come with me?"

"What?" Kelly didn't move, her eyes burning holes in him.

"Please, Kelly. I need you to see this."

She blew out an exasperated breath. "OK."

Jason led her into the garage and the Porsche. Kelly rode in silence in the passenger seat, her curiosity growing as he parked in front of an upscale apartment building and led her across the lobby to the elevators. "Where are we, Jason? Who lives here?"

Jason didn't answer her as the elevator arrived and they rode up together.

Monday being Mitzy's day off, they found his mother lying in bed in her room. The room was pleasant; the walls painted a pale lemon, windows filling one wall overlooking the gardens. The large adjustable hospital bed dominated the space. A door wide enough to accommodate a wheelchair opened into a bathroom. A large spray of white and yellow roses stood in a vase on the nightstand. They looked to Jason a little tired, and he wondered how much longer he could go on buying fresh flowers every couple of weeks.

One of the day nurses, Jason couldn't seem to come up

with her name at the moment, was just finishing feeding her lunch, which his mother more or less would eat as long as it didn't require much chewing and someone spoon fed it to her. "Hi Mr. Taylor. So nice to see you again." Another member of the thousand watt smile club.

"Hi. Can I finish feeding her?" He gestured to small plastic bowl that she held half filled with chocolate pudding.

"Of course," she handed it to him, "just leave the dish on the nightstand when you're done." She collected the rest of the lunch tray and carried it out of the room. The door sighed shut behind her on a pneumatic hinge.

Jason hooked his toe around a chair leg near the bed and pulled it under him as he sat down. "Hi Mom, this is Kelly. I've told you about her."

"Hello Mrs. Taylor." Kelly said coming around the far side of the bed. "So nice to finally meet you." She placed her hand upon the woman's hand which was resting on top of the covers. She found it as responsive as a lump of clay. Kelly looked at her closely, the slack skin on the expressionless face, the eyes open and unfocused. She also couldn't help but notice the flattened bedspread where the hump caused by her right leg should have been. "Mrs. Taylor? Jason, is she alright?"

"No, but she's been this way for a very long time." He filled the spoon with pudding and held it against his mom's lips. She opened her mouth slightly, and he slid the spoon inside. The mouth worked slowly, and he pulled it out a moment later clean. Kelly had had a doll that did that when she was a child.

"What's wrong with her?"

"Most of the doctors called it early onset Alzheimer's,

though some called it something else, I don't remember what. It doesn't really matter. She didn't respond to any treatments and here she is." He saw that she had noticed the missing leg. "They amputated her leg, um, about a year and a half ago, just after Christmas. Poor circulation, not enough movement, and diabetes, they just couldn't save it."

Kelly looked at the room around her. She had a million questions she wanted to ask, about his mother, about his childhood, about why he had never told her, but she had already figured out the answer to the most important question herself. "This is it, isn't it? This is why you need the money. It isn't about the house at all?"

Jason was quiet as he finished feeding her. The spoon clattered in the empty dish when he set them on the nightstand. He allowed himself a small smile. "It's always been all about her, since I was fourteen years old." He picked up a forest green linen napkin that was folded on the bed and used it to wipe the corners of her mouth. He kissed her on the forehead. "I probably can't explain that to you as well as I'd like to." He paused. "If some day you want to sit down and hear all about, well, all of this, I can try, but I need your answer now. In a week and a half they're going to move her to some shithole of a state facility unless I can pay the bill. I'm out of options here and I'm out of time."

"We don't know anything about Ricky. I don't trust him."

"Neither do I, but I don't have a choice." He stood and reached across the bed taking Kelly by the hand, looking deep into her eyes, "I need your help, Kel."

She put a hand on his hand, knowing that she couldn't get Jason to let go of the money, unable to think of any other alternative, "OK, Jason." She smiled, "Someone has to watch out for you."

Jason put his other hand on her hand on his hand, "Thanks, Kel."

They arrived back on the house to find Chip sitting nervously on the couch. He jumped to his feet as soon as they came in. "Where did you guys go?"

"Long story," Kelly answered, wondering what, if anything, Chip knew about Jason's mom. "What have they been doing?" she asked, referring to Ricky and Deirdre who were still out by the pool.

"Nothing at all. Deidre came in and asked for some water and I gave her a glass. I hope that was OK." He looked nervously from Kelly to Jason, "So?"

Jason gave a weary smile, "Kelly is going to help us."

Chip held out his arms, "That's great! Group hug!" He swept them both up in his arms, lifting Kelly clean off her feet and pulling Jason to his toes.

When he let them go, Jason walked out to the pool with Kelly and Chip in tow. Ricky was laying on one of the lounge chairs with his shirt off, his shirt and jacket in a pile on the table next to him. Deirdre was standing at the edge of the pool looking down into the water.

Ricky turned his head to look at Jason, a reflection of the sun off his sunglasses catching Jason squarely in the eyes, making him squint. "So?"

Jason looked to Kelly who gave a nearly imperceptible nod.

"You're in," Jason said reluctantly

"Outstanding."

*****

They had all moved indoors and gone upstairs to the guest bedroom. Kelly sat at the desk with the laptop in front of her as she spoke. "OK, the problem is finding the format that the banking computers accept for account information inquiries. There might be a couple of ways we could do this, but the way that makes the most sense to me is to watch a legitimate account inquiry and see what format it takes."

Jason leaned in over her shoulder, "You mean like filing for a home equity loan or something?"

She looked up at him, "Exactly."

Her fingers moved over the keys. She opened a number of windows, and in one of them started a search for online loan companies. "We're going to want a pretty small company. If their packet volume is too high we'll never be able to find the one we're looking for in all the traffic."

Kelly found a company that suited their needs and in another window wrote a packet sniffer that directed copies of all incoming packet traffic to that site to their laptop. As soon as she ran the program the screen filled with messages, each with a time and date stamp. A counter in the corner that monitored the packets as they came in quickly passed one hundred.

"That's a lot of traffic," Chip said.

"Yeah, even small sites can log up some real bandwidth, but ninety-nine percent of it is probably garbage as far as we're concerned; web surfing, email, connection maintenance protocols."

"How are you going to sort it all out?" Jason asked.

"Some of it will be obvious by the format. Email will be easy to spot, as will html and video files. The rest we're just going to have to sift through. Grunt work, but it should pay off. Timing will be important too. When we send in our loan form, we'll look at the message traffic for say, the next fifteen minutes."

Jason shook his head. "I don't know, Kel. Are you sure it will be in there?"

"No, but it's a pretty good bet. If not, we'll check the next fifteen minutes, and the next fifteen after that until we find something. We'll need to use someone's account information that we know well so we can compare the packets to it. Some of the information is likely to be encrypted in some way, so it might be a little tricky to spot. Can we use your account, Jason?"

"Sure, let me get you a bank statement." He left the room.

Kelly called to him, "Bring that little thermal printer of yours too, and a ream of paper. It might be easier to sort through it all if we can hand it around."

While they waited Kelly sifted through some of the packets they had already collected. She wrote a small subroutine to delete html documents as they were received to cut down on the traffic, and another one to isolate email messages, figuring that the information could, but almost certainly would not, come through as an email.

Chip sat down on the bed.

Ricky went to the window and lowered the shade the inch he had raised it earlier, cutting off anyone from the outside trying to look in as he had done.

Jason came back with the printer, paper, and bank

statement. He handed the bank statement to Kelly and started hooking up the printer while she entered the information in a loan request form.

"Wow, you really are down to your last two hundred dollars."

He shrugged, "Uh-huh."

Kelly cleared the packet buffer, noted the time, and hit enter. As they watched, the counter climbed to three hundred seventeen in the next fifteen minutes. Kelly dumped those into a file, and then let the buffer accumulate again.

"OK, let's print it."

They waited in awkward silence as sheets ran out of the printer.

"Hey, I've got one." Chip broke into the silence.

"One what?" Deirdre asked.

"Shoot." Jason said.

"Marilu Henner and Peggy Lipton." Chip waggled his eyebrows.

"Marilu Henner was Nardo on *Taxi*, right?" Kelly had turned from the keyboard and was resting her head in her hand, her elbow on the desktop.

Jason leaned against the wall with his head down, "Uh-huh. *Taxi* had a lot of people go a lot of places. I think we should come at this one from the other side. Peggy Lipton didn't do all that much, at least not that I know of. There was *The Mod Squad*. Who made if off of that show?"

"What are you talking about?" Deirdre looked at the three of them.

"It's a game. You try to get from one actor to another using TV shows that they both acted on." Chip explained.

"Oh, so like Judd Hirsh was on *Taxi* and *Dear John*."

"Yeah, like that."

"But who else was on *Dear John*?"

"That's for you to figure out."

"Oh." Deirdre scratched her head.

"Tony Danza went from *Taxi* to *Who's the Boss*." Kelly pointed out.

"Yeah." Jason nodded. "Katherine Helmond was on *Who's the Boss* and *Soap*."

"*Soap*. I loved that show!" Deirdre started humming the theme song. "This is the story of two sisters, Jessica Tate,"

"And Mary Campbell." Chip continued for her.

Jason was shaking his head. "That's another show that had a million people on it who came from and went on to other shows. We'd never sort them all out. Wasn't Peggy Lipton on *Twin Peaks*?"

Ricky was incredulous, "How much TV do you people watch?"

Chip missed the criticism, "Lots."

"Ugh," Kelly groaned, "That show made no sense at

all."

Jason nodded his head, "Yeah, Peggy Lipton played the dead girl on *Twin Peaks*."

"How do you play a dead girl?" Deirdre asked.

"You'd have to see the series." Chip replied.

Kelly added, "Don't waste your time."

"Benson came off of *Soap*." Deirdre said.

"Yep," Jason added, "and he was also on *Sports Night*. Wow, Chip, this is a tricky one."

"That it is," Chip smiled happily.

"This is the dumbest game I ever heard of," Ricky shook his head.

Deirdre asked, "What was the name of the guy with the puppet on *Soap*?"

"I remember the puppet's name was Bob." Kelly said.

Jason smiled, "How pathetic is it that you can remember the puppet's name, but not the guy who ran it? The guy's name was Jay Johnson and he played Chuck."

"I think I've lost my train of thought," Jason said, "What was I trying to find again? A link between Peggy Lipton and?"

"Marilu Henner." Chip answered.

"Right." He paused in thought, "Uh, right."

"Hate to break up the party," Kelly said as she pulled a

sheaf of papers from the printer and banged the edges against the desktop to even them, "but the printer is done."

"Give up, Jase?" Chip asked.

"We'll pick it up again later."

"OK"

Kelly handed pieces of the stack to Jason and Chip. "You might see Jason's name or part of it. You might see a piece of his account number. You might see his account balance, or maybe the name of his bank, Bank of North America. Frankly I don't know what you're looking for exactly. Just look them over and see what you see." She split the remaining stack between Ricky and Deirdre. They took their pages and set to work.

Going through all those packets, many of them just meaningless strings of numbers, was mind-numbing. After three hours the numbers just flowed past Jason's eyes in a nearly homogenous stream. It was almost impossible to keep focused on the task, the poor print formatting making it difficult just to follow the data from one line to the next. Jason had his pile spread over much of the floor while Chip had taken the bed. Ricky and Deirdre had taken theirs downstairs to the living room.

Chip leaned back against the wall and rubbed the stubble on his cheeks. "I'm near the end of my stack and I haven't seen anything, but I could have missed it. It's all a blur to me."

"Me too." Jason added.

Kelly ran both hands through her hair. "If it makes you feel any better, the computer program hasn't found anything either. Maybe we should move on to the next fifteen minutes?"

Chip and Jason both groaned.

"Hey, I think my idea can work. It's just going to take some time. If you want to go back to cracking banks, I'll get out of your way."

"No, Kelly, it's not that. It's just that Chip and I have already been at this for two days straight. It's a little draining."

Cries of "I found it! I found it!" called up to them from downstairs. Deirdre came into the bedroom holding one of the papers with Ricky right on her heels.

"What have you got?" Kelly asked.

"Right here," she held out the paper and pointed with a lavender-lacquered fingernail. "That's your bank balance."

Chip looked over her shoulder, "She's right, but the rest of the page is jibberish."

Kelly took the page and scanned it with her eyes, "It's not jibberish. It's encrypted. I guess they do that to any part of the data that might be useful to someone intercepting the message. We should count ourselves lucky that they didn't encrypt the whole thing."

"This message includes my bank balance." Jason commented. "Doesn't that mean that this is the bank's reply to the info request?"

"Yeah, it does. Still, finding the request now shouldn't be too hard." Kelly rewrote her search routine to scan the other packets for number clusters common to the one Deirdre had found, discounting all packets that had arrived after the bank reply to lessen the number of packets that the computer actually had to sort through. In less than a minute the computer chimed indicating it had found the right one.

Kelly split the computer screen into two windows and displayed one packet in each. "There are several number clusters common to both. Probably your name, your social security number, your address and stuff like that. There's also the requesting institution's identification code, and the code of the bank they want to query. There should be enough information here to build a routine that will figure out the encoding method and decode these messages. Then we can make up our own messages, encode them in the same fashion, and follow the money."

"How long will all that take?" Ricky asked.

"I don't know. The math is complex but this is a pretty fast computer. We might have something tomorrow morning. You know," she looked at Jason, "it might be faster if we had a larger data set of encrypted messages to work with."

"You want to do all this again using other loan sites?"

"It shouldn't take too long this time. The programs to collect the packets and search for the number clusters are already written."

Jason shrugged, "Sure. What do I care? With my bank balance and lack of job they're going to refuse the loans anyway."

"Cool. You order Chinese food for dinner, and I'll get to work."

"Deal. I'll get the take-out menu." Jason headed out of the bedroom and downstairs.

"Happy Family for me," Kelly shouted after him.

Chip got up from the bed dumping the papers from his lap onto the floor, "I don't think he heard you." He put a hand on Kelly's shoulder, "You're pretty damned smart."

She looked up at him and smiled. "Thanks."

Chip went after Jason. Ricky and Deirdre drifted out shortly thereafter.

Kelly continued to work on the computer, the light leaking in around the drawn window shade turning gray with the approaching dusk.

*****

They were all back in the guest bedroom.

Kelly sat at the computer, an open take-out container of Happy Family mixed with white rice on the table next to the keyboard. She had chopsticks in one hand and was pecking at the keys with the other. Jason, Chip and Deirdre sat on the bed, Chip and Jason with take-out containers of their own. Deirdre was eating pizza with Ricky, who was sitting on a chair he had brought up from the dining room table.

"Kel?

"Um-hmm?"

"Want to trade?" Jason held up his container.

"What do you have?"

"Beef with broccoli."

"Sure." She picked up her container from the desktop and held it out to him. He took hers and handed his back, which she put back on the desktop untouched.

"You need any help?"

"No, the program is just grinding along. It might take a little longer than I thought. I mean, we know for example that your bank account number is encoded in the data, but we don't know where. The program has to try to fit it into the data somewhere, and then develop an algorithm that matches the encryption pattern. It then reverses that algorithm and applies it to decoding the rest of the data and sees what it ends up with. In this case I have it looking for your name in the resulting decoded message. If it doesn't find your name, it fits the bank account number somewhere else in the data and tries again. It's a pretty long process."

"How long do you think it will take?" Ricky asked, wiping his mouth with a greasy napkin.

"No easy way to know. It could find a match in the next two minutes. It could take hours. I think one way or another it will be done by morning."

"And after all that you still have to use it to find the money, which will take even longer, right?"

Kelly picked up the take-out container and speared a piece of broccoli with a chopstick, "Hey, if you've got a better way to find it, I'd like to hear it."

Ricky held up his hands in mock surrender, one hand still holding the crumpled napkin, "I'm just asking."

Kelly turned back to the computer without comment.

"What's Chinese food like?" Deirdre asked.

Jason chewed and swallowed a prawn, "You've never had Chinese food? What planet are you from?"

"Ever hear of a place called Red Mountain?"

"That's out towards Death Valley. More like a trailer park than a town. I drove through it once." Chip said.

"That's the place. My mom's car must have run out of gas on the way through town, because we actually lived there."

Jason was digging around in the container looking for another prawn, "No Chinese food?"

"No restaurants at all."

"Oh, well, Chinese food is, uh, kind of hard to describe. It's Chinese food."

"Can I try some?"

"Sure. This is Happy Family. It's sort of a mishmash of everything: chicken, prawns, pork, some Chinese vegetables."

Deirdre made a face, "Maybe too adventurous for me."

"I've got lo mein. It's sort of a Chinese spaghetti." Chip held out his container.

"What was the other one?" she asked.

"Beef with broccoli."

"That sounds more my speed."

Jason reached out with the happy family container, "Kel?"

Kelly held up the beef with broccoli container over her shoulder without turning from the computer. Jason took that container and gave her back her original one. She chucked it onto the desktop without looking at it.

He passed it to Deirdre and she took the white carton and looked inside. "What's all the sauce?"

Jason shrugged, "Soy sauce, plum sauce, ginger, probably some beef stock. I don't know exactly. Oh, here," he held out his chopsticks.

"I don't know how to use those."

"Are you a lefty or a righty?"

"Righty."

"Give me your right hand."

Deirdre held out her hand and he twisted her fingers around the chopsticks. "Now to grab something you kind of move your thumb and forefinger a little like this." He manipulated her hand so the chopstick tips met and separated. "Give it a try."

Deirdre experimentally opened and closed the chopsticks in the air and then tried grabbing a piece of beef, but it slipped free and fell back into the container before she could get it to her mouth. She tried a couple more times, finally managing to get a piece of beef quickly to her mouth by lifting with the chopsticks and simultaneously ducking her head to the container.

She chewed, "Wow. It's salty."

Chip nodded, "I guess most Chinese food is kind of salty."

"But it's also kind of sweet. I think I like it."

"There, you've expanded your horizons. Tomorrow night you'll try haggis." Jason smirked.

"What's haggis?"

"Trust me," Chip was laughing and wiping sauce from his chin, "you don't want to know."

Jason laughed with him.

"Seriously," Deirdre looked at them, "What is it?"

"I'll tell you another time." Jason took a drink from a soda can that he had propped between his knees.

"You want this back?" Deirdre offered the container.

"Not if you want it. I've had enough."

"Thanks." She settled back on the bed, poking around in the container with the chopsticks.

"So, Jason," Chip swallowed a mouthful of food, "Marilu Henner and Peggy Lipton."

"Oh, hey, right. I forgot."

"If you guys are going to start that again, I'm going to get some beer." Ricky chucked the partially eaten slice of pizza he had been holding back into the box, got up from the chair, and left.

"Where was I?" Jason wondered aloud.

"*Taxi*." Kelly said.

"*Soap*." Deirdre said.

"*Lost*." Chip said, and laughed at his own joke.

Jason was silent for a moment and then snapped his fingers. "Of course! All I needed was a little time to think about it. Peggy Lipton played the dead girl on *Twin Peaks*. Miguel Ferrer played an FBI agent. He was also a cop on the Stephen Cannell series *Broken Badges*, with Jay Johnson playing a cop with a puppet sidekick. And, uh," he ran a path in the air with his eyes as he fit all the connections together, then raised his eyebrows, "that's it."

"Boy, I really thought I had you there." Chip said, shaking his head as he sucked up a lo mein noodle.

"I thought you did too. I just kind of saw it all at once."

"I still don't think I have it." Kelly was turned around in the chair now.

"I don't think I do either." Deirdre was practicing opening and closing the chopsticks.

While Chip explained I to them, Deirdre started humming the theme song to Soap. Chip picked it up a moment later.

"What are you going to do with your share of the money?" Chip asked Jason suddenly.

Jason leaned back on the bed against the wall, "Oh, I don't know. Pay off the house, the car, the credit cards."

Kelly though it significant that he didn't mention his mother.

Jason continued, "I don't really want to think about it. We haven't found the money yet, and we might not find it at all."

"But we might." Deirdre said hopefully.

"Yeah, we might." Jason shrugged, "Of course, finding it and getting it are two different things."

"How so?"

"A lot of ways. You have any ideas about that Kel?"

Kelly shook her head, "None yet. I kind of figured we would burn that bridge when, and if, we came to it."

Deirdre looked from Kelly to Jason, "What's the problem?"

"Well," Jason began, "the biggest problem is that the guy who actually owns the account is dead. The instant his body turns up, the government will freeze all his bank accounts. That would end this paper chase right here."

"Where's his body?" Deirdre asked.

"We don't know. Ricky said that you were down at the docks. I thought you might know."

"I was asleep in the car."

"Maybe Ricky knows?"

Deirdre gave that some serious thought, and then shook her head. Jason thought that meant she didn't know. To Kelly it meant that she knew, but wasn't going to say.

"Anyway, even when we know where the money is," Kelly leaned her arms folded along the back of the chair, "that doesn't mean that we can just walk into the bank and get it. First of all, you have to find a bank that has over seven million dollars cash on hand. Not that that's unheard of – there are probably at least fifty banks in the state of California alone with that kind of cash in their vault and more – but we have to interrupt the transfer program somehow and move the money into one of those banks. I haven't figured out how to do that yet."

"The other problem," Jason continued the thought, "is getting the bank to give us the money. I thought at first that we could reroute the money into one of our bank accounts directly and withdraw it from there, but the more that I think about it, the more I'm convinced that that will leave a trail that can be followed to us. Ideally I'd like to just walk into the bank with a fake ID and walk out with the money. All that leaves the bank with is a faded Xerox of a fake passport and a grainy video of the withdrawal. But I suspect we would need an exceptional fake ID to withdraw seven million dollars. I had a crappy fake driver's license in college to get into bars, but I don't know where to get that kind of quality."

"I do." Ricky was standing in the door of the room holding a six pack of beer in one hand. He came into the room and plopped down in the chair, pulled one can from its plastic retainer ring, and popped the top. "I'll make a few phone calls tomorrow."

"I don't know," Jason frowned, "We might also need a credit or social security card. It's got to be good enough to make the bank think one of us is Ryder."

"I can get you enough ID to convince the Vatican that you're the Pope."

"Fake IDs. I don't think I like that." Kelly said.

"I don't like any of the options I've come up with so far, but we have to actually take possession of the money somehow. If you come up with any other ideas, I'll be glad to hear them."

Kelly pressed her lips into a thin line but didn't say

anything.

"But it's all academic if we don't find the money." Chip said, dropping his chopsticks into the empty take-out container and putting it aside.

Jason nodded, "First we have to find the money."

5 Days Earlier

Scott and Miller stood against the wall in the morgue. A body lay on a gurney under a starched blue sheet, only the grayish soul of one foot uncovered, the toe tag hanging off the big toe from a loop of wire. The fluorescent bars on the ceiling glared at them, reflecting off the stainless steel table surface and instruments on the tray nearby, the industrial beige tile on the floor, the urine yellow of the block walls.

"How did you hear about this one?" Miller's voice sounded funny, nasal. He was breathing shallowly through his mouth, avoiding the constant smell of rot and sewage that permeated the very concrete of the building.

"Came over the police scanner. Found by a couple of hikers."

Miller leaned in close, his voice a whisper, though there was no one in the room but the dead to hear him, "Think it's Ryder?"

"It would be bad luck if it is. I figured the canyon we put him in, he'd be lost for at least a week. Still, gotta know."

"What do we do if it's him?"

"I don't – Doctor." Scott addressed the man who had just walked into the room through the double doors at the end.

The medical examiner was a tall man, thin to the point of gaunt, a fringe of hair near his ears and forming small caterpillars over his eyes on an otherwise hairless skull, his scalp dotted with liver spots. "Gentlemen," his voice was surprisingly firm given his emaciated appearance, "what can I do you for?"

"We're here to see your next autopsy." Scott said. "He

might be a missing witness from a case we're working on."

"Well," the doctor took a quick glimpse at the toe tag, "the body came in without ID. If you guys can identify him it will save me a boatload of paperwork."

"And we can stop looking for him," Scott said.

"This one might not be pretty. Tag indicates some animals got to the body first. If either one of you thinks you'll be sick, I can get you vomit bags. I'd rather not have to mop the floor later."

"We're fine," Scott answered for both of them.

"Suit yourself." The medical examiner said, and without further word whipped off the sheet.

"Jesus!' Miller said, clamping his hand over his mouth and turning away.

The body was bloated and yet collapsing in on itself at the same time. The skin was bluish-gray, with missing patches where animals had taken their snacks. They seemed to have concentrated on the face: one eye missing completely, the other hanging by threads of the optic nerve, most of the nose gone, as well as one missing cheek, exposing the jawbone on that side and giving the corpse a permanent rictus smile.

"Is this your guy?"

Scott worked some saliva in his mouth, determined not to look away, "This guy's a floater."

"Yeah, washed up the beach in San Clemente last night. A couple walking on the beach found him. That must have been a fun ending to a romantic evening. A couple miles further South and he wouldn't even be my jurisdiction.

Currents are funny that way. Looks to be two, maybe three days in the water – of course, the crabs make it look worse than it is. Still, give him a good look; you might be able to identify him."

"I heard on the scanner that he was found by hikers in some valley to the North."

"Oh, wrong body. That one just came into the shop. I won't be working him until," he looked at the watch, "three, maybe four hours. I'm really backed up here. You want to see that autopsy, come by after lunch."

"We don't need to see the autopsy, just the body. Could we do that now?"

"I don't see why not. This way." He led them out of the room, stopping at a rack of equipment to retrieve a plastic specimen pan and hand it to Miller, "Here. You look a little green."

Miller accepted the container sheepishly.

They went down the hall and through a large stainless steel door that looked like it would be to a meat locker, which essentially it was. Inside there were rows of doors in the wall that would open and slide out body racks on rollers. The booming business of death in Los Angeles had caused an overflow of several bodies that lay on gurneys around the room.

"Cold in here," Scott commented.

"When the body is a couple of days old, believe me, you don't want it warm. Let's see here." He took a clipboard off the wall and scanned down the page, then turned to the next page and scanned again. "Newcomer. Doesn't even have a room yet. He should have made a reservation. He's on gurney six."

The gurneys were numbered on a vertical strut near the head. They found number six against the far wall.

The doctor consulted the clipboard, "This guy was shot and wrapped in plastic. They left the unwrapping to me with instructions to try and lift some fingerprints, so it might be tough to ID him through the plastic. He also apparently took a face shot. Still, worth a look."

Scott and Miller exchanged a glance.

The doctor put his hands on the sheet and looked at Miller, "You good?"

"Good." Miller swallowed.

The doctor made a drum roll sound with his tongue and then whipped the sheet off with a flourish.

Scott examined the body through its heavy plastic wrap. After a few days in the sun, fluids from the body had fogging the inside of the plastic and desert dust still clung to the surface. Through the thick wrapping, identification was out of the question. Except that the body was that of a black man.

Scott shook his head ever so slightly, "Not ours. Ours was white." Scott marveled at the violence of a city that would see at least two guys shot in the face, wrapped in plastic, and dumped in the trash-strewn wilderness outside the city in a single weekend.

"Better luck next time." The doctor wadded up the sheet and left it on the floor next to the gurney. "If you'll excuse me, I have bodies piling up."

Out in the hallway the doctor turned right and went back through the double doors.

Miller put the plastic container down on an empty gurney parked just outside the door. "Until we saw the body, I was sure that was going to be him. How many people you figure get shot in the face, wrapped in plastic, and dumped in a single weekend?"

"I was just thinking the same thing," he was interrupted by the shrill ringing of his phone. Scott grabbed the phone off his belt and checked the display. "Hmm, who's number is this?" he asked himself as he let the call go to voicemail.

Not wanting the trail of an outgoing call on his phone to a number he didn't know, they looked for an found an empty office where Scott could use the desk phone anonymously. He dialed the number, and then waited while it rang. "This is Scott," he said when the phone was picked up.

"Agent Scott, this is Jerry Sikes. I wanted to give you an update on that hard drive of yours." The man was almost shouting, the whine of the vacuum pumps loud in the background.

"What have you got?"

"The system managed to recover the FAT during the night."

"Fat?" Scott wasn't sure he heard correctly.

"File Allocation Table. I have a complete directory of the hard drive in front of me now. Do you know the name of the file you're looking for?"

"No, I don't know the name."

"Do you know what kind of file it is?"

"What kind?"

"Yes, like a text file or a Microsoft Word Document or an Adobe Acrobat file. That sort of thing."

"No, I don't." The whine of the pumps was starting to give him a headache.

"Then I'll have to pull off everything on the drive that's not operating system and let you look through it. Is that OK with you?"

"Sure. How much data are we talking about."

"Well, the machine appears to be almost brand new, and the hard drive is mostly empty. Maybe only fifty or seventy-five megabytes of junk to sift through."

"How long will it take to recover it?" Scott felt his own voice rising to compete with the pumps.

"I'm not saying that I can recover all of it. I'm still not sure what the bullet obliterated. All I can tell you now is that the FAT is intact and I have it. I'm running a sector scan now to find the disk alignment. Until that's done, I won't know what part of the disk the bullet passed through."

Scott sighed into the phone "And how long will *that* take?"

"About a day."

"Thank you very much. I'll expect to hear from you tomorrow." He hung up the phone before the other man could reply. He sat in the chair in front of the empty desk and massaged his forehead.

"Good news?"

"I'm not even sure. The hard drive file listing has been recovered, but that just says what was on the drive; it doesn't tell us what can't be recovered because of the damage. To know that is apparently going to take another day."

"So we wait."

"I can't think of anything else to do." He clipped his phone back onto his belt.

They went outside. Miller looked at his watch as they traversed the parking lot towards Scott's car, "Your shooting review board starts in an hour."

"Yeah, no big deal. Did you get the report on the dock shooting to Dorado?"

"First thing this morning. I made it pretty sketchy. If he complains I'll tell him that he didn't give me enough time to write it, but I can't stall him forever. That whole scene is not going to look right."

Scott stopped, took Miller by the forearm, and turned to face him, "I told you not to worry about it. The scene looks fine. What Dorado thinks and what he can prove are two different things. But I'll tell you one thing – by acting all strange about it you're looking suspicious. We just need to hold it all together for a couple more days, OK?"

"OK."

"I'm going to grab a bite and do the review board," Scott said as he crossed a few more aisles and reached his car, unlocking to door with the fob. "I want you to go back and rewrite the report. Write about every single piece of physical evidence in excruciating detail, but don't draw a single conclusion. Fill it up with lots of bullshit, make it long. Give Dorado something to chew on for a few days."

Miller hesitated, then said, “Will do.”

“Attaboy!” Scott slapped him on the shoulder and got into his car. He sped out of the parking lot leaving Miller breathing his exhaust.

*****

“Come and get it!” Kelly stood at the counter in the kitchen ringing a triangle that she held by a leather strap with a metal stick about the size of a pencil. Arranged on the counter in front of her was a bowl of eggs, a package of cheddar cheese, mushrooms, scallions, and ham wrapped in white deli paper.

Chip roused himself from the couch, throwing off the sheet he had been laying under, and came into the kitchen. “What are we? On the Ponderosa?”

“You don’t like the triangle?” She gave it a few more dings.

“It’s a little early. Where did you get it?”

“I found it in a drawer while looking for the coffee.”

“I wonder where Jason got a triangle?”

“I’ll have you know that I played first triangle in the school orchestra.” Jason said from the kitchen archway. “My teacher told me that I was the best triangle he ever heard.”

Chip laughed, “You played triangle in the high school orchestra?”

“No, not high school. Sixth grade. I never throw anything away.” He took the triangle from Kelly. “I shall now give you a command performance worthy of kings and presidents."

Kelly turned around and leaned the small of her back against the counter. She folded her arms under her chest, making it absolutely clear that she wasn't wearing a bra under her T-shirt.

Jason swallowed. He counted silently, keeping the time by bobbing his head. He tapped the triangle. Then bobbed his head some more, then a single tap, then some more bobbing, then a double tap. He looked up at them.

"That's it?" Chip asked.

"Hey, I think that was Wagner. I can't remember the name of the piece."

Kelly laughed.

"Try and imagine the whole orchestra around me."

"Uh-huh." Kelly said.

"Well, whatever." He pulled open a drawer and threw the triangle and striker inside with a clatter, then closed the drawer with his hip. He walked over and looked past Kelly at the food on the counter. "Kelly, you didn't have to do all this."

"I like a big breakfast, and I was up all night futzing with the program anyway. I would have made coffee, but I couldn't find any."

Jason opened the freezer and looked at the permafrost inside, "Hmmm. I might be out."

"Hey, campers. How goes our program?" Ricky had appeared in the archway holding a Styrofoam coffee cup with the words 'Mountain Grown' printed across the front in green.

Jason jumped and slammed the freezer door. “Christ! Don’t you know how to knock?”

Ricky knocked on the wall next to him. Once, and again, without humor.

They stood around awkwardly in the silence that followed.

“What do you want on your omelet, Chip?” Kelly asked with forced cheerfulness.

“Mushrooms and scallions?”

“Can do.” She cracked two eggs one-handed into a bowl, added a little milk, and began whisking them.

Chip watched her. “You know, Jason, we started to talk about this yesterday. I still don’t understand what Ryder was trying to accomplish with the whole bank account thing.”

Jason was back looking in the pantry for coffee. “He was worried about bringing all the money to the drug deal. He was afraid he would be killed for it.”

“Worked really well,” Ricky laughed and drank his coffee.

Chip persisted, feeling he was on the verge of understanding something. “So, he doesn’t bring money to the drug deal. He puts it in a bank account, and wires it out when the deal is done. But why hop the money all over hell and gone?”

Kelly dumped the eggs into a hot pan where they sizzled and threw up a gout of steam. She put a lid on the pan and adjusted the burner under it. "I guess he was also afraid of being killed and then having someone else do the wire. If the money keeps moving, only you know where it is, and you have to be alive to recover it."

Chip shook his head, "But how long does a drug deal take? You only need the money hopping that long – once, twice, maybe half a dozen times."

Jason stuck his head out of the pantry, "Where are you going with this, Chip?"

"I'm not sure. I just think that more than a couple of hops and there's no point to it."

Kelly had started chopping mushrooms. There was a steady thock, thock, thock as they thought about that. She stopped chopping. "That kind of fits with what I was thinking. How did he plan to get this money back? I mean, the wire program is running off in cyberspace somewhere. It won't stop until the end of the bank list. I don't think he could just stop it. I'm not certain that I'll be able to stop it if we find the money, and I'm sure I know more about computers than some movie producer."

Ricky leaned against the wall, "Maybe he didn't expect to get the money back. If he gets killed, the money would do just what it's doing now. It keeps moving, and no one can ever get it. Kind of a big parting fuck you."

Jason frowned, "This guy had money, cars, a big house. He's not planning on what to do if he gets killed. He's not planning to get killed at all."

"So what was he thinking?" Deirdre asked.

Kelly lifted the lid off the pan and threw in mushrooms and scallions, then closed the lid again. "That's the seven-million-dollar question."

Later Chip was eating his omelet. Kelly and Jason were eating a giant ham, cheddar and mushroom omelet that Kelly had cut in two. Ricky and Deirdre were just drinking their coffee. They were all sitting around the dining room table.

Chip gestured with his fork, "Try and put yourself in his place."

"OK," Jason said, "I'm a movie producer trying to make a drug deal. Now what?"

"You tell me."

He leaned back in his chair, pushing the partially finished omelet away from him, "OK, I'm a movie producer trying to make a drug deal," he began again, "I'm afraid of getting killed carrying seven million dollars in the trunk of my car."

"So you set up the money in a bank account," Kelly picked up the narrative, "with the plan to wire it to the drug dealers. It keeps the money out of your car."

"Right," Jason continued, "but even that doesn't feel very safe. I tell the dealers that I'm going to wire the money, and then they kill me and wire the money anyway."

"What keeps them from killing you after you wire the money?" Chip interrupted.

Jason twirled his fork on the tabletop, "I guess at some point you have to figure the deal is done, right?" He cocked his head, "They have the money, and you have the drugs. Presumably if you've survived up to that point, you're OK."

Chip nodded, "That makes sense."

"So, you set up the program that moves the money from location to location. They need you alive to get the money now. The deal should be safe." Jason stopped there, uncertain where to go next.

Kelly was pushing the last few bits of omelet around on her plate, "But the program he's set up has hundreds of banks listed, maybe thousands. Why go to all the trouble if you only need a few hops?"

"Which brings us back to where we began." Chip said glumly.

"Not exactly." Jason turned to Kelly, "All the extra hops must have been for something. Everything he's done so far has been to keep him alive, and I think this does too. Now, I'm on the dock, I've got the wire account, I've got the money moving. The drug dealer shows up. What happens if the deal goes wrong now?"

"Heh," Ricky barked a short laugh, "Then the shooting starts."

"If you're not going to say anything helpful," Kelly looked at him.

Jason interrupted her, "He's right. You've done everything you can think of to make the deal go smoothly, and yet it doesn't. The shooting starts. What do you do now?"

"Uh, run?" Chip shrugged.

Jason pointed a finger at him, "Exactly. These guys want you dead for whatever reason. You can't go home. You can't even go to the bank safely. You've got to keep moving."

Kelly understood, "And the money keeps moving too."

"Drug dealers don't forget shit. Take it from me." Ricky was rolling the coffee cup in his hands making a faint squeaking sound. "They'll hunt you to the ends of the earth. If that money ever stopped, and Ryder went to pick it up, they would be waiting for him."

"So the money keeps moving, and it moves in some kind of pattern, so some day he knows what bank to walk into and pick it up. Yeah, that works." Chip finished his omelet.

"Well, it sort of works. As I said yesterday, lots of these banks are too small to provide that kind of cash. If you need to pick up this money, why move it through banks that are too small to give it to you? Unless," Jason got up from the table and carried his and Kelly's dishes into the kitchen to load them into the dishwasher.

"Unless?" Chip called after him.

"Well," Jason came back and sat at the table, "if he simply downloaded a list of banks from somewhere, then unless he purposely edited out banks that are too small, they would be caught in the matrix by default. He keeps a copy of this list with him, and goes into a bank that is large enough to withdraw the money when it comes up on the wire schedule."

"That sounds like a good theory," Kelly said, "but something tells me you have another 'but' coming up."

Jason sighed and nodded, "But if he just downloaded a list of banks, wouldn't it be alphabetical, or at least some other pattern that was simple to spot? We haven't seen that pattern yet, so I don't know. Maybe Kelly's program will help with that."

Kelly drummed her fingers on the tabletop. "I figured I would bring this up after we were all done with breakfast.

We've got another problem with my program. The decoding program works great. We can simulate account requests and decode the replies without difficulty, but we can't run it until tonight."

"Why not?" Ricky demanded.

Kelly's first instinct was to be defensive, a feeling that she quickly quashed. She chose to ignore him and spoke to Jason. "We can make the account requests look like they come from the loan site. The bank computers in turn will automatically respond to the site making the request – it accomplishes that routing through the institute ID number. See the problem?"

"All the requests you make are going to show up on their computers, and they'll know they didn't make them." Jason replied. "Can't you just reroute the response message as well so the loan company will never see it?"

"I won't know which of the incoming messages are the ones we're looking for. I'd have to reroute everything, and then they'd know something is wrong because they won't be getting responses to their own requests. Our best bet is to run the search at night when their traffic is low. We reroute everything, look at the data, and forward on the packets that are intended for the loan company. There will be a delay in the forwarded packets, but I can't see as we can avoid that. I'm hoping that it's such a small loan site that it doesn't do much business at night so there won't be much to forward. Still, this is the internet, and everyone does business twenty-four seven."

"We should try and get some sleep then. It looks like an all-nighter."

"I'm going to go by my apartment. Finish packing for the move and grab my laptop. It might help us if we had one computer handling the codec and another doing the routing. I'll take a nap while I'm there." She took her purse off the counter and paused. "You guys can clean up?"

Chip looked at Jason and nodded, "We can handle it. Thanks for the food."

"Anytime. Well, any breakfast time. See you later. Oh, wait." She dug into her purse, pulled the picture of herself out and handed it to Chip.

"Wow, Kel. Wilma Dearing in the flesh."

Jason looked over his shoulder, "Zowee!"

Kelly smiled. "Glad you like it. I've got to go."

They heard the sound of her opening and closing the front door as she left.

Jason put the picture down on the dining room table and gathered up the remaining silverware and loaded it into the dishwasher. As he did so he gave Ricky and Deirdre a tight smile, "It's been lovely having you two over. If you'll let yourselves out, I'm going back to bed. Busy, busy night."

Ricky threw his empty coffee cup into the garbage, "Get dressed. You're coming with me."

Jason put the silverware in the sink, "Wow. You sounded just like Joe Friday when you said that. Didn't he, Chip?" He stepped towards Ricky, the counter between them. "Just where do you think we're going?"

"You wanted ID, a passport, driver's license, to get the money out of the bank. I made a few calls this morning from the motel, and it's all set up."

"So, go get the ID."

"You need to be there for the pictures."

Jason pointed to himself, "I'm going to be Ryder? Your connections, your ID. Why don't you be Ryder?"

"It's your idea to walk into the bank and get the money - you do it. You'll have the best fake ID made."

Jason was shaking his head. Ricky continued, "What if they ask something about the account? How would I know what to say? Besides, do I look like a guy who has seven million dollars in the bank? There's no way a bank is going to let a guy like me walk out the door with that kind of cash. You put on a pair of slacks and a dress shirt, you'll look like any other dot com millionaire dork. They'll never give you a second glance."

The crack about the dot com dork aside, Jason had to admit that Ricky was right. "Let me get in the shower."

*****

Jason came down the stairs wearing blue jeans, a white dress shirt, tie, and blue blazer.

"What's all this?" Ricky gestured at him.

"I'm the one going on the passport, right?"

"So?"

"I figure a guy with seven million dollars dresses nicely for his passport photo."

Ricky rolled his eyes, "Sure, why not? Let's go." He opened the door and stopped short going through it. "One more thing, give Dee the keys to your car."

"Yeah, I'm giving the keys to my fifty thousand dollar sports car to your girlfriend. Give her your keys."

"We're taking my car."

"We'll take my car."

Ricky shook his head, "The neighborhood we're headed into, you don't want to take your car."

"It's got an alarm system."

"I'm sure it's a very nice one. They'll almost certainly take it when they strip the rest of the car."

Jason blew out his breath. "What does she need the car for anyway?"

"To get our stuff from the motel. No point in paying for the room since we're here all the time."

"Who said anything about you moving in?"

"Just being practical. We're all in this together, and we're going to stay here until we find the money. You've got plenty of space. We can break into the empty house across the street and stay there if you would prefer."

"Crap." Jason muttered under his breath as he turned away.

He found Chip in the livingroom. "I don't have time to explain it all now, but could Deirdre borrow your car?"

"Sure, I guess so."

"Thanks." Jason would have offered Chip the Porsche, but knew that his friend couldn't drive a stick. "Problem solved." he said as he went by Ricky and out the door.

Deirdre came out behind them with Chip's keys. She wore cut off jean shorts, a man's white dress shirt knotted at her waist, and knee-high, low-heeled cowboy boots. Jason thought she looked like a blonde Daisy Duke impersonator.

She got into Chip's car. Ricky and Jason got into Ricky's.

As he was closing his door Ricky said, "One second." and got back out, jogged over to Chip's car, and leaned in the driver's side window.

Out of sight of Jason he slid the gun from his belt and pushed it under the seat between Deirdre's feet. "Keep an eye on this for me."

"What are you doing with a gun? After 'Frisco you said no more guns."

"I changed my mind. Seven million dollars on the line, you bet your sweet little ass I have a gun."

"I don't want it." She started to reach under the seat.

Ricky's hand shot out and grabbed her forearm, clamping down on the soft flesh painfully. "Look, the guys I'm going to see don't like guns, and I don't want to take the risk that they might see me carrying it. In a choice between upsetting them or you, I choose you. Now shut up and do as you're told."

He released her arm and she rubbed it where a bruise was already appearing. "Fine." she said and gave the ignition key a viscous twist.

Ricky went back to his car.

*****

They drove into an area just outside of downtown LA so deteriorated that it took Jason by surprise. He didn't think anything like it existed outside of third-world countries or post-apocalyptic action movies. Building after building was abandoned, some with plywood nailed over the windows and doors, others with the plywood ripped off, doorless doorways and glassless windows gaping. People had taken up residence in some of these shells; a black teenager watched with hooded eyes from an open window frame three stories up as they drove by. They passed one block where nothing at all stood, the space strewn with broken piles of brick and steel and concrete.

Ricky slowed at the intersections, sped up again in between. Jason thought that he was looking for a street sign, which Jason found kind of funny given that he hadn't see a standing sign pole, streetlight, or parking meter in over five blocks, though stumps sheared off near ground level indicated that they had once been there.

"I hope the food is good, because the atmosphere is shit," Jason said.

Ricky looked over at him, "What the fuck are you talking about?"

Jason recoiled a little involuntarily, "Just a joke."

"Yeah, well, you joke with these people," he turned his attention back to the road, "they'll cut your tongue out."

"What lovely people you know."

The desolation continued for some distance, the glass and steel towers of downtown always visible in the distance, shimmering like a mirage.

Ricky finally pulled over at a building that was distinguished only by the fact that some of its window glass was intact. The lowest floor had once been a neighborhood grocery store, its two big plate glass windows covered by plywood covered in graffiti. A stocky man was leaning against the building entrance wearing jeans and a flannel shirt with the sleeves torn off, his arms and shoulders covered with slabs of overlapping muscles like armor. His head was shaved bald and oiled so that it gleamed whitely in the sun.

He heaved himself away from the building and walked to the car, looking every bit like the proverbial brick shithouse. Jason rolled down his window and the man leaned into the car, his forearms resting on the frame. Jason noticed a tattoo of a black widow spider on the back of one hand, on the web of skin between his thumb and forefinger.

"No parking, gentlemen." His voice was surprisingly soft, almost feminine. Jason wondered if steroids caused that.

"I'm Ricky. I'm here to see Frank. I called ahead."

"Hold on." He stood up and pulled a cell phone from the breast pocket of the flannel shirt, dialed, and spoke for a moment. He hung up and leaned back into the car. "Go on in. Leave the keys in the car."

Ricky turned off the engine and got out of the car.

Jason waited for the man to step back so he could open the door, but it became clear after several seconds that he wasn't going to. Jason opened the door just a little, careful not the hit the man, and wormed his way out of the car. Standing up next to him Jason realized he was an inch or two taller than the other man, but probably a third as wide.

"Your keys too," the man held his hand out to Jason.

"It's not even my car."

"Keys." The man demanded.

"Fine, whatever." Jason dug his keys out of his pants pocket and tossed them to the man who snatched them out of the air.

Jason realized he has lost whatever chest thumping, hunter apeman contest has just transpired, and lost badly. Fuck it, he thought, as he joined Ricky and they entered the building.

The inside was in much better condition than Jason had expected. Fresh drywall, neither painted nor taped, hung on the walls. Bare bulbs in ceramic sockets suspended from the ceiling every dozen or so feet provided adequate lighting. This building had electricity, Jason realized, while most of the other buildings along the street didn't appear to.

A doorway at the end of the hallway opened and they walked into a room that looked a whole lot like a Kinkos – fluorescent light bars along the ceiling, computers, large printing and copying machines, and binding and laminating equipment. An incredibly fat man was at one of the computers. A huge bodybuilder leaned against the wall and could have been a twin for the man outside, except that his skin was the color of a ripe eggplant.

"You Frank?" Ricky asked.

The man at the computer spun around on his chair's casters, "You're Ricky. Tim said you were OK, or you wouldn't be here, understand?"

"Yeah, well, Tim's a good," Ricky began.

"Friend, cellmate, butt-buddy, whatever." Frank

interrupted. "No special deals for friends of friends. You wanted the full ID package. That's passport, driver's license, and credit card. The passport will be perfect, right down to some entrance and exit stamps, because a worn passport always gets less attention than a crisp, new one. Driver's license will clear a records check, and simply show a California resident with a clean driving record. The credit card will just be a Visa with a five-thousand-dollar credit limit. You pay the bills and the card is as good as any other. We take the pictures now, and it will all be ready in about an hour. Twenty-five hundred dollars now, another twenty-five hundred when they're done, cash or credit cards are fine."

"Great." Ricky nudged Jason with an elbow, "Pay the man."

Jason swallowed, his throat suddenly dry. He smiled weakly. "Just a second." He took Ricky by the arm and walked him back to the door. "Pay him? With what?"

"Ricky looked at Jason like he was retarded. "Put in on a charge card."

"Hello? Does a two hundred dollar balance in the bank ring a bell? House payments I can't make? Car payments I can't afford? My credit cards are so maxed out that they couldn't get me into a Sunday matinee at the Bijou."

"Shit!" Ricky hissed.

"Maybe he'll let us put in on the new charge card once he gives it to us?"

"Is there a problem?" The fat man had rolled up right behind them without either of the noticing. "I don't want to hear that you came here without the money, that I've wasted my time. And Tim vouched for you, which makes him look bad, which probably won't make him too happy either."

"We," Jason started to say, with no idea whatsoever what the next word out of his mouth would be.

"I'll take the watch." Frank said suddenly.

Jason blinked. "What? This?" He pointed to his watch. "It's a Fossil. Thirty-nine ninety-five at Macys."

"Not your watch. His." He pointed to Ricky. Ricky pulled up his sleeve and Jason got a flash of gold and diamonds. "This is a Rolex. It's worth way more than five thousand dollars."

"What it's worth here is five thousand dollars, plus safe passage. Now, do you hand it over, or should I have Milo take it from you?"

Ricky puffed up, "I'd like to see him try."

"As a matter of fact so would I, but don't flatter yourself. Milo has a third degree black belt in taekwondo, and he's armed, which you're not. Trust me, I know. You walked through a metal detector built into the walls of the hallway. If you had set it off we would have opened the door just far enough to stick out a shotgun barrel and pull the trigger. Shoot first, ask questions and replace the sheetrock later."

Jason understood now why they had taken his keys. It probably avoided a lot of unnecessary sheetrock work.

Ricky undid the catch on his watch and handed it to the man, who bounced it in his hand twice, feeling the weight, and then slid it into his pocket. "Outstanding. Let's take some pictures."

An hour later they left the building, Jason carrying a

Ziplock bag with the passport, license, and credit card in it. He was amazed that, although he was certainly no expert, the passport looked genuine to him. Holding the license side by side against his own, he was unable to tell the difference.

They both blinked as they exited the building into the bright sunshine.

"I'm taking the price of that watch out of your share."

Jason shrugged, "Yeah, whatever."

"That watch cost way more than five thousand dollars."

"Uh-huh." He gave Ricky a small smile and looked up and down the street. "Where's your car?"

Ricky looked around, realizing for the first time that both his car and the guy who had been there were gone. "Fuck!" He shouted. He turned to go back inside but then remembered Milo and decided not to. He stomped up the street to the end of the block and glanced both ways and, evidently not seeing his car, stomped back.

Jason stayed right where he was in front of the door. He didn't feel safe standing there, but he knew it was better than walking ten blocks through no man's land to get back to any semblance of civilization, the image of the teenager looking down at him firmly in mind. He also knew he didn't want to be there when night fell, though he had a few hours before he had to start worrying about that. He wished he had his cell phone with him, but he had left it charging on the nightstand this morning.

Jason was surprised at how quiet the street was without the background of normal city noises – voices, other cars, air conditioners, construction machinery. There were no birds or other animal noises either. It was probably quieter on this street corner less than five miles from downtown Los Angeles than in even many rural areas.

They didn't wait long. Both car and man returned about fifteen minutes later, the car covered in a thin layer of dust but otherwise undamaged. He pulled the car to the curb where Ricky stood fuming and Jason just stood.

He got out of the car and held the door open for Ricky like a valet returning a car at a restaurant. "You're low on gas, and the timing sounds off. Did you replace the timing belt at 120,000 miles?"

Ricky got in without a word and pulled the door closed.

The man shrugged and said, "Your keys are in the glove compartment" over the top of the car to Jason.

"Thanks." Jason said just to say something, and because his mother had drummed courtesy into him at a very young age.

Ricky pulled the car away from the curb almost before he was completely inside.

*****

Deirdre drove on autopilot, the cars around her barely registering on her consciousness. If the SUV in front of her had chosen that moment to slam on the brakes, she probably would not have reacted until lodged in its trunk. Instead almost all her attention was focused on her seat, which actually felt warm to her, as if the gun underneath were highly radioactive.

At the motel she stuffed things at random into the garbage bags that served as her luggage. She pondered the situation.

Question: What did Ricky want a gun for? OK, that was a stupid question. He wanted the gun for the same reason he did everything – it made him feel in control.

Next question: Was he going to shoot anyone?

She carried the bags out of the room and threw them into the backseat two at a time.

Her first answer, that he was manipulative but not a killer, shriveled and died on the vine. The Ricky she had seen over the past few days – consumed, driven to the point of obsession – was a Ricky that she was having trouble predicting. And though the little voice in her head refused to put it into so many words, the cold feeling that was forming in the pit of her stomach spoke volumes.

Ricky would kill for seven million dollars.

As she finished loading the car and walked to the motel office, she ran through her options.

Do nothing? Not an option. What if she just got rid of the gun? Well, he would get another one. Could she leave, just take Chip's car and go? Beyond the usual problem that she had no cash, she had to admit to herself that the pull of the money was strong. If they found it, if they got it, then she would find a way to get her share and get away from Ricky once and for all.

At the office, she tossed the room keys onto the counter, then went back to the car, started it, and nosed out into midday traffic. She remained no more certain of what to do than an hour ago when she had started thinking about it.

Given the neighborhood the motel was in, she came upon another option almost immediately. A nearly-abandoned strip center had a run-down Laundromat at one end and a pawn shop at the other, half a dozen shuttered stores between them. The pawn shop exterior was stucco painted a faded blue, with big plate glass windows across the front displayed a bicycle, a bag of rusty gold clubs, an exercise machine, and a large fluorescent orange sign with black letters a foot high that read "GUNS."

She pulled into the parking area and into a space in front of the pawn shop. The "GUNS" sign filled her windshield. He had a gun, so she would get a gun – that made sense, right? Could she shoot him? If he was going to shoot her, she was damn sure she could, the problem being how much warning she would get. What if he was going to shoot someone else? There she was a good deal hazier, and as she sat in the car looking at the sign she realized that this idea was half-baked at best. Still, better half-baked than not baked at all.

There was only one other car down at this end of the lot that she assumed belonged to an employee. She hoped the employee was male, and alone – if female or one of those mom and pop shops, she would have to look for another pawn shop, and she didn't have a lot of time. If Ricky got back from his errand before she did, she probably wouldn't be able to come up with an excuse that would satisfy him. All she was supposed to do was go to the motel, get their stuff, and come back. Even she, he would gladly point out, couldn't fuck that up.

She didn't have any cash, but if there was a living breathing male employee in that store, she didn't think that was going to be a problem. She had used her body to get things for herself in the past, and more recently for Ricky. Her body was a tool, the best she had, and she would use it in whatever way necessary.

Deirdre tousled her hair and touched up her lipstick using her reflection in the car rearview mirror to check the results. The gun would probably cost several hundred bucks; she had better go with the hard sell. She unbuttoned and untied her shirt, and then retied it just below her breasts. The cups of her bra pulled down a little and the bra straps off her shoulders, and the dress shirt became almost like a bikini top with only the knot holding it closed. She smiled at the mirror, blew herself a kiss, shrugged her shoulders and giggled – all systems go.

With a lot of hip rolling she walked into the shop. An electronic chime sounded as she opened the door, but the squeal of the rusty spring on the door was almost as loud.

There was no one else in the store that she could see. Three rows of wooden shelving broke the space into four aisles that ran from front to back. Deirdre walked down the nearest aisle, the sound of her boots deadened on the worn linoleum floor tiles. The shelves were crammed with merchandise from all eras. Manual typewriters gathered dust next to electronic models. Boom boxes were jammed in next to old transistor radios, their cases yellowed with age, and sleek Walkmen in bright metallic colors. One shelf contained a jumble of Barbie dolls and accessories, including a hot pink motor home that could have been the one she had had as a little girl. Another held an Atari game system and a stack of game boxes, their colors faded with age.

She approached a glass case that served as a counter at the back of the store. A flower print curtain covered a doorway behind it leading to some other space beyond. No one had as yet appeared in response to the chime. Maybe she could just take what she needed and leave?

Rifles and shotguns were in a wall rack behind the counter, a length of chain running through and around their trigger guards closed with a padlock. Jewelry, mostly large pieces made of gold-colored metal and cut glass, was visible through the greasy top of the case in front of her. She moved to her right to another section of the case that held guns and various knives. Several large-barreled revolvers and a matte black semi-automatic were all too large to keep concealed from Ricky. A smaller revolver, maybe a snub-nosed 38, looked so rusty Deirdre thought it might not fire. Next to that however was a brushed nickel-plated semi-automatic. It was very small, probably a 22, and though a little dusty looked to be in a good condition.

Was the case unlocked? She looked again at the unmoving curtain. Down at the end of the counter a video camera hung on a wall bracket, its amber light glowing softly. Was anyone watching? She edged farther to her right, breathing shallowly, the cut through the counter lying in that direction.

The curtain rustled and parted, and an old man shuffled out leaning heavily on a metal cane with a rubber tip that squeaked on the floor as he moved. He was old, but not ancient, probably somewhere in his seventies. He had a full head of hair that was closer to white than gray, and cut in a simple bowl shape around his head, covering the tops of his fleshy ears. He was soft but not fat, his skin hanging in loose folds on his face, giving little or no clue as to what he might have looked like when he was younger.

Deirdre knew that she had done much, much worse.

"I was upstairs watching TV. Figured if you were here to rob the place you'd be long gone by the time I made it down all those blasted stairs, and besides, the camera would catch you." He indicated the camera on the wall with a bob of his head. "And if you were here to buy something it wouldn't kill you to wait five minutes." His voice was surprisingly strong, through all his consonants were rounded off by the presence of maybe only a dozen teeth in his head.

"Well," Deirdre said, her voice modulated carefully into a sort of breathy Marilyn Monroe, "My crazy ex-boyfriend won't leave me alone, and I need to get a gun."

"I have some guns," the man said lamely, as if the guns weren't in the case right in front of both of them. "He do that to you?" He pointed at her arm with the hand not busy with the cane.

Deirdre looked at her arm and was surprised how dark the bruise from Ricky's hand had become. It didn't hurt that much. She swallowed audibly, nodded, and made her eyes big, "Uh-huh." She leaned one arm on the counter and rested her chest on her arm, pushing her breasts even farther up and out of her shirt. "But I'm afraid that I don't have much money."

The way his eyes locked right in Deirdre knew that she had him.

"If you don't have any money, what do you have to, um, trade?"

Without a word Deirdre came around the counter, took the old man's hands, and put them on her chest. The cane fell to the floor with a ringing sound. His balance upset, the man stumbled back, clutching at her breasts for balance until he regained his footing, his back against the rifle case. The length of chain around the guns rattled. He leaned forward to kiss her, his mouth making wet, smacking noises. She put a hand on his chest to stop him, then went down onto her knees and opened his pants.

She took him in her mouth as he clung to the rifle stocks. His mouth hung open and he made a huh-huh-huh-huh sound like a car with a dying battery trying to turn over.

As he finished, only a minute or two later, his knees buckled and he slid down the wall. His penis pulled from her mouth with a sound like a cork from a bottle, and his semen dribbled down the front of his unbuckled pants.

He breathed heavily from his seat on the floor. “Hell of a thing. Just when you get up and think it’s going to be a day like every other. Here are the keys.” He unsnapped a ring of keys from his belt. “It’s the fifth key on the ring past the bottle opener. Take any gun you want; I wasn’t selling anything anyway. Shit, I haven’t had a customer except you in nearly three weeks.”

Deirdre counted to the fifth key and found, though stiff, the lock popped open. She reached in and took out the small automatic. It took her a little searching to find the release and pull the clip. She ratcheted the slide to make certain the gun was empty – it was. After reinserting the clip she thumbed the safety and dry-fired the gun several times. It sounded OK to her. She had pretty much just exhausted everything she knew about handguns.

She put the gun in her purse, which was standing on the counter, picked it up, and started to leave.

“If you want some bullets for that gun,” he had pushed himself up the wall to a standing position and buckled but did not bother zipping up his pants, “that’s going to be extra.”

Deirdre sighed to herself and turned back, all smiles and bright eyes.

The man was taking shuffling steps towards her without the cane, his hands grasping open and closed in front of him and his half-flaccid penis hanging from his fly. He looked to her like an escapee from Night of the Living Perverts.

She arched her back and thrust her chest out at him, “What would you like, sugar?” she said in a Southern Belle accent.

“Let’s see them titties.” the man smiled toothlessly.

*****

The gun carefully secreted in her purse, the depths of which Ricky had never shown a particular desire to plumb, and having arrived home before Ricky and Jason, Deirdre put on a tiny gold bikini and decided to lie by the pool for a while.

It was nice. Very nice. The pool was nothing special, just an oval gunite hole in the ground, but it was positively palatial compared to anything she had ever known.

If they found the money, could this be her future?

It was the first thought she had had of a future that didn't involve prison bars or a shallow, unmarked grave somewhere in the desert in a long time.

She heard the sliding glass door open and Jason and Ricky came out to the pool.

"Did you get the papers?"

"We got them." Ricky grumbled. "Christ, I need a beer." He went back into the house, slamming the slider closed behind him.

Though wearing sunglasses, Deirdre shielded her eyes from the sun with her hand and looked up at Jason. "What's wrong with him?"

"They took his watch for payment."

"The Rolex? Ooh, no wonder he's in a bad mood."

"Did he pay a lot for it?"

Deirdre barked a laugh. "Plenty. Lemme see." Deirdre held out a grasping hand.

Jason fumbled with the plastic bag and gave her the license, passport, and credit card.

She glanced at the license then flipped open the passport. “A pleasure to meet you, Mr. Ryder.”

He bowed, “The pleasure is mine.”

“Wow, a real, live charm school graduate.” She noticed the credit card. “Oooh,” she squealed, “I’m going shopping.” She mimicked tucking it into her bikini top, and then handed all the papers back to him.

He put them back into the sandwich bag and zipped it up.

“Do you think you can find the money?”

Jason moved to sit down on the chaise lounge and Deirdre scrunched over to make room for him. “The more I think about Kelly’s idea, the more I like it. It’s fast, and far more elegant than the brute force hacking I was doing.”

“She’s smart, huh?”

“About computers? One of the best.”

“And she’s very pretty.” Underneath her sunglasses Deirdre looked sideways at Jason, carefully gauging his response.

He squirmed. He didn’t understand why that statement from Deirdre should make him uncomfortable, but it did. There was a bottle on the ground near his feet and he picked it up, mostly just to have something else to look at, other than Deirdre, so she wouldn’t see his discomfort. It was a bottle of suntan oil.

“Oil me up?” Deirdre asked. She flipped onto her

stomach on the chaise and untied her top.

He paused, and then shrugged internally. The suntan oil was warm on his hands from the bottle sitting in the sun. Deirdre sighed contentedly as he rubbed her shoulders. He worked down her back, increasingly conscious of how little clothing she was wearing. The smell of coconut oil rising off her skin was making him lightheaded.

"Mmmm. That feels nice. You have strong hands."

"Lots of typing."

She laughed, probably more strongly than the joke warranted. "Do you think I'm pretty?"

In point of fact, Jason thought that Deirdre wasn't just pretty, she was beautiful. In comparison to Kelly's clean, girl-next-door beauty, Deirdre radiated the raw, sexual heat of a centerfold. Applying a metaphor that generations had been using for years, he felt like he was in his own, personal Ginger/MaryAnn dilemma. "Sure." He replied, and then inwardly kicked himself. 'Sure' was just one microscopic step up from 'Neat-o.'

"All finished." He wiped the slight excess oil off on her forearms.

"Aren't you going to do my legs?"

"OK." He started down at her feet. He calves were firm, and her thighs taught and muscular. When one hand accidentally slipped between her thighs she closed her legs together, trapping it there. Jason jumped, startled, and pulled to free his hand, which came out easily because of the oil.

Deirdre laughed again, throaty and sensual.

"Um, look, what's going on here?"

Deirdre rolled partially onto her side. "What do you want to have happen?"

In her present position Jason couldn't help but notice that one breast was almost fully exposed, and Jason was caught between a carnal urge to stare and a Catholic upbringing that made his avert his eyes.

"Am I interrupting something?" Kelly said, standing a few feet away.

Jason's head whipped around; he hadn't heard the door open. He looked from Kelly to Deirdre and back again without thinking of anything to say.

"I figured that since we're going to be working all night, you guys might want to do dinner. Chip told me that you were out here, and, um, you two can talk it over and we'll be inside when you decide something." Kelly moved at a fast, awkward walk back indoors.

Jason jumped up to stop her, but the door slid closed before he had gone more than a few steps.

"Jason." Deirdre called.

He looked back.

She was clutching her bikini top to her chest. "I'm sorry."

He held his hands up in a stop gesture, then turned and went inside.

*****

Dinner, take-out Mexican for all, was a little awkward

to say the least. Ricky was sullen, still upset about the watch. Kelly was unusually quiet, answering questions from Jason about the codec in simple yes's and no's, and she couldn't be drawn into a game of TV trivia by Chip. Jason interpreted her mood, not as angry or jealous, but disappointed, though possibly he was projecting his own feelings somewhat.

It hadn't helped matters that Deirdre had continued to wear her bikini through dinner with only a small T-shirt thrown on top. Chip, and Jason, and even Ricky couldn't help but keep glancing at her out of the corners of their eyes. Jason heard Kelly mutter "Men," under her breath more than once.

When Kelly finally announced that it was probably late enough for them to run the codec, it came as a relief. They moved to the upstairs bedroom and got started.

4 Days Earlier

Jason and Kelly sat side by side at the small desk, each with a laptop open in front of them, so close together that their shoulders nearly touched. Jason could feel Kelly beside him as a warm presence, as though she emitted heat from some great internal source. He could see her profile out of the corner of his eye, and he found himself often turning to look at her, her teeth clamping down gently on her lower lip, a strand of dark hair hanging down one cheek unnoticed as she worked. If she noticed him staring at her, she gave no indication. His face felt hot.

It had been almost six hours now, encoding account requests and decoding the responses. Kelly did the bulk of the encoding. Jason did the decoding, as well as sending on packet data that they intercepted unintentionally as part of the internet forwarding program. True to Kelly's prediction, the loan company had very little web traffic at night, and so the number of packets that needed to be passed on was mercifully few.

Starting with the first bank, both to test both Kelly's program and Jason's computer hacking, they had followed the money through more than two hundred banks. Jason's shoulder's ached and his head felt stuffed with cotton, but they were making real progress.

Chip, Ricky, and Deirdre had begun the night watching them work with rapt attention, as though they were some great sporting event. After six hours, Chip was pacing around aimlessly, Ricky was sitting on the bed staring at his shoes, and Deirdre, having changed from her bikini into jeans and a sweater, had curled up in a ball on one end of the bed like a cat and fallen asleep.

Jason dissected another packet using a text editor and then ran it through the decoding program. "Bank of America, account number 2153628184."

"2153628184" Kelly mimicked as she typed.

The response packet came in almost immediately, and Jason set about decoding that one.

“Anyone want some coffee?” Chip asked.

“That would be great,” Jason said. Kelly simply held up her empty coffee mug, continuing to type with the other hand.

The program finished decoding, “Bank of America, account number 2153628184. Damn, there it is again.”

Kelly looked at Jason’s screen, “That’s no error. It’s got to mean something.”

“What’s up?” Chip leaned over Jason’s shoulder.

“I’m not sure. We get a transfer request from one bank to another here, see?” he pointed to a wire transfer request open in a window on his computer screen. “Then the next transfer request seems to start and end in the same bank account,” he pointed to another transfer request in a different window, “but that’s nuts. Why would you wire a request to transfer from an account to the very same account?”

“And that’s not a mistake?”

Kelly shook her head, “That’s the third time it’s happened. The first couple of times I thought it might be an error in the encoding program; maybe I wasn’t clearing the buffer correctly between executions. Now I don’t know what to think.”

“I’m going to print this one out.” Jason squared a stack of paper and loaded it into the printer. “It’s even stranger than that, because the next transfer request is going to be the same, or at least it was the last two times.”

Kelly encoded the wire information request and sent it off. When it came back, Jason decoded it.

He nodded, "See, another wire transfer request from account number 2153628184 to account number 2153628184. I'll print this one too."

Ricky leaned forward on the bed, "So let me get this straight. The money is transferred into a bank account, then there are two transfers that appear to take place within the bank, then the money is sent on to the next bank."

Jason pulled the two printouts from the printer, "That's about the size of it." He held them side by side, looking at them.

"So, they're doing something with the money while it's at the bank."

"That's pretty obvious, but what?"

"Beats the shit out of me. That's for you geniuses to figure out."

"What about some kind of internal account transfer," Chip asked. "Like transferring the money from savings to checking."

"It's not a bad idea," Kelly had turned in her chair and was resting an arm on Jason's shoulder. "But checking and savings accounts would have different account numbers."

"You said it's happened three times. Once per day since the drug deal?" Chip pulled at his lower lip with thumb and forefinger.

Jason and Kelly looked at each other. "I'm not sure," Jason began slowly. "We could check the data and see."

Kelly looked at the clock in the corner of her computer, "We can do that later. It's after 5AM now, and I want to let the internet forwarding program go by 6, before the traffic picks up."

The light outside was a muted gray. Dawn would not be that far behind.

Jason handed off the last account data to Kelly who encoded the next request, the response to which Jason decoded. They felt that they were under the clock now, and picked up the pace. Jason's head became a whirl of account numbers, banks, and decoding matrices. He was almost completely on autopilot, glancing only at the bank name and account information before moving on, and therefore almost missed completely what a decoded packet displayed forty-five minutes later. It struck him absolutely speechless.

"Jason, do you have the next account location?" Kelly asked.

"Holy shit." He said softly.

"What?"

"There it is."

"There what is?" Kelly looked towards his screen. When she saw what he had seen, she said, "Holy shit is right!"

"Is that what I think it is?" Chip asked. He leaned over between them, clutching at Jason's shoulder so tightly that a half-moon of fingernail turned white on each finger. Jason looked at Chip's hand.

Ricky got up from the bed so see, jostling Deirdre awake as he did so. She sat up and blinked sleepily, before joining them around the small laptop screen.

The account balance showed seven million, two hundred seventy three thousand dollars and change. They crowded against each other, as if by getting closer to the computer screen they were somehow closer to the money.

"Get it! Get it!" Ricky said excitedly.

Jason looked at him. "Get it how?"

"Transfer it into one of your bank accounts or something."

"That would leave trail for someone to follow later. That's why we got the passport and driver's license, remember?"

"Besides," Kelly continued typing as she spoke, "we're just in the account information database. We can't actually move the money. The account wire transfer protocols are much more secure."

Ricky was hunched forward, shoulders tight, a bundle of energy without release. "So what can we do?"

"We can watch it transfer out."

A moment later the account balance rolled down to zero. They all, except Kelly, sagged slightly as if deflated. Kelly tapped out a few more keystrokes and hit 'Enter'. The screen cleared momentarily and then again displayed the account balance of more than seven point two million dollars.

"Look, it's back." Chip observed.

"No, I just followed it on to the next bank." She opened an internet browser in the corner of her screen. "This one's actually a small credit union near Ojai; total assets of less than three million dollars. The money passing through is going to make quite a blip on their balance sheet for twenty minutes."

"So what can we do?" Ricky tried again.

"I told you, we can't do anything. What we have is almost three hundred banks the money moved through over the last four days. If we can find the pattern, we can find the money – simple as that."

"But the money is right fucking there."

Kelly chose to ignore him and looked at her watch, "We done here?" She asked Jason.

Jason sat with his hands clasped and his fingers laced together on the desk in front of him. He hunched forward, his head rested on his hands, his eyes at the level of the screen. He didn't answer her.

She nudged him, "Jase?"

"Hmm?"

"It's after six. We should let the connection go."

He frowned, "I was just thinking."

"Thinking what?"

"Maybe I could open a dummy account, transfer the money into that, then from that into one of our accounts. When I delete the dummy account, the trail would be broken."

Kelly noticed the packet traffic to the site starting to pick up, as if the internet was photoelectric, and the rising sun was bringing it to life. She started using her computer to forward the rerouted packets. She spoke as she worked, "The account would still be logged, as would the transfer in and the transfer out. It would just take a little longer to follow the trail, but it would still be there."

"What about starting our own wire transfer program, and running the money through a couple of hundred banks before retrieving it."

Traffic was really starting to pick up. Kelly knew it was only a matter of time until someone noticed the packet lag and started searching for their forwarding routine. "We've already followed the money through hundreds of banks ourselves. You don't think someone else, or the government for that matter, could do the same? We need to close the connection before someone discovers us."

Jason drummed his fingers on the desktop. "Maybe we don't need the pattern. We could transfer the money to a dummy account and then use the passport to go in and get the cash that way."

"We still don't have the wire transfer protocols. And what if the protocols are logged? Then as soon as we move the money it flags right back to this computer."

Jason thought about that for a moment.

The bandwidth meter on the modem ran up into the red. The packet traffic was exceeding the DSL line capacity. Shit, Kelly thought to herself, I thought this was a small loan company. Her fingers flew over the keys in a blur. She misrouted a packet and sent it off to god knows where, never to return. How long before someone noticed that?

"What if I-" Jason began.

"Jason!" Her voice held and edge, fear and warning at the same time. "We've got to close the connection!"

"But maybe-"

The modem locked up, packets jamming up on their IP, the DSL bandwidth much too low to handle the server traffic. Her screen was awash in data packets she could no longer make heads or tails of. Her keyboard was sluggish as the CPU stuttered and peaked.

"No!" She reached past him and yanked the modem cable from his computer. The open windows on computer screen closed slowly at first, then with increasing speed as the CPU cleared the data backlog until she was left with just the root window and its blinking cursor.

"You know, I think I could have," Jason began.

"Let it go, Jason." She scrubbed her hands against her face and stopped with her fingers pressing against her eyes. "Just let it go."

*****

Everyone was silent as Kelly unplugged her laptop, folded the screen down, and placed it within the shaped nest of the nylon carry bag. She ran the zipper around the circumference closing the case. The mouse and power cord went into a pocket on the side.

"So, what do we do now?" Chip asked.

"Well," Jason had left his laptop running and was scrolling through the routing records they had generated, "we look at the banks, find the pattern, find the money. Right, Kel?"

"What I do now is I go home and get some sleep. The

money will still be out there later."

Ricky spoke from where he was leaning against the wall, "How can you be sure? What if someone else finds the money first?"

Kelly shrugged, "Yeah, I guess if someone else is looking for it and they find it, or some bank computer flags the account activity it and pulls it out of circulation, then it's gone."

"Gone? And that's it?" Ricky made a slashing motion with his hand.

"Yeah, gone." Kelly put the strap of the computer carryall over one shoulder and went for the door. "What do you want me to say?"

Ricky moved to stand in her path. "I want you to say that you'll get the money back. We had it right there."

"You don't know what you're talking about. You act like there was a suitcase full of money lying on the bed and I threw it out the window. The money was caught in a financial routing program. There was no way to just get it." She curled her fingers in the air like quotation marks around the word 'get.' "Maybe Jason can explain it to you. I need to get some sleep."

Ricky didn't get out of her way. "You're not going anywhere. You're staying here and finding the money."

"No," Kelly said with exaggerated clarity, "I'm going home." She turned her head to look at Chip sitting on the bed. "Jesus, did he just crawl out of a bad gangster movie?" She pitched her voice low and goofy, "You're not going anywhere, Mugsy."

Ricky stepped up close to her, way inside her personal

space. With his greater height he leaned over her, yelling down on her. "Is this all some fucking joke with you? That money was as good as ours, you worthless bitch, until you lost it! Now sit your ass down in that chair until you get it back!"

Kelly managed to fight the urge to step back, but it took every bit of her will. "You have no idea what the fuck you are talking about," she began, but Jason pulled her aside and stepped in front of Ricky. Jason's face was so red that Kelly wondered what his blood pressure must be at that moment.

"What the fuck is wrong with you?" Jason yelled into his face at point blank range. It was actually Ricky that took a half a step back. "This whole approach was all Kelly's idea. She got us here! She found the money! If we were still going my way we'd be two hundred banks in the past, so just shut up and back the fuck off!"

Ricky's eyes burned with rage but he said nothing.

"Can you write an IP tap and execute a bidirectional reroute in real time? Can you build and fill a direct memory map of unformatted and unspecified data types at full system bandwidth? What the fuck do we even need you for? If you're giving me a choice between her and you, I'll take her hands down!"

"You don't get that choice," Ricky smirked.

Jason ground his teeth and clutched his aching head with both hands. He felt like he was having a stroke and thought for a moment that he might welcome it. He squeezed his eyes shut. "Get out," he said simply and in a completely normal tone of voice.

"What did you say?"

Jason eyes snapped open. He dropped his hands from his head and his voice exploded. "You heard me! Get out!"

"You can't tell me to get out."

"Are you deranged or just stupid? Of course I can! I want you out of my house!"

Ricky stood stock still with the muscles in his face bunching as he worked his jaw. A hundred angry responses balanced on the tip of his tongue, but he realized that he had absolutely no way of winning this confrontation and everything to lose. Without another word he spun on his heels and left. A moment later the sound of the front door slamming shook the entire house.

Jason stood with beads of sweat on his face, his hands clenched in shaking fists at his sides.

"Jase, are you all right?" Chip was at his side.

"I don't know. I don't know. I think so. Can you go make sure that he's gone?"

"Sure." Chip jogged out of the bedroom.

Jason turned to Kelly. She had her back to him, her head bowed, her shoulders trembling. He put a hand on her shoulder and turned her to him. Tears ran down her cheeks.

"Are you okay? Did he hurt you?"

"I'm sorry. I can't do this." She sniffed loudly. "This is all a mistake."

"Kelly, he's gone."

"And you don't think he'll come back? Of course he's

coming back."

"I'll deal with that when it happens."

She shook her head violently. "No. You can't possibly trust him. I can't. I can't do this anymore. I must have been insane." She shoved past him towards the door, lugging her computer case like it weighed three hundred pounds.

"Kelly, what about the money?"

She stopped at the doorway and turned back. "Forget about the money, Jason. That fucking psychopath is living in your house. And while you're sitting around waiting for Ricky to come home, you might want to ask yourself how he knew that you had only $200 left in your checking account."

"What? I don't understand."

Kelly shook her head sadly, "You've really lost it, Jason. Seriously. And I'm not going to stay and watch. Have a nice life."

Jason tipped his head down and ran through the conversation in his mind from when Ricky had first come knocking on his door – was that only a day ago? How *had* he known my bank balance? When he looked up, the doorway was empty. "Kel?" He began, but when he heard the front door close he knew that it was too late, that she was already gone.

He sighed and leaned his back against the wall, and then slid down it until he was sitting on the floor.

Deirdre spoke to him from her spot on the bed from which she hadn't moved during the entire exchange. "Is there anything I can do?"

Jason had almost forgotten she was there at all. “No. I think I could use some breakfast though. Are you hungry?”

“Not really.”

“There’s leftover Chinese food.”

“For breakfast?”

“You’ve never had cold Chinese food for breakfast? That’s right, you never had Chinese food before last night. Trust me, leftover Chinese food is the breakfast of champions.”

“I’ll take your word for it.”

“I’ll go grab it.” Jason climbed slowly to his feet and left the bedroom.

“Could you bring me my purse?” Deirdre called after him. “It’s downstairs on the kitchen counter.”

As he came down the stairs, he ran into Chip coming in the front door.

“He’s gone; at least I think he is.” Chip said.

“He’ll be back; I’m sure of that. I just don’t know when.”

“What should we do?”

“I don’t think there’s anything we can do. He knows too much to cut him out, and in a twisted kind of way he has as much right to this money as we do. He’s just such an asshole.”

Chip shook his head sadly, “This is pretty fucked up.”

"Yes, it is," Jason replied. "Did Kelly say anything to you when she left?"

"No, not even goodbye. What was she supposed to say?"

"Nothing. I don't think she's coming back."

"Why? What happened?"

"You heard what happened."

"I mean after I left."

"She said she just couldn't do it. Believe me, I understand how she feels."

"I'll go talk with her."

Jason blew out his breath. "OK. Thanks."

"I'll be back later." He went out the front door.

Jason collected the takeout containers from the fridge plus two pairs of chopsticks. He retrieved Deirdre's purse from the counter, surprised at how heavy it was, and carried it and food upstairs. "Here." He handed the purse to her. "What do you have in there? Rocks?"

"Girl stuff."

"Heavy girl stuff."

"It does build up. I need to empty it out." She opened the catch and dug around inside, carefully keeping the gun out of sight. She removed a pack of cigarettes with a hot pink Bic lighter jammed into the cellophane sleeve and held them up. "Do you mind?"

"Can I have one?"

She shook two cigarettes from the pack and handed him one. "You smoke?"

"I did for a little while in high school." He held the tip into the flame of the lighter when she thumbed the wheel. "Gave it up in college. Still, it's like riding a bike, right?"

"I guess. I never had a bike. I once dated a guy who owned a motorcycle if that counts."

"No Chinese food, no bike. It doesn't sound like much of a childhood."

"It wasn't." Deirdre said seriously.

Jason frowned, "Sorry."

She waved her hand dismissively, the cigarette leaving a trail of smoke in the air, "It's in the past. Water over the damn parade."

The mixed metaphor struck Jason as kind of funny. He took his first drag from a cigarette in over five years, and exploded into a violent fit of coughing. "Maybe it's more like falling off a bike."

"You OK?"

He looked at the pack of cigarettes, now lying beside her on the bedspread. "Filterless Camels? You'll have to forgive my lungs. My cigarettes always had training wheels."

"Huh?"

"Never mind. It's another bike riding metaphor." He took another drag, this one shallower. It went down easier.

He affected a bad Humphrey Bogart impersonation. "So, what's a nice girl like you doing in a place like this?"

Deirdre laughed and batted her eyes, her voice a falsetto, "I'm trying to find seven million dollars. And yourself?"

"What a coincidence. Me too." The humorous tone drained from his voice as he thought about Kelly and what she had said. Was she going to come back? Could he find the money without her help?

Deirdre sensed the rapid change in his mood.

Poking around at the Chinese food with the chopsticks, neither of them ate very much. They sat instead and smoked the cigarettes down in silence, using an ancient 3.5" floppy disk Jason had found in a desk drawer as an ashtray. When they finished, Jason took the butts and ran them under the faucet in the hallway bathroom to put them out, then threw them and the floppy disk into the garbage pail under the sink.

When he got back to the bedroom she asked "You mind if I crash? I really need to get some sleep."

"Help yourself." He stood up, gathering the takeout containers in his arms.

She sat on the edge of the bed and reached behind herself to undo her bra. After shifting her shoulders and arms, in what almost looked like a magic trick to Jason, she pulled the bra out of one sleeve of her sweater without taking the sweater off.

"Tada," he said.

"What?"

“I’ve never seen a woman do that before.”

She looked at her bra, winked at him, and then tossed it on the floor. “Now who had the deficient childhood?”

She quickly undid her jeans and pushed them down and off, then swung her legs under the covers. Jason caught a flash of white satin and long, tan legs that made him instantly, almost in some primal, instinctual way, hard.

“I can’t sleep in them; they’re too tight.”

“Oh,” Jason said, unable to think of anything else.

“Tell me a bedtime story.”

“OK. Um. Once upon a time,” he began, and then stopped.

She looked beautiful, the fan of golden hair on the pillow, the outline of her body clearly visible under the thin covers. His attraction to her was undeniable, but at the same time the way things were with Kelly left him with a palpable ache. He felt like everything was spiraling out of control.

Deirdre shifted her position on the bed. “Doesn’t that even come with a ‘The End’?”

“Huh?”

“That has to be the worst bedtime story ever.”

“What? Oh, I’m sorry.”

“I’m kidding.” She reached out and pinched his side. Jason squirmed away. “I’m a little too grown up for bedtime stories, or hadn’t you noticed?”

"Yeah. I just have a lot on my mind."

"About finding the money?" she asked hopefully.

"Something like that." He got up and unplugged the laptop, wrapping the cables around the case. He moved to the room door carrying the computer and food. "You want this open or closed."

"Open is fine."

"I'll be downstairs. Call if you need anything."

"Good night, or I guess good morning." she called as he left.

But he didn't respond.

Deirdre sighed and lay on her back, staring at the ceiling.

Downstairs Jason dumped the laptop onto the coffee table, chucked the food back into the fridge, and threw the chopsticks into the sink. His head ached and his nerves felt scraped raw. He thought about trying to take a nap; maybe it would help clear his head, then stopped and stood at the bottom of the staircase with his hand resting on the newel post.

He had another thought.

He went out the front door, pulling his car keys from his pocket as he left.

He drove through the dawn-empty streets, arriving at his mother's nursing home just as morning visiting hours began. He went straight up to her room and to her side without acknowledging another human being.

"I don't know what to do, Mom." His voice was muffled by the covers into which he pressed his face. He sat in a chair leaning forward with his head against the bed, breathing deeply the scent of whatever fabric softener the nursing home used while trying futilely to recall the scent of his mother that had brought him such comfort and security as a child.

He lifted her hand from where it lay motionless on the covers and placed it upon his head. Realizing that it was probably crazy to do so, he nonetheless felt a little bit better.

Time was running out. Kelly was gone, and he didn't think he could find the money again without her. Chip had gone after her, but he didn't think he could convince her to come back. Ricky was out there, doing what he had no idea, cruising with the same casual intent of a shark, preparing to unleash a destructive force he could only guess at. And what did Deirdre want from him anyway?

"I can't find the money. I don't know how to get it even if I could. Kelly is probably right in leaving. It's the smart thing to do. Maybe if I'm lucky she'll convince Chip to stay away as well."

He thought back over the choices that had brought him to this place. He felt stupid and weak at the realization that if he had it to do all over again, he would probably end up here anyway. What else could he have done? What other options had he truly had?

"What happens to you if I just walk away? What would Ricky do if I just walked away? Would he even let me?" He murmured into eight-hundred-thread count Egyptian cotton.

He started when he felt a hand upon his shoulder. Mrs. Real spoke from behind him, "Mr. Taylor, are you alright?"

How long had she been standing there? What had he said, and what had she heard? He replied without lifting his head, "I'm fine, Mrs. Real."

"Yes, well, Mr. Taylor, we really need to discuss arrangements for locating a new facility for your mother."

"One more week, Mrs. Real." He groaned. "I told you two weeks, and that still leaves me one more week."

"I understand completely Mr. Taylor, but I think it prudent to," she began.

He lifted his head, his mother's hand sliding off and slumping back onto the bed, and looked at her, his eyes rimmed red from lack of sleep, dark circles under his eyes, "One more week, Mrs. Real." He said firmly. "You will have your money in one more week."

Her lipstick today was a fluorescent shade of violet. She must be colorblind, Jason thought.

Mrs. Real swallowed, clearly uncomfortable. "Very well, Mr. Taylor." She beat a hasty retreat from the room.

"One more week," he said again.

*****

Kelly took a cobalt blue coffee mug down from the shelf over the sink and wrapped it in a sheet of newspaper, taped down to ends with strips of scotch tape from a dispenser, and fit the package into a cardboard box on the counter. A tear slipped down one cheek, and she wiped it away irritably, leaving a black smudge of newsprint on her face. As she reached for another mug the doorbell rang.

Kelly navigated past mostly-packed boxes to the front door and found Chip standing there when she opened it.

"Hi, Kel, I, um," He just kind of petered out, uncertain of what he wanted to say.

She stepped back from the doorway and waved him inside, taking another swipe at her damp cheek as she did so.

He came in moving carefully past the boxes, looking around the living room and into the kitchen. "It's funny, but I never made it over here before. We always seemed to meet out somewhere or at Jason's. Wow, this is a really nice place."

"Thanks, I always liked it."

"You sure you can't keep it?"

"I've looked at the numbers a couple of different ways. The money just isn't there."

The mention of money opened up the yawning chasm between them of the subject they really didn't want to discuss.

Kelly went and looked out the window at the restaurant across the street. The air was warm and filled with the smell of warm tortillas; the breakfast crowd was just starting to drift in. She felt tired to the bone, the wasted night at the computer wearing on her heavily. More tears slid silently down her cheeks.

Chip stood with his hands in his pockets.

"I," She began, but at the same time Chip said, "We."

Kelly wiped at her eyes and turned from the window to rest her butt against the sill, her hands on the sill at her sides.

Chip laughed, Kelly smiled flatly.

"Go ahead," he said.

"I don't know why I'm acting this way. Jason's a big boy; he can take care of himself. But I'm worried."

Chip frowned but didn't say anything.

"He's going to get himself hurt. You both are."

Chip was touched by the irony of having himself included as an afterthought. "We need this money, Kelly."

"Don't you see?" She pushed away from the sill and approached him, "You only think you need it."

"If he doesn't get it, he's going to lose the house."

She spun away from him and went into the kitchen, snatching a mug from the shelf and quickly balling it up in a sheet of newspaper. "I know exactly what Jason stands to lose, but there's nothing I can do about it." She paused for a moment and then placed the mug into the box with great care. She looked at him, her eyes sad, "What about you? You've got a job; you've got a place to live. Can't you just let it go?"

"You want to know something funny?" He came into the kitchen, reached past her and took down a mug, and started wrapping it. "When I was lying on the boat at the dock and I heard about the money, the very first thought through my head was 'This money could really help Jason.' Swear to God, that's what I thought. But you know what? I'm tired of being good old Chip, everybody's friend Chip, poor old Chip. You and Jason. Ricky and Deirdre. What about me?"

Kelly was shaking her head, "Oh, Chip, I," she began.

"No, let me finish." He cut her off. "I look at me, I look at you, I look at Deirdre, and I know. OK? I know. I've lived in this body an awfully long time. It's the way I'm always going to be. You know what's going to make this body not matter anymore? Money, and lots of it. And not the kind of money I'm going to make at the fucking plastics factory."

"You're a nice guy, Chip."

He went right on as if he hadn't heard her. "Have I told you how much I hate working there? I'm still running the same injection-molding machine that I was running when I used to work there summers during high school. I haven't moved an inch in that place in ten years. And my dad's there, with the learning-the-business-from-the-bottom-up and someday-all-this-will-be-yours bullshit. He can keep it. I don't want it. I want this money. It's as simple as that. I want it."

Chip stood, practically panting, as if drained. Kelly was stunned at this side of Chip she had never seen before.

"No one likes to work, Chip," she began cautiously. "You think I like listening to my alarm go off? You don't think I'd rather spend my days at the beach or playing volleyball or reading or doing some cool coding; just doing what I want to do every day, and not planning my life from weekend to weekend? Even CEOs probably grumble about the two days a month that they get called off the golf course. It's part of life."

"Not for me. Not anymore."

Kelly couldn't think of anything to say to that, so she started packing plates, wrapping them individually and then stacking them in the box next to the mugs.

Chip sighed. "This isn't what I wanted to talk about at

all."

For several minutes the only sound in the room was the rattle of newspaper and the zip of the tape dispenser as they finished packing the rest of the dishes.

"So," he looked around at the boxes, "when are you moving?"

"Tomorrow afternoon."

"Do you need any help?"

"No. I'm only moving the little stuff. I have a moving company coming to take what little furniture is mine."

She folded over the flaps of the box they had been packing and wrote 'DISHES' on the side with a black magic marker. She rested her forearms upon the box.

Chip toyed with the serrated edge of the tape dispenser. "I told Jason that I would try to get you to come back and help us. I don't think he can find this money without you."

She shook her head, "I'm not so sure you'd find it with me, but it's not going to happen."

"I kind of knew you were going to say that, but I had to try." He shrugged. "I guess I'd better go."

A sudden, overwhelming feeling that it was all going to end horribly consumed her. Kelly threw her arms over his shoulders and hugged Chip fiercely. She leaned against him, the top of her head barely reaching his chin.

He awkwardly put his arms around her and patted her back. "It's going to be all right. It's going to be better than all right."

He let go of her, but she held onto him. He gently took her arms off his shoulders.

She swallowed down a lump in her throat. “Please,” was all she managed.

“We’ll call you when we find the money.”

Kelly tried to control her breathing. Chip turned from her and left the kitchen. “You don’t have to,” she started, but then stopped when she heard to sound of the apartment door closing.

She leaned back against the counter, put her head in her hands, and silently started to cry.

*****

Nothing fit. No pattern existed. There was no alignment in the data, neither alphabetical nor numerical, in street, town, zip code, county, longitude, latitude, phone number, assets, credits, debits, cash flow, customers, or any of the more than one hundred vectors that Jason had tried. The banks were large and small, North, South, East, West, in big cities and tiny towns. With the list of almost three hundred banks now before him on the computer, the only factor that remained patently obvious was that all the banks were in California.

He pushed the laptop away from him on the coffee table and leaned back on the couch dejectedly. He had been hoping that after the night’s work the pattern that had eluded him would become clear. In retrospect he could see that there was no reason to expect that the pattern in three hundred banks would become obvious where the pattern in one hundred had not. Still, the failure, and with it the realization that he could not find the money, would very likely never be able to find the money, was awesomely depressing. The lack of sleep wasn’t helping his mood, either.

Chip came in, closing the door behind him, and flopped onto the recliner across the coffee table from Jason.

"Did you talk to Kelly?"

"Yes, and before you ask, it didn't go well."

"Oh." He paused. "She won't help?"

"Not hardly. How are you doing?"

"Awful. It's not like this guy was a mathematician or a code-breaker from World War II. He was a movie producer. Any pattern he used should be easy to spot."

"But you haven't."

"No. I'm starting to think," he stopped as Deirdre came down the stairs, dressed in the same jeans as before but wearing one of Jason's polo shirts.

"I hope you don't mind that I borrowed a shirt. Do you have any aspirin? I've got a raging headache."

"The shirt looks good on you. There's aspirin in the drawer in the kitchen under the microwave." Jason started to get up.

"I can get it." She went into the kitchen. They heard her open the drawer, open a cupboard, and fill a glass with water from the tap.

"Did you get any sleep?" Jason asked her.

She came into the living room carrying the glass of water and the aspirin bottle. "Yes." She lied. She tipped three aspirin out of the bottle and tossed them into her mouth, followed by a gulp of water.

"We haven't seen Ricky yet."

She swallowed with a little difficulty. "He'll be back. You can count on that." She slumped down on the couch next to Jason and drank some more water. "Have you found anything?" She gestured at the computer with the glass.

No." He ran his index finger along the corner of the computer. "As I was just telling Chip, this guy wasn't Einstein. Any pattern he used should be a simple one. Either that, or else."

"Or else what?" Chip prompted.

Jason shrugged his shoulders, "Or else there simply is no pattern. He just built a list of banks in any old order that suited him and loaded it into his program."

"But then how do we find the money?" Deirdre asked.

"We don't." He closed the laptop with a decisive click. "We can't."

"We found it last night without the pattern. We could do it again, right?" Chip was almost pleading.

"That was with Kelly. I can't run the program alone, and it would take me a month to teach one of you to run it." He got up from the couch wearily and moved towards the stairs. "And Kelly is probably right. Even if we could route the money out of the program and into an account we control, it couldn't be done in a way that wouldn't be traced right back to us."

As he started climbing the stairs Chip called to him. "What are we going to do?"

"You have a job, Chip. Go back to it." He continued climbing the stairs and went down the hallway, his voice becoming echoed and distant. "I'm going to start looking for work in the morning. Maybe I can get some unemployment benefits."

Deirdre jumped off the couch and went up the stairs after him. She caught up with him at the doorway to the master bedroom. "I don't have anywhere to go."

He looked at her, brushed a strand of hair behind her ear with his hand. "Then stay. Mi casa, su casa. Go wild. Trash the place. Unless a buyer suddenly materializes out of the woodwork, the bank is going to own it all in twenty-six days anyway."

"Jason, I," her eyes were wet with unshed tears.

"Hey, it would have been great to be rich, but it's not going to happen. I can't make it happen. It's over."

He left her standing there, closing the bedroom door firmly in her face.

*****

He opened the sliding door quietly, stepped in, and eased it closed behind him. Ricky stood still, absorbed the hush of the house around him, breathing silently as his eyes adjusted. The figure asleep on the couch was most likely, from the size, Deirdre, and as he concentrated he could just pick up a hint of her scent. He didn't see anyone else.

He sat down in one of the recliners, the chair creaking slightly as it took his weight. In the past he had slept in cars and on benches outside; the recliner wouldn't be a problem.

His earlier loss of temper had been stupid. Here he was in a position that allowed him to just sit back and wait for the others to find and retrieve the money with no risk or effort on his part at all, and he let that bitch Kelly push his buttons. She wanted him to lose it; she wanted to get rid of him to get his share of the money.

He took a deep breath and let it out.

He wouldn't let that happen. If he played it cool, they would bring the money right to him, and then he could take it all.

And he had decided that he was definitely going to take it all.

He smiled to himself as he drifted off to sleep, despite the gun jabbing him uncomfortably in the stomach under his shirt.

3 Days Earlier

He was having a nightmare; even inside the nightmare itself he knew that, and yet he couldn't wake up. The nightmare was indistinct, filled more with feelings than actual images. There was something small, perhaps a flower like a daisy; light, nonsensical musical was playing, glass wind chimes. Something big was coming, ominous music flowing into the dream like heavy, black tar. A giant black bowling ball rolling down on the flower, slowly, ever so slowly. The surface wasn't simply black, it was darker than black. There was no light reflected, no sheen to its surface. The motion could not be seen so much as sensed, the blackness blotting the sky as it approached. Jason could feel the weight of the ball on his chest, a crushing weight, a two-hundred-ton bowling ball. The flower would not be merely flattened, but obliterated, mashed into an unrecognizable liquid pulp. The flower sat unaware in a field of grass. Completely unaware.

His eyes snapped open suddenly in the dim light. It took him a moment to realize that he was in his own bedroom. His head pounded so intensely that his eyes ached. He felt as though there was sand in his eye sockets as he looked over at the clock on the nightstand, six-fifty showing in the cool blue LED segment display.

He lay in the bed very still, breathing shallowly.

He had the answer.

They had spent so much time checking and cross checking addresses and phone numbers, assets and allocations, that they had missed the most natural organizational scheme of all.

He got up from the bed and pulled on a pair of gym shorts. In the spare bedroom he flipped on the light and moved to the papers on the desk. Chip sleeping in the bed scrunched up his face and rolled away from the light to face the wall.

When Jason dumped over the garbage can and started picking through the crumpled balls of paper on the floor, Chip rolled back and squinted at him. "What's got you up at," he lifted his wristwatch to his face, moving it in and out to try and find focus, "whatever the heck time it is in the morning?"

"I've got it, Chip. I know I have. I think we have some paper here somewhere."

Chip snapped wide awake. He got down on the floor with Jason and started pawing at the scraps, "What am I looking for?"

"I can find this easier online." He got up leaving Chip kneeling on the floor and pulled out the desk chair. He hit the power switch on the computer to start the boot up process.

"Find what online? What's the pattern?"

"Wire transfer numbers."

"What about them?"

"That's the pattern. It's only hard to see because they're nine digits long, and including only banks in California they're not consecutive. This computer takes forever to boot up. Can you get me the printer? It's downstairs on the kitchen table."

Chip went to get the printer. When the computer came up Jason opened the internet browser and did a search on wire transfer numbers. In minutes he had a half dozen banking sites open as he looked for what he needed.

Chip came back carrying the printer, Ricky and Deirdre following behind.

"Chip said you figured it out." Deirdre said breathlessly.

"Yeah, I," he paused when he saw Ricky, frowned to himself, then continued. "They're called ACH numbers," he said, scratching the letters ACH on a scrap of paper nearby with a stub of pencil. "We got all caught up trying to find a pattern in the banks," he paused again, opened up a search window, and typed 'ACH numbers California' into the search box. "The pattern is the wire transfers themselves."

Chip leaned over his shoulder, "It's a little early. What are you saying?"

"Just this." He turned the laptop so the screen faced Chip. To Chip it showed a nearly endless list of banks.

"What am I looking at?"

"The pattern. Banks wire money to each other using a unique ID number called the Automated Clearing House number or ACH. Ryder downloaded a list of California banks organized by ACH number, and used it to feed his wire transfer program. He has the money converted to cash and moved into a safe deposit box at the first bank on any given day that can handle that kind of a transaction."

"So you can find the money?" Chip's voice was very loud in Jason's ear.

"Uh," Jason scrolled the list up and down, "I need to print this out." He set up the printer and sent the file to it.

Deirdre stood speechless with her hands clasped to her chest like a heroine from a 1920's movie. Ricky hung on the corner of the chair with a crazy light in his eyes. They watched the pages roll out of the printer.

Jason gathered the papers together. “Three banks an hour, seventy-two banks a day, five days and,” he checked his watch, “three hours, thirty-seven banks on a page, brings us to,” he flipped through the pages to the eleventh page and ran a finger down the list.

They all leaned forward expectantly around him.

“There’s a Union Pacific Bank in Goleta that will have the kind of cash on hand.”

“Goleta?” Deirdre asked.

“Small city near Santa Barbara.” Chip answered.

“Three, four, five, six,” Jason counted banks on the page. “The money will be there between nine-twenty and nine-forty this morning.”

Like a farce they all looked at their watches at once and then at each other.

“That’s less than two hours from now!” Chip’s voice cracked.

Jason stood up from the chair and was out of the room like a shot.

“Where are you going?” Ricky shouted after him.

“To get dressed. Anyone not in the car in five minutes gets left behind!”

*****

The grip of the gun was warm against his hands. Scott stood with his feet shoulder-width apart, his weight distributed evenly, his back straight, but not tense, his head up. The orange-tinted safety glasses he wore maximized the contrast of his vision in the harsh fluorescent lighting of the indoor shooting range. He sighted at the man-shaped outline of the target thirty yards away and let his breath out slowly.

He pulled the trigger twice in quick succession, then a third time a moment after that. Three holes appeared in the target, two in the vicinity of the heart, the third in the head. It was a shooting technique taught to him by an instructor at Quantico who had been a Special Forces guy in Vietnam. He fired the spread again, with its distinctive pattern of bang! bang! pause, bang! It was guaranteed to be fatal, with death occurring so rapidly that the target never even uttered a sound. Scott regretted that the only place he got to use the technique was on the shooting range. Surely any shooting review board would look at the wound pattern and see it as so wantonly brutal that they would pull his badge in a Los Angeles second, 120 of which you could fit into a New York minute.

As his gun carried six in the clip and he kept one in the chamber at all times, he let the remaining round fly in a single head shot. He then removed the bulky hearing protectors and started to reload the clip from the pile of bullets that rolled loose on the countertop in front of him.

"I was wondering when you were going to take those off," said Miller from behind him. "Sikes texted us about five minutes ago."

Scott finished loading the clip, slapped it into the breach of the gun and chambered a round. He then pulled the clip and inserted one more round, slamming the clip home again when he was finished. "Let's go."

They made their way through the rabbit's warren of hallways, finding the door to the lab unlocked when they arrived. Inside the vacuum chamber was silent, like some mechanical beast hunched down at rest.

Jerry Sikes saw them enter from the desk across the room, and pulled a stack of pages from the printer as he came over to them, “I was just about to try your cellphone. The recovery process completed last night. We managed to salvage data from 68% of the hard drive, which is pretty amazing considering that the bullet directly removed 14% of the hard drive platter. In fact, statistically-”

Scott waved his hands to cut him off, “Did you find the file we were looking for? One that looked like it might be bank accounts?”

“I believe so. I just finished printing that one out.” He handed Scott the sheaf of papers.

The top sheet showed a list of banks and numbers running solidly down the page. Scott flipped through the pages quickly and saw the list continued on page after page.

“I think that’s it.” Miller said from over his shoulder. He couldn’t keep the excitement out of his voice.

Scott rolled the papers into a tube and rapped it against his palm. “This is perfect, Jerry. It really is. It could blow the case wide open. We’re going to follow up on this immediately.”

When he turned to leave Jerry asked, “I have the rest of the recovered data burned to a CDROM. What do you want me to do with that?”

“Just drop it into interdepartmental mail. Thanks.” The door closing behind them cut off the last word.

They went upstairs to their slot in the cube farm, where Scott took off his jacket and threw it over the back of his desk chair. He spread the pages out on the desktop while Miller grabbed an atlas out of the bookshelf.

"All the banks are in California?" Miller asked.

Scott looked at the pages, "Yeah, it looks that way."

Scott dragged the desk chair in behind him with his ankle and hunched over the papers, "The deal took place at 4AM five days ago. It's now 7:15, which makes at three banks an hour, seventy two banks a day, uh." He opened the desk drawer and took out a small calculator and punched some buttons. He marked every tenth bank on the list to make it easier to count off. "The money has gone through more than three hundred and fifty banks."

"So where is it now?"

"Bank three-sixty-nine is a Citizens Bank in Sacramento."

"That's pretty far away."

"Three-seventy is in Redding."

Miller checked the atlas, "Way up North. Beyond San Francisco. That's even farther away."

"Three-seventy-one is Oakland, three-seventy-two is San Jose, three-seventy-three is back in Sacramento. Bank three-seventy-four is in Goleta."

"That's near Santa Barbara. We can get there in two hours." Miller looked at his watch. "We'd never make it before the money moved again."

Scott grabbed his jacket off the chair and gathered up the list, "I'll drive."

Miller dropped the atlas on the desk and followed him out of the cube farm and down the hallway. "What's the point? We can't get there in time."

"Because I want to know for a fact that the money went through there. What if this whole list is bullshit? Before I make some serious plans to get this money, I want to make sure it's there to get."

"By driving all the way to Goleta?"

"It's either that or wait until late afternoon when it hits a bank in San Diego, and I want to know now. We can always check the bank in Goleta, then make it back to San Diego in time for that one."

They decided to forego the elevator and took the fire stairs to the parking garage, their shoes echoing sharply off the concrete walls of the stairwell. They climbed into a light-colored, nondescript government sedan that was exactly like the other hundred parked around it, Scott behind the wheel. The keys were already in the ignition. Scott took a sign-out slip off the pad on the seat and started to fill it out.

"How are we going to get the money? I mean, how are we actually going to pick it up?" Miller said fastening his seatbelt.

Scott shook his head, "I haven't figured that out yet, but if that money is actually there, I'll come up with something. You can bet your life on that."

*****

He rifled through the sheets of papers; dozens of them covered in dense print, crimped at one corner with a heavy black binder clip. Dorado placed the papers down on his blotter. "This it?"

Jerry Sikes stood in front of his desk shifting his feet nervously like a six-year-old who needed to pee. "That's the contents of the file that I recovered for them."

"But what does it mean?"

"Clearly the data represents bank accounts, over twelve hundred of them. What's in them, whose bank accounts they are – I don't know. I did notice that they're all in California, if that's any help. Oh, and another thing: no bank is on that list twice."

"What do you mean?" Dorado picked up the list and pointed to two adjacent Bank of America listings, "Bank of America is on the list twice right here."

Jerry shook his head, "Same corporation, but different branch locations. For all I know that list represents every commercial bank and branch location in the state. The guys from treasury could probably tell you more."

"Hmmm." He tossed the sheaf of papers back on the desktop. "Anything else on the hard drive?"

"Nothing that seemed to stand out. Everything that came off the drive is on the CD that I gave you."

Dorado fingered the clear plastic jewel case that sat on the blotter next to the list. "Well, thanks for keeping me in the loop. If Scott or Miller come to you for anything else, let me know?"

"Sure thing." He walked to the door of the office and opened it. "Open or closed?"

Dorado was already deep in thought, running an index finger down the list. He looked up, "Huh?"

"Do you want your door opened or closed?"

"Oh, closed, thank you."

Dorado hardly heard the click of the door latching shut.

Every bank in California was probably on the list, and that meant... He found the bank he was looking for about halfway down the third page, a First California Federal Credit Union in Fresno. A friend of his from college was the manager. He picked up the phone and dialed the bank's number, which was also on the list.

A collection of pops, clicks, and pauses as the call routed through the California in-state dialing system finally resulted in ringing, which was answered promptly by a woman with a sunny, young-sounding voice "First California FCU, how may I help you?"

"I'm looking for Steven Windsor."

"Mr. Windsor is on another line. Would you like to wait, or should he return your call?"

"I'll wait. This is James Dorado. I'm a personal friend."

"Yes, sir, please hold."

The call switched over to canned muzak, some sleepy version of *Heard it Through the Grapevine*. He found himself humming along to it by the time the phone was picked up again.

"James? Holy smokes! I haven't heard from you since the class reunion, what, four years ago."

"Yeah, well, I've been busy. Deputy director of the DEA in Los Angeles now."

"Deputy director! Wowee! Helen must be happy."

"We divorced. Three years ago now."

Dorado could hear the hiss of static on the line in the

ensuing silence.

"I'm sorry about that."

"Well, the work was demanding more and more of my time, and Helen wasn't willing to-" He stopped himself. What was the point in telling all this ancient history to a distant classmate? "Anyway, I have a little favor to ask."

He could almost hear the gears shift in Steve's head, "Shoot."

"I have an account number at your bank. I'm hoping you can tell me about the account."

Steve sucked in air through his teeth, "I dunno. Regulators are very picky about personal account information. Can you get a warrant?"

"It's not even part of an official investigation. More an investigation into opening an investigation."

"Wellll." He dragged the word out. "Give me the number."

Dorado gave it to him.

He said "Hold on." Dorado heard the clunk of the receiver hitting the desktop, followed by the squeak of the wheels on the desk chair as they rolled back, and the sound of hard-soled shoes clicking into the distance.

He hummed *Heard it Through the Grapevine* while he waited.

The return of the shoes, the squeak of the desk chair, the intake of breath as Steve picked up the phone and started to speak, "Not much to tell you. The account was opened six days ago electronically by a Mr. Peter Ryder.

Lists his address in Los Angeles, out your way."

"What's in the account?"

"Nothing."

Dorado sat up straight in his desk chair and leaned his elbows on the desk, "Nothing?"

"Nothing. Nothing in it. Balance zero. Nothing has ever been in it."

"Why would someone open an account and not put money in it?"

"Oh, it happens all the time. Usually someone moving into the area opens an account and then transfers in the balance from their old bank. Sometimes they wait a week or two for overlap, or pay cash to print the first order of checks and then keep their old account open until they show up. Though I don't see an order for any checks having being placed, and usually people opening an account deposit something, if only a couple of hundred dollars."

They both sat listening to the hum of the phone line.

Dorado rubbed his thumb and forefinger against his closed eyes, "So, that's it. Peter Ryder's account is empty, and it's always been empty."

"That's about the size of it. Does that help you?"

"It might. Thanks very much, and give my best to Patty."

"Will do. You drop by if you come out this way. We'll do a barbecue."

Dorado promised he would, though both knew it would never happen, and he hung up.

He leaned back with the list on the desk in front of him, the chair groaning under his shifting weight.

The laptop clearly belonged to Ryder, not the drug dealer as Scott and Miller had claimed. Why they were interested in Ryder's bank accounts, if in fact all the accounts on the list were Ryder's, was a mystery. Where the agents had come up with Ryder's computer was also a mystery. All Dorado knew for certain was that, whatever had happened down on the docks that night, it wasn't the story contained in Miller's report. Beyond that, he had precious little to go on.

*****

The bank sat at one end of a strip mall, the other end anchored by an Albertsons supermarket, with a Hallmark store, pet store, a sub shop, and beauty salon sandwiched in between. The strip mall was constructed as one continuous building; beige simulated stone face and Spanish tile roof. Tired palm trees were planted in the lane dividers in the parking lot.

They drove into the parking lot in Ricky's car with a slight squeal of the tires at 9:31AM and pulled into a no parking zone in front of the bank.

"It doesn't look like a bank that would have seven million dollars in it." Chip observed looking through the car side window.

"According to the computer it does. Santa Barbara isn't too far away, and there's lots of money there. Maybe that's why it keeps so much cash on hand." Jason replied.

Ricky looked at his watch, "Get a move on."

Jason checked his pocket to make sure he had the passport and driver's license. Deirdre got out of the car and tilted the seat forward so Jason could climb out from behind her.

"Good luck." She kissed him on the cheek.

He nodded to her, and then to Chip sitting in the back seat. He walked up to the tinted glass doors of the bank. His vision seemed to be on overdrive, every facet and characteristic of the doors magnified a hundred times. He could see fine pitting in the chrome work on the door handle, the result of the acids from tens of thousands of hands opening the door. A slight wrinkle in the glass tinting caught his attention, the thickening of the coating, the tiny rainbow gleam of the sunlight diffracted by the wrinkle. A blob of bright green bubblegum was flattened on the sidewalk beside his foot, the crosshatch pattern of a sneaker imprinted on the surface.

He looked back at the three of them sitting in the car behind him and time expanded. They were motionless. The whole world was motionless around him. Across the parking lot a man was frozen as he wrestled with three golden retrievers on leashes, their hindquarters tense, their tails up, their muzzles to the ground following scents that only they could detect. A woman leaned over a stroller, a small fist reaching up from inside. Cars waited at a red light at the nearby intersection. Heat haze rising off the concrete and the cars was unmoving.

His head turned slowly back towards the bank as though on a pillar of stone. He reached out and grasped the handle, slightly warm to the touch, and pulled the door open, causing a small squeak and a pneumatic hiss of the door mechanism. The hiss and the clunk of the door closing behind him broke the spell. He was inside the bank.

Tellers' windows were to the right, a line of four people

waiting for service in a serpentine of green felt ropes. A small seating area was to the left near an array of wooden desks, divided by wood-framed glass panels, at which sat the bank managers and assistant managers.

He stood in the entranceway feeling rooted to the spot, his breathing very loud in his ears. A bank guard flanking the door he had come through coughed into his fist, and Jason wondered how suspicious he looked standing there immobile. How long had he been loitering? He checked his watch: 9:32. He had less than eight minutes left.

Forcing his feet to move, he walked stiffly to the seating area and sat on the nearest chair. He was the only one waiting. He flipped through the magazines on the table in front of him unseeingly, and then leaned back in the seat crossing one leg over the other at the knee.

Three of the four desks were occupied. One had a woman on the phone, her gray hair coiled on top of her head, narrow glasses with blue frames attached to a gold chain that hung around her neck giving her a matronly air. A man in a brown blazer shiny from wear sat at another desk working at a computer, his thin brown hair grown long and combed across the bald spot at his crown. A woman at the third desk, flashing white-capped teeth and big gold earrings under a huge pile of chesnut hair, spoke in low tones to a couple, pointing at brochures in front of them with the tip of a silver pen that flashed in a beam of sunlight coming through a nearby window.

9:34.

The man at the computer typed as if oblivious that Jason was waiting. The woman remained on the phone. The couple nodded at the smiling woman vacuously.

9:35.

Jason shifted so the other foot rested on the other knee, then sat forward with both feet on the floor. He again flipped through the magazines, glancing at titles and cover stories that would not have been more opaque to him had they been written in hieroglyphics. He looked back at the guard standing by the door rocking slowly on his feet.

9:36.

“Can I help you?”

Jason hadn’t seen the matronly woman hang up the phone and come over to him. He stood too quickly and felt a brief moment of lightheadedness.

He dug the passport out of his pocket and held it up, opening it like a badge case. “Peter Ryder. I’d like to make a cash withdrawal from my account.”

She frowned at his odd behavior, but quickly recovered her professional smile. She took the passport from his slightly shaking hands, “Certainly,” she glanced at the passport, “Mr. Ryder. If you’ll just step over to my desk, it will only take a second.”

She stepped away from him walking backwards, as if backing away slowly from a dangerous animal. She gestured to the chair in front of her desk while she took her own seat behind it and tapped on the computer keyboard.

Jason moved to the chair, feeling tense and spastic, imagining that he must look like a poorly operated marionette. He rested his arms on the desktop and glanced in what he hoped was a surreptitious manner at his watch: 9:38.

Each second ticking by on the digital display was punctuated in Jason’s mind with a clap of thunder that echoed and overlapped with those of seconds past and seconds lost yet to come.

"I'm sorry, Mr. Ryder. That account was closed and the funds transferred out via wire order."

Jason looked up and blinked. "They what?"

"We received a wire order at 9:20 to recollect the cash balance and transfer the funds. Is there a problem?"

Jason's mind was a whirl. 9:20? He was twenty minutes off.

The woman had continued talking, but Jason wasn't registering any of it. He started mumbling something about his secretary and a misunderstanding. He stood and thought about shaking her hand but his own were slick with sweat, so he shoved them into his pockets instead.

He headed for the door, the woman calling to him from behind. He didn't hear, couldn't understand; blood was roaring in his ears.

The bank guard stepped away from his post into Jason's path, one hand out in front of him, motioning Jason to stop. The guard was saying something to him. What? What! Jason couldn't sort it out, all his fuses blown. Was his other hand moving to the butt of the gun on his hip, a big ugly-looking revolver jammed into a sweat-stained leather holster? Jason thought about making a break for it, bowling past the guard and running for the car. They didn't know who he was. All they had was the fake passport.

He stopped, his overworked brain holding up that one shining clear thought like the hand of a drowning man breaking through to the surface.

He turned, the woman behind him holding it out to

him, “Mr. Ryder, you’ve forgotten your passport.”

Jason took it feebly between slick, numb fingers, all his will going to keeping his hand from shaking.

“If there’s been some problem perhaps you would like to use a phone? We could call the institution that received the funds.”

“No, I, it’s OK,” was all he could manage. He turned back to the door and almost cried in relief to see that the guard was returning to his spot, no longer standing in his way.

He shuffled out the doorway, so completely drained that it was almost beyond his capability to lift his feet off the floor.

Deirdre got out of the car when she saw him coming and tilted the seat forward for him to get in. “Where’s the money?”

As he flopped into the back seat Chip asked from the seat beside him, “Did you get a bank check?”

“The money’s not here.” He said softly.

“What?” Ricky asked.

“The moneeey,” he dragged the words out, “isssss nooooot heeeeeere!”

“Then where the fuck is it?”

“It’s not here. Just drive.”

“Where’s the fucking money?”

“Drive!” Jason yelled.

Ricky looked over the seat at him, his nostrils flaring, his face etched with anger and hatred. He spun in the seat and slammed the car into gear. They flew out of the parking lot in a peal of rubber.

No one spoke for the entire two-hour ride back.

*****

Miller and Scott walked into the bank. Miller stepped aside to have a few words with the bank guard while Scott surveyed the teller area and manager's desks. He found it hard to believe that seven million dollars in cash had been in this bank forty-five minutes ago. If they had been just a little bit faster...

Miller came over to him, "The guard says the bank manager's name is Dorothy Farmer. She's the woman over there with the gray hair and glasses."

Mrs. Farmer was currently helping an elderly lady fill out the forms to open an account. Scott and Miller went over and stood just behind the elderly woman's chair, arms folded across their chests, looking like centurion bookends.

Mrs. Farmer looked up at them from her chair, "Can I help you?"

Scott pulled out his badge and snapped it open with a well-practiced flip of the wrist, "Special agents Scott and Miller, DEA. We have some questions regarding an account at this bank."

"Yes, well, I'm with a customer. If you will be so kind as to take a seat I'll be with you shortly."

Scott deflated slightly. Still, it's not as though he expected her to throw the customer out onto the sidewalk. They sat on the edges of their seats and waited as the old woman stared at brochures through watery eyes behind glasses twice as thick as Coke bottle bottoms, and filled out forms with a torturous, palsied hand.

When she was finally finished and assisted out the door by the manager and bank guard, the woman returned to her desk and asked, “Now, what can I do for you?”

Scott and Miller got up from their chairs and stood across the desk from her. “We have questions concerning an account at your bank.”

“That’s no problem, if you just submit your request to our corporate legal counsel with the proper warrants, we can get any account information to you within ten business days.”

Scott shook his head. People could be so stupid. “We would like at this time to do this as quietly as possible. We are tracking the funds of a very dangerous drug dealer, and believe we have someone within our department tipping him off. If we try and go through channels, he’ll know we’re onto him and he’ll be back in Mexico before sundown.”

Miller was amazed at the line of bullshit his partner could come up with when necessary.

“Be that as it may, I can’t violate this institution’s policy on your say so.”

“Fine,” Scott said tightly, “then in order to contain this leak, I see as we have no choice but to seal this bank and hold you all as material witnesses until we can get a judge to issue a warrant.” He made a big show of looking at his watch, “You’ll all miss lunch or course, but we should have you out of here in time for a late dinner.” Without looking at him he said, “Miller, go inform that guard to seal the doors. As of this instant no one leaves this bank.”

Scott's story was a self-conflicting mess, but it was so convoluted the woman was almost certain not to figure it out, especially with Scott staring down at her and Miller moving towards the guard.

"If you'll just let me call the regional director." She reached for the phone.

Scott put a hand on hers carefully but firmly, pinning it to the phone handset, exerting pressure so she couldn't lift it, "I'm afraid I can't allow any phone calls out either. I'm sure you understand that's because of the leak."

"You can't do that," she tried to tug her hand out from under his lightly.

"Uh-huh," Scott released her hand, which she pulled back and cradled in her other hand as if burned. He removed a small notepad from his jacket pocket and wrote something in it, "Just like we're not doing it right now."

She and Scott held each other's stares in a battle of the wills she was certain to lose quickly.

"Please, stop. Tell your partner to stop."

"Miller." Scott called to Miller over his shoulder, who came back to stand beside him.

"If this drug dealer is as dangerous as you say, then I think as a good citizen it's my job to help you catch him. I have a niece just starting high school, after all."

Scott smiled emptily. Whatever justifications she told herself, it didn't matter to him in the least.

"What is the name of the account holder?" She held her hands at the ready over the keyboard.

Scott looked at his notebook, “Peter Ryder. I have an account number if you need that also.”

She didn’t touch the computer keyboard, held her hands hovering over the keys, “He was just here.” She said breathlessly.

Scott and Miller exchanged a quick glance. Scott put his hands on the edge of her desk and leaned forward, towering over her. “Who was just here?”

“Mr. Ryder. Sat in the chair just behind you not fifteen minutes ago. Tried to withdraw money from the account, but the account had been emptied by wire transfer earlier.”

“How do you know it was Peter Ryder?” Miller asked.

“He had a passport.”

Miller’s jaw hung open. He looked at Scott who shook his head minutely.

“How much money was in the account before the wire transfer?” Scott asked.

“Oh my God, he was right here.” She was bunching her hands under her chin.

Scott snapped his fingers in front of her face. When she focused on him again he spoke slowly and calmly, “It’s OK. He’s gone, and the money’s gone. He won’t be coming back. How much money was in the bank account?”

She made a visible effort to collect herself, “I don’t know exactly, a little over seven million dollars. I can get the number in just a moment.” She started typing, clearly taking great effort to concentrate sufficiently to remember the commands.

"No, no, that's not necessary. If you'll excuse us for a moment." He took Miller aside back into the seating area.

"He's dead. We know he's dead." Miller whispered.

"Don't be an idiot," Scott hissed, "of course he's dead. Someone else knows about the money and is trying to get it using a fake passport."

"Who?"

"I don't know, but they obviously don't have the money yet. If they did, they'd be gone already and we'd be screwed."

"Shit! I don't like it."

Scott was rubbing his forehead with his fingers, trying to fit this into his plan quickly. "It might be OK. Wherever the money is tomorrow, you can be sure he'll be there also."

"But we don't know what he looks like. We could miss him completely."

A sudden thought occurred to Scott and he looked around, finally spotting what he knew he would find over Miller's shoulder.

He walked back to the desk. The woman was clutching a picture frame that held a picture of two small children, a boy and a girl, probably grandkids. "We're going to need to see your security camera tapes."

She looked up from the picture, "Yes, of course."

*****

The lock turned, the door opened. Jason came in,

swinging the door wide, letting it bounce off the doorstop mounted on the wall and start to swing shut again. He jogged up the stairs.

Ricky caught the closing door with a stiff arm and followed Jason up the stairs, taking them two at a time. "OK. I waited until we got back here. Now, where the fuck is the money?"

Chip and Deirdre came in together, Chip closing the door behind them. They went reluctantly upstairs where Jason could be heard shouting. The words could not be understood, but the volume reverberated quite clearly down the hallway.

Jason went down the hallway and turned into the guest bedroom. "If you'll just shut the fuck up for a second, I'll figure that out." He threw back over his shoulder at Ricky. He snatched up the bank list and a pen, counting down the columns with the tip of the pen.

Ricky waited about two whole seconds. "So?" he demanded.

"Shhh!" Jason had lost count. He began again on the first page of the list.

Chip and Deirdre came into the bedroom and stood near Ricky. The three of them watched as Jason counted down the list once, twice. He made some hash marks in the margin and counted down the list a third time. He nodded to himself, satisfied, and tossed the list and pen down the desk. "I miscounted." He announced.

Ricky's eyes bulged, incredulous, "What do you mean you miscounted? This isn't some fucking game! We're talking about seven million dollars!"

"Hey! This morning when I figured all this shit out I

didn't have a lot of time to double check the numbers. I got it wrong, OK? Simple as that. The money was there between nine and nine-twenty, and we couldn't have gotten there in time anyway. Do you want to know where the money will be tomorrow morning, or do you want to yell some more?"

Ricky said nothing, his face flushed.

"Where will it be?" Chip asked.

"Community National Bank in Riverside, tomorrow morning at 9AM."

"You're certain?" Ricky hissed.

"Certain." Jason paused. "Unless someone else finds and gets the money between now and then."

Ricky stomped out of the room.

Jason smiled tightly at his back. A part of him almost hoped that they didn't get the money, just to see how much it would piss Ricky off.

*****

Scott and Miller came out of the bank over three hours later. They had interviewed all the bank officers, the security guard, and even the tellers – anyone who might have seen the man claiming to be Peter Ryder, the car he had come in, and person or persons who might have been with him. Despite the considerable time they had spent, they had very little to show for their efforts.

The bank manager had given them copies of the copies of the man's driver's license and passport, insisting she had to keep the original copies for the bank's files unless a court order told her differently. The copies themselves had not been all that great, and the copies of the copies were very poor, the photographs too small to be of any use. Scott folded the papers into thirds and slipped them into his inside jacket pocket.

A teller returning from mailing a letter at the post office down the street had seen the man get into an older model car in a dark color, probably black. The young woman was further certain that the man had gotten into the passenger side of the car, indicating there must have been a driver, but she couldn't describe anything about that person at all.

The security guard said that he had noticed the man's eyes were gray. He revealed this tidbit during the interview covertly, leaning forwards and whispering out of the side of his mouth like a spy in a bad 60's espionage film, like it was the clue that would crack the case wide open. Miller feigned interest and jotted it down in his notebook, but was certain it would be of little use.

One thing of possible significance that they did have, as they walked out of the bank and got into their bland government vehicle, was three printouts of frame captures from the bank surveillance videotape – one full length shot (that could perhaps be used to calculate the subject's height using items nearby in the frame), one medium shot face front, and one fairly close up in profile taken as he sat in the waiting area. The surveillance system recorded the video on a stack of old VCRs. Scott was shocked the bank hadn't converted over to a digital format years ago, but the analog system still worked, more or less, and corporate saw no point in paying to replace it.

The tapes ran in a rotating format, and probably hadn't been replaced in years. As a result, the image quality was awful. Perhaps with a few thousand computer hours, the pictures could be enhanced and a match found in the California Driver's License database. All of that would have required paperwork and they wanted to keep their paper trail to a minimum.

Scott and Miller instead were formulating a different plan, as they drove back to Los Angeles, and it was based on the one other piece of information they had gotten while at the bank. Shortly after being wired into the bank account, a second wire instruction had arrived directing the bank to convert the money into ready cash. So the bank had, with some difficulty, converted the account to cash and held it in their vault. Nearly twenty minutes later a wire instruction had arrived to return the money to the account, followed by a routing instruction to another bank.

They were stunned! The money had been held as cash for almost twenty minutes! The bank manager assured them that, while it was an unusual request, she had known of several instances in the past when some of the bank's wealthier customers had availed themselves of that service. The subsequent reprocessing and transfer were stranger still, but again, not unheard of.

As they approached the outskirts of Los Angeles, lunch hour traffic slowed them to a crawl. A mile of red taillights stretched ahead of them on the 101, shimmering in the heat haze rising from the pavement. This department vehicle, like many of them, came without working air conditioning.

Miller rolled down the window letting in a blast of oven heat and car exhaust, "Seven million dollars. I can't even imagine what a stack of seven million dollars must look like."

"Sure you can," Scott said loosening his tie and unbuttoning the top button of his shirt, "What about that bust in that factory near Chinatown last summer? That was at least ten million in cash."

Miller nodded, "Yeah, that's right. But still, to think that it was right there."

"That's true. It was all right there. And I'll do you one

better."

"What's that?"

"I think the money is there every day."

Miller frowned, "I don't follow you."

"Let me put it this way. You're a movie producer who gets involved in a drug deal that you're worried might go wrong. What do you do?"

"What, to protect myself? I guess I'd hire some guns, a few bodyguards."

Scott shook his head, "Can't do it. Who can you trust? Millions of dollars are involved. No, what you make are plans to run if it all goes to hell, hence all the hopping bank accounts. The other thing you do is get the bank to have your money ready for you when you come for it. The cash is just waiting there, and you run in, grab it, and run out."

"You think the account is converted to cash at every bank?"

"No way. How many banks have that kind of cash on hand? But maybe a couple of times a day. I bet if we go back and look at the list, we'll be able to find out which banks handle that kind of money, and which don't. Tomorrow we stake out the most likely bank, and wait for the money to come to us."

"But even with the money in cash, it's still in the bank. How do we get it?"

"We don't." Scott tapped the photocopied picture on the seat between them. "He does."

2 Days Earlier

The Community National Bank was a single-story building with a flat roof and fake stone facing. A monstrous air conditioning unit squatted on the roof, looking as through a stubby cubical alien ship had docked with it. Scott and Miller pulled into a Winchell's Donut Shop lot directly across the street at 8AM and backed into a space towards the rear, but that still gave them an excellent view of the front of the bank. The shop gave them ready access to coffee, donuts, and a bathroom. It was definitely one of the more luxurious stake out locations they had worked.

A large number of other panel vans, colorful business logos painted on the sides, came and went with the morning coffee and donuts, and their van blended in with perfect anonymity. The lot had the further advantage that it sat on the corner of two major roads, so they could easily follow their subject in any of three directions when he left the bank. A concrete barrier between the East- and West-bound lanes in the roadway between their location and the bank would make it difficult to tail the subject east, but that couldn't be helped. It was a moot point in any case as Scott hoped to attach a tracking beacon to the car – he was rolling the roughly quarter-sized device in his fingers while they waited – which would allow them to track the subject up to fifteen miles away. He planned to follow the subject and take the money in some less public location.

"If I were going after this money," Scott blew the steam off the surface of his coffee, "given that I had missed it at the last bank by less than twenty minutes, I would have pitched a tent on the bank's front lawn to make sure I didn't miss it again. Wouldn't you?"

"If I were going to go after this money, I would have picked it up five days ago, before some bank computer could possibly flag the account as suspicious." Scott replied.

"Why didn't they?"

“Pick it up five days ago?” Scott shrugged. “Who knows? I’m not even sure what this guy’s relationship to the money is. Maybe he only just found out about it. Maybe whatever information he has is wrong or incomplete, and that’s why he missed it. It’s possible that he won’t be here today at all; that he doesn’t know enough.”

“We’ll find out in less than forty-five minutes. What if they don’t show up? How do we get the money then? Do we go to a Monday bank and wait there?”

Scott shifted in his seat, “We’ll burn that bridge when we come to it.”

*****

Everyone was in an exceedingly good mood, and why shouldn’t they be? This was the day, and they were well on their way to the bank and the seven million dollars.

Traffic was light early on Saturday morning as they headed east. Ricky drove, keeping his thoughts to himself, with Deirdre in the passenger seat. Chip, behind Ricky, had Jason, sitting behind Deirdre, stuck somewhere between Patrick Duffy on *Dallas* and Elizabeth Berkeley on *Saved by the Bell.*

Jason hadn’t watched much *Saved by the Bell*, and so had little idea of who else had been on it, let alone what other series they might have come from or moved on to. “There was that guy, what was his name, Shriek?”

“Screech.” Deirdre offered from the front seat.

“Whatever. Didn’t he do another series when he was younger, but no less annoying?”

Chip smiled and said nothing.

"One of the guys went on to do some cop show, I think." Deirdre said.

"What guy? What cop show?"

She shook her head. "I don't know."

"You're some help." Jason said in jest. "You know," he said to Chip, "you wouldn't have even heard of Elizabeth Berkeley if she hadn't done that lesbian porn thing with Verhooven."

"You mean *Showgirls*?" Chip frowned. "It was so boring, it wasn't even worth watching for the nudity."

"But you did anyway."

Chip laughed. "But I did anyway."

Jason was thrown against the back of the front seat, and then across the back seat into Chip as Ricky banged on the brakes and swerved across three lanes of traffic.

The CHECK ENGINE light lit. The engine quit, and the power steering and brakes failed with it. Ricky wrestled with the car furiously to steer it into the breakdown lane.

The car lurched to a stop and Jason was thrown back into his seat. "What the fuck was that?"

"How should I know? It just died." Ricky pulled the hood release and got out of the car.

"Everyone OK?" Jason asked.

"Fine." Chip replied.

"I'm OK." Deirdre pushed her hair out of her face. She was wearing her seatbelt.

Jason looked at his watch. "We don't have a lot of time for this."

The three of them got out of the car and went around to the hood. Ricky was leaning inside wiggling wires and checking belts and hoses.

"Tempus fugit." Jason commented.

"Huh?" Ricky looked at him.

"Latin. We don't have much time."

"You don't think that I know that?" Ricky growled as he pulled the oil dipstick and examined the end.

"So?"

"So, I'm working on it. Dee, go turn the engine over."

Deirdre went and sat in the driver's seat with the door open. The engine cranked, but didn't start.

"We have gas, right?" Chip called to her.

"Of course we have gas." Ricky snapped.

They waited while Ricky removed the air cleaner, checked the carburetor, and wiggled the battery cables.

Despite the fact that they had left the house with plenty of time, it was running quite short now.

"We can't wait." Jason pulled out his cell phone, looked up the number for nearby cab company, and called them. "I'm going to need a cab to take me to my bank in Riverside. I don't care about the surcharge for leaving the city limits. Tell the driver there's an extra hundred in it for him if he can get me there before 9:20." He shifted the phone from one ear to the other and looked around. "I'm, um, on the 101 eastbound, I think between exits eight and nine. I'm right next to a big, black, broken down car – you can't miss me. I'll be here." He hung up the phone and put it back in his pocket.

Ricky was leaning against the fender. "I can't leave the car. It will be stripped down to the frame by the time we get back."

"Then stay with it. As soon as that cab comes, I'm out of here."

Ricky moved to stand in front of Jason. He pointed a finger, "When you get the money, you go straight home. I'll meet you there."

"Yes, Dad." Jason turned away from him, far too busy concentrating on each passing minute to be intimidated by Ricky's posturing. He watched the cars whipping by, hoping to see the cab coming.

"Are we going to make it?" Chip asked standing next to him.

"I don't know." He looked at his watch again. "It's going to be close."

*****

Miller looked at his watch for the tenth time in the past two minutes. "Five minutes left." He sat in the passenger seat, looking past Scott in the driver's seat and out the driver-side window.

"Would you give it a rest?" Scott said without looking at him, "I don't need updates every ten seconds."

"Sorry." Miller was jittery, subconsciously bouncing

his knee rapidly. It was practically making the whole van shake. "I just think he should have been here already, you know? Why wait until the last minute? Who would pass up a chance to pick up seven million dollars in cash? Could we have missed him?"

Scott looked down at the grainy still picture from the bank surveillance tape. "I don't see how. There have been only fifty or so customers since the bank opened."

"What if he sent someone else to pick up the money for him?"

"That's nuts. Who would you trust to pick up seven million dollars in cash and bring it back to you? Besides, only the guy with the ID can access the account." His answer seemed to placate Miller somewhat, but as soon as it was out of his mouth Scott reconsidered.

The guy claiming to be Ryder clearly had a fake ID. Couldn't some other guy get a fake ID as well? He closed his eyes and tried to run through in his mind all the male customers he had seen that morning. Had any of them been carrying a bag or suitcase that could hold the money? It was futile. He hadn't been looking for it, so he couldn't remember, and even if he could, the head start would have been too great – the money would be long gone. When they had first pulled up, he had debated with himself about setting up a video camera and pointing it at the front of the bank to record everyone who came and went, but had decided they already had a picture of the guy they were looking for, so what purpose would it serve? He regretted that decision now.

Another possibility they had already discussed was maybe this guy was working from incomplete or incorrect information. That would explain why he had been late to the bank yesterday, and maybe why he would be late to the bank today, if he showed at all. And maybe, just maybe, they would never see the guy again. If that were the case, then the problem of actually getting the cash out of the bank fell back into Scott's lap again.

At the words "He's here." from Miller, Scott's head snapped up. He looked out the window to see the man from the bank photos stepping out of a taxi onto the sidewalk in front of the bank. There were two other people in the car, a man and a woman, but because of the angle between the van and the taxi and the fact that they were both looking the other way at the man on the sidewalk, Scott couldn't get a good look at either of them.

Miller sat at the camera snapping off pictures.

"They came in a taxi. That's smart." Scott said to himself out loud. Coming in a taxi meant that no one would be likely to identify your vehicle later other than to say that you had come in a cab. And even if some observant witness did notice the cab number and company, you could always arrange to have it pick you up and drop you off at some anonymous location, like a supermarket or a shopping mall, and then your trail would end there.

"Not so smart." Miller held up his wrist with his watch so Scott could see it, "They're too late."

Sure enough as Scott watched the man took a step towards the bank, looked at his watch, then turned back to the taxi. He spoke with someone in the back seat, and then got back inside. The cab pulled away from the curb. Scott started the engine and drove out of the parking lot after them.

"Who are these guys? Why are they always late?" Miller asked.

Scott was wondering exactly the same things, but he didn't have any good answers.

Following them did not prove difficult. All the way back to LA the traffic was sparse, and the van was completely ordinary, a style owned by trade workers and businesses of all sorts. Besides, Scott was pretty good at the tailing game – pulling close, dropping back, changing lanes, even once passing the taxi for a stretch of highway that Scott knew had no exits, and then letting it pass him a few miles later.

They followed, not to a parking lot somewhere as Scott has expected, but into a moderate to high-end residential development on the outskirts of LA. When the cab stopped in the driveway of a house, Scott glided by without slowing down while Miller noted the house number.

They pulled over to the side of the road a little ways down and watched out the back windows of the van. Miller got the tripod turned around and took some better pictures of the other two people from the cab as they walked into the house.

"Nice house. You figure they worked with Ryder?" Miller asked.

"Either that or they were in league with Nick. I guess either is possible, but neither one really feels right."

"No, it doesn't." Miller agreed. "So now what?"

"Now, we watch and see what we see. I'd like to plant a listening device in that house if we could."

"The house across the street looked empty."

"You noticed the newspapers on the stoop too?"

Miller nodded.

"OK, we'll give it a look." He made a U-turn and drove

back up the road. He swung the van into the driveway of the empty house and eased to a stop all the way at its end near the back door. They both climbed out, Scott carrying a tool bag. He was about to try the electric lockpick on the back door when Miller tried the knob and found it unlocked.

"Hello. What's this?"

"Ordinary B and E?" Scott dropped the lockpick back into the bag.

"Maybe." Miller twisted the knob and let the door swing open.

They both stepped inside, Scott putting the bag he was carrying down just inside the doorway. Through the archway beyond the kitchen they could see the smashed table, broken vase, and scattered mail on the floor of the front hall. They both immediately pulled their sidearms.

"DEA. Is anybody here?" Miller called.

The house was quiet.

Relatively certain that the house was empty they split up. Scott covered the ground floor while Miller checked upstairs.

When Miller had completed his sweep he found Scott in the dining room looking out the window. "If this was a burglary, it was the neatest burglary in history. The upstairs looks untouched."

"Same down here, except for the front hall." Scott replied.

"I found an itinerary for the owners in an upstairs desk. They're not coming back for almost a week."

"That's nice to know." Scott answered distractedly. He looked back at the dining room table, then again at the windows.

Miller looked past his partner out the window. The view almost directly across the street was the house they were interested in. "Good view."

"Uh-huh."

Scott picked up one of the dining room chairs and found that the feet fit perfectly into indentations in the carpeting in front of the windows. Miller saw what his partner was thinking and picked up a second chair, which fit into a second set of indentations next to the first.

They sat down in the chairs side by side and noticed they were angled in front of the windows to look directly at the house across the street.

"Well." Miller paused. "What do you think this means?"

"Beats the shit out of me, but I'm sure it means something."

*****

Something was going on with Scott and Miller, Dorado was utterly certain of that. What, he had to admit, he just flat didn't know. He was fairly sure that it was all somehow connected to the shooting at the docks six days ago.

He had read over Miller's incident report about the shooting. It fit the crime scene facts, if only just barely, and it offered absolutely nothing beyond what could be discerned from the raw physical evidence. Why a drug dealer would hang out on the dock at 4AM without an apparent buyer was a mystery. Why he had decided to shoot it out with a DEA agent, when he had to know that they had no probable cause to search him or his vehicle, was also a mystery. A common street dealer might get jumpy, but veterans of the drug trade knew the ins and outs of the law as well as, and sometimes better than, the police pursuing them. Nick Sandesci had been moving product at some point or other in the food chain for going on twenty years. It just didn't fit. And why Miller had acted to shoot as he did – a single low-caliber round that had left Nick up and around for at least a minute, according to the medical examiner's report, when the dealer's weapon had been positively discharged three times, was maybe the biggest mystery of all. Where was his service weapon? Why only the single shot? Finally, the petty dealer who had sent them to the docks, whom they definitely had been following the night before the shooting as evidenced by the request for a license plate check, was missing, disappeared, Casper in the wind. Until he turned up dead or alive, there was no action for Dorado to pursue in that direction.

Dorado fingered the report on the blotter in front of him, one corner already dog-eared from two dozen readings. He knew what the report said without opening it. Why was the drug dealer out there? No answer, not even conjecture. Why had the dealer fired upon Miller? No answer again, other than to state that the dealer had definitely fired first after Miller had identified himself as a DEA agent. Where was his service revolver? Back in the van with Scott – this forced him to use his backup to defend himself. Why had he left his primary weapon in the car? No answer. Where had the dealer's three rounds gone, as an examination of the rest of the dock, nearby boats, and the dockmaster's shack which Miller claimed he had been hiding behind had not turned up any of them? No answer, the implication being that at a distance of less than thirty feet all three shots had gone high and sailed out into the water, lost forever. And finally, why had Miller fired only once? Here, in complete conflict with the medical examiner's report, Miller claimed that the wound had been swiftly fatal.

Dorado got up from his desk and stood, holding the report, and looked out the window at the lot below, nearly empty of cars on a Saturday morning. All of it was suspicious, improbable, and highly unlikely in fact, but none of it was damning.

Some of these questions Dorado could get answers to at the shooting review board that was scheduled for Thursday afternoon, but he had a sinking suspicion that events were accelerating, that time was running out. The feeling seemed akin to superstition to Dorado, because he had no idea whatsoever what time was running out on, but it persisted nonetheless. He was tempted to call Miller into the office and simply nail him with some of these questions point blank; he was sure Miller's story would crack. But of course, that would have been a violation of Miller's rights under the union regulations. Dorado ground his teeth, turned, and slapped the report down on the desktop.

Still, nothing in the regs said that Dorado couldn't keep an eye on Miller's activities, and so he had.

They had checked out a car the previous morning and returned the previous evening, logging almost exactly two hundred miles. Dorado pulled a map of California and a compass from his desk. Consulting the scale at the corner of the map, he drew a circle with a one-hundred-mile radius centered on the agency parking lot. If they had taken a circuitous route or driven to more than one location then this analysis was doomed to fail, but if they had made a beeline to wherever they went, Dorado liked what he saw. Geography was with him.

LA, because it was on the coast, sliced half of the circumference of the circle off immediately as likely destinations because they were in the Pacific. To the south and east was San Diego, but it was more like 130 miles to that city – a little too far. Ditto Palm Springs. San

Bernadino due east was too close. Barstow was about 100 miles to the north and east. Not a big city, but not insignificant either. Nothing lay 100 miles to the north but uninhabited desert, Edwards Air Force Base, and the tiny city of Mojave, so small that it was hardly the size of a pinhead on his map. Northwest? Well, to the northwest lay Santa Barbara. Dorado smiled – that seemed likely.

He slid the list of banks from under his blotter. He didn't know what the list of banks meant either, but he thought it was the key to all of it, if for no other reason than it was the sole piece of evidence in his possession that he knew Scott and Miller had lied to him about, claiming instead that they had been searching the laptop for a list of associates. There were roughly a dozen banks and credit unions scattered throughout the list that had offices in Santa Barbara or Goleta. If he called those offices, would he have his answers? Dorado thought it likely, but on what authority could he make such calls? He didn't know, and so had reached another dead end.

What could he make out of the single bank account that he did know something about? Peter Ryder, the owner of the account, was also by no small coincidence the owner of the home Scott and Miller had been staking out seven days ago. A call this morning to his friend at Pacific Union Bank revealed that the account continued to have zero balance. And what of Mr. Ryder himself? His office hadn't seen him, and while everyone thought that strange, especially in the last critical shooting weeks of a movie, no one thought enough of it to actually worry, or look for him, or God forbid contact the police. A call to his home found a wife utterly unconcerned that neither she, nor anyone else, had seen her husband for going on six days now. He drank, consumed vast quantities of recreational drugs, had a mistress, dabbled in gambling and prostitutes, and it wasn't the first time he had disappeared for days at a time. She was certain he would turn up. He always did, a bad penny incarnate. And could Dorado please excuse her as she had shopping to do and a lunch date with friends at eleven? Thank you. Click.

The last piece of the puzzle that Dorado had in his possession had arrived in his 'In' box early this morning. A report from the equipment supervisor stated that after returning the car Scott and Miller had again checked out the surveillance van, night scope, telephoto camera, microphone, this time including a remote tracking system late last night. They were watching someone, but who, where, why? Dorado found the lack of information frustrating.

He looked down at the list of banks. It was all about the bank list – it had to be! It was the only thing that Scott and Miller had blatantly lied about. He tapped his index finger on the pages. The very first bank, the one that maybe started it all, was a Bank of America right here in LA. Maybe as the regional director of the DEA he could make a call. He knew that in that direction lay some very thin ice. An officious bank officer could demand to know on what authority he wanted to see confidential bank information, and of course he really didn't have any. A complaint could be lodged against him with the treasury department which, while not a career killer, could prove to be an enormous pain in the ass. On the other hand, one helpful banker could give him the wedge he needed to crack this nut wide open.

Dorado sat down in his chair and drummed his fingers on the desktop. He looked at his phone then glanced at the clock face set in a marble paperweight nearby, a ten-year service award. It was 11:35 on a Saturday morning; many banks closed at noon. Tomorrow was Sunday, and then no matter what he knew or suspected there was very little chance that he could find anyone to call or talk to him until Monday morning.

He knew Scott and Miller were up to something, right? He knew it involved the banks, right? Time was running out, the second hand sweeping out circles inexorably.

He picked up the handset and dialed.

*****

Several hours later a tow truck arrived at the house and dropped off another man, leading Scott and Miller to the conclusion that it had been car trouble that caused them to arrive too late at the bank in a cab to get the money. They didn't recognize the man – tall, black hair, dark featured – and Miller took a few pictures.

They had yet to identify any of the people in the house, a process they could have started by simply calling the DMV about the Toyota in the driveway. As close as they were to the money, they were hoping to leave as little official paper trail as possible, so they had chosen not to. What they had done was use a reverse directory to identify the owner of the home as Jason Taylor. Whether Taylor was the one pretending to be Ryder, whether the Toyota was his, and whether he was involved at all, they didn't know.

Until they had an opportunity to get into the house and look around, and maybe plant a few bugs, they were pretty much shit out of luck. All they could do was watch and see what they could learn.

*****

Ricky returned to find them all sitting around in the living room.

"Before you even ask," Jason said from one of the recliners, "we didn't get the money. The taxi wasn't fast enough."

"Fuck!" Ricky slammed his fist against the wall.

"Hey! Easy on that! I'm still making payments." Jason

shouted.

Ricky looked deflated. “So, where is it going to be next?”

“I’ve checked the list. Monday at 9AM it will be at a Greater Pacific Bank in Menlo Park.”

“New Jersey?”

“That’s funny. Chip asked the same thing. There’s a Menlo Park in California, up North, near Palo Alto.”

“We can drive up Sunday night,” Chip said from his seat on the couch, “and stay at a hotel. We simply get up and get it the next morning.”

“Not in my car we can’t.”

“What happened to the car, Ricky?” Deirdre asked.

“Timing belt went.”

Jason snorted a laugh, and then swallowed it when Ricky gave him a venomous glare. The bodyguard at the passport maker had warned Ricky about the timing belt, a fact that Ricky didn’t want to be reminded of.

“The timing belt went,” Ricky began again, “and the engine ate itself.”

“We can’t all fit in either car.” Deirdre pointed out.

“We’ll have to take both.” Ricky replied.

Chip shook his head. “Not to rain on your parade, but my car’s not all that dependable. If we take my car, we’re likely to have a repeat of today.”

"We sure as hell can't all fit in the Porsche."

Jason shrugged, "So some of us will go and get the money and bring it back here."

"Oh, and who goes and who stays?" Ricky sneered.

"My car, and I have the passport, I'll go. Chip can go with me."

"Yeah, right." Ricky laughed sourly. "And Dee and I will just wait here while you take off."

Jason moved forward to sit on the edge of his seat and pointed at the floor, "This is my house –" He stopped and stood up, waving his hands in front of him. "You know what? This has been too long a day already, and I don't have the energy to fight with you now. We have until tomorrow evening before we have to leave, so we'll figure it out tomorrow."

Ricky began to object, but Jason ignored him and went upstairs.

*****

The list of banks and a scratch pad of notes sat on his lap, but he had stopped looking at them long ago. Jason knew that this time they would get it right. He sat sideways on the bed in the guest bedroom with his back against the wall and his legs out straight.

Chip passing by in the hallway stopped when he saw Jason and came into the room. "I was wondering where you were. Is something wrong?"

"No." He put the papers aside and rubbed his eyes with the heels of his hands, then dropped his arms to his sides. "Just thinking."

"About what?"

Jason smiled ruefully, "Mostly Kelly. I feel like she should be here after all the work she put in. I don't want her to be left out. And I think I kind of miss her."

"Call her."

"After what happened? She won't talk to me."

Chip shook his head, "Call her."

"You think?"

"What can it hurt?"

Jason picked up the phone off the nightstand and dialed Kelly's number.

Chip watched as Jason waited, frowned, then hit the disconnect button and dialed again. "What's up?" He asked.

Jason held up one finger as he listened. He hung up the phone and got up from the bed. "I get a message saying the number has been disconnected without forwarding information. I must have the number wrong."

He passed Chip and headed towards the master bedroom. Chip turned slowly to follow him, a dawning understanding of what was going on.

He found Jason in the master bedroom, his cell phone held to his ear. After a moment he took the phone away from his ear and turned it off. He tossed the phone onto the bed. "She moved today."

Chip nodded.

"Did she give you her new number or address?"

"No," Chip shook his head, "You?"

"No."

"Call her work number."

"Her work number was her home number."

Deirdre came into the room. "Why the long faces?"

"Nothing," Jason said distractedly.

"Then smile." She came over to Jason and used her fingers to push up the corners of his mouth. "In a day and a half, we're going to be rich! Let's go out and celebrate!"

Jason looked over at Chip who shrugged, "Sure, why not?"

"Wow. Aren't you guys fun? I'm going to change. You know a good bar around here?"

"Yeah," Chip nodded, "I think we know a place."

*****

When they stepped into the bar it took a moment for their eyes to adjust, as the room was mostly in darkness except for the stage at the far end that was bathed in the smoky beams of blue and white spotlights.

Chip leaned over to Jason, "Tonight's the night they start the live music thing."

"Yeah, right." Jason nodded. "Blues or something."

"As long as they have beer, they can whistle polka

music out their assholes for all I care." Ricky said as he pushed past Jason and Chip to take a chair at a nearby empty table.

Jason looked back to see Deirdre standing in the doorway, her silver dress glowing almost ghostly in the dim light. She glided past him, her silence emphasizing the feeling of the ethereal, and sat in a chair next to Ricky. Chip and Jason took the remaining two chairs at the table, Jason next to Deirdre, and Chip between Jason and Ricky. The waitress came by and everyone ordered beer, Ricky with a shot of bourbon.

They sat watching the people at the tables around them, feeling already somewhat disconnected from reality. In two days they would all be rich. What would that feel like? Nothing seemed real anymore, everything floating unanchored in the middle distance.

The buzz in the room quieted as a band took the stage. The bassist picked up a guitar and plucked a few chords, adjusting the tension of the strings to the pitch in his head. The drummer sat down on the stool and shifted its position around as he picked up the sticks. Jason looked down when he heard the clunk of the waitress putting the beer bottle on the table in front of him, and then looked back up to see that a woman had appeared on the stage while he was distracted. It was as if she had come out of nowhere.

She had on a long, jet-black dress made of some shimmery velvet, blue highlights from the spotlights racing liquidly along the fabric. Her hair was likewise black, long and trailing over one shoulder and down her chest, rippling like satin. She took the microphone in one slender hand, her nails painted brilliant red like her lips, her skin luminously pale.

The music began behind her, something slow and bluesy, lots of deep bass and cymbals. Jason took a swallow of beer.

We've had a lot of fun, baby
There's no denying that's true
But our love is over
And there's nothing we can do
So I'm packing up my suitcase
I'm going to hit the road
I have to leave us behind, baby
It's hurting me more than you can know.

"Would you like to dance?"

Deirdre was smiling at Jason, and he felt his heart flutter in his throat. "Well, I-" he stammered.

"Come on." She stood, took him by the hand, pulled him up out of his seat.

He looked over at Ricky who was smoking a cigarette in violation of about a hundred city ordinances and sipping at the bourbon. "Do you mind?"

Ricky waved at him absently with the hand holding the cigarette and shook his head.

She led him weaving through the tables to the open area that had been cleared in front of the stage. Jason's thoughts were a blur, the silver figure of Deirdre leading him ahead like a Siren, adding to the unreality of the evening. When they got in front of the stage Jason realized that it wasn't really set up as a dance floor – it was just a space without tables, and they were the only couple in the space when they got there.

Deirdre turned him towards her, draped her arms around his neck and leaned in close, her body warm and pliant against his, contacting him completely from his chest all the way down to his knees.

He put his arms around her awkwardly, his hands resting on the bare skin of her back, the intimacy of the naked skin sending a rush of blood to his face. He moved his hands downwards, seeking the security of a layer of fabric between her and him, going all the way to her ass before sliding across the glassy surface of the satin. He pulled his hands away quickly as if he had touched something hot, and settled for putting them on her back.

She laughed against his throat, her face nestled in the crook of his neck. She began to sway her hips with the music, a maddening friction against him.

I'm leaving us behind, baby.
I'm leaving it all behind.
You know I'll always love you, baby
I'm leaving it all behind.

He smelled her hair, a combination of cigarette smoke and lilac. She was shimmying down his body now, her head at about the height of his groin. He reached down and took her by the shoulders, stood her up, and she melted against him again laughing.

"Hey, could you-" he tried to gently move her away a little, get a wedge of light between them, "Could you tone it down about a thousand watts? I feel like I'm getting a lap dance."

She pulled her body back from his, to Jason it felt like the breaking of a vacuum seal on a jar, and moved into a sort of modified waltz. She was a surprisingly graceful dancer. Jason relied on dimly remembered dancing lessons he had taken before his senior class prom.

"I don't know how to relate to you." She said quietly, her mouth close to his ear.

"What do you mean?"

"All my life guys have only wanted one thing from me. But you're different."

"Nice guy syndrome."

She shrugged, a small motion he could feel through his arms, "Yeah."

"Nice guys finish last."

"They don't have to." She shook her head. "They won't this time."

Jason digested this bit of Zen wisdom. It meshed naturally with his Catholic upbringing of 'the meek shall inherit the earth,' and made him feel that just maybe she was right.

"That's some dress."

Deirdre put on a bad Southern accent. "This old thing? It's just a little something I threw on."

He noticed a dark smear of grease down near the hem. "What's this?" He started to lift the fabric to get a better look.

"It's nothing." She pushed his hand aside, letting the fabric fall back into place.

She leaned back in his arms, causing him to dip her, albeit awkwardly, as they danced.

"What are you going to do with the money when you get it?"

He shrugged. "I've been working so hard that I really

haven't thought it all through. I'd like to pay off the house and the car, but how would I account for all the money to the government?" Jason thought about getting his mother the care she needed, but didn't think this was the time, and didn't know Deirdre well enough, to bring it up.

Deirdre bit her lip and shook her head, but didn't say anything.

"I suppose I could deposit it as cash nine thousand dollars at a time, because cash deposits under ten thousand dollars aren't flagged. Still after a million or so dollars it would have to raise some eyebrows, not to mention that it would take me a good chunk of a year to deposit it all, and that's if I did nine thousand every single day. Split four ways we get one point seven five million apiece."

Even saying the number aloud sounded unreal to Jason.

They were still alone on the dance floor though many people watched them dance, many of the men watching Deirdre's figure closely.

"What do I want a house for, anyway? I've got no job here, not much of a life. I could move somewhere else where no one knows me, maybe buy a house quietly for cash. Like I said, I don't know; I haven't thought it through enough. What are you and Ricky going to do when you get the money?"

"I don't give a fuck what he does," Deirdre said bitterly, surprising Jason with her anger. She paused and swallowed, then began again. "This money is going to let me get away from him. Far, far away."

"He doesn't own you. You could have left any time you wanted to. What does the money change?"

"I would have thought you would understand more than most people. The money changes everything. Look at what you've done for it. I need it too, and I can't run a computer. Shit, I can't even type. I left Red Mountain with Ricky before I had even finished high school."

"So where are you going to go? What are you going to do?"

"I don't know."

The silence stretched between them as they swayed to the music.

Deirdre looked up suddenly, catching Jason's eyes with her own. "Do you think that maybe we could 'I don't know' together?"

Jason opened his mouth to speak but nothing came out.

The song finished and the audience applauded. It echoed in his head and made it hard for him to think. They had stopped swaying and stood transfixed.

The applause died down and the next song began.

Deirdre blinked. "Forget I asked." She broke away from him and moved back towards the table, leaving him standing alone.

He waited just a moment and then trotted after her, catching her by one arm. "Deirdre, wait."

She turned back to him, no expression on her face that he could read.

"I, that is to say, I wanted to," he took a deep breath and tried again, "This has been kind of a wild week for me;

I lost my job, committed about three hundred felonies, found a fortune. It's all been moving so fast that I've stopped thinking about the future really; I'm just trying to hang on tight and get through now. Do you understand?"

"OK." Deirdre said noncommittally.

"What I mean to say is, after we get the money and Ricky leaves, you can stay at the house for as long as you'd like. I'd – I'd like you to stay."

Her smile lit up her whole face. "I'd like that too."

He couldn't help but smile back at her, though his nerves jangled as with a low electrical current. "And you'll find the rent very reasonable."

She punched him lightly on the shoulder, and then kissed him on the mouth, her tongue darting between her lips to touch his. "Maybe we can work out something in barter."

Jason swallowed. Deirdre took his hand and put it around her waist, and walked back to the table. It was difficult maneuvering the narrow aisles around the tables that way, but she wouldn't let go of his hand.

Ricky had watched the whole exchange between them carefully, as he had been quietly doing for days now. If sniffing around Deirdre's crotch kept Jason searching for the money that was just fine with Ricky. As for Deirdre, maybe she needed a little reining in – it wouldn't do to have her getting ideas, start thinking about her own future.

In the long run, of course, it didn't matter, Ricky thought as he tossed the shot of bourbon, his third, down his throat and felt the warm acid rise, which he then cooled with a swallow of beer. He had decided several days ago that he was going to keep all the money for himself. Every penny. Fuck Deirdre and the rest of them.

*****

They came out of the house and crossed the street, walking quickly, but not so quickly as to attract attention. They were both dressed nicely, and the slim black case that Miller carried would be mistaken for a businessman's briefcase at a distance.

At the front door Scott rang the doorbell once, though they had seen the four of them leave, and their surveillance convinced them to a near certainty that no one else was in the home. He fitted the electric lock pick into the door. He had it open inside of ten seconds. They stepped inside and closed the door behind them. Scott started his wristwatch stopwatch function – he planned to be in and out in less than five minutes.

"It would have been nice to wire the cars, but they took them both." Miller commented.

"It doesn't matter. We know where they're going to pick up the money."

Scott moved into the kitchen. He took the phone off the wall and unplugged the wire leading to the handset. He clipped off the modular jack end with a pair of wire cutters, and then crimped on a new modular plug that also contained a transmitter using tools from the case. It would relay both sides of any phone conversation as well as any number dialed on the phone to recording equipment they had set up in the house across the street.

As he hung up the phone Miller called from the living room. "In here."

Scott found him on the floor near a bookshelf with a

college yearbook open in his hands. He taped a picture. "Jason Taylor. He's the one pretending to be Ryder."

"Any of the others in there?"

"Not that I could see."

"OK. Let's look around upstairs."

Scott moved upstairs. Miller followed him after shelving the yearbook. On the way down the hallway Miller looked into the spare bedroom and called Scott back.

"Check it out." Miller stepped into the bedroom, noticing the map on the wall, flipped through the papers on the desk. "Busy little bees. Give me one of the flat bugs."

Scott opened the case and handed Miller a microphone and transmitter about the diameter of a quarter and twice as thick with an adhesive strip on the back. It would pick up anything said in the room, even the smallest whisper, and transmit it up to a mile on a rotating frequency band. The battery was good for ten days. Miller pulled out the desk chair and leaned underneath the desk, mounting the bug on the underside of the desk surface. Scott took pictures of everything with his phone.

That finished, they moved down to the master bedroom. Scott opened the doorway to the closet, which he noted was open a crack when he got there.

"How do you know this is his closet?"

"His house, master bedroom, his closet. What have we got?" He knelt down and looked at the shoes arrayed on the floor. There were only two pairs: sneakers and docksiders. "We'll wire them both."

Scott opened the briefcase on the floor, and they got to work. He used a small drill to bore a tiny hole into the sole of one docksider, then handed the drill to Miller who started on a sneaker. A small vacuum cleaner from inside the case sucked up the tiny bits of rubber. He pulled the tracking device from a small vial. It was a sphere only a few millimeters in diameter and would transmit a beacon to a specialized receiver nearly five miles away, depending on the geography. Its internal battery would last a week.

He dropped the sphere into the hole in the shoe. A row of bottles in the briefcase held rubberized compounds of various colors. Scott picked a brown closest to the color of the sole and carefully filled in and smoothed over the hole with a metal spatula. He dried it using a heat gun. The repair would be nearly invisible and also waterproof.

He checked his watch, "Three minutes."

"Not a problem." Miller was smoothing the filler over the hole in the sneaker.

He dried it with the heat gun while Scott put everything else back into the case.

The shoes went back into the closet and the door was left open a crack. Everything was just as it had been when they got there.

"Test it."

Miller took a flat case that looked like an iPhone with another smaller box mounted on top out of his jacket pocket. He turned it on and the screen flashed a moment during warm up, and then displayed a local street map on the LCD screen. Two small X's blinked on top of each other, a number next to each X indicating an ID number sent by the tracking device. Miller played with the zoom feature, expanding the view until it contained just the street they were on, and then zoomed back out until it showed half of Los Angeles County.

He turned it off and dropped it back into his pocket. "A-OK."

Miller picked up the case and they stepped back, scanning the carpet for anything they might have left. Satisfied, they went back up the hall the way they had come, stopping at the second bedroom to check that room also looked as it should. Scott stepped in and pushed the desk chair back in, crouching down to align the feet with the grooves in the carpet as best he could.

"We good?" Miller asked from the doorway.

Scott stood up dusting off his hands on each other, "Yeah, we're good."

They left the house four minutes and fourteen seconds after they had entered it.

*****

They came in through the front door laughing, more than a little drunk. Deirdre with her arms thrown around Jason's neck, up on the toes of her high heels, her cheek resting against his shoulder. Jason flipped on the lights with one hand, the one not around Deirdre's waist. Chip followed them in also laughing, his face flushed, his hands holding his stomach. Ricky came in last. He was not laughing.

Jason and Deirdre fell into a heap on the couch, the pirouette of their fall wrapping the front panel of her dress around both their legs, exposing her nearly to the crotch. Chip flopped into the recliner on the opposite side of the coffee table, his laughter reduced to wheezing giggles. Ricky closed the door.

Jason leaned his head back against the cushions, an arm thrown over his eyes. The room spun slowly around him. Deirdre lay with her head to one side, a cascade of blonde hair spilling across her face.

Ricky stepped forward and grabbed Deirdre by the hand. He hauled her to her feet, her dress unwinding from Jason with a whispering sound.

She fell against Ricky and clung to him unsteadily, her eyelids half open. "Hiya, sailor." She said, and laughed.

He turned her around and sent her up the stairs with a smack on her behind. "You guys can sleep down here. The adults are taking the bedroom."

Jason waved an arm in the air at nothing. Chip was already asleep.

Ricky followed her upstairs. She wove uncertainly down the hallway, her hands sliding along one wall and then the other as she found her way into the master bedroom. He caught up to her, kicking the door shut with his heel as he wrapped his arms around her from behind, his hands finding the open slash in front, probing through to her breasts.

She turned to face him, pushed away from him lightly with her hands, "Wait here."

She crossed to the radio on the nightstand, her hips already swaying to the music in her head. She turned it on and spun the dial until she found something that kind of matched her rhythm.

She moved back to him, danced around him with her body close, her hands trailing below his waistline, feeling him hard through his jeans. She turned her back to him, lifted her hair from the nape of her neck. "Do you mind?"

He undid the tiny hooks at her neck and waist. She dropped her hair, her arms forward, the dress skimming down her body into a pile at her feet. The slide of the silk against her skin made her feel sexy. She stepped out of the pile, wavered unsteadily on her heels for a moment, and then started swaying to the music wearing nothing but the thong underwear and the shoes.

His hands trailed up her as she danced in front of him; buttocks, crotch, waist, breasts. He picked her up easily like a child, one arm at her back and the other under her knees. He spun her around and Deirdre felt the blood rush to her head; maybe she passed out for a moment.

The next thing she felt was a drop of sweat falling into her eye, Ricky's face above hers, him ramming into her relentlessly, the warm alcohol haze leaving her. The stinging made her clench her eyes shut, and Ricky's metronomic thrusting reminded her of going white water rafting as a teenager, the water a heavy froth around her, flattened molars of rock poking through the surging green water. Keeping her eyes closed, she could almost hear the white noise booming of the river off the canyon walls.

Her hands felt his back, the muscles of his shoulders bunched underneath the skin as he supported his weight. His mouth clamped suddenly against hers, his jaw prying, his tongue darting between her lips as her mouth opened, his breath beery and with the underlying sharp tang of bourbon. She inhaled shallowly through her nose, each breath quickly forced out of her as he drove her repeatedly into the mattress.

Ricky shifted his weight to one side, holding himself in a one-arm pushup as the other hand clutched savagely at her breast, the thumb and forefinger crushing the nipple. She whipped her head to the side, breaking her mouth free of his, gasping for air and at the sharp pain in her chest. Ricky apparently took this as encouragement, accelerating his tempo to a fever pitch; Deirdre could count the springs pressing into her back from the mattress.

She turned her head back and opened her eyes to find him staring at her, his dark eyes boring into her. She saw a flicker of emotion in those eyes, anger or hatred, something cold and reptilian coiling in the irises, so dark brown they were nearly black. A tendril of fear unwound in her stomach, climbing into her throat like a choking vine. She put her hands against his shoulders to push him off. In a flash his hands gathered hers at the wrists, pinning them above her head to the bed. His weight entirely upon her for a moment, the air pressed from her lungs leaving her gasping.

She thrashed. He crossed her wrists allowing him to pin her arms with a single vice-like hand, the other hand again finding her breast and twisting the nipple savagely. Her ribcage creaking, she sucked in air to scream. His hand left her breast and covered her nose and mouth. She tried to breathe and could only draw a thin stream of air through his fingers.

Her chest felt tight, his eyes locked with hers, his thrusting as merciless as the pounding ocean, her shoulders screaming with the strain of her arms stretched and pinned above her head. She tried to turn her head to the side, break the hold on her mouth, but he clamped down harder, cutting off all air and pressing her head down into the pillow.

Blood pounded in her ears, her vision narrowed as if she were looking through a tunnel, Ricky's grunting becoming echoed and distant. She twisted her wrists within his grasp, waved her fingers, and bucked feebly to try and throw him off. Ricky at the end of the tunnel grinned sadistically.

His hand slipped off her mouth to her throat, crushing down on her windpipe. His mouth mashed against hers, his tongue probing. Deirdre thought she tasted blood, but wasn't sure. The world was going dim, as if someone had just turned off an old tube television, the world shrinking down to a dimming dot. Her eyes slid away from his, her mind a jumble of colors and disconnected images. She was looking at the creamy white of the wall nearest the bed, but black spots like birds swooped and circled across its surface. They grew and joined, the birds coming closer, the wall more dark than light. Time slowed to a crawl, each beat of her heart marking seconds that stretched out into infinity.

And then Ricky was gone.

She lay motionless for some time before realizing that his weight was off of her, had to consciously form the thought that she should take a breath before her lungs reacted. At the first shuddering inhalation, the cool air burned in her throat like fire. She drew her arms down from overhead, heard both shoulders pop as the joints realigned and rolled onto her side to hang her head over the edge of the bed. Every heartbeat was an agony that pounded in her temples, but the blackness receded, the colors becoming too bright, the edges of the bed frame sharply defined, now a television with the contrast too high. She maybe felt nauseous, but she wasn't certain; the signals coming from her body were all jumbled.

She found that she had to concentrate for each breath as if her body had forgotten how. The carpet and bed frame was bright, then dim, fuzzy, then sharp, her sight like a car with a sprung suspension slowly returning to equilibrium.

There was a dampness on one cheek. She trailed a numb finger along her mouth and held it in front of her face – blood. Probing around her lips she found a ragged tear, probably from being forced against her teeth, or his. The cut was sore now, but her senses were still coming on line, and she was certain it would hurt much, much worse later.

Ricky was breathing behind her, slow and even, a bear at rest in its lair.

She thought about getting dressed and going downstairs, stealing the keys to the Porsche and driving away. She thought about getting the gun from her purse, she could see it in the corner of her vision lying on the floor across the room, and blowing his dick off.

She can picture herself doing it, rolling into a sitting position, walking across the room naked past the clothing strewn on the floor, bending over and getting the purse. She rummages through it, finally feeling her hand wrap around the cool metal grip. She drops the purse, the gun in her hand, the burnished nickel finish glowing softly in the dim room light.

She walks back to the bedside, clutching the gun now in both hands, looking down at Ricky, fear and self-loathing churn within her, toss her, a small flower caught in a whirlwind. She reverses the grip in her hand, her thumb in on the trigger, brings the gun up and puts the cold, oily barrel in her mouth.

Deirdre, lying on her side on the bed, felt as if something had broken within her. A deep tremor started in her stomach and traveled upward to lodge in her throat like a hard, hot ball. She swallowed against it, refused to give it a voice. Tears started streaming down her cheeks unnoticed, mixing with the blood on her cheek to stain the pillowcase near her head pink. Her body was shaking and she could not stop it.

“Sleep tight. Don’t let the bedbugs bite.” Ricky, apparently not asleep, said from the other side of the bed.

Deirdre does not, cannot, answer him. She drew her knees up against her chest. As the sheet slid away she felt his semen cooling and drying between her thighs.

She wrapped one arm around her knees, bowed her head, and prayed for sleep.

1 Day Earlier

Twenty minutes. Seven million dollars. Twenty minutes. Seven million dollars. The two facts flashed alternately in Dorado's mind like neon signs, and had been doing so ever since he had gotten off the phone yesterday. He had lain awake all night sifting, sorting, discarding theories, and finally climbing out of his twisted sheets as the very first hint of gray dawn was visible in the cracks around his window shade, arriving at his desk at dawn.

Dorado sat at his desk on Sunday morning, rolling a Styrofoam cup half-filled with hot water between his large hands. Intending to have tea this morning instead of coffee, he had forgotten to put the tea bag into the cup at all. So far he had drunk about half the cup and had yet to notice the error. He was a little preoccupied.

Twenty minutes. Seven million dollars.

From the phone call yesterday he had learned that Peter Ryder's account – the first one on his list anyway – had held over seven million dollars for exactly twenty minutes 7 days ago, four-twenty to four-forty AM. Wired in, wired out.

Twenty minutes. Seven million dollars.

What up until that moment had seemed an impenetrable curtain beyond which all the answers lay, had suddenly, as Dorado had hung up the phone, sprouted a single thread. If pulled just right, he was certain everything would unravel.

He had snatched up the list of banks. It was no longer just a list of random banks in California; it was a timeline – twenty minutes a bank, three banks and hour, seventy-two banks a day. Scott and Miller had checked the car out at 7:40 and possibly driven to Santa Barbara. Where was the money two hours later when they got there? Dorado made some hasty hash marks on the desk blotter, then relented to a lifetime as a C-minus math student and pulled out a small solar-powered calculator that he kept in his desk.

Failure. Bank number three seventy six, by his calculation, was in San Francisco. Why had they gone to Santa Barbara?

He had stared at the list until his vision telescoped down, highlighting the few entries around number three seventy six. That was when he noticed that bank three seventy four was in Goleta. Scratching his head he looked at the map of California on his wall. The money had been in the Goleta bank from nine to nine-twenty. Even at seventy miles an hour they could not have made the trip by nine, and that ignored Friday morning traffic that would have held the 101 at a standstill. And yet they had rushed to get to a bank they couldn't get to in time, when they could have gotten to, say, bank three ninety in San Diego with plenty of time to spare. What made that bank so special?

Dorado knew that he was pushing his luck – not every bank officer he called would be sympathetic to his inquiries – but this was the call that he felt could answer everything. Luck was still with him as he caught the bank manager at her desk and more than willing to talk about her very unusual Friday morning with the deputy director of the DEA, even if he was calling seventy-five miles outside of his jurisdiction. Her story of seven million dollars wired into the account and then converted to cash via another wire order, only to be wired away twenty minutes later was astonishing. Seven million dollars, cash! Twenty minutes! More astonishing still was Peter Ryder arriving only minutes too late to withdraw the money. And the icing on the cake, ladies and gentlemen? Miller and Scott charging in with a story about a federal investigation and a drug dealer, demanding account records, bank surveillance photos, and interviewing everyone in sight. A thousand possible scenarios unfolded in his mind so rapidly that, as he hung up the phone, he swore he could feel his head expanding to fit them all.

He swallowed another mouthful of hot, flavorless water unnoticed and thought he finally had a picture that fit the facts, as he knew them.

Scott and Miller saw a small time drug dealer at the party, ran his plates, gotten his address, and pinched him at home. Faced with prison, or whatever other threats they chose to deliver, the little fish turned in the bigger fish – a big deal going down at the docks. Poor Tommy, he had given up his source, so he blew town, ergo one missing drug dealer. Down at the docks Ryder was buying from Nick, using his laptop to wire the payment, only Miller showed up and shot Nick. Ryder set the money in motion, probably with a routine already set up for just such an emergency, and ran. Scott and Miller used data from the laptop to follow Ryder and the money. It all fit perfectly.

Dorado shook his head and grumbled to himself. No, it didn't.

It didn't explain why Miller shot the drug dealer at all, let alone only once with his backup gun and not his service weapon, nor did it explain who shot the computer and why. Ryder to destroy his trail? Why not just take it with him? Maybe of the three shots Nick had fired two had been into the computer. None of the scenarios Dorado had assembled so far had a sound reason for Nick to shoot the laptop, and even if he shot the laptop, the bullets should have been dug out of the dock somewhere. In fact, no matter who shot the laptop, the bullets had to have gone somewhere. That remained an unpleasant and unexplained facet that still baffled him.

Why, as he continued to play devil's advocate with himself, had Ryder arrived too late to get the money? He wrote the program – he certainly should know where the money was going to be and when. And why had he waited so long to get it?

Holes. Even his newest theory had lots of holes.

Still despite the holes, there were many things that the theory could perhaps illuminate for him. Just for starters, it told him that the routing program sometimes moved the money into cash.

Seven million dollars in cash! But only for twenty minutes!

Again, looking at the list of banks, Dorado realized that not every bank on the list could produce seven million dollars cash on short notice – most of them actually. The routing program must take that into account, as well as the fact that there would be no point in converting the money to cash outside of business hours, when the banks are closed and Ryder can't get to it. So maybe only a couple of times a day, or better yet only once a day, the money is converted into cash form for quick withdrawal. That explained why the Goleta bank was so important – it was the bank that did the cash conversion that day. When would it happen next? Monday morning, 9AM, a Greater Pacific Bank in Menlo Park near Palo Alto could process that transaction. Dorado put a felt tip pen mark next to that bank. And the next? He counted ahead seventy two banks and found a branch of the farm workers credit union near Napa Valley. Unlikely. Next, however, was a California Savings and Trust in Redding – the money would be there between nine-twenty and nine-forty – that he suspected could do it. He made another mark. He went through the entire list, past and future, marking the banks between nine and eleven AM that he thought kept sufficient cash on hand.

What could he do with this information? Maybe plenty.

Like most federal agencies, the DEA offices were largely closed for the weekend, but there were ongoing investigations and undercover operations that required a certain degree of support. The divisions providing that support remained open 24/7. He found the number for the electronics division in the interdepartmental phonebook and dialed.

"Electronics, Tollson speaking."

The voice on the other end of the phone sounded young. Dorado made his voice gruff. "This is Deputy Director James Dorado."

"Yessir," Dorado could almost hear the man snap to attention over the phone.

"I just got dragged out of bed by some yahoo over at the BATF. He claims he has an agent in deep cover, and he thinks two of my agents may have his agent under surveillance as part of one of their investigations."

"Wow, wouldn't that be a fuckup." Tollson gave audible swallow. "Pardon me, Sir."

"Yes it would. I need the present GPS coordinates of the surveillance van checked out by Agents Miller and Scott on Friday evening."

"Yessir. Just a moment, Sir."

Several years ago GPS trackers had been installed in all the department surveillance vans. It helped to reduce exactly the problem that Dorado had cited – investigations from various agencies stepping on each other's toes – by allowing them to know where the vehicles were at any time. As a fringe benefit, it cut down on agents using the heavy-duty vehicles as personal moving and cargo vans. Finally, it had helped in the fortunately poorly publicized and rapid recovery of a surveillance van containing over a quarter of a million dollars in electronic equipment stolen off a street corner while an agent was away answering the call of nature.

While he waited Dorado took a sip from his cup. He grimaced at the blandness and noticed the cup contained only hot water. “What the hell?” He muttered.

“Sir, did you say something?”

“Nothing important. You have those coordinates?”

“Yes, Sir.” He gave them to Dorado who jotted them down on a Post It note.

“One more thing. They also checked out a number of tracking devices. Would it be possible to get another unit that would track those devices? I’d love to tell the BATF that my agents planted a bug on their man.”

“I can check the log and configure another unit for the same tracking device IDs. It would only take about an hour.”

“That would be fine. I’ll pick it up later today. You’ve been a big help, Mr. Tollson. I’ll be sure to make a note of it.” Dorado hung up on the man’s ‘Thank you, Sir,’ and looked again into the clear depths of his cup. He shook his head and put the cup aside on the desktop.

Unrolling a map he found the surveillance van apparently parked in an upper middle class neighborhood East of LA. Was that where Ryder was hiding out?

The desk chair creaked as he leaned back and tried to figure what his next move should be. If Dorado took as a given that the money was going to be moving through the Greater Pacific Bank in Menlo Park at 9AM Monday morning, and if Scott and Miller were going after it, what could he do about it?

*****

The rain fell steadily but not very hard; the sky colored a flat iron gray much darker than it would normally have been at this hour in the evening. They stood next to the Porsche in the driveway. Jason opened the driver side door and tucked a backpack with a change of clothes and a toothbrush behind the driver's seat.

He stood in the open doorway and, throwing a glance over to the other side of the car where Ricky was talking to Deirdre, leaned towards Chip and spoke in low tones, "You're going to be okay here?"

"I'm just going to be waiting here for you to bring the money back. You're the one doing the dangerous part."

Jason thumped his hand on the doorframe, "Yeah, well..."

"Besides, we can't all fit in the Porsche. Go. Drive safe. I'll be here."

Chip stepped back from the car. Jason stood with one foot in the car and one foot on the ground, feeling as if there was something more he wanted to say.

"Go." Chip said.

"Going. Going." Jason slumped into the car and closed the door. He twisted the key and the engine purred to life.

Chip knocked on the window and Jason lowered it.

"One more thing: Fred Gwynn and David Doyle."

Jason laughed and shook his head. "I don't have time for that now."

"Think about it on the trip. It's a super-hard one. I'll give you the answer when you get back."

"I'll have the answer when I get back."

"Ten thousand bucks says you don't."

"Ten thousand?"

"Hey, you'll have seven million in the trunk. I figure we can afford to up the stakes."

He smiled. "OK, Chip. You're on."

The window whined up, cutting off the space between them.

*****

Deirdre was wearing a white sleeveless turtleneck sweater, white cotton skirt, and white high heels. She looked very bright against the gray background of the evening. The turtleneck sweater hid the bruises she had found on her neck when she woke up this morning. She wore a wide bracelet made of hammered brass to cover the bruises on one wrist.

Ricky was standing close, towering over her, "You get the money tomorrow morning, and you come right back here."

"What else would I do Ricky? Where would I go?"

"Nothing and nowhere, and I don't want you thinking otherwise."

"Ricky, if you want to go get the money, then I'll stay here and you can go."

His eyes, usually so steady and penetrating, slid away from hers. "I've got some things I have to do here."

She felt a familiar cold tingling in her stomach that convinced her not to utter the question "What?" that was waiting on the tip of her tongue. "Okay." She said instead, "We'll be back tomorrow afternoon."

His eyes came back to hers, fierce, and maybe, she thought, nervous? "You bet your ass you will."

She got into the car and closed the door, Jason backing the car out of the driveway as she buckled the seatbelt, the tires hissing on the damp pavement. He gave quick one-handed wave to Chip and then popped the car into gear and accelerated down the street.

They wove their way out of the development as the dark thickened around them, passing between the pillars swathed in streamers of fog. The rain picked up as he came to the on ramp of the 101, which would take him north where he would transfer to the 5. He planned to cut back west to the 101 near Gilroy for the rest of the way into Palo Alto. He switched the wipers from intermittent to steady.

*****

They stood on the sidewalk watching the taillights of the Porsche disappear around the corner.

"Well," Chip turned to Ricky, "dinner?"

Ricky shrugged. "Sure. Why not? What are you thinking of?"

They walked up the driveway and into the garage.

"Let's see what's in the fridge."

As Chip opened the door between the garage and the house, Ricky spotted the red plastic gas can on the floor by the door. It fit into his coalescing plan to take the money for himself and burn everything to ash in his wake perfectly. He surreptitiously nudged the can with his toe, and it slid several inches – it was empty. Not perfect, he thought to himself, but that could be rectified.

"I'll tell you what." Ricky began slowly. "Lend me your car keys and I'll buy pizza."

"It's a deal." Chip dug out his keys and threw them to Ricky. "No anchovies."

Ricky caught the keys out of the air. "No anchovies. Got it. You want anything to drink?"

"I think there's Coke here."

"Okay."

They stood awkwardly for a moment, Chip finally going into the house and closing the door. Ricky took the gas can and put it into the truck of the car.

He filled it up at a Circle K he had noticed several miles away. Luck was with him – he had just enough cash left over after buying the gasoline, plus three rolls of duct tape bound together in a cellophane wrapper that he found in a bin near the cashier, to get the pizza.

*****

Scott stood in the window across the street watching the scene with binoculars. The shades were fully open, but all the lights were off in the house around him and he had little fear of being spotted. "It looks like the girl and Taylor are going."

"How can you tell?" Miller was in the window next to him working a telephoto camera on a tripod, though he had yet to take a picture. "I can't see shit."

Scott had to agree. He had tried the starlight scope first, but it had flared horribly due to a floodlight mounted on the siding next to the garage door, and yet there really wasn't enough light for the regular binoculars either. With all the technology, there just wasn't a good way to surveil a backlit scene. Still, even poorly lit it was easy to pick out the girl's figure, and the man getting into the car with her wasn't the fat one and it wasn't the bulky one; a process of elimination. Plus, he owned the car and the fake ID. "I can tell. Look at the shapes of the two guys left behind."

The Porsche backed out of the driveway and headed up the road.

Miller checked a display near him. "OK. I've got movement. He's wearing the shoes. I still think we should follow them."

Scott sighed. They had been over their plan a hundred times, and this remained the point of greatest contention between them. The tracking device would allow them to follow all the way to Palo Alto, and the money, at a discrete distance. For that matter, they knew where they were headed and could have waited for them at the bank. Miller argued that it would be easy to force them off the road and take the money somewhere on the trip back. Scott felt that most of the trip was going to be made on the 5, a very public and high traffic road for such a maneuver, and, just their luck if a state trooper happened along just as they made their move. No, Scott liked waiting to take the money here in this big, quiet subdivision, in that big, quiet house. Even if a gunshot inside could be heard outside the house, he suspected that there would be no one in the neighborhood on a Monday afternoon to hear it.

Scott thought that argument was over and done, but

Miller continued now to press his case. "I mean, you have that car and that piece of ass and seven million dollars, are you coming back?"

"All he had was a backpack. He'll at least come back for more clothes." Scott talked, the binoculars pressed to his face.

"With seven million dollars he could buy more clothes."

"I don't mean clothes exactly. I mean personal stuff – pictures, letters. This guy isn't a drifter – he owns that house. He's coming back to it. Besides, we've been listening to them for more than a day; all they talk about is meeting back here once they have the money, and – hello, where are you going?"

Scott watched as Ricky put the gas can into the trunk and got into the car. Miller got back to the camera in time to see him drive away.

"Where's he going?"

"I don't know. He took a gas can with him."

"A gas can?"

"Yeah. A five-gallon red plastic model. Maybe he needs gas for the lawnmower."

"Ha. Ha." Miller popped an Oreo cookie into his mouth from an open package on the windowsill. "I don't like it."

"Neither do I, but the money is coming back here, so we wait and stick with the plan."

They watched when Ricky returned less than half an hour later and lugged the now clearly-full gas can into the garage along with a small paper bag, and then carried a pizza into the house.

"Looks like he might have a plan of his own."

Scott, now leaning back in a chair with his legs stretched out in front of him crossed at the ankle, unscrewed an Oreo cookie and paused with the iced half near his mouth. "We'll see." He stuffed the half into his mouth whole.

*****

The only sound in the car was the vibration of the engine, and the thump of the wipers. Deirdre was silent, looking at her own reflection in the car window. Jason, driving with one hand, started looking at the list of music on his Ipod.

"I'm sorry about Kelly." She said quietly. "I didn't mean to come between you."

Jason stopped, the iPod balanced on one knee. "Kelly and I were," he paused. "Well, we were. You didn't come between us. I'm not sure there was any us to come between."

"Yeah, well, I'm sorry."

"Don't be."

They both sat and listened to the rain spatter on the windshield.

Deirdre fingered the collar of her sweater. She pulled it back and could see the bruises in her reflection livid against her neck. "Something is different about him. He's always been devious, but now I'm worried."

Jason had trouble following the conversation.

"Worried about who? Worried about Ricky?"

She tried to sort out her thoughts, put into words the iciness she felt in her veins, the feeling that disaster was closing in on them. What was Ricky going to do? Wasn't he just going to take his money and go? Had he said or done anything to make her think any differently?" Ricky, she reminded herself, had a gun.

"Deirdre?" Jason looked over and tried to catch her eyes in her reflection.

She dropped them to her lap. "Forget about it."

Jason opened his mouth, but then closed it again when he couldn't think of a good question to ask. He slowed as rain and fog wrapped around the car, the taillights of the car in front of him barely visible ahead.

"Do you think you could love me?"

The question struck Jason completely blindsides. He gaped, uncertain what answer he wanted to give, what she wanted to hear.

She continued softly before he answered her, "I've fucked up so many things. What was I supposed to do?"

"What?" was all he could think to ask.

She slid off her heels and swung one leg over his so she was straddling him kneeling, his face to her chest, a thin slice of the roadway visible over her shoulder.

"Deirdre!" The car swerved in its lane before Jason got it back under control.

"Shhhh." She pressed one finger against his lips, then trailed her hand down to his groin, opening his jeans and expertly stroking him to arousal. She lifted her skirt, wearing nothing underneath, and lowered herself onto him, gasping as he entered her. The penetration was sharply painful; Ricky had bruised her badly.

They rocked gently with the thrum of the car on the roadway, Deirdre kissing his forehead, silent tears falling in his hair. Neither of them spoke as she rode him, her rhythm augmented by the sway of the car.

Jason, for his part, was too stunned to speak. He really wasn't thinking anything at all, his whole body awash in feelings and senses almost too complex to process. He hadn't been a virgin before, but sex while driving a car at fifty miles per hour was definitely a new experience for him. It was really just about all he could do to keep the car on the road.

As he climaxed, Jason took one hand off the wheel and hugged Deirdre to his chest. The car swerved again and then steadied in its lane. He had no idea what people in other cars in the lanes around his car had seen, nor did he really care. It was a small miracle that a cop hadn't pulled them over.

Deirdre slid off him, tucking him back inside his pants and running the zipper up. She smoothed her skirt down and climbed back into the passenger seat, sitting as far away as possible against the door, looking out the window.

Jason wanted desperately to talk with her, but couldn't think of how to begin. He cleared his throat several times, opened his mouth, and then closed it. His shoulders slumped. He started *Barenaked Ladies* playing on the stereo, then stopped it a minute later. The bouncy, happy music seemed at odds with the mood in the car, whatever that was.

Jason found the pervading silence combined with the

road noise oppressive, but the remaining four hours of the drive passed without Jason discovering a means of breaking it. He felt tense and uncomfortable.

God only knew what Deirdre was thinking. She might have been asleep for all Jason could tell. As Jason checked into a Best Western near Palo Alto, she remained in the car.

The hotel was shaped like a large, two-story, letter C, the inside filled with a courtyard and a pool. A picture window from the lobby looked out upon it, narrow concrete paths winding around with landscape lighting at ankle height. No one was in the pool at this hour, the water still, its surface like a dark mirror.

He returned to the car and drove around the outside of the C and parked in front of their room. When he turned off the engine they sat, only the slight ticking of the engine as it cooled breaking the silence.

"Well, we're here." He opened his door and grabbed the backpack from behind his seat. He unlocked the room door with a swipe of a keycard.

Deirdre, almost hesitantly, followed him inside.

He threw the backpack onto one of the two double beds and turned to her, "Deirdre, I-"

"I'm sorry," she said quickly.

"What?"

"I'm sorry."

"For what?"

"Um," she paused, "everything?"

The way she turned the statement up at the end, making it into a question, would have made Jason bust out laughing if she hadn't looked so sad and serious. "Everything?"

She nodded. "I'm sorry." She repeated.

"Why do you keep saying that? I wish you wouldn't."

"I'm sorry." She smiled a little. "It's just that I can't help it. Because I am. Sorry, that is." She ducked her head a little like a turtle, a shadow of her subconscious belief that she would be hit.

"Don't be."

He took her face in his hands and kissed her forehead, then her lips, then her lips again. Taking her hand he led her to the bed and swept the backpack onto the floor, lying her down on her back on the coverlet.

This time, he was on top.

Zero Day

Jason's alarm went off a few minutes after the wakeup call, while they were still lying in a pleasant half-asleep daze wrapped in each other's limbs. He reached out and fumbled with the buttons until the shrilling stopped, then turned on the TV and carefully synchronized his watch to the clock in the corner of the CNN channel. No matter what happened today, he wasn't going to be late again.

He lay in bed smoking a cigarette with the sheet pooled in his lap, watching Deirdre as she got ready. She moved about nakedly, unselfconsciously, the play of light and shadow on her body like a work of erotic art. Feeling himself wake up in more ways than one, he jumped into a quick, cold shower.

When he came out of the bathroom Deirdre was already dressed. She sat in one of the room's two chairs and watched him dress, her gaze cool and appraising. Jason, never ill at ease with his own nudity, blushed profusely.

They went down to the lobby to check out. The complimentary motel breakfast consisted of over-brewed coffee and some tired looking donuts crammed into a greasy cardboard box. They each grabbed a bitter cup as they ran out the door.

The sky was a deep and flawless blue. Jason felt imbued with a crystalline clarity of purpose, suffused with a feeling that nothing could go wrong. His senses were sharp and fast. He was living in a hyper time, the entire world at a crawl around him. The Porsche inching down the freeway at near seventy, the other cars changing lanes in slow motion. He could feel his heart beating leisurely and evenly in his chest, the rush of the wind into the car with the top down blowing Deirdre's hair into a golden fan. The man in the next car was talking on a cell phone; he had nicked himself shaving and there was a small square of toilet paper held on with a dot of blood. The woman in the car on the other side was putting on lipstick, a maroon so dark it was almost brown, while she drove. Jason could see it all, split seconds stretching out to minutes. He felt as cool as an ice floe and faster than a speeding bullet.

The Greater Pacific Bank was a freestanding brick building with white trim and three gables across the front, leaning towards an architectural flavor that would have better matched New England than the California business district in which it stood. Jason's Porsche blended well into the parking lot filled with other Porsches, Mercedes, and BMWs.

He stopped the car and blew out a breath, flexing his fingers on the steering wheel. "Hopefully this won't take long."

Deirdre leaned over and kissed him on the cheek. Then she removed her sunglasses and took his chin in one hand, turning his head to give him a long and lingering kiss on the mouth. "Good luck."

He got out of the car and walked into the bank. Once inside he moved immediately into the seating area near the managers' desks, and sank into a green leather chair that was so soft and deep it was almost uncomfortable. The clock on the wall read 9:02AM.

After a few minutes the fresh-faced college graduate at the nearest desk looked at Jason and said, "What can I do for you?" His pale blonde hair parted and combed carefully over, his muted red tie with small blue chevrons was knotted tight up against his throat in a full Windsor – the consummate bank professional. The placard on his desk read 'David Beal, Asst. Manager.'

Jason got up, with difficulty, and moved to one of the chairs across from him. He slid the passport and slip of paper with the account number from his hip pocket onto the desk. "I'd like to make a cash withdrawal from my account."

"Certainly." He reached for the passport and opened it, turning to his computer. He looked down at the passport and then at Jason, then down at the passport again.

"Is there a problem?" Jason let just a hint of the tone of a harried executive delayed by underling into his voice.

"Oh, no. It's just that. Are you *the* Peter Ryder? *Undressed to Kill*? *Acts of Vengeance*?"

Jason was stuck for a moment on how to reply. The account certainly belonged to that Peter Ryder. Would the bank computer somehow indicate that? Jason didn't know. He also had no idea what Ryder looked like, and wouldn't know anything about the movies if asked. He figured there had to be other Peter Ryders in California. "No, I'm not," he said, and then added for the hell of it, "but I get that a lot."

"I'm sorry. I don't know what I was thinking. Ryder, the other one, that is, has been making movies for more than ten years. You're not much older than I am." He busied himself with the computer. "Everything seems to be in order. The money has been prepared for cash withdrawal as per the wire request. I'm going to need to see a second picture ID for verification purposes."

Jason pulled the driver's license from his wallet and laid it next to the passport.

The man examined both side by side and then looked at Jason. "This is fine. Cathy?" he called.

An oriental woman came over with dark black hair clipped pageboy style. She wore a cream silk blouse and blue business skirt that was much too short for an office worker in any other state, but fit in just fine in California.

"Yes, Mr. Beal?"

"Please make copies of Mr. Ryder's documents while I assist him with his withdrawal."

"Yes sir." She took the passport and license and teetered away on improbably high heels.

Mr. Beal sat up slightly in his chair and looked over the desk at Jason's feet. "Did you bring a bag?"

"For what?"

"To carry the money." The man cocked his head slightly, "Have you ever seen seven million dollars before?"

Jason almost laughed at the absurdity of the question, but then just shook his head, "Not in cash."

"Here, follow me."

He lead Jason across the bank lobby and then down the row of tellers to a cut through at the end. They went through a heavy steel door and down a flight of stairs, the air becoming noticeably cooler as they descended. The man's black dress shoes clicked sharply on the tile flooring.

At the bottom the stairs opened into a room that was empty, the far wall housing the bank's vault. The door was highly polished, at least a foot thick, and swung open on massive hinges. Stainless steel locking shafts as thick as Jason's wrist were retracted into their guides all around the door perimeter. A set of bars, not unlike prison bars, blocked the doorway beyond leading into the vault.

The man removed a key card from his pocket and swiped it through a scanner mounted on the wall. He blocked Jason with his body as he keyed in a passcode on the keypad. A buzzer sounded, and he pushed open the bars and stepped into the vault.

Jason stayed outside the vault, uncertain if he should step in. From where he stood he could see the entire wall was lined with steel utility shelving stacked with currency, some in plastic wrap, some in banded stacks piled into cubbyholes built into the shelving.

He took a clipboard down from the wall. "Ryder, shelf 17, sections B, C, and D. These three are yours."

The shelving he indicated was about four feet wide, divided into quarters by partitions, each labeled with a small metal plate riveted to the front edge. The three on the right labeled B, C and D. They were completely filled with banded stacks of cash.

Jason's eyes widened to the point that he felt they might fall right out of his head. He wondered briefly how they could have possibly counted and stacked such a large amount of money on such short notice. They must have machines for that kind of thing.

"I'm sorry if it's more than you were prepared to carry, but with the request coming in as unexpectedly as it did, we were unable to fill the withdrawal entirely with hundreds, which would of course be the usual denomination to use in such transactions. Even then, the total account balance was," he checked the clipboard, "seven million, two hundred seventy three thousand, eight hundred and six. As hundreds that still would have been more than seventy-two thousand bills. The best breakdown we could do for you in this case was fifty-three thousand, five hundred hundreds, thirty-one thousand two hundred fifties, sixteen thousand two hundred and fifty twenties, five thousand eight hundred tens, one hundred sixty-one fives, and one single. The total comes to one hundred six thousand nine hundred and twelve bills. Is that satisfactory?"

The man's accounting has been no more than a distant droning in Jason's head. The vault actually smelled like money, paper-dusty and faintly sweet. He had to think for a moment before he could answer, "Yes, that's fine."

"We don't usually wish to part with this much cash on an average business day. Are you absolutely certain that a bank check would not be satisfactory? We could write an associated letter of solvency if need be."

"I'm purchasing a certain piece of art, and the buyer has specified cash. I'm sure you understand."

The man folded his hands in front of him, reminding Jason oddly of a funeral director, "Of course. I can provide nylon carry bags for the money, if you would like. They look kind of like gym bags, plain beige, nothing fancy."

"That would be fine."

"I'll have a bank officer pack up the money and bring it to you upstairs." He ushered Jason from the vault.

Jason glanced at his watch: 9:12. He wondered what would happen if the wire instruction came in to transfer the money while he was still in the bank. He didn't want to think about it. As they climbed the stairs he asked, "I'm already running late for my appointment. Would it be possible to have me on the road in five minutes."

The man checked his own watch. "I don't see why that should be a problem."

True to his word, at 9:17, all of the paperwork had been attended to and a guard carrying two bulky, beige cylindrical bags by the shoulder straps stood beside Jason and the assistant bank manager in front of the doors leading outside. Jason reached out and took the two bags, surprised by the weight of each.

"Would you care to count it? We could provide you with one of our counting machines and a private room."

"No, that won't be necessary. As I've said, I'm in a hurry."

"Of course. One of our guards will escort you out to your car."

Very conscious now of the passing time, and not wishing to let the guard get a look at his car, he said, "No thank you. I'll be fine."

"Well, thank you for doing business with California Federal, Mr. Ryder." He held out a hand to shake, realized that both of Jason's were full, and simply held the door open for him.

Jason had to turn sideways to maneuver himself and the bags out the door.

He made his way across the parking lot to the car at a pace just short of running. Deirdre knelt on the driver's seat and called out, "You got it?"

"I got it!"

He put one bag on the ground and fumbled with the keys with shaking hands. He opened the trunk and stuffed both bags inside. It took some shoving to get the trunk to latch. Another couple of hundred thousand and it probably wouldn't have fit. The thought made him laugh a little unsteadily as he got into the car.

Deirdre had pushed herself back into the passenger seat. "What's so funny?"

"Nothing. Everything!" He leaned over and kissed her quickly. She grasped the back of his head and kissed him back more slowly.

He pulled away from her, "We've gotta go." He could see the assistant manager and the guard talking to each other through the glass doors, and wished for a moment that he had parked the car somewhere out of sight around the side of the building. Nothing he could do about that now.

He started the car and pulled out, resisting the urge to push the pedal all the way to the floor. They melted into the surface street traffic, and merged onto 101 South, quickly accelerating to exactly 57 miles per hour. Jason planned to spend as much time watching the speedometer as the road – he wasn't about to get picked up for a traffic ticket and give some cop a reason to look in the trunk.

He dialed up *Incubus* on his iPod, and by 9:24 they were long gone.

Chip stood at the stove cooking an omelet in a large cast iron frying pan. He had found some mushrooms and cheese left by Kelly several days ago in the refrigerator.

Ricky came downstairs wearing his jacket. He had stayed, though slept very little, in the master bedroom the previous night. When he woke, he dressed, carefully tucking the gun at the small of his back. He put on his jacket and looked at himself in the mirror, pleased that the gun was almost invisible.

With a potholder underneath, Chip put the pan onto the dining room table and sat down to eat directly from it. "There's no mushrooms left, but there's cheese and eggs if you want to make something."

"No. Too big a day to think about eating. When do you

think they'll get back?"

"It's about three hundred fifty miles to Menlo Park. Jason drives fast, call it five hours. The bank opens at nine," he glanced at the clock on the microwave, "They should be getting the money right about now."

As if on cue the phone rang. Chip jumped up and hurried over the lift the phone from the wall mount. "Yo."

The shout of 'Chip, we got it!' over the phone was so loud that Ricky could hear it.

"Wahoo!" Chip yelled. "We'll be here waiting for you! Great!" He turned to the wall and hung up the phone. "They got it, and they're on their way back. No problems."

"Outstanding."

In one fluid motion Ricky pulled the gun from his belt and swung it at Chip, catching him in the forehead just as he turned back, opening a gash and spilling blood down his face. Chip fell to his hands and knees, blood pattering on the floor between his hands. Ricky raised the gun, holding it by the barrel, and brought it down towards Chip's head. Chip jerked back onto his heels, and the gun swished by in empty space. He launched up and forward, largely blinded by blood, and grabbed Ricky around the waist, pinning the gun between them, and ran him into the wall. Ricky battered the back of Chip's head and shoulders ineffectively with his free hand. Chip stood up suddenly, smashing his head into Ricky's jaw, snapping Ricky's head back against the wall.

Ricky, dazed, struck out with lefts and rights, driving Chip away from him. He then stepped forward and drove his knee into Chip's stomach, and brought the gun up into Chip's face as he doubled over, opening a second cut over one eye. Chip flopped onto his back out cold.

Ricky wiped his mouth and came away with blood. "Goddamn fuck!" he shouted, and kicked Chip in the side. He went to the table and picked up the napkin that Chip had been using and cleaned the blood off his face, then stuck the gun back into his belt.

Out in the garage he retrieved the gas can and duct tape. He rolled Chip over on his stomach and, after wrestling with the cellophane wrapper for a moment, he got the package of tape open and taped Chip's hands behind him. He dragged Chip to the couch by his armpits, and wound tape around his ankles, knees, chest. He finished with several turns over Chip's mouth and around his head. All told, he used two rolls of tape on Chip. He figured to save the last for Jason and Deirdre.

He put the gas can down near one of the chairs across from the couch and sat, propping his feet up on it, to wait.

It was only twenty minutes later that Ricky started to get restless. Maybe he had jumped the gun a little by cracking Chip's skull while the money was still hours and hours away. It would have been better to wait, as he was now stuck keeping an eye on Chip until Jason and Deirdre got home.

When he had heard the money was on its way he had just lost it for a moment. Ricky admitted that to himself. Still, everything was fine. He was in control, Chip wasn't going to be a problem, and it was all going to work out just as Ricky had planned.

He went into the kitchen and got a beer, then sat down at the table and ate the omelet. Chip came around just as he was finishing.

Chip didn't say anything, didn't make a sound. He just stared, which Ricky found unnerving. More so because the blood from the gashes in Chip's forehead had gummed one eye shut, so it was just the single eye looking at Ricky, and that was driving him nuts.

Ricky walked over and grabbed Chip's head. Chip grunted and tried to turn his face away, but Ricky held on and forced the stuck eyelid open with his fingers, soundly poking Chip in the eye with his thumb at least twice as he did so. It was not particularly an improvement, as Ricky soon found out, because Chip continued to stare, the second eye now peering out of a socket caked with blood. Ricky ignored him as best he could, settled into a recliner, and turned on the TV.

He found Monday morning television an intolerable mix of talk shows, game shows, and news. He finally found an old *I Dream of Jeannie*, which wasn't vastly better but at least Barbara Eden had a nice rack. When that ended *Hogan's Heroes* came on, which was OK too, but that was followed by *My Three Sons*, which was a show that Ricky despised.

It was still at least three and a half hours until the money would arrive, and Chip was staring at him again. Ricky fingered the gun at his belt and considered killing Chip outright, but he had planned to keep Chip alive in case he needed the threat of killing him to keep a handle on Jason. He didn't want to change his plan now, though he was sorely tempted. No, he decided. He was the one who had clubbed Chip too early, and he would have to deal with the consequences.

The seven-million-dollar paycheck that he was going to get at the end made the waiting easier.

Halfway back to LA, a bone-deep exhaustion overcame Jason as all the stress and hours of work of the past week caught up with him. Deirdre took over driving near

Bakersfield and Jason lay listlessly in the passenger seat in a sort of dream haze. Without the money in front of him it was difficult to believe that it was real. He was tempted to tell Deirdre to pull over so he could check on it, but resisted.

As they hit the outskirts of LA, the 'LOW FUEL' light lit on the dashboard. Jason didn't want to stop. He figured they had enough to get home, even if they would probably have to use Chip's car and the gas can to get some when they got there. It was nearly all over. Ricky would take his share and leave. Deirdre would stay. He couldn't wait to see the look on Chip's face.

Deirdre didn't want to stop either. Her feeling that Ricky might do something was intensified by her own reaction at seeing the two huge bags that Jason had carried to the car. That money was everything she needed to fix her life, and what she thought she would do to keep it, from the moment she had laid eyes on it, frightened her. She was convinced, to a near certainty in the last fifty or sixty miles, that Ricky wasn't going to be satisfied with just his own share. He was going to take her share as well, and quite possibly all of it. How far he would go to get it, how far she would go to stop him, she didn't know. Though the thought of confronting Ricky scared her, way deep down inside scared her.

Jason was out of the car almost as soon as the front tires hit the driveway, before it had stopped. He stumbled, but then caught himself and ran into the house.

"Jason, wait!" Deirdre called, but he was already inside.

She set the parking brake and got out of the car, hiking her purse over one shoulder as she did so. She slipped her hand inside and gripped the gun.

Across the street Scott and Miller had had some advanced warning of Jason and Deirdre's return, owing to the tracking device in Jason's shoe.

"They're back." Miller announced pointlessly from his position behind the camera.

Scott could see perfectly well that they were back. He stood in front of the window in his shirt sleeves, his gun in the holster and his jacket hanging over the back of the chair nearby.

"How do you want to play this?" Miller asked.

"Let's wait until we're sure they have the money."

"They said they had it on the phone. And the way Taylor ran inside? Of course they have the money. It's probably in the trunk."

"Let's wait until we see it." Scott picked up and strapped on his holster.

The hours wore on Ricky, and he dozed off. Chip, wrapped in three hundred feet of duct tape and his head throbbing, had been unable to do anything.

Ricky had been expecting to be alerted by the sound of the garage door going up, and so was surprised when Jason came running in.

"Hi, honey, I'm-" the word 'home' died in his throat as he took in the scene of Chip, on the couch wrapped in tape with his face crusted with blood, and Ricky just getting to his feet from one of the recliners, drawing a gun from his belt as he did so. He skidded to a stop with a squeal of his sneakers on the hardwood floor. There was a gas can on the floor at Ricky's feet. "You've got to be fucking joking."

"Do I look like I'm joking?"

"The money is in the car. Just take your share and go."

"Yeah, funny thing about sharing," he scratched his chin with the barrel of the gun, "I always sucked at it."

Deirdre came in through the front door, kicking it closed behind her. She pulled the gun from her purse and pointed it at Ricky without hesitation. The car keys were pulled out of the purse in the same motion and fell to the floor with a nerve-jarring clatter. "Let him go, Ricky." She regretted that her confidence was already betrayed by a shaking hand and a quaver in her voice.

"Oh my!" Ricky clapped a hand to the side of his face and opened his eyes wide in mock horror, "Deirdre's got a gun." He began to sing it to the tune of *Jamie's Got a Gun* and do a little dance. "Deirdre's got a gun. Deirdre's got a gun."

She put her other hand on the gun to steady it, but that didn't seem to help much. "I'm not bluffing, Ricky."

He stopped his little dance in mid step. "Of course you're not bluffing," he sneered, walking towards her. "It takes intelligence to bluff, and you don't have the fucking brains."

He reached out and Jason stood paralyzed, certain he was just going to take the gun from Deirdre's shaking hands. Instead he slapped her openhanded across the face, hard. The sharp, flat sound echoing off the walls.

Her head rocked back but she didn't stumble. A small bubble of blood appeared at one nostril and grew until it burst, running in a thin rivulet down to the line of her lips.

"You like that? You want some more? Because I'm just the man to give it to you." Ricky moved to stand beside her, spittle from his lips spraying her check, her unsteady aim was now pointed at nothing but the far end of the living room. "Don't you get it? I own you. Can't you get that through your thick, blonde, cunt skull? Put the gun away before you hurt yourself, or maybe you'd like to me to jam it somewhere for you? Bet you'd like that." He moved back, purposely putting himself in front of her gun, daring her to pull the trigger. He was so close that the barrel was pressed against his chest, and that steadied it somewhat. "You're not a killer, Dee. I don't see it in your eyes. Inside you're still the scared little twat that I dragged out of that shithole trailer two years ago. If you want to see what the eyes of a killer look like," he leaned towards her over the barrel of her gun staring deep into her eyes with his own, "look at mine."

Without looking away from her but with the steady assurance of a compass pointing due north, he swung his gun around almost behind him, pointed it directly at Chip, and pulled the trigger. The gunshot was hugely loud in the room. Chip didn't even have time to suck in a last surprised breath as the bullet blew off the top of his head and sprayed it all over the wall behind the couch.

In the deafening silence that followed, the sounds of some of the larger pieces of Chip's brain sliding off the wall and hitting the floor could be clearly heard.

"Chip!" Jason shouted, and took two running steps towards his friend, though there was clearly nothing he could do.

Ricky swung the gun around and slammed it into Jason's stomach as he tried to go past. Jason doubled over, and Ricky shoved him aside into the wall, where he fell to the floor in a ball, gasping shallowly. Ricky picked up the roll of tape from the coffee table, "Barbecue time!"

The sound of her gun going off started everyone, possibly Deirdre most of all.

Ricky looked down at the hole in his left bicep, the blood spreading down his arm, incredulous. He began to bring his own gun up and she fired again and again without aiming, the remaining bullets striking a tight pattern in his arm, shoulder, and chest.

Ricky stood as Deirdre continued to dry fire, unable to find the strength to raise his own gun, his shirt blooming crimson. His mouth moved, lips working soundlessly. He fell to his knees, then forward onto his face, his arms stretched out in front of him. His last breath rattled in his throat.

Though Scott and Miller had been unable to understand anything that had been said because the bug had been planted far away in the upstairs bedroom, they could tell that there was shouting, and the gunshots could be heard quite clearly.

"Those sounded like gunshots." Miller observed.

Scott smiled wryly, "Sounds like they're having a little difficulty dividing the money."

He waited, listening to the white noise hiss coming from the speaker for several moments. "Come on." He went out the front door and across the street, Miller trailing behind. "You take the front. Wait ten seconds for me to get around the back and then go in."

Miller approached the front door, his partner drawing his gun just as he disappeared around the corner of the house. Miller drew his own weapon and counted ten in his head.

Jason found the pain tremendous, debilitating, unlike anything he had ever known. He wondered if it was possible to die from a single blow to the stomach. It was nearly impossible to take a breath, and he was becoming quite light-headed from the lack of oxygen.

From his position on the floor he looked up and over at Deirdre. She still stood with the gun pointed at the spot where Ricky had been standing. At some point she had swiped at the blood on her upper lip, and it was now smeared across one cheek and the back of her left hand.

Ricky lay motionless in an enormous, and still spreading, pool of blood.

Jason didn't have the nerve to look back over his shoulder at Chip. Though his defense mechanisms were working hard to blot out the image, he still had a pretty good idea of what that looked like.

Miller kicked in the door and entered, gun extended in one hand and badge case in the other. "DEA!"

Deirdre started to turn as Scott came in through the patio door, his gun also drawn. "Gun on the floor, lady, nice and easy."

She crouched slowly and put the gun down.

Jason looked from one man to the other from his position on the floor. When and how had the DEA gotten involved?

"Go over and sit on the couch." Miller ordered Deirdre.

She looked at Chip's body and the mess on the wall behind the couch, clearly reluctant. Scott moved forward with his gun ahead of him. With his free hand he grabbed her roughly and shoved her onto the couch. She sat down with an alarmed squeak as her weight caused Chip's body to slump over against her. Without wanting to touch or look at the body, she pushed it from her so it slumped the other way.

Miller nudged Jason with the toe of his shoe. “You shot?”

“No.” Jason said weakly.

“Then get up.”

Jason struggled onto his hands and knees, any movement of his stomach muscles an agony. Maybe I’ve got cracked ribs, he thought. I wonder what a punctured lung feels like. He didn’t know if he could actually get to his feet.

Scott became impatient. “Never mind him.” He pointed his gun at Deirdre’s face. “Where’s the money?”

Certain that it would ordinarily be a terrifying experience to look at a gun barrel pointed at her from just inches away, Deirdre nonetheless felt almost nothing, the adrenaline fire having burned through and left her empty. “In the trunk of the car.”

“Keep an eye on them.” Scott moved to the front window and looked past the curtains to the Porsche parked in the driveway. The street was empty at the moment, but it was mid-afternoon and a little too public out there. He cocked a finger at Deirdre.

She got off the couch and went to him, only too glad to be away from the body. “What?”

“I want you to go outside and pull the car into the garage. Can you do that for me?”

“I need the keys. They’re on the floor over there.” She pointed.

"Miller." Scott called.

Miller took a step and kicked the keys, which skittered across the floor to stop against Deirdre's shoe. Mechanically, she picked them up.

As she moved towards the door Scott took a handful of her hair and pressed the gun against her skull behind one ear. "Get into the car, and pull it into the garage. Nothing funny."

"No."

"Good girl." He released her and she went out the door.

From his position bent over on the floor on elbows and knees, Jason was breathing a little easier. His stomach felt awful and the muscles quivered, but he was starting to believe that maybe nothing was broken.

As the pain subsided, he could think more clearly about what was going on. These DEA agents, if in fact they were DEA agents at all, sure weren't behaving like they were making an arrest. It looked to Jason like they were planning to take the money, however they had learned about it, for themselves. And now Jason had heard one call the other by name, and that could only mean that they didn't care if Jason or Deirdre could identify them, because they wouldn't be around to do any identifying.

He turned his head fractionally to look up at the man called Miller. Miller stood to Jason's right, gun in hand pointed rock-solid at Jason's head. "Could you get me an ambulance? I think I have internal injuries or something."

Miller looked at him utterly without emotion. "I don't think so."

Jason knew they were going to kill him and Deirdre, but saw absolutely nothing he could do about it. He hoped that Deirdre realized it, and when she got into the car she just floored it out of there, and to hell with whatever they did to him. That hope dissolved when he heard the garage door roll open and the car engine change pitch as it pulled into the enclosed space.

Scott moved from the window to open the door to the garage and stepped inside.

Ricky was livid. The bitch had shot him! He had that stupid cunt coming and going, and yet she had still shot him. He was going to teach her a lesson, Ricky thought, the last lesson she would ever learn.

The world came back to him as just a few bits and pieces. Most of his body was completely numb, though his right foot felt twisted around and ached. Trying with all his might he couldn't move it to straighten it out. Also, as he thought about it, he was pretty sure that he wasn't breathing, though he couldn't seem to do anything about that either. How badly was he hurt?

Ricky opened his eyes and saw the floor stretching away from him, one side of his face pressed to the living room hardwood. There was blood on the floor near him – was that his blood? He could also see his own hand still holding the gun, and just like that he could feel it, warm and solid, each line of the waffle pattern on the grip pressing into his palm.

And there, at the end of his vision, the door to the garage opened and he saw the Porsche drive in with Deirdre behind the wheel. When this was all over he was going to get himself a car like that. The car rolled to a stop with her almost exactly in line with his gun. Concentrating his every thought, a cry of vengeance burning in his throat without the air to utter it, he raised the nose of the gun an inch off the floor to put her fucking whore face dead in the sights.

Then someone stepped in the way, blocking his shot. He wanted to wait until the person moved so he could see her face cave in as the bullets smashed home, but someone was screwing with the lights because it was getting dark, and the gun felt like it weighed about a million pounds. Fuck it, he shrugged internally, whoever it was would get out of the way when the shooting started.

As Deirdre pulled the car into the garage, the door to the house opened and the man stepped into the doorway. He pushed the button on the wall and the door trundled down behind her, his gun leveled at her head. In that instant, the uneasiness that this was like no arrest she had ever been a part of crystallized into a granite certainty that these guys, DEA or not, were simply going to kill them and take the money. Though she found herself entirely without an idea as to what she could do about it.

Scott heard the first shot from behind him at the same time as he felt it rip through his thigh. His leg buckled under him and he fell, a second bullet catching him in the shoulder. He let the impact momentum spin him to one side and used his still-working leg to propel himself out of the doorway as more shots passed through the space he had just occupied.

Miller jumped more than a foot when the gun went off at his feet. Like some horror movie, he stood transfixed as the dead body on the floor, a huge puddle of blood pooled out around it and already congealing, clutched a gun in hand, the finger spastically pulling the trigger over and over. It took a moment for him to recover and step forward. He kicked the gun out of the hand and delivered two shots to the head at point blank range, sending up a shower of blood and bone and wood splinters as the bullets smashed through and struck the floor.

Both actions had been pointless: Ricky had fired the gun empty and died on his own several seconds earlier.

In moving to shoot Ricky, Miller had put himself directly behind Jason on the floor. Sensing an opportunity Jason kicked straight out behind him with his right leg. It wasn't a very strong kick, and it glanced off the side of Miller's knee, but it was enough to unbalance the man. Miller stumbled into the coffee table and then fell over it, arms pinwheeling, and landed flat on his back on the floor. The gun flew from his hand and slid under the dining room table.

Jason scrambled over on hands and knees and knelt on Miller's chest. He grabbed two fistfuls of the man's hair and slammed his head into the floor as hard as he could – one, two, three times. He then dove off Miller and under the dining room table, reaching for the gun.

Deirdre looked over as Scott fell out of the doorway and stared straight into Ricky's eyes. For his final act on earth, Ricky wanted her dead. Pinned down in the car by his gunfire, she shifted low in the seat, squeezed her eyes shut, and thought herself as small as possible.

Remarkably, she was not hit, despite one round passing through the window, through her hair, and out the roof, and a second grazing across her stomach, tearing her shirt and leaving a red line on her skin, and lodging in the back of the passenger seat.

When she opened her eyes Ricky was dead, the other man standing over him firing into the back of Ricky's head. The man who had held the gun on her was on the ground next to the car, bleeding from thigh and shoulder. She opened the door with no more plan in her head than to kick the living shit out of him, but he recovered too quickly, when she only had one foot on the ground, and leveled the gun at her.

He fired.

Head pounding and ears ringing, Miller wrapped his arms around Jason's legs. He released with one arm and latched onto Jason's belt, pulling Jason away from the gun and himself towards it at the same time.

With only an inch to go before he could reach the gun, Jason found himself sliding back, unable to break the other man's grip. Abdomen twisting and cramped with pain, this was a wrestling match that Jason knew he would lose.

Then he saw the handle of his big cast iron frying pan and a corner of a potholder hanging over the edge of the table above him. He suddenly pushed in the same direction that Miller was trying to pull him and slid out from under the table. Jason grabbed the panhandle in both hands and, on his knees, swung the pan for all he was worth.

Miller skidded forwards when Jason slid back, and found himself kneeling right next to the gun. He picked it up and turned, putting his temple right in line with Jason's swing.

The impact sounded like a heavy gong and sent Miller tumbling back into the chairs on the far side of the table. He ended up dead on his back, his arms and legs tangled in a pile of chairs, his skull clearly flattened and misshapen where the pan had struck.

Jason held onto the pan, unable to put together enough coherent thoughts to pick up the gun, and headed towards the garage at a stumbling run.

Deirdre let gravity pull her back into the driver's seat. Scott's first shot passed harmlessly through her hair and out the car roof. The big blonde hairstyle, that Ricky had loved and took her a can of hairspray to build each day, might save her life yet.

She pushed the clutch in and jammed the stickshift into reverse, then popped the clutch and mashed her foot down onto the accelerator. She figured she would pull out of the garage right through the closed door, then drive forward again and run the bastard down.

She didn't get that far.

The tires spun on the smooth concrete floor of the garage and then grabbed. Scott fired, missing as the car rolled back and shattering the passenger-side window. The explosion of the high caliber weapon echoed in the garage. He corrected his aim and fired again. The bullet smashed through Deirdre's jawbone so her mouth hung askew and took an upward path through the roof of her mouth, shattering teeth, and passing out Deirdre's right cheek just below her eye. She was thrown towards the passenger seat, her foot coming off the gas and the car stalling.

The last of the car's momentum rolled it backwards into the closed garage door, denting the two lower door panels and knocking the door out of the track.

Scott lurched forward to look down at Deirdre in the car.

The pain was much less than she thought it would be. She knew her face was ruined, could feel pieces of bone and teeth on her tongue. A thin stream of saliva and blood ran from her open mouth.

She tried to roll her eyes to look at her attacker. The right eye, pinned by the swelling and the damage to her cheek, did not move, and her vision doubled sickeningly. She threw up weakly onto her shoes and the floor of the car. With her hands she managed pushed herself around, her head lolled back against the headrest. She could see the man looking at her.

"Shit, lady, I really fucked up your face."

She tried to sit up, to do something. Her thinking was in slow motion, the man raising the gun towards her. She managed to lift her head off the headrest.

Scott held the gun at arm's length, just a few inches from Deirdre's left eye, the sclera turning red with blood, and fired a third time, blowing bone and brains out the back of her head.

Jason was still far across the living room when he saw Scott stand over the car and fire through the window, saw the blood and other things that he didn't want to think about spatter onto the windshield.

He screamed wordlessly with such pain and fury that it almost couldn't be recognized as human.

Scott spun on his heels, but was unbalanced by his injuries and his first shot at Jason went wide.

Jason dove to the floor and slid, the next bullet passing over his head. When he reached the garage door he slammed it shut, scrambled to his feet with his back to the wall next to the door, and wrenched at the deadbolt. He had never used it as long as he had owned the house – it had probably never been used by anyone ever – and it was jammed.

Scott fired low through the door, where he thought Jason would be. The shot easily perforated the steel-skinned foam-core door, but left a surprisingly small hole, and Scott was disappointed that he wasn't rewarded with a wounded scream from the other side. The slide on his gun stuck forward; the gun was empty, his spare clips back in his jacket across the street.

He threw himself against the door and it opened a crack, Jason on the other side fighting to keep it closed.

The shoving match over the door ended when Scott's wounded thigh gave on him, and he fell back against the car with a grunt. Jason heaved on the deadbolt, which finally slid home with a metallic squeal.

"Yessss!" He said through gritted teeth.

Jason rested for only a second, then got to his feet and ran outside, frying pan still with him. He had to find some way to block the garage door or deal with the man when he opened it up. But when he got to the driveway he found exactly what Scott was discovering at that moment from the inside. The car had bent the door and derailed the lower corner completely out of the track. Scott tried pushing and pulling the door experimentally, but quickly realized that, without a hydraulic jack or some other tool, that door wasn't going anywhere.

Jason went back inside and put the frying pan down on the counter, and picked up the gun. On the way by he put a hand to Chip's neck, knowing it was stupid to be looking for a pulse with the ragged bullet hole near the center of his friend's forehead, yet unable not to. Chip was already noticeably cool, his skin rubbery. He ignored a hammering sound from the garage – Scott pounding on the doorknob with the butt of his gun – and closed his friend's eyes and said some jumbled collection of prayers.

He moved across the living room and sat on the floor with his legs crossed facing the door to the garage. It surprised him that the man wasn't shooting his way out.

"Run out of bullets?" he called.

No answer came from the garage, not that he had expected one. He looked at the gun in his hands. With the adrenaline fading, and with three dead bodies around him, he didn't know if he could look another human being in the eye and pull the trigger.

Scott sat on the floor of the garage near the damaged door and tried to figure out just how fucked he was. He was out of ammo, and locked in a garage, his partner probably dead. Uninjured he was sure he could break down the deadbolted door, but not now. The shoulder wound wasn't bad, though it hurt like a mother. It was the thigh that had him worried. It continued to bubble dark blood and was numb from the hip down. He whipped off his belt and twisted it tight around his thigh just above the wound. It hurt a little, but not as much as he thought it probably should, and that worried him more. He took a quick mental inventory – he didn't feel shock or woozy from blood loss, which was good.

He dragged himself over to the car door and reached past the woman's body to get the keys from the ignition, then went back to the trunk. The collision with the door had done little more than scratch the paint, and the trunk popped open as soon as Scott found the correct button on the fob. He dropped the keys on the garage floor and wrestled one of the nylon bags out and onto the floor next to him, and ran the zipper. It was full of thick, banded stacks of money. Scott pulled a stack out and riffled it in front of his face, inhaling deeply with his eyes closed. The money smelled sweet to him.

"You've got the door locked, but the money's in here with me. What say we make a deal?" He yelled.

Jason looked up from the gun in his lap when the voice called from the garage.

When he didn't answer the voice continued: "Fifty-fifty. Plenty for both of us."

The money. He could picture the two nylon bags open, packs of money sticking out in all directions like a bouquet of flowers. Would the money bring Deirdre back? Or Chip? Or Kelly?

Scott tossed the stack back into the bag. The seepage with the tourniquet around his leg had nearly stopped, but maybe he felt just a little lightheaded. Not good. "What the fuck is wrong with you? There's seven million dollars in here!" He yelled.

He looked around and decided to try a different tack. "Hey, you know what? Your girlfriend is still alive, but it doesn't look like she will be for long if you don't open this door and help her."

Jason looked up when he said that, fresh adrenaline coursing through his veins. Deirdre was dead; he was sure of it. The gore splattered onto the windshield was sharply visible to him even with his eyes closed, burned into his retinas.

He found that he now did not simply want to kill, he wanted to torture, mutilate, rend skin from muscle and flesh from bone. "I'm going to kill you." He said loudly and clearly.

The voice laughed at him. "Come on in and give it your best shot."

He bounced the gun in his hands, feeling the weight of it. Jason had never had particularly strong feelings either for or against guns. He figured that people who wanted them could have them, but had never had a desire to own one himself. He had never fired one in his life either, not even so much as a pellet gun as a teenager. Jason certainly wasn't planning to go in there and bet his life on his first-ever gunshot.

Crossing the living room he picked up the gas can and found it almost completely full. He walked carefully towards the door leading to the garage, all his concentration on keeping his shoes from squeaking on the floor; he didn't want to alert the other man to what he was doing. His heart was racing and that, and the gas fumes, made him lightheaded. He looked ahead to the door, which appeared to him to be down a corridor a mile long but in reality was only four steps.

When he reached the doorway he opened the container and poured gasoline out slowly onto the floor without splashing noises. The weather stripping at the bottom of the door kept the gasoline out of the garage, and it puddled in the hallway. He poured nearly two gallons there.

He sped quietly and quickly through the kitchen, grabbing paper towels off the roll as he passed, and out the patio door. Around the side of the house he crept to the window in the side of the garage.

Underneath the window, he raised his head slowly until he could just see through the lower edge. The gristle clinging to the Porsche windshield was more than he had wanted to see. He hadn't seen the man who had killed Deirdre during his quick look.

He put the gas can down near the window and jammed wadded paper towels into the opening. Then he went back into the house through the patio door, grabbing another few paper towels in the kitchen, and stopped in the hallway.

He pulled the plastic lighter Deirdre had given him from his pocket and thumbed the wheel.

Scott hefted the tire iron he had pulled out of the trunk, planning to brain the man when he came in. There hadn't been any sounds from the other side of the door for several minutes. What could he be planning? Could he have left?

Scott had to find some way out! He looked again at the ruined garage door, and then the locked door to the house. No help there. That left only the small window in the side of the garage. It looked a little too small, but he would have to squeeze his way through, injured or not. He picked up one of the bags with his good arm, his shoulder shrieked at him from the change in balance. His thigh and leg felt nothing at all, like dead wood dragging behind him, as he made his way towards the window.

Jason lit the paper towel and let it flutter to the floor. The deep puddle of gasoline ignited instantly, almost exploded in the hallway, building a wall of flames from floor to ceiling.

He ran around the outside of the house again. Picking up the gas can he noticed that the paper towels had absorbed a great deal of gasoline – were almost sopping wet with it, and he was afraid to light it. He gave himself no chance to chicken out, thumbing the wheel, touching it to the end, and pushing the gas can through the window, breaking the glass in the process.

The gas can hit the floor and erupted in flames so quickly that he had to jump back to keep from being burned.

Scott had almost reached the window just as the gas can was pushed through from the other side. It burst as soon as it hit the floor, spattered burning gasoline on his pant legs, which he slapped at to put out.

He left the bag and went back the house door. It sounded like a good-sized fire was burning beyond that door as well. What maniac would set fire to the house with seven million dollars in it? It was all nuts.

Jason waited by the garage door. Inside the house was no longer safe; the living room was fully ablaze, and the fire was spreading towards the kitchen.

Scott moved from door to window in a shrinking orbit as the flames advanced, crouching down to avoid the smoke that was roiling above.

Desperate and trapped, he tried to think fast, but found

he kept focusing uselessly on the spreading fire. He had never been inside a burning building, and he found it terrifying to the point of paralysis. The smoke was so thick, the flames spread so quickly, the heat too intense.

The car! He could use the car to batter down the garage door! He yanked at the body behind the wheel, something in his shoulder tearing and blood flowing freely once more, but he was beyond noticing. The body only came halfway out, the woman's foot wedged behind the brake pedal. He pulled and heaved, choking and his vision going gray. Dropping her upper body to the floor, he snaked past her and worked the foot free. He scrunched into the driver seat, kicking the body the rest of the way out as he did so. She had driven with the seat was all the way forward and he couldn't find the mechanism to slide it back. It didn't matter; he just managed to wedge his much larger frame uncomfortably behind the wheel.

Reaching for the keys, he only then remembered that they were lying on the floor by the trunk.

He screamed in frustration and pain, the air far too smoky to breathe. The door to the house had become hot with the fire beyond it and was roasting him from just a few feet away.

He tried to pull himself from behind the wheel, couldn't get his knee and numb leg past the steering wheel, and his big feet untangled from the pedals on the floor. He started to sob, pounding on and cracking the steering wheel with his fists, breaking several small bones in his hands, the horn sounding over and over.

The screams from inside the garage brought a smile to Jason's face. The sobs soon after wrenched at something inside him. Another human being was dying in there.

As the car horn sounded, he backed away slowly, then more quickly, making his way around the side of the house farthest from the flames. By the time he reached a perch high up on the hillside, the horn had stopped.

Ever After

Jason's heart was hammering, his pulse throbbing deep in his head, his breath coming in thin gasps, burning in his throat and chest. His feet were slapping heavily against the pavement along the shoulder of the roadway as he moved in more of a stumbling headlong rush than a run. How far had he come, and where the hell was he going?

Leaving it all behind, baby, baby
I'm leaving it all behind.

Sweat dripped from his forehead stinging as it found his eyes. It ran down his back, plastering his shirt to his body. He slowed from a run to a jog, a jog to a walk. He plodded along with his head down, breath whistling through his open mouth, his hands on his waist, fingers digging into the stitch starting in his side. Fuck, but he was out of shape. Looking around he saw the Circle K where he would stop to buy milk sometimes on the way home from work. He figured that he had come maybe five miles.

Water. He needed water. And when was the last time he had had anything to eat? The cup of coffee this morning? And he hadn't even finished it. He stopped at the point where the roadway slanted upwards to hit the entrance to the Circle K parking lot and went through his pockets. The fake passport and driver's license was in his jacket pocket, another pocket held the pack of cigarettes and lighter, his own wallet was in the rear pocket of his pants. He pulled the wallet out and opened it. Two dollars. And, and, he dug into his pockets and felt around for change, and pulled out a dime, a nickel, and two pennies. Two dollars and seventeen cents.

He laughed and shook his head, drops of sweat flinging from his face and hair to spatter on the pavement at his feet. He thought again about the seven million dollars in cash burning in the trunk of the Porsche back at the house. And then he thought of Deirdre in the car also, very dead, and he stopped laughing.

He sat down quickly on the curbside, his legs splayed out nearly into traffic, his shoulders slumped, his back bent forward in a curve, his head hanging, his arms lying at this sides. Maybe a few tears joined the droplets of sweat on the pavement.

Nausea wormed its way up from the pit of his stomach and he turned his head to the side and dry heaved a few times, but there was nothing to bring up. He worked up some saliva and spat into the weeds of the dirt strip that ran next to the cracked sidewalk.

He felt cold and dizzy, and he started to shake all over, his teeth chattering. The sun was too warm, baking his skull where it struck the crown of his head like a leaden fist. He thought he might pass out. Maybe, he thought, this is what shock is like. The chrome of the passing cars was too bright, the glints felt like needles in his eyes. He dropped his head again and pressed his hands to his face, his skin felt slick with greasy sweat.

A car tire rolled up and stopped just in front of him; he heard the sound of an electric window rolling down. He figured he must look either drunk or crazy slouched down on the side of the road.

"Jason, get in." The deep voice that called to him from the car was entirely unfamiliar to him.

He whipped his head up and looking into the car. A big black man sat behind the wheel, crisp white shirt unbuttoned at the throat, gray suit jacket that fit him well across the shoulders despite his size. Jason had absolutely no idea who he was.

"Are you talking to me?" Jason asked, as if there was anyone else in the immediate area that the man could be talking to.

"Come on, Jason, get in. I'm blocking traffic. You and I have a lot to talk about."

"Are you a cop or something."

The man smiled, at once warm and still somehow menacing, "Or something. Let's go."

Jason looked left and right along the street. If there was help out here, if he needed help, he didn't see it. He got up, and then felt suddenly dizzy again and fell forward. He put out his hands to brace himself against the car roof, the cactus spines in his left hand digging in deeper as his hands hit the car.

"Fuck!" He pulled back his injured hand, clutching it at the wrist with the other one. He danced in a little circle, holding the hand away from his body as if that would distance the pain from him, "Fuck! Fuck! Fuck! Fuck! Fuck!"

"What's wrong?"

Jason held up his hand to the open window so the man could see, "Cactus spines."

The man sucked wind through his teeth, "That looks bad. We'll have to get you cleaned up. Fortunately we have some time."

The sting of the cactus needles had cleared his head. Jason felt steadier, more in control of himself. "Am I under arrest?"

"Have you done anything I should arrest you for?"

Jason had to think about that for awhile. All the stuff with the computer was well hidden, and the computer itself was almost certainly destroyed by now. The money was burning up, so how could he be charged with that? He had beaten a guy to death with a frying pan at his house, whoever he was, but the guy was trying to kill him. That was clearly self-defense. He had set fire to his house with someone locked inside; a jury would likely take a dim view of that, even in the man had just shot Deirdre.

"No." he replied. It seemed the simplest answer to give.

"Then you have nothing to worry about. Get in."

Jason looked up and down the road one more time, wondering if someone driving by at this moment would be watching the news later and see 'Unidentified body found in vacant lot,' and think of Jason getting into this car on this street at this time. Probably not. He opened the car door, which he noticed was a silver Chrysler LeBaron, and sat in the padded comfort of the red velvet interior. As he closed the door the man sped away from the curb and into traffic.

They drove in silence for a while. Jason ran his right hand through his hair, the sweat pasting it back against his skull. He hung his head out the window like a dog and felt the sweat drying on his face and neck.

"Water?"

Jason looked over to see the man holding out half a bottle of Evian. He took the bottle and fumbled the cap off with his injured left hand. He tipped the bottle back, the water cascading down his throat, stale and warm as piss but wonderful just the same. Water splashed out of his mouth and down his neck and the front of his shirt.

He dropped the empty bottle on the seat between them. "Thanks."

"Uh, you're welcome," The man flicked his eyes from

the road to the empty bottle. "We could stop and get more, but I'd rather wait until we get there."

"Get where?"

"We'll talk about that later."

"OK. I can wait."

They sat in silence again. Jason thought about him and Deirdre in the hotel last night, and felt his groin stiffen in response. He shifted in his seat, uncomfortable with his reaction and the thought that she was now dead. It made him feel sick and sad and angry all at once.

"You've had a busy week." The man said suddenly.

"You don't know the half of it."

"I think I know a great deal more than you think, Jason. Perhaps I even know more than you do about some things."

Jason looked over at the man driving. He drove easily, one hand on the wheel, the other lying on the door armrest. His eyes were watching the road ahead without a moment's glance at Jason, as if he were discussing the weather or the score of last night's baseball game. Who the fuck was this guy?

"Who are you? Do I know you? How do you know me?"

"James Dorado, DEA deputy director, Los Angeles division." He took the wheel in his left hand and held out his right to Jason. Jason made no move to shake it. Dorado flicked his eyes from the road to Jason, shrugged, and put his hands back on the wheel. "I'll let that go. You've had a bad day."

"Uh-huh." Jason's voice was flat, without emotion.

They drove on in silence again, which was fine with Jason, lulled by the road sweeping past, as he thought about Chip, also dead. He wondered what he would tell Kelly, if he could find Kelly. If Kelly was still talking to him. Dorado exited the road they were on and merged into the stream of traffic headed north on I-5. This was the same road he and Deirdre had driven on last night.

Dorado sighed. "Look. I'll level with you. I know about the bank accounts. I know about the money. I know about Ryder, and I know about Scott and Miller."

"Who?"

"Scott and Miller. They were two of my agents. They're dead at your house now."

"There are a lot of people dead at my house now," Jason looked down at his hands, poked gingerly at the swollen palm of his left.

"Uh, yeah. The firemen told me that. I must have gotten to your house just ten or fifteen minutes after you left," Dorado said awkwardly, and then lapsed back into silence.

The sun was setting now. If they had been driving on the Pacific Coast Highway they could have seen it dropping into the ocean, spreading rays of gold and orange, coloring the undersides of the clouds pink. This far inland, there was only a pale glow to the left deepening in hue towards full darkness across the hemisphere of the sky.

"How did you find me?"

"How's that?" Dorado seemed jarred out of his own thoughts by the question.

"How did you find me? You said you got to my house fifteen minutes after I left. The house was burning, no one alive there but the firemen. How did you find me?"

"Oh, that." He reached over into the back seat without looking and felt around, grabbing something that he handed to Jason. It looked like a big iPhone, with an LCD screen and a small box, about the size of a pack of gum, attached to the top with an antenna sticking out of that. "Homing device. Scott and Miller must have put it on you, probably in your shoes."

Jason furiously pulled off his right shoe and looked at it, then his left. He threw both shoes out the window of the car. Dorado pulled over to the side of the highway quickly to the blare of a horn from the car behind him. He slammed the car into park.

"What did you do that for?"

Jason thought about that for a second, looked down at his socks and wiggled his toes, and then started laughing, "I don't know."

Dorado started laughing with him. The two of them laughed for a long time, Jason doubled over, Dorado leaning his head back against the headrest with an arm thrown over his eyes.

When the laughing had subsided to just a few chuckles Dorado said, "Go get your shoes."

"OK."

Jason got out of the car and ran back in his socks. It was nearly dark, and it took the headlights of the passing cars to find his shoes, which fortunately had ended up lying near each other in the breakdown lane. He put them on and returned to the car. Dorado checked his mirrors and accelerated back into traffic.

As the car was still accelerating, Jason said suddenly "I killed your agents. One was trying to kill me. The other had killed Deirdre."

Dorado looked at him, again just the flick of the eyes from the roadway. "I had my suspicions that Scott and Miller had gone rogue; I just didn't know how badly. I think the money made them crazy. I'm sorry about your friend."

"So am I."

This again halted their conversation. Jason stared out the window; Dorado flexed his fingers on the steering wheel.

"This has been a pretty crazy case for me," Dorado began. "I put most of it together just this morning. The thing that I can't figure out is, how did you find out about the money?"

Jason turned to him, "How did *you* find out about the money?"

Dorado ran his tongue around inside his lips, "OK, fair enough. Scott and Miller brought a laptop back from the drug deal at the dock. They said it was the drug dealer's, but I'm pretty sure now that it was Ryder's. The account information was on the machine."

"My best friend was at the dock when the deal went down. He heard the whole thing, including Ryder calling his bank on his cell phone. He took the phone, and we ended up working from there."

Dorado nodded to himself. "With Ryder missing, presumed dead-"

"Presumed dead? Don't you know?" Jason interrupted.

"His body never turned up, but I'm pretty sure he's dead."

"He was killed at the drug deal."

"Dead?"

"From my friend's story, yeah, very dead."

"Well, somebody got rid of his body. I think Scott and Miller had a hand in that, but it's a little hard to ask them now. With all the scrub desert around, he may never turn up."

Jason couldn't think of a comment to make to that, and so didn't say anything.

"So," Dorado continued his previous thought, "with Ryder dead, how did you get the bank to give you the money."

Jason dug into his coat pocket and came out with the fake driver's license and passport. He handed them to Dorado.

Dorado glanced at the license and then opened the passport against the steering wheel. He looked down at it as he drove, flipping through the pages. He rubbed a page between the thumb and index finger of his right hand, and then handed both documents back to Jason. "They're not bad. Not great, but not bad. You walked into the bank with those and they just handed you seven million dollars in cash?"

Jason looked at the passport and license, "Yep."

Dorado shook his head smiling, "Amazing."

"Yeah, well, it doesn't matter now." Jason wound up his arm across his body, preparing to throw the documents out the window.

As his arm started in motion Dorado took his hand off the wheel and grabbed Jason's wrist. "Whoa. Whoa. Hold onto those. You might need them yet."

Jason looked down at Dorado's hand on his arm, and then over at Dorado who was looking at him, giving the occasional flick of his eyes to the road now. A tiny light bulb came on in his mind.

"Where are we going, anyway?"

"We're going where the money is going." Dorado said slowly.

Jason shook his head, "The money is going up in flames."

Dorado smiled, "Not exactly."

"Not exactly? I loaded it into the trunk of my car myself."

"Weeellll," Dorado drew the word out while turning his attention back to the road, "It took some doing, but the money you picked up this morning was play money."

"Counterfeit?"

"Not exactly. It's money the government prints up to use in drug deals and whatnot. It looks better than modern counterfeit, but it's all marked to hell so we can pick it up easily afterwards."

"So what happened to the real money?"

"The real money continued on its merry way."

Dorado reached into his jacket pocket and pulled out a sheave of papers that he handed to Jason. Jason looked at the papers. It was a computer printout list of the bank accounts that the money was hopping through. Dorado had put little check marks next to the account that held the money in cash each morning. Jason ran a finger down the list. He came to the Greater Pacific Bank that he and Deirdre had been at that morning. He pictured her leaning across the seat to kiss him as he got back in the car, the money in the trunk. She was smiling, her head tipped back, her mouth open in a silent laugh, her hair shining gold in the sun. Jason felt something catch in his throat, and it took him a moment to swallow it down where it rested in his stomach feeling dark and hollow.

He continued down the list until he came to the next check mark. This one Dorado had also circled in red. "The money is going to be at a California Savings and Trust in Redding tomorrow morning."

Dorado smiled, his teeth shining in the dashboard lights, and said simply, "Yes. Yes it is."

"Where the heck is Redding?"

"About two hundred miles north of Sacramento."

Jason looked at his watch. Before he could speak Dorado said, "We should get there with about four hours to spare."

He was ninety-nine percent certain what Dorado was planning, but it seemed impossible to believe. Jason had to ask, "We're going to pick up this money, aren't we?"

Dorado's response was a hearty "Shit yes! How does fifty-fifty sound to you?"

Afterword

Though Avarice is my fifth published novel, it is actually the first one I ever wrote, and it took over three years to complete the draft manuscript. Way back when, I had been posting the novel online a few chapters at the time, and had an agent who had seen some of them call me. For those who have not slammed their head against the Great Wall of Publishing, this is an unusual occurrence. Ultimately this agent represented the novel, but was unable to make a sale. Plenty daunted but unwilling to give up, I have recently turned to self-publishing which has allowed me to connect, not with agents or marketers or publishers, but directly with readers, and I'm well on my way towards killing more trees and selling more books than I would have ever thought possible.

I may well revisit these characters (or at least those that survived) again in the future, but for the present, this novel is a one off. Most of my focus is on a series of novels about a volunteer firefighter from a small, fictional town in southern New Hampshire who becomes embroiled in mysteries. As a fourteen year veteran of firefighting and a New Hampshire resident, I have woven actual fire calls I have been on as well as a strong sense of New England and the people who live here into the stories. For a sample, please turn the page for the first chapter of the first firefighter mystery, Embers.

Anyone wishing to contact me may do so at psoletsky@gmail.com.

One

It all began with a call for an ordinary house fire, at least to those of us who consider house fires at two in the morning ordinary.

"Fallon, tank up!" Russell Burtran, a grizzled forty-year veteran of the fire department shouted at me over his shoulder from the officer's seat. "As soon as we get there, you're with me on the hose line."

"Right." I hooked my arms through the straps on the air tank built into the seatback and lifted it from the clips. Snapping my facemask onto the regulator, I tightened the straps so the tank rode snug against my back.

Paul McNeil, a kid so new to the department that he wasn't certified on the breathing gear yet, sat across from me, watching me with wide eyes as he struggled to close the spring clips on his jacket. "What should I be doing, Jack?"

"Just get your gear on. Russell will tell you what to do when we get there."

He swallowed; I saw his Adam's apple bob. His face was thin, his cheeks almost adolescently smooth. He was what, nineteen? If he stuck with it, he'd have forty years in the department someday. I had a moment's doubt about the wisdom of joining the Dunboro volunteer fire department at the age of thirty-five.

The house was a two-story colonial with grey clapboard siding, white trim and a hip roof. The right side of the first floor was fully involved. The front bay window and side patio door had both blown out and were pouring columns of thick dark smoke and occasional licks of orange fire into the night sky. So far the second floor appeared uninvolved. As we drove up we could hear the shrill of the smoke alarm going off inside the house. A blue Nissan was parked in the driveway. Russell relayed his observations of the fire scene into a handheld radio as he climbed down from Engine 2.

I jumped out of the back and pulled out the speedlay line, 150 feet of hose and a nozzle folded up in a rack underneath the pump control panel for quick deployment. Running to the bottom of the front porch steps, I fed the line out as I went. Tom Schmitt, the driver, got down from the cab and climbed onto the back deck of the truck to activate the pumps.

"Paul, get a ladder set up to that top window on the left and clean out the glass." Russell pointed at it, "We find anyone in the house on the second floor we're taking them out that window."

"Will do," Paul nodded once and ran off around the side of the truck.

"Tom, when Engine 3 gets here, I want them to get lines into the first floor."

"I'll let them know," Tom shouted over the throb of the big diesel engine.

Russell joined me on the line just as the pumps started, water rushing down the hose at one hundred pounds per square inch. I spun the air tank valve with my facemask on and took my first breath of canned air – cool, dry, and tasting a little rubbery.

We lifted the hose and dragged it up the three steps onto the porch and to the front door. It was like wrestling with a 150 foot boa constrictor.

"We'll hit the fire on the first floor and then head upstairs to look for people." Russell exhaled with a hiss from the regulator reminding me of Darth Vader. I knew as well as Russell did that the presence of the car in the driveway indicated someone was home, most likely in bed at 2:15 in the morning, and possibly overcome by smoke.

I put a hand on the doorknob but it wouldn't turn. I rattled the knob and the door felt loose in its frame. It was probably only locked at the knob without a deadbolt.

"Locked!" I shouted, putting my helmet against his to be heard over the roar of the fire.

It took three tries with my shoulder before the door popped open. We both ducked down as flames rolled over our heads and puddled in the underside of the porch roof. I hit the nozzle while crouched and drove the fire back. Russell put a hand on my shoulder and pressed me forward against the force of the water. We duck-walked into the house.

Even with my flashlight off, I could see well enough in the flickering orange light of the fire. To our left was a dining room with six chairs around a large oval table, bare except for a pair of crystal candlesticks which reflected the firelight onto the table surface. A china hutch stood against the far wall. To the right was the living room: sheets of flame instead of walls, burning couch, burning love seat, the entertainment center a small inferno, the television and stereo components already reduced to shapeless lumps of metal, plastic and glass.

A large patch of the woven rug in front of the couch was burning, sluggishly, like a guttering candle. That struck me as peculiar and I filed the observation away for later. A stairway going up was in front of us. The shrill of the smoke alarm mounted directly over our heads was deafening.

Russell pointed to my right, and I opened the nozzle all the way, throwing a few hundred gallons of water into the living room. The backwash of steam into our faces blinded us. I fumbled with my flashlight and turned it on.

"Leave it for Engine 3," Russell shouted in my ear. "Let's get upstairs."

I closed the nozzle and put the hose down. We crawled up the stairs, the smoke becoming thicker with each step, until visibility at the top was reduced to nothing. When Paul took out the window we could get some ventilation and clear the smoke out. Of course, that might take too long to help anyone who was in the house. We pressed our faces to the floor and groped our way down the hallway.

My questing fingers found a door on the left. It only opened partially, coming up against something solid. I squeezed my upper body through the opening and found a cardboard box wedged behind the door. I felt another half dozen boxes within arm's reach; the room was full of them. Rather than search the room further I backed out, figuring I wouldn't find anyone in a storage room in the middle of the night. I realized that wasn't perfect deductive reasoning, but it was the best I could do since time wasn't, as the Rolling Stones claimed, on my side.

I heard the thump of Paul setting up the ladder against the house. I didn't know what Russell was thinking, but I was wondering how we would get a victim past all the boxes to the ladder if it came to that.

The next door along the hallway was open, and I crawled into the room with Russell right behind me. I bumped into a desk and a chair before finding the bed. I climbed on top and swept the surface looking for the telltale lump of a body, finding nothing but sheets. Russell crawled underneath– not an easy thing with a tank on his back– and also found nothing.

I climbed off the bed and ran a hand along the wall until I found the closet door. When caught in a house fire people have been known to become disoriented and crawl into the closet when they think they're escaping the room. I opened it and reached in and discovered only a vacuum and bucket. We made our way back out and down the hallway.

At the next room the flooring changed abruptly at the doorway from the rough carpeting of the hallway to the hard smoothness of tile.

"Bathroom," I shouted over my shoulder.

I quickly swept across the tile floor and felt inside the tub. Instructors at firefighter training had told me that people in house fires will sometimes seek refuge in the tub, though I've never seen that happen and never personally known a firefighter who has. The homeowner I guess hadn't either, because the tub was empty.

I heard the shattering of glass. Paul had taken out the window. Perhaps it was my imagination but it seemed instantly the smoke was thinner. I could just make out the shape of my glove in front of my face.

The last door on the hallway opened into a room that somehow felt large and open. The master bedroom. We had been crawling around in this house for more than five minutes on top of our response time plus whatever time it had taken for the fire to be called in. I was all too aware that the chances of someone surviving much longer in the smoke were slim.

Quickly we found the bed. Russell scooted under, and I again took the top. Immediately my arms slid over a dead, no, make that inert, shape that could only be a person. My adrenaline level, already pretty high to begin with, shot through the roof.

The person, a woman, was lying on her back, above the covers and even through my heavy gloves I could tell was completely naked. I heard myself panting rapidly into the respirator and fought to control my breathing.

I patted Russell on the shoulder as he came out from under the bed. "I've got one!"

Russell got on the radio. "We have a victim. Second floor, end of the hallway. We'll be coming down the stairs. Have

EMTs meet us on the lawn." He moved away from me, vanishing into the smoke in less than a foot, probably towards the stairway to make certain our escape route was clear.

I slid my arms underneath her and lifted, the body only coming up a couple of inches off the bed before she bowed backwards and I was forced to put her back down. I ran my hands up her body, a moment's embarrassment as I brushed past her breasts, up her arms to her hands which were stretched over her head. I felt metal rings on her wrists, and a chain. She was handcuffed to the headboard! I grabbed the loop of chain in my gloved hands and heaved. The slats of the headboard creaked, but held firm. I let go and felt back down to her feet. Heavy links encircled her ankles and the solid wooden frame of the footboard.

I rocked back on my heels to think for a second. I'd need a bolt cutter to get her loose, or maybe a chainsaw would be quicker. A hacksaw? An axe?

Russell came back to my side and yelled over my shoulder. "What the hell are you waiting for, Fallon? Get her out of here!"

"I, that is she, I'm going to need . . ."

"What?"

"She's chained to the fucking bed!" I yelled.